Daughter of the Kibbutz

GALIA BARON

Copyright © 2014 Galia Baron
All rights reserved
ISBN-10: 150569576

MAP OF ISRAEL

Source: OpenStreetMap.org

A NOTE TO THE READER

This book was written when my parents were still alive. At the time, I was afraid that reading about my childhood would be difficult for them, so I fictionalized it. Today, although my parents are no longer with us, I find that I like the story as it was written. None of the names I use in this book correspond with real people. I also never mention the name of my kibbutz, although it would be easy to find out where I grew up.

Being a daughter of the kibbutz means that I grew up in the communal education system. Therefore, my experiences do not belong only to me – they belong to many other girls who grew up in the children's house and were taught to call themselves *bnot kibbutz* (daughters of the kibbutz).

I based my stories on snippets of events, fleeting memories, and words that organized themselves into a storyline when I started writing this book. It was my attempt at making sense of the past and, sometimes, the present.

This book is the result of the unending support and encouragement I received from my friends: Yael Pardess, Tal Ben Gal, Steven Phenix, Michal Diner, Lina Moretti, Michael Grimmer, Melodie Bahou, Caroline Shaaya, Ofra Eldor, Chris Ortega, Monica Maravelias, Hans Kaindl, and Geraldine Bouchet. And, of course, my daughter, Eliya. Each one, in his or her way, helped me stay focused on the important stuff of life.

Special thanks to Yael Pardess who designed the front cover.

July 2016

For my mother
Mira Bar On

Chapter One

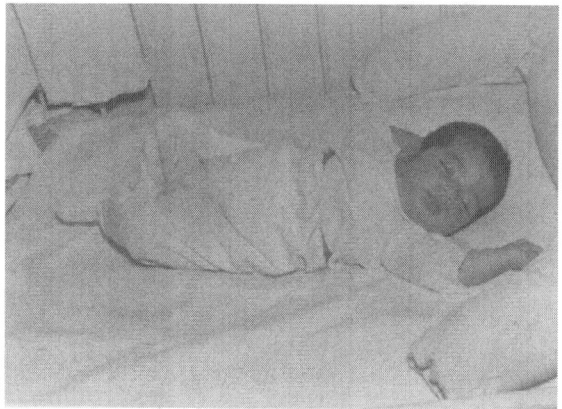

From the beginning I was expected to stay. As a rule, everyone was expected to stay. Staying was as binding as one of the desert commandments. If you were strong you stayed. If you had courage and integrity you stayed. If you were a true socialist you stayed. Only the cowards left, and after them left the weak, the spoiled, and the individualists. Some of them left in the middle of the night without an explanation and without saying good-bye, all their possessions stuffed into one small canvas backpack.

My parents did not mind the secrecy. They knew it would be too embarrassing to succumb in daylight, and besides, they did not want to witness a comrade give up. Especially not a friend who had joined the youth movement a few years earlier with the same conviction that founding a kibbutz near the border was the best way to serve the young nation.

The new kibbutz was located a stone's throw from the Mediterranean Sea at the foot of a mountain ridge that separated Israel from Lebanon. The founding members settled in the abandoned British army barracks conveniently situated near the train tracks that used to connect Haifa to Beirut. The cows were housed a short distance away from the reclaimed barracks, in the deserted British police station that marble floors and high ceilings failed to impress the rugged young kibbutzniks. Tall palm trees, weeping willows, and fig trees provided respite from the sun for those who were preparing the land for planting, and a spring that flowed between the barracks and the train tracks supplied fresh water to the cows and the pioneers.

A year later the pioneers moved up the hill. Several barrack-style houses were built in a semi-circle facing the communal dining hall and kitchen. Each building consisted of four separate rooms and some had running water in the bathroom. Next to the communal dining hall and kitchen the pioneers had built public showers, a laundry house, and a clinic. A cowshed, stable, chicken coop, and barn were raised a short walking distance from the residential area, and a small metal shed was quickly assembled to protect the recently purchased tractor and plow from the unforgiving elements.

When my mother and two other young women got pregnant, the first communal children's house was built. Thirty years earlier, when the very first kibbutzim were founded, communal child rearing was a necessity. Leaving the children under the supervision of one *metapelet* (caretaker) was more efficient, and pooling the meager resources provided the children with better medical care, clothing, food, and housing. However, by the time my older brother, Avner, was born communal child rearing was no longer only a necessity; it was embedded in a revolutionary educational philosophy that promised to abolish paternal authoritarianism and abuse, emancipate women from the domination of their husbands and the "yoke of domestic service," and raise independent, confident, and free-spirited children who would perpetuate the kibbutz communal-agricultural values of work, equality, and personal responsibility.

I was born into this reality. Three kilos, two hundred and twenty-three grams; straight black hair, dark brown eyes. Second child to Boaz and Alma Kidron, the twenty-fifth child born into the kibbutz since its inception in nineteen forty-nine.

During the long delivery, my mother told me, she had never vocalized her pain. She ground her teeth and clenched her fists and resisted the moans that begged to pass her lips, with the tenacity of a true martyr. Unlike other women who screamed behind the curtain in order to chase away evil spirits or their pain, a woman who lived on a kibbutz had to deliver with dignity. She had to maintain the legendary reputation of the strong kibbutznik who possessed ample inner-discipline and pride. According to my mother's tale, I fulfilled the expectations as well. With great consideration not to rob more sleep from her, I started my life in the afternoon, after six hours of contractions and without any complications. Quiet and content, I did not utter the first cry until the hospital nurse patted on my back. Moments later, the kibbutz nurse who accompanied my mother to the hospital called the only telephone in the kibbutz and informed my father that his wife had given birth to a healthy baby girl.

There was no celebration when my mother returned to the kibbutz. She felt a little weak, but was determined not to show my father that she needed help to climb down the pickup truck. She insisted on carrying me in her arms, turning away from the heavy baby carriage my father had left in the shade of a dusty fig tree. It was almost noon. The small parking lot was quiet and deserted. All the members of the kibbutz were still at work and the tractors out in the fields. No one was around to greet us but Ilana, the *metapelet* in charge of the infants' house.

Although Ilana was busy scrubbing the square waist-high bathtub, she stopped working when she saw my mother, wiped her ungloved hands on her apron, and walked with her into the bedroom. The room was clean and cool. The drawn wooden shutters blocked some of the sunlight and heat and created an atmosphere of pleasant tranquility. The smell of baby oil and a hint of Lysol hung in the air. Parallel to the walls stood four metal cribs painted in white oil paint, a straight-backed chair next to each crib, and a spotless white changing table. Three cribs were already occupied by babies who were born in the previous months. At the moment of my entry they were lying in their mothers' arms, attached to their breasts, listening to their soft murmurs and responding with energetic sucking sounds.

Without ceremony Ilana led my mother to the vacant crib, tightened up the white cloth that covered the pink rubber sheet, and stepped out to complete her cleaning chores. The women welcomed my mother in whispers, inquired about my weight, and compared birthing stories with her. My father waited in the next room, folding cotton diapers and arranging them in neat, even piles on a low table. Men were not allowed to enter the bedroom when women were breast-feeding. In those days only Arab women breast-fed their babies in front of men. They did it on city sidewalks while waiting for the bus to come and take them to their villages. Surrounded by small children and plastic baskets full of fruits and vegetables, they held their babies to their breasts and ignored curious stares from passersby.

    Because I was my mother's second child, she knew what needed to be done. She put on a white coat, identical to the one all the other mothers wore when they fed their babies, and nursed me to sleep. After checking that I was breathing evenly, she put me in the crib and tiptoed out of the bedroom. She did not want to stay in the infants' house and eat the special food Ilana had brought from the communal kitchen for the breast-feeding moms. Ilana reminded her that she had to eat even when she was not hungry or risk losing her breast milk, but my mother was too tired to eat or argue. She drank a cup of tepid tea in silence and left the infants' house with my father, who finished folding all the diapers.
    Although my parents' room was only a three-minute walk from the infants' house it took them much longer to get there. When they passed in front of the communal dining hall they ran into several members who were on their lunch break. They were lying on a small patch of yellowing grass, dressed in the kibbutz-issued blue work clothes, smoking Dubek cigarettes and drinking Turkish coffee. Sasha, who knew my father since their high school days in Tel Aviv, wanted to know the name of the new baby.
    "Maya," my father answered proudly.
    "Maminka, where's my Maminka," someone started to sing, giving me my nickname.
    When my parents finally got to their apartment, a mere fifteen-by-eighteen foot room with a modest bathroom on the front porch, they found a homemade poster pinned to the door wishing them *Mazal Tov*. Inside, my mother noted to herself in relief that the floor was recently mopped, the white sheet on the bed was fresh, and the temperature was comfortable enough for sleeping. The table in the corner was covered with an embroidered tablecloth she had never seen before. An empty can packed with freshly picked daisies and carnations enlivened the austere decor of the room. Under the flower canopy glistened a slab of chocolate cake that someone from the kitchen's crew had baked that morning and

brought over along with a plate of colorful hard candies and two bottles of orange juice.

After four o'clock, my mother knew, the members would come to see the new baby, eat cake, drink coffee, and decide whether the new addition to the kibbutz looked more like her mother or her father. She did not look forward to it. She needed more quiet time for herself and for the baby. In the hospital she had to share a room with five other new mothers and a bathroom with more than fifty women. Now, all she wanted to do was to take a nice long shower and wash the hospital smell from her skin and hair. She had dreamed about using her own shower for almost a week and was not going to wait for the kerosene water heater to warm up. She decided to take a lukewarm shower, then to take a nap. She had to collect her strength before four o'clock. Shortly after four my brother was going to arrive from kindergarten brimming with questions and begging to touch his new baby sister.

For six weeks my mother shuttled between the infants' house, the kindergarten where my brother lived, and her small family room which was located at the end of a barrack-style row house built on the edge of the hill. Every four hours, day and night, she went to the infants' house to nurse me, quietly humming her favorite songs and trying to stay awake. During the day, in between feedings, she visited my brother or went for long walks around the kibbutz with me, the sleeping baby, in a heavy carriage. She was so glad I was a summer baby. With Avner who was born in the winter, she found it hard to leave her warm bed in the middle of a rainy night and run to the infants' house to nurse him.

Her only regret was that Ilana Porat was still in charge of the infants' house. Ilana started working with the infants shortly before my brother was born. Since then, her reign of the infants' house was unquestioned and unchallenged. She created a strict set of regulations and made sure that all the parents followed them. She frowned at the mothers who showed up too many times between feedings and dismissed anxious fathers as overly protective. Her prompt response to their concern over long spells of crying was always, "Don't worry, she's all right. She's only trying to get your attention."

My mother did not forget how she used to stand under the window of the infants' house before feeding time, listen to my brother cry, and fight her urge to go inside. She was afraid that Ilana would criticize her in front of everyone for spoiling the child, then explain to her that babies needed to cry to develop their lungs and independence. She did not approve of anything Ilana had said, but now she had to hide her feelings and try to overcome her misgivings. She had no choice. There were no other infants' houses on the kibbutz and she could not ask the work committee to designate another *metapelet* for the infants. The committee had decided that Ilana should be the *metapelet* of the newborns and she had to learn to live with it.

During these weeks my father tried to help my mother cope with her worries by reassuring her that Ilana would not hurt the babies, no matter how short-tempered or bossy she was toward everyone. Every time my mother would complain that Ilana was too slow to change wet diapers or attend to a crying baby, or that her voice was shrill and her hands too rough, my father would remind her that it was not all Ilana's fault. Ilana was simply too busy sterilizing bottles, shuttling between the laundry house and the communal kitchen three times a day, and making sure all the babies ate on time, slept well, and stayed healthy. Reluctantly, my mother would admit that Ilana was not all that bad. She did sing occasionally when she scrubbed the sinks and when she had a moment she tickled the babies and smiled. Then my mother would hear a rumor that Ilana had fed one of the babies their own puke and the cycle would start all over again.

Six weeks after I was born my mother began doing light work in the communal clothing house. At first she stopped the night feedings and worked only four hours a day, ironing and folding clothes. Slowly she added more hours to her workday and cut other feedings. By the end of the third month her breast milk was gone. She was a little sad that she had to stop nursing. She was not ready to give up the frequent visits to the infants' house but she did not dare to challenge the new schedule. The education experts determined that the best way to raise children was to leave them under the supervision of a *metapelet* immediately after birth and she believed every word they said. It was her habit not to question the rules, written or unwritten. She was young and inexperienced and people she trusted convinced her that she was doing the right thing.

When I was about eighteen months old I was moved from the infants' house to the toddlers' house along with my four roommates. By now we were a tight group of five toddlers, four boys and a girl, having to adjust to a new children's house, a new *metapelet*, and a new routine. Two and a half years later we moved again to kindergarten. This time we joined a group of eleven children, ages four to six years old.

Although the building in which kindergarten-age children lived stood on the other side of the fenced yard where I used to play as a toddler, I had never seen what it looked like from the inside. That was why the day I entered kindergarten was so memorable. The kindergarten was huge. While the toddler's house had only one bedroom in which the five of us had slept, in kindergarten there were five bedrooms. There were also three adult-size toilets instead of the one kiddy-size toilet, and the shower room was so spacious, all the kids could fit in there together. Kindergarten also had a separate kitchenette and a large sunny dining room with three tables and so many chairs around them I couldn't count them. There were also two playrooms, one that looked more like a classroom with lot of books and puzzles, and another one full of toys and building blocks. Kindergarten was so big, it had so many rooms and doors and closets, for a moment I thought that if I woke up in the middle of the night and had to go to the bathroom, I would get lost in the dark. Then I remembered I could always wake up the father whose turn it was to sleep in the kindergarten with us and ask him to show me the way.

I was so happy to move into kindergarten I did not mind leaving my bed and my *metapelet* from toddler's house behind. The old *metapelet* had to stay there to receive another group of five snotty-nosed babies who still peed in their beds at night. I knew that living in kindergarten was going to be much better. Now we could go for long hikes all over the place, even as far as the sugar-beets fields and the *wadi* behind the cowsheds and the stable. We could celebrate fifteen birthdays every year instead of only five. We could play in two playrooms or outside in the huge, fenceless playground. So vast was our new playground, it spread all the way up to the mountainside where the kibbutz ended and the wilderness exploded with the constant buzz of insects and the urgent calls of birds.

On our first day in kindergarten we had a party in the playroom. The teacher welcomed us into the ranks and the new *metapelet* gave us cookies and candies for snacks. We played fun games and sang songs and afterwards we helped the teacher clean up the mess. In the evening, after the *metapelet* had turned the lights off and left for the folk dance party at the communal dining hall, we started a pillow fight that ended as soon as the night-watch passed outside, heard the noise, and rushed in to remind us that big kids like us were supposed to go to sleep after lights-out rather than destroy the furniture. That night I fell asleep feeling safe and brave and blissful. I was no longer a finger-sucking toddler seeking the approval of her elders, but a full-fledged member of a wild tribe consisting of ant-eating boys and conspiratorial girls. Of course I still had to respect the unwritten law of seniority or risk a physical confrontation, but as a rule I was never excluded from games or pushed around by anyone just because I was younger.

In our kindergarten all seasons were suited for a celebration. We had so many holidays, some as old as the Bible, others as new as our young nation, one could have gotten the impression that our life was filled with festivals celebrating the victory over this or that enemy and nothing else. We learned new songs and improvised dances with masks, candles, or baskets of fruits and vegetables. We played special games, created artwork and hung them on the windows and the walls. We wore our "Saturday clothes" and ate traditional foods our mothers had learned to prepare at their mothers' traditional kitchens: Honey cakes in Rosh-Hashanah, deep-fried donuts in Hanukkah, Hamen Tashen in Purim, gefilte-fish in Pesach, cheesecake in Shavuot, Tcholent on Shabbat.

The Shabbat was also very special to us, not because of its religious significance, but because it made the grown-ups who worked so hard all week more relaxed and playful. In preparation for the Sabbath, every Friday afternoon the children's house sparkled with an added shine. After lunch the kindergarten teacher covered her desk with a white tablecloth, put fresh flowers in the vase, and read us stories composed by old Jewish sages. We also baked Challah bread, lit candles, and sang about the Shabbat. At four o'clock we left for our parents' rooms, girls wearing skirts and patent leather shoes, boys in ironed white shirts and dark blue pants, all of us carrying a precious brown paper bag filled with carefully counted candies and cookies.

Saturdays displayed a more contemporary edge than Fridays thanks to our parents' revolutionary interpretation of religion. Saturday was the only day of the week we had sour cream and halvah for breakfast. Saturday was also the only day our fathers took turns working in the kindergarten so the *metapelet* could take a break from us and we could take a break from her. Our fathers were ten million times more fun. They let us stay in bed longer, told us funny stories during breakfast, and played piggyback with us. But the biggest treat of all was that on Saturdays we got a bonus of three more visiting hours with our parents: A total of five and a half hours in one day.

And what a glorious time it was.

When a child spends her childhood under the supervision of busy *metapelets* who are rarely sympathetic toward her feelings and her needs, spending an entire morning with her own parents can be quite overwhelming, almost too much to handle for a five-year-old.

She gets up in the morning knowing that after breakfast she is not going to stay in kindergarten, but run to her parents' room and see them and her brother or sister, and she can hardly contain the excitement inside; it's almost unbearable. So she makes a lot of noise when she gets up, like all the other kids, and she runs to the bathroom and pushes everyone in line to get to the sink first, and she drops things, and she chases other kids around the dining room tables and slides on the floor, and she promises everyone to meet them at the beach later on, because she is not used to being away from the other kids for such a long time. Then she goes "home," which is what we called our parents' rooms, and begs her mother to take her to the beach where everyone from the kibbutz is going to be. Her mother asks "Did you remember to bring your bathing suit?" because that was exactly what she had planned to do even before her daughter asked, and, proudly, the little girl says, "yes, I did," and lifts her tank-top to show her mother that she is already wearing her bathing suit under her clothes. Her mother smiles and maybe even gives the little girl a kiss on the cheek if she stands close enough to her. Then her father comes in and asks, "Why for all the ghosts and spirits does it take everyone such a long time to get ready?" and the little girl tells him that she can't find her floaties. Her father helps her search the mess inside the closet on the front porch, while her mother packs the margarine and halvah sandwiches she had prepared and asks her little girl for the millionth time to put on her hat and terrycloth beach robe. Finally everyone heads to the parking lot, where half of the members of kibbutz are crammed into a wooden cart pulled by the gigantic green Oliver tractor, and everyone is waiting for the little girl to climb up already, so they could get to the beach before sunset.

On the way down the hill the tractor's engine roars, the kibbutz dogs chase the tractor, trying to out-bark each other, people sing at the top of their lungs, and the little girl feels that her body is exploding with happiness. She has to hold herself back not to jump off the hard bench she sits on before the tractor comes to a full stop, then she joins the flood of people as they spill out of the carriage and head down the rocks, past thorny bushes and lazy reptiles to the secluded stretch of sand called "The Beach."

My beach.

A beach hidden behind pristine sand dunes and graced by modest coastal lilies that opened their magnificent white flowers only at twilight. A beach where the yellow sand is so soft and pure that I could easily follow the tiny footmarks of beetles and birds after they had concluded the eternal dance of the hunter and the hunted. A beach reaching for a sea so clear and inviting that I could observe the fish sleep in shallow tide pools under translucent seaweed, and the crabs scan the flat rocks sideways, unafraid.

That was the beach I frequented during every summer of my childhood. I knew that beach better than I knew my body. Without a moment's hesitation my feet could find every ledge in the seaweed-covered walls that dropped into the abyss. My hands anticipated every nook and cranny in the rocks and could lead me around them without scraping my knees or elbows. My eyes recognized the smallest caves and tunnels where timid underwater creatures dwelled. My ears kept me from falling into deep holes carved into the rocks when they heard the heavy breathing of the sea. My torso knew the way of the waves as they filled the tide pools from one side and rushed out to the open sea on the other side. I knew the best places to jump from, where it was safe to dive, how to balance on the slippery rocks, which tide pools to avoid. I understood the sea in all its moods.

The only people who swam in these waters were from my kibbutz. Once in a while, a solitary Arab fisherman from a nearby village would stand on the rocks and try his luck with a long fishing pole; but other than the occasional fisherman, there were no strangers on that beach. There was not a paved road or a sign to advertise that secluded beach. One had to be familiar with the hidden footpath that cut through the cotton fields and also know when it was safe to cross them. No one was allowed to walk in the fields after they were sprayed with parathion. Exposure to parathion was lethal, a scary poster adorned with a drawing of a black skull and crossbones would appear on the dining hall's bulletin board after each spraying, warning those who did not see the crop-duster plane.

We children of the kibbutz knew when to stay away from the fields because we always saw the plane. We loved watching it fly above the fields, leaving a white trail of pesticides behind its tail, and tilting its wing in a friendly salute to the people on the ground. Then one day it flew too low, hit the hillside, and burst into flames.

Everyone who saw the accident, but the children who were ordered to stay put, ran to save the pilot and extinguish the fire. Shortly afterwards we learned that the pilot had survived the crash and was taken to the hospital. The next day we made get-well cards for the wounded pilot and begged the kindergarten teacher to take us to the plane.

Knowing that the pilot did not die in the crash made the hike feel like an exciting adventure rather than a morbid pilgrimage to a disaster site. The crop-duster crashed a short distance from the last houses of the kibbutz, on the western side of the hill above the field it was spraying. Slumped on top of burned bushes and limestone rocks, it was tilted to one side, its nose stuck inside the lower branches of a carob tree, its wings blackened and broken. In spite of our kindergarten teacher's somber head shaking and sighing, we all agreed the plane was magnificent. We hoped that our fathers would drag it to our playground where we could climb into the cockpit and pretend that we were brave pilots. For us, even the old carob tree that suffered severe fire damage did not look like a silent witness of a horrible accident. It was a proud monument for courage and survival.

Because of our secular upbringing, none of us attributed the pilot's survival to divine intervention. In those days, all grown-ups appeared to us invincible and immortal. They could cope with any threatening situation. Nothing scared them. Even the packs of wild dogs that occasionally crossed the unmarked border before it was sealed with an electric fence did not make them run away in terror. On the contrary; whenever the emaciated dogs showed up in our cornfields, threatening to inflict us with rabies, the men would rush to the armory and grab a rifle. We children would hang out of the windows and watch the chase. With their tails tucked between their hind legs and their tongues hanging out of their foaming jaws, the dogs would bark in rage or misery, it was hard to tell, and try to dodge the bullets shot in their direction. Sometimes a dog or two would be killed and quickly buried before the kindergarten boys could go to investigate the slaughter fields. For obvious reasons the grown-ups were set on keeping us away from the dogs, dead or alive, no matter how curious we were. However, while the secrecy deprived us from ever seeing the bloody corpses, it did not stop us from offering our total admiration to the men who shot the dogs.

Skinny, black goats also risked their lives when they crossed the unmarked border in their diligent search for new grazing grounds. But the goats never got shot at like the wild dogs. Arazi, the only man on the kibbutz who could speak Arabic with the right accent, was designated to deal with the straying goats and their Lebanese owner. He never failed to round up the goats and guide them back to the herder, in spite of the loud protests from some of the kibbutz members who called the goats "the walking steaks." In return, the grateful herder would give Arazi goat cheese and black olives and promise to watch his goats more carefully in the future. And no, Arazi always reassured us kids that the goat herder was not a spy.

We kids would have given anything to get a close look at the goat herder. We had never seen an Arab from another country, especially an Arab who was supposed to be our enemy. Even when we hiked to the top of the ridge and looked as far as our eyes could see, we had never seen anyone from Lebanon. The villages were tucked somewhere behind the hills and the nearest town glimmered in the distance by the Mediterranean Sea. Once we gave up looking for our mysterious neighbors, we would try to figure out where the border passed and dare one another to cross it just to see what it felt like being in another country. Usually the bravest kid would point at a low cairn, walk past it, and scream, "I'm in Lebanon." We would cheer his courage and practice the few words we could say in Arabic just in case we ran into another goat herder. Then we'd turn around and run down the hill without ever finding out if our friend had really crossed the border.

Chapter Two

Though life was full of fun and adventure in kindergarten not all was splendid. My one obstacle to total bliss was an unsmiling, commanding, omnipresent new *metapelet* who answered to the name Tamara. Tamara was so committed to the new educational theories about communal education–basically that everyone in kindergarten had to do the same thing at the same time, always, regardless of different tastes, internal rhythms, inclination or temper, and without the interference of the parents–she failed to notice that we were only children and quite different from one another.

Shortly after I met Tamara I realized that she was not going to be anything like my former, easy going *metapelet* from toddlers' house, but a strict disciplinarian with a limited vocabulary. No matter what kind of drama gripped the kindergarten residents, all she could ever say was: Sit down, Get Up, Eat, Be quiet, Enough already, Now, Not now, Go to bed, Don't argue, Because, Maybe, Immediately, and No.

Tamara was everywhere. Showing up from nowhere when we least expected her. Yelling at us. Dragging slow kids by the arm. Threatening to punish. Sometimes she gave big punishments, sometimes small ones. Sometimes she punished only one kid, sometimes the perpetrator and her roommates. Sometimes she punished the entire group. Many times it was hard to understand why we got punished at all, but we always heard that it would be a good lesson for the future.

My first clash with Tamara was over tomatoes. In the toddlers' house I was not forced to eat anything. But in kindergarten I had to eat whatever Tamara had put on the table, and tomatoes almost always were part of our breakfast menu along with cucumbers, hard-boiled eggs, cheese and bread. "If everyone can eat tomatoes, so can you," was her reasoning. Emphasis on "everyone." No special privileges, no alternatives.

I couldn't bear the thought of eating tomatoes. Tomatoes made me puke. Their smell offended me, their texture nauseated me, their skin irritated the roof of my mouth. To correct my independent taste, I had to spend hours staring at my salad while the other kids who were able to eat those slimy things left the table and went to play outside. No amount of begging or crying ever softened Tamara's firm conviction that I should eat tomatoes like everyone else. Sometimes Iris, who hated drinking milk, would be sitting at the other table staring out the window, taking tiny sips from her cup, slowly reaching for the bottom and the promised release from the chair. With a sinking heart I would watch her carry her empty cup to the sink and then run outside. Then time would stand still, the voices of children at play would travel inside through the windows, but Tamara would not budge. My aversion to tomatoes was a rebellion that needed to be crushed before it could contaminate everyone in kindergarten. When the simple order "Eat" would fail to convince me, Tamara would circle the table, glare at me, warn me that I'd better eat or spend the rest of the day sitting on my chair. But nothing worked. And for countless days I sat at my table until everybody came in for lunch.

One morning I realized in horror that Tamara had a new idea. She was pushing me into a corner of no excuse, testing my commitment to be different from the other kids. She poured boiling water over one tomato, peeled the thin red skin, cut the tomato into small pieces, put them on a plate and slammed it on the table in front of me. "Now don't tell me you can't swallow it because of the skin," she exclaimed victoriously.

I stared at the boiled tomato and tried to control my revulsion.

"Eat," she yelled.

I licked a piece and put it back on the plate.

"I said eat," her frustration rose into a scream.

My finger went into my mouth.

"Take that finger out of your mouth," she slapped my hand.

I could not tell her that the tiny, slippery seeds disgusted me as well. I watched her struggling to stab a piece of boiled tomato with my fork, lifting the loaded fork, waving it in front of my mouth.

"Open your mouth," she ordered. "I don't have all day to waste on you."

I opened my mouth and a wave of sourness rose into my throat. I covered my mouth with my hands and ran to the bathroom, trying to hold onto the foul liquid that was flowing out of me.

"Now, clean up the mess," she startled me the moment I stopped throwing up into the toilet bowl.

She handed me a wet rag, flushed the toilet, and left. My hands were sticky with vomit, my cheeks were drenched in tears. I took the wet rag by the very corner. Another wave shook my stomach. I wanted to collapse on the floor but the floor was filthy with my vomit. Don't look, don't smell, don't cry, someone in my head was telling me. I wiped the toilet and the floor around it, threw the rag into a bucket full of water, and went outside to play.

None of the kids asked me why I took so long to come outside. They knew. They saw me brood over my breakfast plate almost every morning since I came to kindergarten. And they understood my helplessness. But they couldn't make my problem go away, so they kept running around, spraying water on each other, swinging from tree branches, chasing one another and pretending that Tamara did not scare them. I wanted to make myself invisible and hide from Tamara in the bushes, stay there until four o'clock, then go to my parents' room and tell them that Tamara scared me. Or go look for my mother and tell her that I wanted to stay with her and never go back to kindergarten. But of course, I knew I couldn't do that. My mother would tell me that there was nothing to be afraid of, that I was imagining things, and that once I got used to living in kindergarten I wouldn't be afraid of anyone.

There was nowhere to hide. The low bushes were covered with prickly thorns and more than once we saw black snakes passing through toward the chicken coop. I sat under the chinaberry tree near the sandbox and sucked on my finger until Tamara called the children to come inside. It was time to take a shower, eat lunch, and go to bed for afternoon nap.

Afternoon nap was the biggest challenge of the day. Every day of the week, including Saturdays and holidays, we had to go to bed for two and a half hours and lie quietly, without talking to each other, even in a whisper, and sleep. The kids who couldn't fall asleep were not allowed to look at picture books, play by themselves, and, sometimes, even go to the bathroom for a drink of water. Afternoon nap was sacred to the grown-ups and kids were not permitted to disturb it. During afternoon nap Tamara would fold the clean clothes she had brought from the laundry house and arrange them on shelves, polish our shoes and sandals, prepare sandwiches for the afternoon snack, and enjoy a quiet moment by herself. And those who dared to disrupt the silence always had to pay a price.

My room faced the dining room. Only a few steps away from one of the bathrooms, it was sandwiched between another bedroom and a playroom. During afternoon naps I could sometimes hear the sound of small feet running to the bathroom, a toilet flushed, water run into the sink. It provided some distraction from the stifling boredom on days I couldn't fall asleep. My roommates, Nir and Iris, and I liked to talk in whispers when we did not sleep. Sometimes we would engage in long conversations about what we did in the summer when we went to visit our grandparents who lived in the city. We talked about what it was like to ride a bus, or go to the zoo, or eat ice cream every day. And we always decided that living on the kibbutz was much better, even though city kids could eat ice cream every day. Sometimes we would argue about who was the bravest and strongest boy in kindergarten. We admired the older kids who were going to start first grade and tried to emulate them all the time. They were not scared of Tamara and the dark. They were not even afraid of the mean rooster who lived in the chicken coop. They showed us how to enter the chicken coop and shoo him away with a broomstick before he could attack us. They always came up with new ideas. Once they dug a hole in the ground and told all the kids from kindergarten to pee into an empty can. Then they put the full can in the hole, covered it with branches and leaves, and waited in the bushes to see what would happen. As they hoped, the best happened. Ari from toddler's house fell into the trap and got his foot wet. We got a good laugh out of it. It was such a loud laugh that Tamara heard us laughing during afternoon nap and stormed into our bedroom.

"What's all this noise supposed to mean?" she yelled at us.

Of course we couldn't tell her why we were laughing. It was a big secret.

"How many times do I have to tell you to be quiet during afternoon nap?" she asked.

We couldn't answer that one either.

When she realized that we were not going to answer she told Nir to go sit in the bathroom and close the door. Iris went to sit on the bench in the shower room and I had to stay in the bedroom by myself. I felt bad for Nir who had to spend the rest of afternoon nap sitting on the toilet. If we did not laugh so loudly, Tamara wouldn't have heard us and no one would have had to be punished. I should have thought about it. But thinking about Ari falling into the pee trap was too funny. I did not feel too bad for Iris because the shower room was big and she could walk around and look out the window and maybe even see someone walk by. It was not as bad as being locked in a small bathroom. I promised myself that next time I would try to be quiet and remind my roommates not to laugh so loudly.

During the four o'clock snack Tamara told all the kids that Nir, Iris, and I made noise when we were supposed to be quiet and that from now on anyone who made noise during afternoon nap was going to be punished. And to teach us a lesson we were not going to get our candy bag on Friday. I did not understand why we had to be punished twice but I did not dare to ask. Maybe she thought that what she did to us was not a real punishment. Maybe she thought we needed to be scared.

I was sure that Tamara had forgotten about the punishment when Friday arrived. Nir and I did everything we could to make her forget. All week we behaved ourselves, we did not talk during afternoon nap, we ate everything she had put on our plates, even the split pea soup, and we were first out of the shower. I watched her during the day and tried to guess if she was thinking about our punishment. But it was hard to tell if she was still angry. She was very busy, cleaning the house, going to the kitchen and to the laundry house, and ordering us around. When afternoon nap was over I quickly got out of bed, got dressed, and went to the table. A puffy brown paper bag was waiting for every kid on every chair, with candies, gum, and cookies, but no puffy candy bag was waiting for me, Nir and Iris. I looked at Tamara to see if she was going to say anything to us but she did not. And that was when I started to get really scared.

The desk was covered with a white tablecloth. On top of it stood a vase filled with fresh cut pink roses and asparagus fern and two candleholders with short white candles stuck in them. All the toys and books were arranged on the shelves and our most recent paintings hung on the walls above them. The air smelled of chlorine, soap, and freshly baked Challah bread making our kindergarten feel clean and bright and festive.
It was time to greet the coming Shabbat.
The kindergarten teacher lit the candles and went back to her chair. She was the only person in the room dressed in regular clothes. We children were barefoot, wearing only white cotton underwear. Showered and shampooed, our nails were vigorously clipped by Tamara, and the wax in our ears mercilessly scraped with cotton balls wrapped around ends of matches.
At the teacher's signal we started singing "Today is Friday, tomorrow is Saturday, a day of rest," and banging in complete disharmony on tambourines and cymbals. At the peak of the noise Tamara joined us and sat near the teacher. I thought she was going to tell us that the chocolate cake she was baking for our four o'clock snack would collapse because of the noise we were making, but she leaned back and started singing with us. So I kept banging on my tambourine and singing along.
Every Friday we celebrated the coming Shabbat before lunch. After our teacher finished reading all the blessings, we played "spin the bottle" or "donkey's tail" or "knock, knock, who am I and what's my name?" and afterwards the teacher read us Jewish folktales with important Jewish morals in the end. Sometimes we drew scenes from stories she had read to us and watched them slowly unfold on the wall like a movie through the magic projector.
But that Friday the ceremony was interrupted when Tamara whispered something to the teacher and then instead of starting to

sing another song like she always did, asked: "Children, who wants to go to the shoemaker's workshop?"

I jumped from my chair and yelled, "me, me, me," waving my arm up in the air to catch her attention, forgetting that shouting never got me what I wanted. I really wanted to go. Tamara ordered us to sit down and be quiet. After scrutinizing us squirming impatiently in our chairs, she decided it was my turn to go to the shoemaker's workshop with Nir. But first we had to finish the ceremony.

With utter self-control I listened to the teacher read another blessing from the illustrated Bible. "And on the seventh day God ended his work which he had made. And he rested on the seventh day from all his work which he had made."

I mouthed the words as she read them, looking at Nir from the corner of my eye, making sure he was behaving himself. Nir was my best friend in kindergarten. We had lived together in the infants' house and the toddler's house. Now, we sat near each other at the dining room table, slept in the same bedroom, played near each other in the sandbox, and showered together. I constantly looked after him, making sure he did not get himself in trouble with the older kids.

When the teacher finished reading and closed the book, Tamara looked at me and said, "You two can go now. But don't take long. I'm going to the kitchen to get lunch, so go straight to the shoemaker's workshop and come back quickly. No playing on the way. Understand?"

I promised we would not stop anywhere, grabbed three worn-out sandals Tamara left on the windowsill, and quickly left with Nir.

The shoemaker's workshop was a small, dilapidated cabin surrounded by waist-high weeds and neglect. It stood behind the pine grove at the end of the asphalt road between the coops and an enclosed barn that was used as a packinghouse for tangerines and lemons during harvest season and as an improvised wedding hall when it rained. Broken tricycles, empty oil drums, and wooden crates in different stages of decay were scattered around the cabin and the smell of chicken poop always hung above it.

Because we were in a rush we decided to cut through the pine grove instead of walking on the asphalt road. All the way there we competed with each other who could skip on one foot the longest and talked about what we would like to get for our next birthdays. In the middle of the grove Nir spotted a bird's nest and decided to climb up the tree and take the nest back to kindergarten.

"What if there are eggs or baby chicks in it?" I asked. We were not supposed to touch bird nests unless they were abandoned. Our teacher told us that birds did not like their nests to be touched by humans.

"If it's not empty, I won't touch it," Nir promised.

He tried to climb up the tree, sliding down the trunk, missing the low branches. "I can't climb this stupid tree," he complained and kicked the trunk.

I left him fighting the tree and went to collect pine needles that fell on the ground. It was very important to know exactly which needles to collect. They had to be not too green, yet not too dry and brown, because then they could easily break. After I collected a fistful of pine needles, I cleared a small patch of earth, sat down, and started making rings from them. Above me Nir was making plans how to reach the nest, swinging on a branch on his way up. I was no longer worried about him falling down, the nest being occupied by chicks, or Tamara yelling at us for taking so long. My pretty necklace was getting longer, and I could already hear the girls ask me to let them wear it for a little while.

"Look at me," Nir called. "I'm Tarzan."

His voice and the scary millipede that passed by my toes reminded me of our mission and the promise I had made to Tamara. I put the necklace around my neck, picked up the sandals, and walked back to the narrow dirt path lined by dry, thorny shrubs on both sides. Nir, who was sitting on a branch with the nest in his hand, called me to wait for him. He slid down the tree and ran to catch up, his legs covered with scratches, green pine needles stuck in his blond hair, spider web crisscrossing his white tank top.

"Let me clean you up first or Tamara will know that you climbed on a tree and yell at you," I advised him. I helped him pick the pine needles from his hair, brushed the dirt from his tank top, and waited for him to go hide the nest in a safe place.

Finally, we got back on the road.

The shoemaker's workshop was crammed with wrinkled shoes and old working boots long forgotten by their owners. Pages from old calendars hung on the walls, some of them displayed pretty women in bikinis, others were decorated with pictures of trucks and bulldozers. In a dark corner, a shelf laden with black and brown shoes was leaning dangerously under the weight of the abandoned shoes. The air was dusty and full of shadows. A large wooden table covered with torn up shoes and iron tools faced the door. A glass of tea with a bright yellow wedge of lemon swimming in it stood in the middle of the table and caught the little sunlight that entered through the small window. It was the brightest spot in the tiny room. The shoemaker was sitting on a low stool by the table, wearing a stained apron that smelled of old shoes, wood, and thick glue.

"Shalom," we said, standing at the door.

"Shalom, children," he said in a soft voice, looking at us with droopy eyes. His timid smile was missing some teeth.

The shoemaker did not know our names because he did not live with us on the kibbutz. Every morning he came from a neighboring town riding an ancient motor scooter. I did not like looking at the shoemaker too closely. He was a sad looking old man with a scrawny neck, a balding head with a few strands of gray hair attached to the top, and long pale fingers that ended with dirty nails. He looked lost and foreign in his old-fashioned city clothes, eating by himself in the noisy dining hall, or walking slowly by the laundry house. But inside his workshop he was as comfortable as a king in his own secret kingdom.

We gave him the sandals and stepped back, waiting for him to speak. He caressed the dusty soles then continued hammering nails on the bottom of a working boot that rested upside down on an iron foot. Only then did we ask if he had already put new soles on the shoes Tamara had sent on the week before.

"They'll be ready on Tuesday," he said in his heavily accented Hebrew. "Come back on Tuesday."

We thanked him as we were told and left him with his shoes, the bright lemon wedge floating in the tea cup, and the smell of crumpled leather, dust, and drying glue.

Outside we looked for new adventures. The first thing that caught our eyes was the motor scooter that stood in the shade by the wall. Nir whispered to me to follow him and climbed up the scooter. Without hesitation I climbed to the seat behind him and put my arms around his waist. For a while, imitating the sound of the engine, we pretended to be riding around the kibbutz, and forgot Tamara and the lunch that awaited us. Then Nir got bored so we decided to compete how far we could throw the tiny stones scattered on the gravel path that marked the end of the asphalt road. To my dismay, I realized that Nir, who was younger than I was, could throw the stones farther. I also discovered that my beautiful necklace disappeared. To preserve my pride and my status as the respected elder, and to improve my mood, I had to show him that I was at least as good as he was. I turned to him with a little stone in my hand and pointing at the small window of the shoemaker's workshop, said, "I can throw this stone so high, it will go through that window."

I threw the tiny stone up in the air. It flew up into the cloudless skies higher than the flat roofs of the long cowsheds behind them, and almost fell on my head on its way down. Nir chuckled and clapped his hands.

His reaction made me more determined to show him that I could do it. I picked the smallest stone I could find on the gravel path and threw it with all my might toward the peeling wall. The stone flew up high, crossed the windowsill, and disappeared inside the workshop.

Without pausing to savor my victory, I grabbed Nir's arm and ran to hide behind the scooter. Crouching on the ground and giggling excitedly, we waited to see if the shoemaker would come out to yell at us. But he stayed inside and kept tapping on the old shoes with his hammer. A few minutes later we gave up waiting and decided that he did not notice the stone coming through the window. We picked a handful of little stones from the ground and ran, laughing wildly at our successful mischief, raising dust, and discarding the stones one by one, until we reached the pine grove, where we stopped to fetch the nest that Nir had hid behind a rock.

Lunch was over by the time we got back. Tamara shot us an angry look and told us to "leave that nest outside and run immediately" to wash our hands. In the bathroom, Nir made funny faces at the mirror that hung above the sink and almost forgot why we went there. I had to remind him to dry his hands on a towel and not on his underwear. In the dining room Tamara ordered us to sit at the last table and eat quickly because she already wiped our table and wanted to start mopping the floor.

"Next time you're late for lunch, you won't get your treat bag," she threatened us on our way to bed for an afternoon nap.

When I arrived at my parents' room shortly after four o'clock, my father was sitting on the top of the stairs in his blue work clothes reading a newspaper. I ran toward him and jumped into his open arms. My father laughed, put me back on the ground, and asked if I wanted to go with him to pick up kerosene for the water boiler. "So Ima can take a shower when she comes home," he explained.

What an exciting idea. My father always had great ideas. He could also tell the most interesting bedtime stories. The kids in kindergarten knew it, too. Sometimes during lights-out they would come to my bedroom and ask him to tell them stories about Ali-Baba, and Aladdin, and Gulliver even while their parents were around. Then there were days my father would come to visit us with Zalman, the old horse who carried fresh produce from the fields up to the kitchen, and take us for a ride around the kibbutz in the squeaky wagon. And that was not all. My father could make the best cucumber salad with sour cream. On Saturday, when it was his turn to work in the kindergarten, though he made sure not to give me more attention than to the other kids, I always felt that he noticed what I was doing all the time. Especially during breakfast when he sat at my table and asked if I wanted more sour cream.

"Can we visit Zalman?" I danced on the pavement. I knew he was going to say yes, but I still asked just to hear him say it. All the parents took their children after four o'clock for long walks to visit the cows, pick corn in the fields, play in the barn, get the laundry, bring milk from the kitchen, and visit other members.

"Of course," my father said and went to fetch the jerry can.

While I waited for my father, my brother, Avner, who was trying to teach the neighbors' dog how to open the door of the old bomb shelter, came over and asked, "Want to go with me to the witch's house?"

"The witch's house?" I shivered, already feeling the eyes of the invisible witch follow me through the cracks in the small asbestos hut. It stood at the end of the kibbutz, not too far from our parents' room, guarding the narrow trail to the beach; its only door always locked, the small windows blocked with a thick layer of dust and spider webs. No one ever entered it.

Avner nodded. "Let's scare her. Maybe she'll run outside and we'll be the first ones to see her."

"Even though she's invisible?" I tried to hide my fear.

Avner started to laugh. "Who told you she's invisible? She's not invisible at all. She's old and ugly. She has hair sticking out of her nose and a big mole above her lip. Everybody knows that."

"What are you kids plotting over there?" my father asked when he came back with the kerosene jerry can.

"Don't tell him," Avner whispered in my ear, covering his mouth with both hands.

"Avner said not to tell you," I repeated proudly. I was so excited that he trusted me with such an important secret; I was willing to follow every word he uttered.

"I'm going to get the kerosene," my father declared. "You kids want to go with me?"

I scratched my head, not knowing what to do. Avner said, "no." Then he turned to me and asked, "You coming?"

Avner never asked me to go with him anywhere. If I said no he would never ask me to play with him again. I decided to go with Avner.

We marched to the end of the concrete pavement, and then skipped on the flat stones that marked the path to the witch's house. I was perspiring with fear. I crouched in the tall weeds behind Avner and made little noises, "psst, psst, psst, miaoo, miaoo, psst, psst," hoping to see the witch storm out on a broom or something to see who was making all the noise. But nothing happened. Tired of waiting, I whispered, "What shall we do now?"

"Stay here," Avner whispered. "I have an idea."

I watched him crawl on his belly all the way to the witch's house and take a broomstick that was leaning against the wall. Then I got my idea. I left my hiding place and joined him near the wall. "Let's throw stones on the windows," I whispered.

Avner thought it was a great idea and told me to collect a handful of stones while he banged on the wall with the broomstick. The first stones I threw did not even get near the window, but after some practice they began flying closer and closer to the window. The sound they made as they hit the asbestos wall was hollow. As if there was no witch inside at all.

In our concentration to scare the witch out of her hiding place we did not notice Dotan's father emptying a trash can in the dumpster. He saw us standing by the wall and yelled, "Avner, Maya, what do you think you're doing?"

"We're scaring the witch," I shouted back.

"Stop throwing stones before you break a window," he ordered.

"But we want to scare the witch," I argued.

"There's no witch in there. Who told you there was a witch in there?" he said, walking away. Then he turned around to make sure we stopped throwing the stones, waved his pointing finger at us, and entered his room.

At night, when my father brought me back to kindergarten, I wanted to tell Nir how I threw stones at the witch's house, but my father already sat on my bed with my favorite book. "Which story do you want me to read?"

I leafed through the book and pointed at one picture that showed a herd of goats and sheep, a bonfire, and two men wearing animal skins. I already knew what the story was about but I wanted my father to read it to me again.

My father cleared his throat and started reading in his storytelling voice. "After many years Adam and Eve had two sons. The older one they named Cain, and the younger one was called Abel. Cain worked the land and Abel was a shepherd. One day they decided to sacrifice something to God. Abel brought a lamb and Cain brought vegetables that he grew in his garden. And God liked what Abel gave him more than what Cain put in the fire. So Cain got jealous and killed his brother."

"And then God asked Cain where was Abel and Cain said that he didn't know," I barged in to show my father that I knew what happened.

"That's right," my father said, and closed the book.

"Wait," I said, grabbing the book from him. "We didn't finish yet."

My father looked at Nir's mother, who was trying to get him to bed promising him that she would come later and leave a candy under his pillow, and continued, "God already knew that Cain killed Abel. He was only testing him. Then he cursed Cain and put a mark on his forehead so all the people would know what he did when they saw him. And now I am going to give you a good night kiss, and leave because Tamara is already turning the lights off," he concluded and closed the book.

Once all the parents and Tamara left kindergarten Nir whispered in the dark, "is it true that your birthday comes before my birthday?"

"Yes," I whispered back.

"Then you're going to die before me," he said.

"Not true," I said. "Abel died before Cain and he was younger than him."

"You're still going to die before me," he said.

On Sunday morning when all the kids went to feed our breakfast leftovers to the chickens and the rabbits that lived in a big cage behind our kindergarten, Tamara called Nir and I and asked who threw a stone into the shoemaker's workshop. Nir looked down and began to scratch something between his toes. Watching the grave expression on her face, and remembering the way Dotan's father yelled at me and Avner, I was not sure whether I should show her how proud I was of my success or not. But I did not consider a denial. So I told her that I did it.

"Don't ever do it again," she frowned, waving her pointing finger close to my face.

Nir raised his eyes for a split second and lowered them before Tamara could notice. My heart sank into a deep hole inside my body and I felt my breakfast climb into my throat. I stared at her. I did not know why she had to find out about it. I thought no one but Nir knew about the tiny stone that flew so perfectly through the open window into the shoemaker's workshop and won me Nir's respect.

"But it was a very small stone," I tried to defend myself and apologize at the same time in a small voice.

"It doesn't matter how small it was," she said. "You should never throw stones through open windows. It is very dangerous. You could kill someone," she said, emphasizing each scary word, and staring into my eyes.

That was a thought that did not cross my mind at all. I could have killed the shoemaker. I did not think that my little stone could reach him. He sat too far from the window. "We waited for him to come out and ask who threw the stone, but he didn't even notice it," I rushed to explain the situation without pausing to breathe, hoping to minimize my sin.

She shook her head and made a disapproving sound with her tongue. Then she said: "Ayelet who works in the kitchen was there after you and Nir left and you know what she saw?"

I looked at Nir, hoping he would say something funny and save me from hearing something I was afraid to hear. But he was still busy scratching his toes.

"She found the shoemaker on the floor, half dead, and blood streaming from his forehead. She brought him a glass of water and put a bandage on the wound. He told her that after you and Nir left, a stone came flying through the window and hit him on the forehead. Now, do you understand why I tell you never to throw stones through open windows? Do you understand that you could have killed him with that stone?" she asked with that dangerous expression on her face.

I nodded and tried to control my growing urge to run to the bathroom and vomit. I understood what she said very well. I was a criminal. A murderer. I almost killed the shoemaker. The old helpless shoemaker who did not do anything bad to me. And soon a policeman would come to the kibbutz and take me to jail. I would never see my parents again. And Avner and the kids from kindergarten. And I would never eat candies on Friday. And my parents would be ashamed of me and would regret that I was their daughter. I was just like Cain who killed his brother. I was cursed, forever. Evil. Me. Maya.

Nir did not look up while Tamara talked, but when she went to finish washing the dishes, he whispered, "Don't believe her. She's lying."

I wanted to believe him. But I could not. Grown-ups did not lie. Only little children did. I wanted to die before my parents would find out. But I was afraid to die. I could not eat all day, although Tamara tried to force me to eat and made me sit in front of my plate while she washed all the dishes and mopped the dining room floors. I threw up twice.

I decided not to say anything to my parents when I came to visit them. As long as they did not find out what I had done, I would not have to go to jail, and they would not know I was an evil girl. I even started to think that I could try to be someone else. I thought if I pretended long enough, I would become that other girl and my parents would never notice. A thick disgusting lump settled in my throat. I felt nauseated. Around me all I could see was blood spilled on the ground. Cain killing Abel. God punishing the murderer.

At night I dreamed that a pack of hungry rabid jackals was chasing me. Blood and foamy saliva were dripping from their red tongues and their eyes were full of hatred. I woke up shivering. The jackals were howling far away on the mountain. Someone started to cry and woke up the father whose turn was to sleep in the kindergarten and make sure we were okay. The bedsprings squeaked when "the sleeper," as we called the father who slept in the dining room, got up to calm the crying child. The quiet murmurs in the other room went on until the sobbing stopped, and finally I fell asleep.

The next day Tamara grabbed my arm and said, "Tomorrow you are going to the shoemaker's workshop to bring back the sandals and I want you to apologize to him. Think about what you want to say to him."

My stomach turned upside down.

"Look at me when I'm talking to you," she yelled.

How could I have looked at her and let her see the infinite terror that resided in my eyes? I could not succumb to the ultimate humiliation and weep in front of her.

On Tuesday I went to the shoemaker's workshop to pick up the sandals. Nir waited for me outside. I entered the workshop and mumbled quickly, "I came to take the sandals."

The shoemaker turned down the volume on the radio, and then I heard him say, "they're on the second shelve. Can you reach it?"

If it was another day I would have probably answer proudly, "yes, I can," but I was feeling too timid to talk. I collected the sandals, and then, while my back was still facing him, I said quickly, "Tamara said I have to ask for your forgiveness for throwing the stone through the window on Friday."

He hummed something friendly in Yiddish and said, "You're a good girl. Come here, I'll give you a candy."

I turned to him, my mouth starting to say, "Can I get one for Nir, too?" and saw in the middle of his pale forehead a dark bleeding hole between two deep creases. A circle of dry blood surrounded the hole my stone had punctured in the skin. The color of the blood mesmerized me. The shoemaker was smiling, his long white fingers inviting me to take two round yellow candies from a tin can. A drop of blood was traveling from the open wound down to his nose.

I turned around and stumbled down the steps, my legs shaking so hard, I nearly fell down. As soon as I steadied myself I began to run. Behind me Nir was running, shouting, "Wait for me, wait for me," but I could not stop. I had to run away from the blood and the smiling man I almost killed. The steaming asphalt burned my feet, the bright sunlight blinded me, the sandals slapped my hips, my belly, my chest. My big left toe hit a rock but I did not stop to feel the pain. Long pine needles stabbed my arms and thorny bushes scratched my legs. And still I did not stop. I tried to catch my breath. Gasping for air and panting heavily, I stopped near the laundry house and wiped the sweat from my face. And then I saw her.

My mother. Pushing a laundry cart full of stinky diapers. And the lump inside my throat exploded into thousands of stinging, burning fragments.

"What happened, Maya?" my mother ran toward me, bending down.

"I.... I didn't mean... I... I didn't mean to...," I tried to talk, choking on my tears, my terror, the scary words that floated in my head.

"Maminka, what happened? Did someone hurt you? Tell me. Who was it?"

"I... I... don't...," I kept choking, holding on to her leg. Gluing myself to her body.

"Calm down. You have to calm down. Tell me what happened. Where are all the other kids? Where is Tamara?"

"In ... in... Kindergarten."

"Why aren't you in kindergarten?" she asked, checking my arms and legs for bruises, wiping the tears from my face with her hand.

I started to cry louder.

"You have to go back to kindergarten. Maminka. It's almost lunchtime. Calm down. Look, nothing happened. There are no cuts or bruises on your legs. Something frightened you? Is that what happened? Now everything is okay, Maminka. Do you want me to walk with you back to kindergarten?" she asked, confused, worried.

"No, I want to stay with you," I begged.

Crouching next to me she whispered, "Maminka, I'll take you to the infants' house but you have to stop crying before we get there, okay?"

I nodded, trying to control a wave of hiccups. My mother was going to take care of me. Protect me from the blood. The scary words. Tamara. The tears were already drying in my eyes, and pleasant warmth spread everywhere inside my body. I put my finger in my mouth and watched her picking up bundles of diapers from her cart and throwing them into a large laundry bin.

"Do you want to go inside and help me load the clean diapers?" she asked looking more relaxed.

I shook my head. She slapped on my finger lightly to get it out of my mouth. I put it back in my mouth when she walked away. When she came back with the clean diapers stuffed inside a dark green canvas sack, she asked me if I wanted to sit on top of the pile. I nodded, my finger still in my mouth. She lifted me up high and put me on top of the canvas sack. At last I had found paradise. My mother agreed to take me to the infants' house instead of forcing me to go back to Tamara. I lay on top of the clean diapers and looked at the clouds floating above me, the ground passing under me and dozed into a dreamy place that smelled of fresh soap and dry lawn clippings.

"We're here," my mother's voice woke me up.

I crawled down from my little nest and followed her. "You have to be very quiet," my mother whispered on the way up the concrete stairs.

"Can I go look at the babies?" I whispered loudly, tiptoeing behind her to the changing table.

She took my hand and walked with me to the bedroom. It was quiet inside. Only Yardena was nursing her baby when we came in.

"Can I kiss the baby?" I tried to touch the baby's cheek. "She's so cute."

"Not while she's eating," my mother and Yardena said simultaneously.

We left the bedroom. My mother went to scrub the toilet while I sat on the floor and played with the baby toys. Yardena came out of the bedroom, opened the refrigerator and poured herself a glass of orange juice.

"Can I also drink orange juice?" I asked my mother who started scrubbing the sink with a soapy pad. It was my only chance to drink from a bottle. In kindergarten we never got to drink anything from a bottle, only when we were sick.

My mother turned to me. "And then you'll go to kindergarten?"

"Yes," I promised.

She stopped scrubbing the sink, washed her hands and poured the juice into a plastic cup. I licked the rim, disappointed that she did not let me drink directly from the bottle.

Yardena smiled at me. Her two hands stretched out toward my face, grabbed both my cheeks, and pinched them hard. "Red cheeks, that's what I'm going to call you from now on. Red cheeks."

I hated what she did. Sometimes she called me Peach. Sometimes, Cherry. Sometimes Sweetie. I tried to smile but I think what came out was an ugly face. Yardena squeezed her nose, and piled a plate with fried chicken livers and mashed potatoes that my mother brought from the kitchen, prepared especially for pregnant women and nursing mothers. Standing behind me, Yardena asked my mother in a very low voice, "does Tamara know she's here?"

"I don't think so. I found her near the laundry house and she refused to go to kindergarten, so I brought her here. I'll take her to kindergarten when I go on my break."

"Sooner the better," Yardena predicted, "or Tamara will raise hell."

"It's time she learned to be a little flexible," my mother said in her grown-up voice. I was not sure what the word *flexible* meant, but it sounded like a good word.

I nodded vigorously and sucked on my finger. "My mother promised to give me a cookie," I bragged.

"Maya, I told you not to talk with your finger in your mouth," my mother scolded me from the sink.

"I want to stay here," I said.

"That's what happened when you..." Yardena shook her head and sighed.

"Come on, Maminka, we have to go or Tamara will be very angry," my mother said. She took off her apron and went to the bathroom. When she came back she had a pair of scissors and a roll of white bandage in her hand. "It's time you stop sucking on your finger. Right?"

My mother had funny ideas that were supposed to stop me from sucking on my finger. Sometimes, when she asked me to give her the finger I sucked on, I would give her the wrong finger and she wouldn't even notice. This time I gave her the right finger. She wrapped the bandage around it.

When we arrived at kindergarten Tamara was standing on the porch, polishing our evening sandals and putting them in a row on the windowsill. My heart jumped and sank again. The sandals. I forgot the sandals. Where did I put them?

"Now I see where you disappeared," she said partly to me, partly to my mother, and frowned at both of us.

I looked at the floor, counting on my mother to get me out of the bad situation, and held on to her hand.

"I found her near the laundry house, crying," my mother said.

"Every kid cries sometimes, it's not the end of the world," Tamara said, spreading brown shoe polish on one of the fifteen pairs of little sandals that she had to polish every afternoon while we took our nap. I watched her slide her hand into one sandal and polish it vigorously, the shoe polish staining the back of her hand. "She went to the shoemaker's workshop with Nir and never came back," she explained. Then she looked at me under her thick eyebrows and asked, "Where are the sandals?"

I wanted to put my finger in my mouth but it was covered with a tasteless bandage. "I don't remember," I mumbled.

"How do you expect me to..." Tamara started to scold my mother.

"I don't expect anything," my mother barged in. I didn't know what that word meant but I liked the sound of it. It sounded like she was on my side. "I'm sure the sandals are not lost. She probably left them near the laundry house," she defended me. "I'll go look for them now. I'm sure they are still there."

"I hope so," Tamara said, irritated.

After my mother left without kissing me goodbye Tamara grabbed my hand, looked at the bandage and asked, "did you cut yourself? Who put this on your finger?"

"My mother put it on because I'm already a big girl and I can't suck on my finger anymore."

"What kind of nonsense is this?" she said to herself and ripped the bandage from my finger.

It didn't hurt but I was really sorry that she took it from me because it was a present from my mother. Our little secret. I went to bed pretending that the bandage was still on my finger, smelling the hospital it came from and tried to fall asleep without putting my finger in my mouth. Nir was rocking in bed, banging his head on the bed. Bang, bang, bang. I looked at him for a long time and then I fell asleep.

Fall announced its arrival with the sighting of the migrating storks soaring above the mountainside in search for a landing spot. Even before the storks arrived, the southern slope was luring us away from kindergarten with promise of new discoveries and wild adventures. It was calling us to chase lazy, brown lizards sunbathing on top of warm limestone boulders. It was wooing us to follow secret trails that ran along clumps of sage and thyme and ended inside dark caves swarming with scorpions and spiders. There were capers to be plucked from prickly branches and carobs to be picked from ancient carob trees. There were acorns to collect from oak trees dwarfed by harsh weather and black goats. There was the entire outdoors to discover, map, and claim as ours. But nothing was more exciting than finding a migrating stork, limping tiredly among the bushes, hungry and distressed, helplessly looking for her sisters. We would carry her to the cowshed to rest on a bed of straw, offer her some food, and watch the vet dress her wounds with a bandage.

Only that I could not get excited. The day I ran up the hill to wave good bye to the rescued stork, I saw the shoemaker standing by his workshop, craning his head back to look at a flock of birds flying in formation toward the sea. The shoemaker bowed his head when he saw us and offered his usual timid, "Shalom, children."

And there, in the middle of his forehead, again I saw the mark. A drop of blood lingered below the wound, just above his nose, bright red and congealed. I rubbed my eyes; hoping tears would wash away the awful sight. But they did not. The open wound kept bleeding. I didn't know what to think. It has been many days since I threw that stone and the wound was still bleeding. How long was I going to see that wound bleed on his forehead? I wanted to ask someone why the shoemaker did not put a bandage on his open wound, why he did not wipe the blood. I wanted to tell someone that I was afraid.

During the first break in the rains we went to the pine grove to hunt for wild mushrooms. We were going to prepare mushroom omelets if we could find enough good mushrooms. There, in the middle of the pine grove, I saw the shoemaker walk toward us, and again, I saw the bloody mark gleaming on his forehead. But this time I did not run away in terror. I realized that it was my curse from God. I understood that no matter how many vows I'd keep, how much regret I'd feel, the bloody mark would never disappear. It would be there forever.

Afterwards I saw the wound bleeding in the workshop, near the dining hall, outside the laundry house. Everywhere I saw the shoemaker I saw the mark. I saw it every time I thought of him. The mark kept bleeding regardless of my shame and my honest penitence. There was no way I could heal it and make it disappear.

One morning, while we were building a castle in the sandbox, decorating it with little stones and sticks, I saw the solution to my suffering. It was my chance to disappear, never feel that awful guilt again, never have to see that mark. I felt no fear or sadness. I waited patiently with a dreamy curiosity. Perhaps Nir was right when he said that I was going to die before him.

The long metal irrigation pipe Nir had picked up from the ground and lifted up in the air was too heavy for him. I knew he was going to drop it. I kept digging in the sand, very quietly, without warning anyone, without looking up until the pipe fell on my head.

It didn't hurt. It didn't make me die either. For a few seconds I was suspended in nothingness as the world shrunk into a dense white cloud that enveloped me in total silence. Moments later I was lying in my bed with a pounding headache and a fast growing bump on my head. I heard Tamara send one of the kids to the main kitchen to fetch ice in a plastic bag. I knew that she was nervous and anxious to act fast. It was her duty to keep me alive.

"She is fine," she said to the curious kids who stood at the door ready to offer me solace. "Nothing terrible has happened, she only has a little headache," she explained impatiently and waved them away.

"Shall I call her mother?" Iris volunteered.

"What for? Her mother can't do anything that we can't do. We'll put some ice on her head and she'll be as good as new at four o'clock," Tamara promised. "Now go outside and don't just stand here like a log."

There was no time for emotional outbursts or hugs. For Tamara my accident was just an inconvenience. I could hear it in her voice. It was annoyed, impatient, preoccupied with more demanding tasks. When the ice arrived from the main kitchen, she wrapped the plastic bag with a towel, put it on my head and disappeared to complete her daily chores. I lay in bed and wondered if I would be allowed to chew on the ice cubes. I did not cry or ask to see my mother. I only felt a little dizzy.

The kindergarten was quiet when I woke up. All the kids were napping in their beds. I reached to my head and felt that all the ice had melted inside the plastic bag. I called Tamara and asked if I could go to the bathroom.

"On your tiptoes," she ordered.

While I was gone she took the plastic bag and dumped the water in the sink before I had a chance to see if any ice cubes were left for me to chew on. I climbed back to bed feeling more upset about losing the precious ice than the painful bump that kept growing on my head.

In the evening, when my father came to put me to bed, he heard Tamara's interpretation of the event.

"Maya had a little accident today," she told my father in a friendly tone while he was helping me take off my clothes.

"An accident? She didn't say a word about it to us."

I pretended to be busy with the buttons.

"You know how it is," Tamara sighed, "the children were playing outside while I was washing the breakfast dishes. I can't watch them all the time," she defended herself before he said anything. "I was just going to call them in for the ten o'clock snack when Erez came in and said that Nir dropped an irrigation pipe on Maya's head. But she's fine now," she added quickly and looked at me with her ominous eyes. "Aren't you?"

I felt obliged to nod.

My father looked at me questioningly. He measured the bump with his finger. I groaned even though he touched it very lightly. He tucked me into bed and promised, "Until the wedding day it will go away."

I didn't know whose wedding he was referring to and how long I would have to wait, but the way he said it sounded comforting. I kissed him on his cheek and asked him to tell me one more time the story about the rabbit who sneaked into the vegetable garden and ate all the lettuce. After he left I lay in the dark and imagined that one day when I grow up all my pain would go away and I would live happily ever after with Prince Charming and my father in the same house.

Chapter Three

For many weeks the part of the mountain slope we used to roam in our search for porcupine's quills and turtle shells was flattened and cleared by a noisy bulldozer. A square area was cordoned off by ropes and dug out for foundations. Trucks loaded with rich soil and debris carved a path on the hillside as they lurched downward coughing black smoke and leaving a trail of destruction in their wake. Other trucks unloaded cement blocks and sacks of whitewash powder and concrete, gravel and sand, long steel bars and wooden planks in a surprisingly organized fashion by the side of our chicken coop.

The boys were beyond themselves with excitement; investigating the piles of building materials, getting rides from the truck drivers, and making bets about when the new children's house would be finished. For hours they stood in front of the concrete mixer watching the sand and gravel mixture turn into soft gray concrete later to be carried away in buckets by timid Arab laborers. We girls stayed away from the Arab construction workers, who came from surrounding villages, and avoided the building site. Our common sense had warned us that even while wearing sandals one could easily get her foot pricked by a rusty nail and have to be rushed to the clinic and get a very painful tetanus shot from the frowning nurse. Getting attention from the nurse and the *metapelet* was not a cherished prize. These two knew how to make a kid feel guilty, irresponsible, or plain stupid even when she was in pain.

The work was progressing slowly, changing the landscape we knew so well into a manicured plot we were going to know even better. The chicken coop was dismantled and removed to make room for another playground and the chickens relocated to the new children's farm built on the other side of the kibbutz. I did not regret losing the chickens. Among them lived a ferocious rooster who enjoyed terrorizing us while we fed his harem. No amount of breakfast leftovers ever appeased him. Even threatening him that he would be sent to the kitchen did not intimidate him. He was determined to demonstrate his prowess to everyone around him and scare us to death until the last moment when he was carried away, pecking angrily at anyone who touched him and clucking at the top of his lungs.

Losing a section of the vegetable garden was a different story. Although I did not like eating vegetables, I loved watching them peep out of the damp earth and grow upward, looking so fragile. I loved smelling them, touching their skin and arranging them in my basket. I was a little sad when our vegetables garden had to be reduced to two rows of cucumbers and radishes because the rows of carrots, scallions, and lettuce lay in the way of the planned concrete walkway that was going to connect the new children's house with the rest of the kibbutz.

As a compensation for the crippled garden, the gardener had planted young poplar trees on the northern side of the new building and let us water them with a long hose. Then one Saturday morning we joined forces with our parents and planted grass in front of the completed building. Now all that was left to do was to wait for all the layers of oil paint to dry out and the powerful smell of fresh paint to evaporate.

A week before we were going to start first grade we were given aluminum buckets, brushes, and scrapers and sent to clean the new children's house. It was a hot day and we were going to work in shorts and sandals. The day looked very promising. A lot of water was going to be poured on the floors and windows and that meant we were going to have a lot of fun.

None of us shied away from hard work. We were used to working hard in the garden, in the yard, and in the kindergarten.

We were raised to love to work and often competed who was working the hardest and who volunteered to do the most demanding jobs. Everyone in kindergarten knew that being a hard worker was the best way to elevate your status in the eyes of the *metapelet* and keep her off your back. If she asked you to dust the book shelves and you took off all the books and wiped them, then wiped the cobweb from the bottom of the shelves, then wiped the top at least twice, every time with a different rag, you knew that she would praise your diligence in front of all the other kids and make you feel special. If it was your turn to clean the tables after lunch, you made sure to collect all the crumbs in your cupped hand before they fell on the floor and use a lot of soap on the Formica. And when it was your turn to clean the chicken coop, you took all morning to do it, sweeping every grain of wheat you saw until your nose ached from the stink and your face was covered with sweat. No task was below us we learned very early on. Laziness was the most loathsome trait one could suffer from. We sang about the merits of carpenters and blacksmiths, read stories that glorified ants because they labored incessantly, and covered the walls with drawings depicting our parents at their work place. **WORK IS OUR LIFE**, a hand-painted poster preached in large letters above the dining room window.

All morning we worked on the new house scraping stains of whitewash and dry paint from the floors, scrubbing paint drops from the glass windows and the sinks, dusting closets, washing the tile walls in the two shower rooms. Tamara presided over the operation with the tenacity of a drill sergeant, reminding us that before we get to splash water all over the place we had to finish scrubbing every bit of paint that stuck to the floors, then sweep and collect the garbage that piled up outside, and take it to the dumpster. It felt as if we were never going to get our feet wet. I started wondering when the new *metapelet* would come to relieve Tamara from her duties. After all we were leaving kindergarten and getting new beds, new tables and chairs and even new curtains for the windows. Why not a new *metapelet*?

"What do you mean a new *metapelet*?" Tamara asked without raising her head from a toilet bowl she was scouring with an ungloved hand. "What do you need a new *metapelet* for? I'm not good enough for you anymore?"

"I thought we were going to get a new *metapelet* with the new house," I stuttered stupidly. "Who will be the *metapelet* in kindergarten if you work here?"

"Don't you worry about that," she patted my head with the same hand that touched the insides of the toilet bowl. "There are enough women on the kibbutz who would be very happy to take my place in kindergarten."

This exchange ended with the sound of a big splash of water. Apparently, Dorit decided it was time to wet the floors. Without asking for Tamara's permission, she filled up one of the aluminum buckets with soapy water and poured it in the middle of the dining room. In an instant, Tamara rushed out of the bathroom to see what was going on. I followed her. As I turned the corner and saw the bubbles quickly progress toward my feet, I knew I had to act fast. I ran outside and grabbed a squeegee before there would be none left for me.

"Wait, wait a minute, I didn't say you could start mopping the floor yet," I heard Tamara's desperate call behind me. But it was too late for her to stop what Dorit had set in motion. Eshel and Nir, my old pals from toddler's house, needed very little encouragement to follow suit. They filled up two buckets with water and stood by the classroom door, waiting. As soon as they saw me reaching for a squeegee, they kicked the full buckets and the water spilled all over the classroom floor.

I looked through the window and saw Tamara stand in the middle of the dining room, surrounded by water on all sides, watching Daphna and Iris bring more buckets of water. She did not order them to stop or threaten that there would be serious consequences. She just crossed her arms over her chest and shook her head as if she were having a secret conversation with herself. Seeing that Tamara gave in to the new turn of events, everyone joined in bringing more buckets of water and pouring it on the floor. The water level rose above my toes, cooling down the dusty floor and my feet.

"Children, start pushing out the water," Tamara regained her drill sergeant composure and started ordering us around, her trancelike paralysis completely gone. "We don't have all the time in the world to do it. I'm going to get lunch from the kitchen in a few minutes."

A loud argument peppered by mild pushing and shoving ensued on the front porch around the questions of who could perform the job better and faster and whether those of us who grabbed the squeegees first should hand them over to those who were working too hard to notice that Dorit took the initiative and opened the flood gates.

"Stop arguing and start working," Tamara reminded us. She didn't have to worry about her squeegee. She already had one secured for herself that she brought from the communal kitchen. It was twice the width of our squeegees, designed especially for the grown-ups' dining hall floor that had to be mopped every day after breakfast.

We had only five squeegees and there were ten of us hungry for action. Under the rising pressure from all sides, those of us who were holding on to the squeegees as if for dear life reached a compromise and agreed to share them. We decided that each one of us would push the water from one bedroom, then give the squeegee to another kid who would continue working in the dining room or in the classroom. In a few minutes the bedroom floor was cleared of water. I surrendered my squeegee to Tomer and walked outside. I had nothing to do and my feet hardly got wet at all. There was simply not enough time to start a water war or slide on the floor "accidentally" and so forth. Tamara left to bring our lunch from the kitchen so there was no one to order me to start cleaning the mess left on the front porch. Shortly afterwards she came back from the communal kitchen and announced that we were going to have lunch outside, under the azedarach tree.

We loved eating in the outdoors, sitting on the ground with our plates on our laps, and eating canned food. There is no worry in the world for a child who eats outside. She puts her little rear end on a rock or leans her back on a trunk of a tall tree, folds her legs under her body, and knows that there will be no pearl barley soup, or cooked zucchini, or fried fish full of tiny bones in the aluminum containers. There will be only food she likes to eat, fresh air all around, and blinding sunlight. The birds will be singing in the trees above and ants will be scurrying beneath her feet, busy as ever, teaching their excellent work ethic to the lazy grasshopper.

Tamara opened cans of corn, green peas with carrots, pickled cucumbers, sauerkraut and beef with a small can opener she took out of her apron pocket. In the middle of the tablecloth she put a pile of sliced rye bread and a tall aluminum jug full of lukewarm lemonade. By the time she handed us our plastic plates of food we were impatient, exhausted, and reaching for the bread.

A few days later we met our new teacher, Ora Etgar. She appeared in the new children's house when we were helping Tamara move our stuff. Ora came to stock the cabinets with books, notepads, writing tools, and all kinds of supplies a teacher and her first and second grade pupils might need during the first months of school.

First I noticed her tight lips. Then I saw the rest of her. She wore faded black shorts held by an elastic band, a short sleeved white shirt with prints of blue and brown ladders that went nowhere and flat brown sandals. Her hair was cut above the shoulders, and there was absolutely no makeup on her face, because women in the kibbutz never tried to make themselves look pretty. Like Tamara, she was also efficient, bossy, and a bit frightening.

She was not unknown to me. I knew her, her husband, and her two children just like I knew everyone else who lived on the kibbutz. But I did not know what she would be like as a teacher until the moment she entered the new children's house and put her hand on my shoulder.

"Shalom children," she said above my head.

I did not like her voice.

"Say Shalom to Ora," Tamara commanded from behind me.

"Shalom Ora," I complied, wondering how to shake her hand off my shoulder.

"Are you happy to start first grade?"

She did not notice the faces Dotan and Erez made behind her back. They were about to start second grade and her question was an insult to them. My gut told me it was not a good start.

"Are you happy to start first grade?" Tamara repeated the question, annoyed.

I nodded. Why do I have to be the one to answer all the questions? Can't the other children talk too?

"These children have no manners," Tamara shook her head and sighed.

"Don't worry, we have all the time in the world to teach them everything they need to know," Ora promised, and to my trained ear it sounded like a threat.

On Friday, Tamara announced that we had to take our pillows and summer blankets to the new house and put them on our new beds because the house was ready for us to move in. Everything was already in place. Reading lamps were hanging on the walls above each bed and new curtains were hanging over the windows. We even had new covers for the beds. The dishes piled up on the shelves above the kitchen sink and three square tables stood in the dining room with wooden chairs around them. The blackboard hung on the wall in the classroom and our desks stood in two rows in front of it.

The new children's house smelled of fresh paint and chlorine. There was not a speck of dust anywhere or brown fingerprints on the whitewashed walls. Spring cleaning would be a breeze this year, I thought. Compared with the crowded dining room and the small cubicle we had for a kitchenette in the kindergarten, the new dining room looked like a palace. We even had new pictures on the walls. Nir started chasing Eshel around the dining room tables. Then Tamara entered and yelled at them to stop running around. "Immediately."

Our beds were going to be assigned to us now, she said.

My bed had a green cover with yellow and red and blue stripes. I liked it right away. I jumped on the bed and looked out the window. A cluster of oleanders blocked the view of the last row house in which Dorit and Daphna's parents lived. During summer nights I knew we would be able to hear their voices when they sat outside on the lawn and talked or listened to the radio. It would make us feel so much safer hearing their voices and, perhaps, even seeing the light from their rooms trickle through the bushes into our windows. It was comforting to know that they were there so close to us. We would be able to call them through the window if we had an emergency in the middle of the night.

In kindergarten we could rely on the weekly parent who slept in the dining room on a folding metal bed, but now that we were starting first grade, we were old enough to rely on ourselves. No more sleeper walking around in funny underwear, no more loud snores, no more squeaky bedsprings, I thought of the night Daphna got scared when she heard the jackals howl on the mountain and the sleeper was not around to comfort her. "Don't be afraid," Tomer called from the next bedroom. "Those are not jackals, those are only wolves."

Everyone in the children's house started laughing and Nir made a long howling sound: Ahooo. Did Tomer really think that wolves were less scary than jackals? Didn't he ever hear the story of Little Red Riding Hood?

We never told the sleeper about what had happened that night when he finally arrived, but for years afterwards it was our best joke. Whenever one of the kids became upset about something, someone would say, "Don't worry, it's only wolves," and we would all burst out laughing.

"And this is your nightstand," Tamara pointed at a short cupboard next to my bed. Then she assigned the other two beds to Iris and Nir.

I did not mind having Iris as my new roommate even though she was a little bit spoiled. When she was in kindergarten she used to have bad dreams and then cry for hours. Sometimes her mother, Bruria, would come in the middle of the night and take her to sleep in her room. Then, early in the morning, before Tamara would come to wake us up, Bruria would bring Iris back to kindergarten, tuck her in bed, and whisper to her that she had to keep it as their little secret. "No one has to know you spent the night with us in our room," she would roll the "R" at the tip of her tongue. And Iris would pretend that she slept in her own bed all night.

In the midst of my excitement to claim the bed under the window, I thought of Amiram who was in the toddlers' house with me and Nir. He did not move into the new children's house with us because his parents left the kibbutz in the summer. Before they left each one of us made a painting of the kibbutz and gave it to Amiram as a souvenir. Then his father did some magic tricks like he used to do for us on Saturday mornings after breakfast, and for a moment we forgot that Amiram was leaving us.

I felt sad for Amiram. Now he had to sleep in a room all by himself, without any children to talk to at night; he had to go to a new school with children he had never met before; and he did not even know his teacher. I thought it was better to have a teacher you knew, even if it was someone you did not like very much, than a teacher you have never seen before.

The Israeli flag was flying at the top of the flagpole in front of the communal dining hall, adding a stately aura to the festivities with its uplifting white and blue colors. From a battered record player a woman's voice singing children songs competed unsuccessfully with the loud bangs on a hanging steel pipe calling everyone to assemble on the unpaved square. All school-age children, about thirty of us, were lined up in front of the flagpole, dressed in our "Saturday clothes" and ready for the opening ceremony of the new school year to begin.

The members who were eating breakfast came outside to watch the ceremony. They stood on the other side of the small square and talked to each other about whatever grown-ups liked to talk about when they smoked cigarettes and drank black coffee. Dorit's mother, who was in charge of the kitchen, came outside to watch the ceremony, wearing a stained apron over her shorts. From where I was standing I could see an intricate web of blue veins running up her legs. Her husband, a heavyset blond who hunted wild pigs on the mountain at night, stood near her in his blue work clothes smoking a pipe. His black rubber boots were dotted with wet brown blotches almost all the way up to his knees. Without standing too close to him I knew that a faint smell of cow dung and tobacco hung in the air surrounding him. Nir's mother, who was the kibbutz nurse, stopped on her way to the infants' house to watch the ceremony with Doctor Shapiro. He came to the kibbutz once a week to check on the sick children and give us the shots and medicines we needed. Standing next to the kibbutz members in an immaculate white coat over neatly ironed shirt and tie he looked like someone from another planet.

I searched for my mother in the crowd. I knew that she worked in the toddlers' house and could not leave work to watch the ceremony by herself, so I hoped she would come with the five youngsters. As I was about to give up, I saw her approaching on the cement walkway with her toddlers. She tried to line them up in front of the grown-ups, but they paid no attention to her, so she gave up and made them sit down in a circle on the ground. I waved to catch her eyes, but she was too busy putting hats on their little heads. I let my eyes wander to my brother's class, the oldest children's group in the kibbutz.

Avner was standing closest to the flagpole, dressed in an ironed white shirt and blue shorts, clutching a piece of paper in his right hand. I knew he was going to recite a poem during the ceremony because he had spent all Saturday morning practicing with my father. Avner needed the entire morning and most of the afternoon hours to memorize all the words. I hoped he would not forget anything now that he had to read in front of the entire kibbutz. I always got terribly nervous when we had to perform in front of our parents; my voice shook when we sang and my heart pounded too fast when we danced.

Our teacher opened the ceremony. With a solemn voice she asked us to be quiet then started greeting everybody with lots of important grown-up words I did not understand. She read a long passage from a thick book. It was very boring and I stopped listening. When she finished reading, Kimchi began playing the accordion. Like all the other members, he was also dressed in blue work clothes and leather work boots. He was the kibbutz's designated musician. As on every occasion, Kimchi played with great concentration and fervor. His roughly shaved chin rested on top of the accordion, the deep furrows in his forehead quickly filled with perspiration, his eyes were tightly shut, and his foot tapped the rhythm on the gravel.

I was so bewitched by the speed his fingers moved I nearly missed our teacher's call to come to the table and get our first book. I took the book from her extended hand and not knowing what to do or say, turned around and ran back to my place. I heard applause and laughter and got so nervous that everyone was looking at me, that I forgot to listen to my brother read the poem.

I came to my senses when the children from my brother's class started playing a song on their recorders, making lots of mistakes. After them, Eshel's mother, who was also my brother's teacher, wished all the children good luck and asked the grown-ups to join her in singing the national anthem.

I did not know the lyrics and listened carefully. The song started very quietly, on very low notes that were difficult to hear; the words making little sense to me. Slowly the music rose in a crescendo into such high notes, the older kids who knew the lyrics had to scream the words in order to reach the highest note, and that made them sing completely out of tune. It was quite funny to hear them sing in such disharmony. I wondered how the grown-ups were able to remain so serious. But they did, until the last word.

Finally Ora announced that the ceremony was over. Above the noise of the dispersing crowd I called my mother to wait and ran to show her my new book. She looked at the book cover and gave it back to me. She did not look very interested or happy that I got my first book. Her toddlers were tired, and she had to wipe their noses and make sure they didn't fall and hurt themselves.

"Run to your classroom before your teacher starts looking for you," she patted on my cheek. "When you come home in the afternoon we'll look at your book. Now I don't have any time."

Because we were in two different grades the teacher told us which subjects we were going to study together and which subjects each grade was going to study alone. Then she distributed one pencil, one eraser, a notepad and a pencil-box to each kid. I arranged everything side by side on top of my desk. Our desk, a large wooden box with two heavy lids that opened upward, smelled like sawdust and varnish. Inside, there was a thin layer of dust. I wiped the dust with my hand and waited for the teacher to start teaching. But she said that there was something very important we had to do first.

We were going to pick a name for our group.

Every age group in the kibbutz got a name once they started school. My brother's class was named *Tkuma* (Resurrection), and the group above us, which included third and fourth grade, was called *Yakinton* (Hyacinth). I liked my brother's class name because it made them sound very strong, independent, and fearless. I wanted to be like them, but they were the oldest children in the kibbutz, so the name really suited them. We, on the other hand, were a bunch of kindergarten kids, who hardly knew how to read and write. The teacher said we'd make a list of names and then take a vote.

Right away I thought of *Tzivoni* (Tulip). Tulips were the most beautiful flowers in the world. They grew wild in the middle of the orange groves and on the slopes of the *wadis* that surrounded the kibbutz. They also grew in countries that existed in fairy tales.

They decorated snow-covered palaces in which majestic swans turned after midnight into handsome princes who danced until dawn with beautiful princesses.

"Eshel, what name did you think of?" The teacher's voice startled me out of my reverie about princesses and snow and rain puddles.

"Eshel," he said.

"Yes, I know your name is Eshel. Now tell us what name you have in mind."

"Eshel, Eshel, Eshel," he said.

We started laughing. He wanted the class to have his name. Of course he knew it was impossible. It was a big joke. And it freed us from having to be quiet and serious and thinking about names. The boys lost control and started shouting their names: Tomer, Dotan, Nir, Noam, they competed who could yell the loudest.

"Bulldozer, tractor, pee-pee," they screamed, laughing as if it were the funniest joke in the world.

"Quiet," the teacher shouted.

Immediately the silence returned to the class.

"Those of you who disturbed the order lost their right to suggest a name," she said ominously, looking at the boys with eyes full of rage. "Now we'll start again and I don't want to hear anyone talk without my permission. You will choose a name of a bird or a tree or a flower that grows around here, not in the desert or on the moon, but here, near the kibbutz, understood? And you'll talk only when it's your turn."

"*Tzivoni* (tulip)," I said half-heartedly only because she was looking at me. I was hoping that everyone in the classroom would love my idea and vote for it, and we would not have to think about names anymore and feel bad for those who lost their turn.

"*Narkis* (daffodil)," Iris said.

"*Dolphin*," Hadas whispered.

"*Efroni* (sparrow)," Erez coughed after her, even though he did not have a cold. He was the only boy who did not shout his name because he was always very quiet and shy.

"*Osher* (happiness)," Dorit said, and started drumming with her fingers on her desk. At second grade she was already very poetic. I didn't think the name she chose had a chance. The teacher said we had to pick a name of a flower or a tree. But Dorit was the oldest girl in the class and her brother was the first boy born in the kibbutz, so she felt she could do whatever she wanted.

Daphna could not decide between *Tapuz* (orange) and *Yasmin* so the teacher allowed her to suggest two names.

We took a vote. The teacher read each name and we raised our finger only when we heard the name we liked the most. The name that got the majority of fingers was *Efroni* (sparrow). I thought *Tzivoni* was a prettier name but the boys did not like it. They did not like any of the names the girls chose. They all voted for Erez's name because he was a boy, and since they were in the majority, we had to accept their name. Even the teacher's vote could not help us win another name. She voted for *Tapuz* because we had lots of orange trees growing around the kibbutz, and her husband was in charge of the orange grove. But she lost too. And from that moment on all of us at first and second grade were known to everyone who lived on the kibbutz as the kids from *Efroni* class.

I loved being in first grade. Entering the classroom made me feel grown-up and important. I knew what to do most of the time and how to get what I wanted: appreciation, attention, compliments. It was the first time I felt I was different. In kindergarten I was just one of the crowd, and worse, one of the younger crowd because I was born in the summer. But here I was noticed and called by the teacher to write on the blackboard. I was not shy or afraid when I stood in front of the class. Learning was easy for me. I did not have to struggle to memorize how to spell difficult words or add numbers. The shape of the letters floated inside me and popped out of my head on cue. I felt comfortable in the classroom. I liked to sit there by myself after all the kids went to their parents' room at four o'clock and read, while listening to the soothing sound of the sea.

Chapter Four

Two weeks before we started second grade we moved again to a brand new children's house. It was built on the edge of a clover field, away from the mountainside and the howling jackals, overlooking the Mediterranean Sea. Again we scrubbed and mopped and wiped and carried armfuls of clothes from one children's house to another. Again we were assigned new beds, desks, and roommates. But unlike the other moves, this time we also got a fresh new *metapelet*. I didn't know what kind of *metapelet* Zehava was going to be, but I was sure she would be better than the ever-frowning Tamara. Everyone in the children's house was excited and curious when she came to relieve Tamara. For a few days we exercised good manners at the breakfast table and did not talk during afternoon nap. In return Zehava did not yell at us and complimented our good behavior.

The new children's house offered us also a promotion in status. Not only did we distance ourselves from the surroundings of the kindergarten and the toddlers' house, we now found ourselves living next door to the oldest kids of the kibbutz. They resided in the supreme children's house, a mighty fortress compared with our new, shiny children's house. It stood solitary on the way to the basketball court, unattached to any other children's house, promoting secrecy and courage and utterly inaccessible to anyone younger than its residents.

My brother, Avner, lived there. Since I had no excuse to go inside, the only time I saw him was during the ten o'clock recess, when he played soccer with his classmates. And even then we never mixed. He hardly noticed me or showed me that he noticed me when I played tag with the girls from my class on the unpaved courtyard between the children's houses. The only time we ever talked to each other was after four o'clock when we went to visit our parents.

The fact that the mighty fortress' gates were closed to us did not mean that our doors were closed to the older kids. Perhaps because they were in the fifth and sixth grade and much bigger than us, they had the courage to do whatever they wanted. One thing they liked to do was to sneak into our bedrooms in the middle of the night and smear our faces with pink toothpaste or black shoe polish. They enjoyed making fun of us.

The second time we woke up with crusty toothpaste on our cheeks, the boys suggested we take turns and stay up all night. All the girls, including me, were too scared to stay up alone. What were we supposed to do if we saw someone sneaking in? Scream? Catch him? And what if they fought back and tortured us until we told them all our secrets?

"We'll watch the house in pairs," the boys compromised.

On Saturday night we launched our defense plan. Tomer and Dorit, the oldest kids in the group, volunteered for the first shift. Immediately after lights out they ran to the shower rooms and sat on the small bench in the dark. A few minutes later we all joined them. We stood around and whispered excitedly about what we were going to do if we caught someone and how we were going to show that kid that we were not afraid of him. Dorit brought her little transistor radio and we listened to music while we waited. For the longest time no one showed up. It started to get really late and we were worried that one of the parents would show up and yell at us to go to bed. We also started getting tired of waiting. One by one we left the shower room. In the morning, when we felt the dried toothpaste on our cheeks, we realized that Dorit and Tomer had fallen asleep during their shift. When Zehava saw the dried toothpaste on our sleepy faces she went to Efrat, the *metapelet* of the older kids from the class of Y*akinton* and *Tkuma*, and asked her to try to stop the raids. But the kids from my brother's class were not afraid of their *metapelet* and the raids continued until the nights got colder and the first rains began to fall.

When winter finally arrived, our honeymoon with Zehava was over. We realized that she was not much different from Tamara, our old *metapelet*. Like Tamara, she was always commanding, impatient, and unforgiving. During afternoon nap she ordered us to lie with our faces turned to the wall, and if she caught anyone whispering she would send him to the shower room and make him sit there until four o'clock. She also didn't care that we always ran out of hot water and insisted that everybody took a shower at the same time. And she made us clean the children's house as if it were the dirtiest place on earth. In the mornings we had to make our beds, then take turns mopping the floors of our bedrooms, scrubbing the toilets and sinks, clearing the breakfast tables, sweeping the dining room floor and carrying bags of dirty clothes to the laundry house. After lunch we took turns clearing the tables, washing the dishes, taking the garbage to the dumpster, mopping the dining room floor. On Fridays we had to wash the windows and the screens with soapy water, air the blankets, brush our mattresses and spray them, scrub the floor panels, and dust the shelves. It was endless work that never brought reward. And while we were at work, she would sit at her table, smoke a cigarette, drink her instant coffee, and gossip with the teacher. Sometimes she would bribe us with a promise of a walk to the beach if we finished our chores on time, but then she would snatch it back if we took too long.

There was no escape from Zehava's chores and Ora's homework. Although there were only two of them and twelve of us, we feared them with the same intensity the pious fear the Almighty. With unfailing determination, they were committed to hold us accountable for the smallest transgression, and they had each other for an ally.

To avoid confrontation with the teacher, I always made sure to do my homework on time. I would copy all the questions then answer them quickly so that later, if one of the kids forgot to do homework I could help and our teacher would not have a reason to punish anyone. I did not mind doing it. I liked staying in the classroom by myself after all the kids went to their parents' rooms at four o'clock. It was my quiet time, the only time I could be by myself with no one around to yell at me or tell me what to do. It was only me, my book, the blackboard in front of me and the sound of the waves crashing on the rocks.

It was not an easy task, however. Not everyone cooperated with my plan. Iris, for example, said that she did not care what our teacher would say or do to her when she found out that she did not do her homework. She even turned me down when I offered her my notebook with all the answers. When I tried to persuade her to do her homework after her parents left the children's house, she said, "I'll do it tomorrow before class. It's not my turn to mop the bedroom floor or set the tables for breakfast."

That girl did not care about anything. Barefoot and dressed in pink flannel pajamas, she hugged her knees and waited for Zehava to start reading to us a bedtime story. All the kids were sitting in a semicircle in the dining room, some scratching between their toes, others swallowing a yawn. I could not relax and enjoy the new adventure Thor Heyerdahl was having in the middle of the ocean on his raft, Kon-Tiki. All I could do was fidget in my chair and try to picture what would happen during Bible class when our teacher discovers that Iris did not do her homework.

The next morning our teacher was fifteen minutes late. She went to donate blood in the clinic and Iris borrowed my notebook to copy the homework. At least that was what I thought when she gave me back my notebook.

The chapter we were studying was about the angels' visit to Sodom. I knew how the story was going to end because my father used to read to me from the illustrated Bible we had in kindergarten, and many times I saw the picture of burning Sodom and the woman who turned into a pillar of salt because she disobeyed God. In class, though, we had to learn the meaning of all the difficult words, memorize important idioms, draw maps and know who said what to whom and why. It was very boring to sit in the classroom and listen to our teacher explain a story, so to make the time pass faster I entertained myself by drawing seashells and fish and an octopus in my notebook. In the background I could hear my four classmates take turns reading aloud from the chapter we were studying, which meant that soon I was going to read too. Reading aloud was a good distraction from boredom. I waited for my turn only half listening to the voices around me.

"Maya, continue reading," the teacher's voice jerked me out of my drawing.

At last. Quickly I scanned the page to where the men of Sodom told Lot to kick the angels out of his house so they could torture them. My finger stopped at the last verse Hadas read. I started reading Lot's response. "Behold now, I have two daughters which have not known men; let me I pray you bring them out onto you and do ye to them as is good in your eyes; only onto these men do nothing; for therefore they came under the shadow of my roof." I read loudly and clearly, paying little attention to the terrible meaning of Lot's words (take the kids, leave the grown-ups alone). I wanted to prolong my reading as much as possible, enjoy the limelight. But the inevitable moment came and the teacher asked me to close the book. It was time to check our homework.

"Nir, read the first question."

Nir read the question then read from his notebook: "Lot to the angels."

"Good," she said, and asked Hadas to read the second question, even though it should have been my turn because I sat next to Nir.

"Me?" Hadas asked in a tiny voice. She was procrastinating because she was afraid to make a mistake in front of everyone and be ridiculed by our teacher. The teacher had no mercy for slower students and always made them feel really bad and stupid whenever she had a chance. But Hadas had no reason to be worried. She was not going to make a mistake because I let her copy the answers from my notebook.

"Yes, you," the teacher sighed. For a change she did not raise her voice or gave her a look. Perhaps because it was the first lesson she was not too exasperated yet.

Hadas read the question then very carefully answered it with another question. "The angels to Lot?"

The teacher nodded to herself and marked something in her small black notebook which she kept under lock in her desk drawer. Whenever we talked during class she liked to tell us that our grades were calculated there and could be changed at any moment depending on our behavior. Eshel stuck his elbow in Hadas' waist. Hadas did not respond to the first provocation, but when he tried again she slapped his hand.

"What do you think you're doing?" the teacher accused her without even looking up.

"He started," Hadas whispered.

Eshel did not protest. He knew he was guilty.

"Next time you will have to leave the classroom," the teacher threatened.

Hadas did not argue. There was no use arguing with that teacher.

"Maya," the teacher said without elaborating.

I read the question and answered, "The men of Sodom to Lot." A tiny hangnail on the side of my thumb started to hurt me badly. I tried to pull it off.

"Very Good," the teacher said when I looked up. She always praised me even though these questions were easy. I did not have to spend a long time to look for the answers. As a matter of fact, it took me longer to copy the questions than to answer them. For Hadas it was different. It took her much longer to do her homework. But the teacher never praised the slower kids. She had no patience for them.

While I was trying to pull the throbbing hangnail she asked Eshel to answer the next question. He read the question, then the answer, which was "The angels to Lot." I could tell that he was bored too.

"Good," the teacher said. She praised Eshel even when he did not deserve to be praised because his mother was also a teacher and she taught our teacher's son, Yoav.

Finally it was Iris's turn. She was sitting at the front where Daphna and Noam from third grade usually sat when they did not go to math class. She was playing with the ring her grandmother sent her for her birthday. She always got jewelry for her birthdays. Necklaces with small pearls, gold earrings and bracelets with little animals dangling from them. This ring had a small round stone that sparkled like a diamond and two red stones on each side of the diamond. Iris was definitely more interested in her new ring than in the lesson. It worried me. Tomer from third grade, who sat next to her during all the other lessons, was also in a math lesson, so there was no one near her to help out in case she did not have the right answer.

"Iris, did you do your homework?" The teacher asked.

"Who, me?" Iris asked.

"Yes, you."

Without acknowledging that she had heard the answer, she opened her notebook and leafed through it. We waited silently until she stopped, leaned over her notebook and said, "The angels to Lot." She leaned back on her chair and raised one side of her lips in a contemptuous half smile that implied she could care less about what the teacher would say about her answer.

"You have to read the question first, like all the other kids," the teacher said, slowly, as if she were talking to someone very stupid.

"I didn't copy the answers," Iris responded. No trace of anxiety in her voice.

I raised my hand.

"Yes, Maya," the teacher asked with an impatient sigh.

"I can read the question." I wanted to divert the storm from engulfing Iris and the rest of the class. I hated Iris at that moment for putting us through this. Why couldn't she copy the questions like everyone else? She knew she had to do it. It was not the first time we had to do homework.

"Why didn't you copy the questions?" the teacher turned to Iris, completely ignoring me. Now I hated her too.

"Someone wiped the blackboard before I had a chance to do it," she shrugged.

Stupid girl. How did she know what the answer would be then?

"Then how did you know what the answer was?"

Of course the teacher had to ask her that.

"I saw the questions before I went to my parents' room," Iris lied with a straight face. I wanted to yell at her to shut up. That was the stupidest excuse I have ever heard. How could she remember them? Someone please say something, I prayed silently, but not to God because according to the Bible God killed liars, thieves, adulterers, and those who did not believe in him.

"I wrote the answers before I copied the questions, then someone wiped the blackboard before I had a chance to do it."

Good. She corrected herself fast enough and her new explanation sounded much better. The teacher might even believe her. Someone did wipe the blackboard before all the kids came back to the children's house from their parents' rooms. The kids liked to play tic-tac-toe on the blackboard before story time. They did it every night.

"Eshel, read the question," the teacher said. I felt so relieved I wanted to applaud Iris. It seemed like the teacher accepted her story. That girl had real talent.

"Up, get out of this place, for the Lord will destroy this city," Eshel read in a loud and confident voice. I was so glad he could read like that. Things seemed to fall back into place and peace was returning to the classroom.

"Iris?" the teacher's voice reminded me that the crisis was not over yet.

"The angels to Lot," Iris said with a shrug and an intonation impregnated with apathy and mature sophistication. Her blank gaze announced to the class that these questions did not match her intellect, that they were insultingly simple. She read the answer as if she had known it all her life, as if it were the only possible answer, as if it were the most obvious answer to anyone who possessed the tiniest brain. She read it as if it were the correct answer.

But it was not!

I didn't know what to do with myself anymore. I pulled the hangnail and peeled the skin around it. It hurt so much, but not as much as the rest of me. I wanted to get out of there. Get out and scream. Whatever I did to save that lesson did not work out. It was a waste of time. What else could I have done to make that woman happy? I can't take it any longer. I can't, I can't, I can't.

"This is not the right answer, Iris." The teacher's voice was flat and frozen.

I wanted to go to the bathroom and throw up. She didn't have enough time to copy all the answers, so she made up an answer like a total idiot. Or maybe she tried to guess. I don't know. All I knew was that whatever I did was a complete waste of time, because there, again, we had to face our teacher's wrath.

"Nir, do you know the right answer?" The teacher asked through clenched teeth, completely ignoring Iris, as if she was not there at all. As if she was completely invisible.

"Lot to his sons in law," he sang the answer.

I loved his voice. The crisis was over and the day was going to proceed as if nothing horrible had happened. I put my thumb in my mouth and sucked the blood. I was in a different peaceful world now where no one could bother me, talk to me, or scare me. I was all by myself, alone and safe. I was inside and she could not reach me. No one could touch me when I went there. I was not even going to listen to what the teacher was planning to do. I did not care anymore.

The sound of loud conversations in the dining room reminded me that I was still in the classroom. The older kids came from math lesson and were sitting down for breakfast. I could hear Zehava telling them to be quiet and their voices changed into loud whispers. The teacher glanced at her watch. For a moment she hesitated, put the watch next to her ear and listened. Then she started winding it.

"For the next lesson I want you to prepare a drawing of the story we read," she said and kept winding her watch. "You don't need to read the rest of the chapter," she added and to my relief stopped winding the watch.

I already knew I was going to draw Lot's wife after she turned into a pillar of salt because she did not do as she was told. I closed my notebook and put it in the drawer.

"Iris." The teacher's voice stopped me.

She was going to punish Iris now. But I did not care. I closed my drawer and listened carefully. She told Iris to write all the questions on a clean sheet of paper, with the correct answers, and give them to her before lunch, which meant that Iris was going to stay in the classroom during the ten o'clock recess. She was not going to play with us outside. That was not a very big punishment. Not as bad as going to bed at eight o'clock instead of nine o'clock. Not as bad as getting slapped on the face. I shrugged to myself and got up. Then I heard the teacher telling her that she also had to copy the chapter we read in class and show it to her the next morning. A whole chapter. We didn't even read the whole chapter yet.

Iris would certainly have to ask someone to help her. There was no way she could do all that by herself in one day. She couldn't write that fast. But I was not going to help her. And I did not care if she said that I was selfish. Or, maybe I did care, a lot, but no one had to know.

In the middle of the winter I lost my cherished spot by the window. I loved sleeping by the window. When I looked out I could see different shades of blue all the way to the horizon, from the deep blue of the Mediterranean Sea to the translucent turquoise of the cloudless sky. Sometimes a large cargo ship would pass in the distance, heading south toward the Bay of Haifa or north toward the ports of Lebanon, Syria, and Turkey. On lucky days a plume of gray smoke would curl above the ship, making it look like the ships I drew in my notebook during boring lessons, with tall chimneys and smiling fish swimming underneath.

At night I would lean my chin on the windowsill and look out. When it was too dark to tell where the sea ended and the sky began, I would look for the yellow lights of fishing boats twinkling in the distance like beads in a huge chain that connected Mount Carmel with our mountain. Sometimes I would see the headlights of a lonely car rushing up the asphalt road leading to the navy base at the border checkpoint. Other than the occasional vehicle heading for the border crossing only stray dogs and tractors graced that road. Its faded black tar hugged the bottom of the hill on which our houses were built on, and cut through corn and alfalfa fields only a stone's throw from the beach, before it made the final climb to the top of the mountain. It was a dead-end road that only a selected few needed to use. Sometimes I could hear the sound of the engine of a coming car before its headlights pierced the darkness, and I would try to guess who was driving it and how many people were sitting inside.

What did they look like? What were they going to do up there so late? Where did they come from? Was it a UN truck full of blond soldiers from far away countries or an army jeep? It was too dark to tell whether the car was brown or white, only how big it was by the sound of the engine.

The last time I spent sleeping by the window I did not look out for cars. The wind was whistling above the children's house and the rain was pounding sideways. The wooden shutters were closed and the curtains were drawn to keep the rain out and the heat inside. Yet, I could not get warmed up. After all the parents left the children's house and my roommates started breathing evenly, I took the small electric heater that stood behind the door, put it on a chair at the foot of my bed, and turned it on. Immediately I felt warmer and drifted off to blissful sleep.

The fact that I was not allowed to put the heater so close to my bed did not stop me. Neither did the very explicit order to use it only during afternoon nap. During the day four kerosene-heaters kept the children's house warm. Every morning Zehava would light them outside, drag them into the chilly house, and place them in the dining room. Every morning we would choke on their foul fumes as we huddled around them, shivering, our hands spread above the iron gates to feel the heat. At four o'clock, before we left for our parents' rooms, Zehava would drag the heaters outside and throw a wet rag on each circle of fire. The heaters would hiss and pop, spit suffocating fumes and stinking smoke, and finally die with a sickening rattle.

Now that we had the luxury of owning space heaters that could be turned on and off with a push of a button, it was such an expensive treat, we hardly ever got permission to use them. But during that stormy night I succumbed to my weakness and turned the heater on.

I woke up in the middle of the night. The children's house was completely silent except for the soft murmurs and sighs of the sleeping children. Outside, the rain was coming down in full force, slamming into the windows relentlessly. I tried to go back to sleep but a strange smell entered my nose. I sat up, pulled my knees up to my chin and looked around. The little light that penetrated the children's house from the front porch enabled me to see the source of the bothersome smell.

On the other side of my bed, where my warm feet were lying only a moment ago, a thin feather of smoke was rising toward the ceiling. The far corner of my heavy blanket was lying on top of the heater, covering the blazing coil. Without pausing to assess the damage to my blanket, I reached for the switch and turned off the heater. Very quickly I realized that turning off the heater would not make the hissing orange dots and the stinky smoke go away, and if I did not act fast enough the entire children's house would be on fire. And what about the sleeping children? Should I wake them up?

No, I couldn't do that.

I got out of bed, put the heater back on the floor, and ran to the kitchen sink, where I filled two cups of water and carried them back to my bedroom. I poured the water on the orange dots, then some more, until I could see no more tiny flames. The blanket hissed and smoked, and in the places where I saw the orange dots there were now black holes.

I went to the kitchen and put the cups upside down in the dish dryer. On my way back to bed I thought I heard someone climbing up the stairs. It could have been the night watch or one of the parents coming to check on their child. I moved the curtain and looked out to see who it was but no one was there. Only rain and wind and the poplar tree branches beating against the wall. Back in my bed, my feet felt like ice cubes, but I was glad the house was not on fire and all the kids were still asleep. I lay under my blanket and tried to fall asleep. But the smell refused to go away. And there was a wet spot on my blanket where my cold feet were lying. I wondered what I was going to tell the *metapelet* in the morning when she saw the mess. I had no excuse, except for being cold and that, I knew, was not a good excuse.

I was going to be punished, but how, I didn't know.

I started shivering all over but not from fear. My teeth chattered so fast they hurt my jaws. I rubbed my feet against each other but they refused to get warm. The smell made me want to puke. I had to get out of the room or the night would never end. I grabbed two thin blankets from the large drawer under my bed and a pillow, and went to the next room where Hadas, Iris, and Noam slept undisturbed under their heavy cotton wool blankets. Thick, dry blankets, I thought enviously. But I could not dwell on it for too long without making myself feel worse. I spread my thin blanket on the floor, lay on it, and covered myself with the second blanket.

Every cold molecule that floated in the children's house chased me into my refuge and settled inside me. The chill crept from under the beds, wrapped itself around me, and dug into my flesh. For a moment it took my breath away. I closed my eyes and goaded my body to fall asleep. But I couldn't. My arms and legs were numb with the cold and the chatter of my teeth was making too much noise inside my head. I tried to keep my mouth shut tight and hold my jaws together but with little success. I lay on my side and tried to relax. I noticed that when I was able to relax my teeth stopped chattering and my body felt as if it were melting away. After a moment or two my body tensed again, my teeth started chattering and my muscles twitched.

That was when I decided to pretend. I pretended I was lying on the beach in the beginning of the summer. The sea was calm, the air was full of light, the sun was hanging low and bright in the sky caressing my shoulders, my arms, my chest, my legs. The southern breeze carried the smell of drying seaweed and salt water; the cold hard floor beneath me felt soft and warm like sand. I buried my toes in the sand and wiggled them inside the little hole. Slowly my feet got warmer and warmer until the numbness left them and the spasms stopped. I kept my eyes shut tight to protect them from the blinding glare of the sun and fell asleep.

The moment I woke up I braced myself to meet my destiny. The radio was on, broadcasting the daily morning exercise program, the lights in the dining room were glaring, and the sound of heavy metal heaters being dragged on the tile floor told me that the *metapelet* was in the children's house. Soon she would enter each bedroom, turn the lights on, recite her loud morning call "*boker tov.*" It was too late to sneak back to bed and hide the incriminating evidence.

"What are you doing on the floor?" the *metapelet* asked, partly surprised, partly disapproving, as soon as she turned the lights on in my new adopted bedroom.

What did she expect me to say? That I was afraid of the thunder? No one was afraid of the thunder. Perhaps I could lie. Tell her something she could believe. But what? I had no idea. Perhaps I shouldn't lie. After all, look what happened to the people of Sodom. They perished because they were liars and mean to each other.

"I... I... the heater ... it burned my blanket," I stuttered.

"Burned? How?"

Why did she have to make it so difficult? What does it matter how? It burned. Hadas, Iris, and Noam, who had just woken up, were lying in their beds, their sleepy faces peeping out from under their heavy warm blankets, watching me squirm on the floor in my pajamas and thin blanket. I decided to act dumb. Iris always acted dumb when things were going against her and a few times it even worked. I shrugged, mumbled something, got up from the floor and nearly fell down. Being frozen stiff, my knees bent and gave way. I swayed dangerously, like a scarecrow in the wind, and made my near collapse look like I was bending down to collect the blankets from the floor. At that moment Hadas and Noam got out of their beds, and the *metapelet* turned away from me to tell them that it was their turn to change the bed sheets.

It was my chance to escape. Without wasting a second, I quickly left and went to get my morning clothes. I started getting undressed and the feeling of an imminent threat slowly subsided. But Zehava could not be easily fooled or distracted. She followed me to my room and told me that I still "owed her an explanation," but since I had to get dressed and mop my bedroom floor before the beginning of classes we would have to have "A Talk" after breakfast. Now my knees were shaking again but not because of their stiffness. These Talks were never fun, especially when the kid talking was the one on the defensive side. I knew that acting dumb would not save me during The Talk. She knew that I was not dumb.

I watched her go to my bed and reach for my blanket. My blanket was lying in a messy heap, its burned side twisted in a lump. The *metapelet* lifted it, straightened it and finally saw the holes. I could already hear her asking me all the unanswerable questions during our Talk. She let the damaged side of the blanket drop and looked around. The electric heater was standing on the floor as if it had never left its spot. If only I could invent a believable story, I would have told it, regardless of what had happened to the people of Sodom and Gomorra. But my mind went blank when I saw the murderous look on her face.

"Take off the sheet and brush your mattress," she said, pulling the sheet by the corner from under the mattress. "It stinks." She opened the window, even though it was still raining outside. "Then hang your blanket outside on the railing," she commanded on her way out of the bedroom.

By the time I finished all my morning chores and sat down for breakfast, the kids were leaving the table. Pools of gray cocoa, tiny squares of tomatoes and cucumbers, wilted pieces of lettuce, bread crumbs and olive pits were scattered all over as silent witnesses of the commotion that took place in my absence. It made me think again of Sodom and Gomorra. The grown-ups always spoke of Sodom and Gomorra when they saw the mess we made. "What's going on here?" they used to ask, "the destruction of Sodom and Gomorra?" meaning, "will you clean up the mess?"

I looked around trying to decide what to eat. The vegetables left in the salad bowl were drowning in their own juices, the boiled eggs were cold, the breadbasket was nearly empty and the *kolboinik* overflowing with scraps. Not too often did I come to the table late when most of the food was gone, spilled, or discarded. But that morning was different because it was Wednesday and on Wednesdays the kids ran to the table and fought for the food because that was the only day of the week we had rolls and butter for breakfast.

All other days we ate bread and margarine, but Wednesdays were special and we looked forward to them. Sometimes the *metapelet* got more than one roll per kid so the fast ones, usually the boys, got to eat two rolls. They also made sure to spread a thick layer of butter on their rolls before all the butter was gone. The *metapelet* always told them to be more considerate and leave some butter for the slower kids who did not get any. The fast ones would scrape the butter from their rolls and hand the knife with the used butter to the slow ones, laughing. The fast ones also liked to snatch the roll from slower kids. They would take a bite, chew the dough and spit it on the table. They thought it was the funniest thing in the world. To hide their embarrassment, the slower kids would try to grab their roll back and laugh at the chewed pile in front of them, making ugly faces and sounds of disgust.

I did not think that what these kids were doing was funny at all. I also did not like butter. The *metapelet* knew that. I even asked her to remember to bring me bread and margarine on Wednesday.

"Whatever we do for you is not good enough," she scolded me when I reminded her that I did not like butter.

I looked at my knees.

"Don't expect me to go to the kitchen now and bring you margarine," she accused me.

I shook my head. She got up from her chair at the center table, came to my table and pushed the almost empty butter dish toward my plate. "Everyone I know likes butter. Only you have to be so special. Can you tell me why you always have to be so different?" Her face was too close to mine. I could smell her coffee breath, but

I was not going to do anything to worsen the situation before The Talk.

"In India children are starving and she doesn't like butter," she said to the teacher on the way back to her seat.

"We spoil them too much," the teacher said.

"Our sour-cream children can't appreciate what they've got," the *metapelet* agreed.

"I can go to the kitchen to get bread and margarine," Iris offered. She was sitting near the teacher, two tables away from me, picking at the food in her plate and watching us. Her sudden burst of generosity did not surprise me. She volunteered to do it because I always helped her with her homework. And she probably hoped to see her mother in the communal dining hall. She always looked for excuses to go visit her mother at work.

"No, you can't," the *metapelet* said.

The teacher looked at her watch, put it next to her ear, listened for a couple of seconds. "The next lesson is starting in ten minutes," she told Iris. "You don't have enough time."

"I can run," Iris insisted.

I did not believe her. The *metapelet* did not believe her, and, certainly, the teacher did not believe her. We all knew that if the teacher allowed her to go to the dining hall, she would be late for history lesson, which was probably the real reason she was so adamant about going there at the first place. I took the last roll from the plastic breadbasket, cut it in half and spread cream cheese on it. The butter left in the dish was melting and I did not dare touch it. I collected a few tomato squares that floated in the salad bowl, arranged them in a triangle on the cheese and bit into the roll. It tasted awful.

"See, I told you she'd be fine," I heard the *metapelet's* contemptuous assertion, as I tried to swallow the gook that filled my mouth.

Iris sent me a disapproving look. She collected her plate and cup, took them to the sink and left. Now it was just me, the *metapelet* and the teacher sitting in the dining room. I chewed slowly. I knew that if I made one move toward the door, Zehava would tell me to come back, so I did not bother to get up or finish my breakfast quickly. After a few excruciating moments she got up and came to my table with her coffee cup and an ashtray. She sat down across the table from me and lit a cigarette. I waited for her to start. From the other end of the dining room the teacher watched at us.

"Can you tell me now how your blanket got burned last night?"

I stared at her. Although I knew The Talk was inevitable I forgot to prepare myself for it. Stripping my bed and brushing my mattress kept me too busy to think about anything. As a result, I failed to concoct an explanation about how my blanket got burned, and now I was stuck with the truth.

"Nu, did you swallow your tongue?"

"I was cold."

"So?"

There was no sympathy in her voice.

"I couldn't fall asleep," I tried again.

"And?"

She was forcing me to say it. She wanted a full confession. It was better to get it out and be done. "I put the heater near my bed." There. I said it. From then on it was out of my hands. My destiny would be revealed at any moment.

"Did you hear that?" she asked the teacher who was listening very attentively to our Talk. "She put the heater near her bed," she repeated every word I said as if the teacher was deaf. There was mean laughter in her voice, as if I had told a bad joke. "And who gave you permission to do it?" she turned to me, sucking on her cigarette.

"No one."

For a moment she was speechless. My simple answer had caught her completely off guard, even though I could have sworn that she knew what I was going to say. But, then, maybe she was pretending to be speechless. "No one?" she regained her voice.

Suddenly the Talk stopped scaring me. The worst was over. I told the truth and all she could do was punish me. I knew that I could take it. I was ready. And I was calmer than I thought I would be. I didn't know if she wanted me to answer her question but I answered anyway. "No one."

"Don't be smart with me," she threatened, wiggling her pointing finger at me.

"I didn't try to be smart."

67

"Don't argue," her voice rose. "You know that we do not allow you to turn the heaters on or move them around."

I nodded. It was better to say nothing. Let her do all the Talking.

"You know that you will have to bear or suffer the consequences."

Consequences, shmuncequences. Always, consequences. I broke the rule, I had to be punished, let us get it over with, just be fair with the punishment you choose for me.

"Those heaters are too dangerous," she said to the teacher.

Not as dangerous as the stinking kerosene heaters, I thought, but I wasn't going to argue.

"Your blanket could have caught on fire and burn the entire children's house. You're lucky nothing terrible had happened. Yes, this is the best solution. If we move your bed away from the window you would not get so cold and you wouldn't be tempted."

Temptation? Did she think I was that stupid? Did she think I was going to turn on the heater in the middle of the night again, after what I've been through? The teacher nodded in agreement and Zehava put out the tip of her cigarette on the bottom of the ashtray, signaling to me that she had nothing more to add to our Talk. My bed was going to be moved away from the window; my most cherished place in the children's house.

"You'll change places with Nir," she said, getting up from her chair.

We went to my bedroom. My metal bed stood stripped under the opened window. The tightly packed straw mattress, dressed in dark blue canvas, was leaning on the wall, exposing the wooden platform I dusted and wiped thoroughly with a wet rag before breakfast. Outside the window I could see that the storm had moved east and a large streak of mud was slowly painting a wide area of the sea in deep brown. The *metapelet* lay the mattress on the platform, grabbed one side of the bed, lifted it, and told me to lift the other side. Silent, I took hold of the bed and lifted. The teacher stood at the door watching us dragging the bed to the middle of the room. "Now let's move Nir's bed under the window."

It was a sad moment. I was losing my cherished spot under the window. But I was glad it was Nir who got my spot. He would let me sit next to him on his bed and watch the headlights of the cars driving to the border in the middle of the night.

Suddenly I heard the teacher behind me. "We should remove all the electric heaters." That woman never had enough with one punishment.

Zehava turned to her. "You're right. We can't trust these kids. You tell them not to turn them on at night and it's like talking to the deaf."

She unplugged the heater and left the room. I chased her into the next bedroom. She was going to unplug the heater and take it out, too. She was going to take all the heaters out of the children's house. I had to do something. I couldn't let everyone suffer because of me. Everyone would blame me. "Maybe we could keep the heaters in the dining room," I tried to negotiate with Zehava.

She turned and looked at me. "It's time for you to go to class."

"But we need the heaters," I insisted.

"Yes, we do," she said and went to the next room.

At lunchtime Zehava announced that she had taken all the electric heaters to the electrician. After telling him what had happened in the children's house they decided that he would shorten the electric cords and hang the heaters high above the windows. Closer to the ceiling where we could not reach them. "And don't anyone dare touch those heaters without permission, or there would be no heaters at all."

All the kids turned to look at me. It was a most embarrassing moment for me but I felt that they were not mad at me. It could have happened to anyone. I was not the only one who ever did something we were not supposed to do. But I was the only one who had a real accident and everyone could understand it. Some kids chuckled quietly and Nir whispered, "Maya burned her blanket, Maya burned her blanket," and chortled.

I didn't tell my parents about what had happened in the children's house. I already decided that if they asked during *hashkava* (bedtime) why my bed was standing in a different place, I would tell them. But if they didn't notice it, I was not going to alarm them, or give them any reason to take the *metapelet's* side and explain to me what could have happened if the house caught on fire.

It was getting dark when I got to my parents' room. My brother was sitting at the writing desk building an airplane model. My mother was sitting in her armchair knitting a dark green ski-cap for an anonymous soldier serving on the border somewhere. My father was sanding the two wooden storks he carved out of a piece of olivewood. I took off my coat and plopped on the other armchair.

"Your shoes are covered with mud," my mother said, looking at my feet.

Without saying a word I got up, went outside, and took off my shoes. I did not feel like sitting outside to scrape the mud with a knife. It was too cold on the stairs.

"Where were you until now?" my mother asked without lifting her eyes from her knitting when I entered wearing only my socks.

"In the classroom."

"What have you got to do there at this hour?" she asked, frustrated, and without waiting for an answer turned to my father. "Boaz, you have to talk to her. She can't be coming home so late every day."

"Come, sit near me." My father patted the rug. I sat on the floor next to him. He gave me a piece of sandpaper and a round piece of olive wood and asked me to sand it for him. It was going to be the base for his sculpture, he said.

I worked near him, glad to be able to help. The record player was playing a symphony in the background. Whenever my father did not listen to the news we listened to classical music. He enjoyed the music so much, sometimes he would start whistling with his eyes closed and make funny finger movements as if he were a conductor, then, when the music stopped, he would open his eyes and ask me and Avner who composed the piece we heard. My brother always knew the answer before I could think of any name.

"We had some storm last night," my father suddenly said.

"Tavori said that the bomb shelter in front of house number four got flooded all the way to the top," my mother replied. "He spent all day pumping the water out."

"Where is house number four?" I asked.

"It was the house we lived in when you and Avner were very little," my father said. "Do you remember how you entered that bomb shelter through the air shaft and got scared in the dark and we had to break the lock on the door to get you out?"

"No." How could I remember something that had happened such a long time ago? I hardly remembered even coming to visit my parents in that house.

"He said that three trees were knocked down by the wind behind the communal showers," my mother continued.

"Yes, it was a strong storm," my father consented. He was examining the long beak of the wooden stork he was holding, moving his finger along the smooth surface.

"Luckily no one was outside, otherwise, I promise you, someone would have gotten hurt," my mother said to the ski-cap.

"Right," my father agreed.

"I know someone who was outside last night and I also know that nothing happened to him," my brother mumbled under his nose.

"Who?" My mother put down her knitting and frowned at him not with curiosity but in disbelief.

"Someone from my class," my brother said.

"And may I ask you what he was doing outside after lights-out?" she asked with the same tone of voice my *metapelet* used when she was starting to get angry and you knew that she was already devising a punishment for you and that you should not tell the truth.

"I forget," Avner said.

My mother did not press on, thinking, perhaps, that Avner had made the story up only to annoy her. But I knew he did not make it up. Avner never lied. Later, when we went to eat dinner (in second grade I stopped having dinner at the children's house and joined my parents at the communal dining hall) I asked him what the kid from his class was doing outside in the middle of the night.

"Only if you promise not to tell anyone."

I swore. "By the life of God and the book of the Torah."

"Yariv and Udi decided to go paint your faces after lights out," he whispered in my ear. "Because of the rain, they said there was no chance they would ever get caught."

My brain was shuffling bits of images faster than light. As far as I knew, no one from my class woke up in the morning with dried toothpaste or shoe polish on the face, which meant that... "So what happened?"

"They said that when they got there they heard someone walk inside, so they ran away."

"Did they see who it was?" My knees were weak with anticipation.

Avner shrugged and shook his head. "Probably one of the parents."

I could not believe it. It was the most amazing thing I have ever heard. Me, Maya, the girl who was too scared to stay up during the summer to catch the kids from *Yakinton* class when they came to paint our faces, saved the honor of Efroni class. Because of me, these boys ran away without even daring to enter our children's house. I remembered the footsteps I had heard when I was standing by the sink. They heard me walk around the kitchen and thought I was one of the parents. They couldn't tell it was just me. Ha, ha, ha.

Suddenly the ordeal I went through the night before was not a traumatic incident with many sad consequences, but a sweet victory. The memories of the cold hard floor and the uncontrollable shaking and teeth chattering dissolved and a warm feeling of great achievement enveloped me. Even picturing my bed standing by the door did not make my heart heavy. It was worth it. Every second of that long and dreadful night was full of glory. If I could only tell someone.

"What are you smiling to yourself about?" my father asked, giving my shoulder an affectionate squeeze.

"No reason," I shrugged, using all my willpower to control the strongest urge to hop on the cement walkway and shout at the top of my lungs: "We won, we won, we won."

Chapter Five

Ora Etgar was my first true enemy. For months she came to the classroom wearing the same blue shorts. They were held by an elastic band at the top and the bottom, making her look like a walking blue balloon. Her thick spectacles distorted her blue eyes and made them look huge. Ominous. Plotting. She had sharp knives behind her glasses; not real eyes. I was afraid they would shred me to pieces if I dared to look up before I finished writing two hundred times in my notebook: "Out of the eater came something to eat, and out of the strong came something sweet."

My hand hurt. I stopped to sharpen my pencil and rub the callus on my middle finger. I bit into the hardened skin and chanted silently: I hate you, I hate you, I hate you. I hated my teacher more than anyone in the kibbutz.

"Are you done, Maya?" she asked without raising her eyes from her desk drawer. None of her curls moved when she bent over to peer inside. There were no hairpins or a bow in her hair, not even a rubber band to decorate it. Only efficient, disciplined curls that grazed the back of her neck and her pedantic shoulders.

"I'm resting," I murmured, staring at the words I wrote in my notebook. All the words were carefully written, evenly spaced. A few gray smudges marked the spots in which I abused the paper with my pink eraser. I was determined to keep even spaces between the letters, even though my hand was getting tired and my pencil dull.

I stole a quick glance at Iris. She was sitting on the other side of the classroom biting her lips, writing slowly in her childish handwriting. I felt sorry for her. Again, she did not do her homework. When the teacher asked her during Bible lesson to explain the meaning of "Out of the eater came something to eat, and out of the strong came something sweet," she said she could not remember. The teacher knew she was lying, but still gave her time to think about the answer. While she was thinking, I quickly wrote on a piece of paper that it was a riddle Samson had told the Philistines about the lion he had killed with his bare hands, and later found a swarm of bees and honey inside the lion's carcass. Then I made my final mistake. I whispered Iris's name before passing the note to her. I forgot that Iris was not a name to be whispered.

I did not try to help Iris because I liked her. She was not my best friend or anything like that. I just did not want to hear the teacher ridiculing her again. Whenever Iris failed to do her homework, the teacher would kick her out of class and later tell us that she was a stupid girl. She even slapped her a few times. And Iris was such a delicate girl. I always wished I were as pretty as Iris, with big brown eyes, a pointy nose and a long, thick braid.

A year ago, when we were still in third grade, Iris started to laugh in the middle of history lesson because Nir farted a stinky one. The teacher, who did not hear the fart, marched to Iris' desk, grabbed her by the arm and dragged her to the front porch, hissing something under her breath. Then we heard her yell, "Go to your room and stop wasting *our* time," as if we cared that she laughed.

Later, during recess, Iris showed us her upper arm. Right below her shoulder, near the little bump of the muscle, there were four bloody dimples the teacher's nails had carved in her flesh. It was a scary moment. We realized that we had two serious problems on our hands: our teacher had lost her mind and we could not get rid of her.

We had a bad reputation. The grown-ups said they had never seen such a "problematic" group of children like *Efroni* class, which was what we called our age group when we started first grade. "Juvenile delinquents," was what they called us when they caught us hiding in the bushes behind the communal dining hall, stretching our necks as high as we could, desperately trying to catch a glimpse of a forbidden movie. Instead of telling the teacher to let us watch the movie, they'd complain to the Education Committee that our teacher had no control over us. Whatever we did, even when we were right, our parents blamed us. They did not even care that the teacher beat us up when she was angry. They believed only what she said, just because she was older.

That was why we were stuck with Ora Etgar. She knew that none of our mothers could teach us, because in the kibbutz no woman could supervise her own children. So slowly she became more and more powerful, more and more dangerous.

One morning we gathered under the children's house to plan a mutiny. We could no longer sit back and let her humiliate us. The older kids said we had to save our honor. "We have to beat her up or something," Dorit whispered bravely, making her hand into a fist.

All of us cheered her great idea, but no one volunteered to do it. We returned to the children's house hoping that someday one of us would dare to beat her up, show her that she could not torture us forever. Maybe Dorit herself, since she was the oldest. We had no one else to defend us. It was us against the rest of the world.

A loud screech on the blackboard reminded me to stop and count my lines. I put the pencil down and stretched my aching fingers; they felt as if they were made of wood. The teacher was writing on the blackboard with a new white chalk she found in her desk drawer. I leaned back and took a deep breath, quietly, making sure she would not catch me taking a break. When she started teaching us, she warned us that she could see everything we did behind her back because she had invisible eyes in the back of her head. I believed her. I was sure she would not lie to us. According to her, lying was a crime that could make small children feel terribly guilty even if they did not get caught. It called for the personal intervention of God himself, she warned.

The letters she was writing on the blackboard were turning into words, then into sentences: Explain in your own words who spoke to whom, why, and when. Straight even lines. Perfect spacing. I had to admire her handwriting in spite of my hard feelings. It was even prettier than mine. Well proportioned, tidy and elegant. "Iris," her menacing voice startled me. "Come here with your notebook."

She was going to give Iris a break. There was no way Iris could have finished writing her quota so quickly. She could not write that fast. Iris moved her chair and dragged her red sandals on the floor in short hesitant steps.

"Put it on my desk," the teacher ordered.

Iris obeyed and stepped back. She stood by the teacher's desk and stared at the ceiling, playing with her long braid. The teacher sat down and started counting. "One, two, three, four..." I began to wonder if Iris would have to stand there until the teacher finished counting.

"Forty three, forty four, forty five..." the teacher continued. Iris's eyes traveled around the classroom and fixed themselves on the beehive our nature teacher brought to class and attached to the window. For a moment, I looked at the industrious bees making honey. They were buzzing to me over and over "Out of the strong came something sweet."

Suddenly I knew what I was going to do. Like Samson who embarrassed the Philistines with his riddle, I could also show the teacher that I was not afraid of her. I could write that riddle more than two hundred times. I could write it again and again, and again, forever. By the time I heard the teacher count, "one hundred one, one hundred two," I had already written it two hundred and twelve times. My handwriting was not pretty anymore and the letters were collapsing into each other. But I did not bother to use my eraser. I was showing her that she could not scare me. I was going to write that riddle three billion times. A trillion times.

"Maya, put down your pencil and come here with your notebook," she finally called me. My heart was pounding, my head was spinning, but I felt strong and brave like Samson. I'll show her, I thought to myself, and wrote the riddle one last time.

"I said put down your pencil," she ordered me again, impatient this time.

I threw my pencil on the desk and it rolled down to the floor. My hand was weak; my callus looked bigger, but I felt no pain. I took my notebook and went to her desk, unafraid, knowing she could not ridicule me. I was so much faster and stronger than she could ever imagine.

I dropped my notebook in front of her and returned to my chair without asking her permission. Her eyes scorched my back but I did not stop. I sat down and waited for her to count my lines. All of them. She stopped somewhere in the high sixties and told Iris, who was still staring at the bees, to leave. Without looking at me, Iris turned around and walked out of the classroom.

The teacher was counting, "One hundred ninety eight, one hundred ninety nine, two hundred, two hundred and one, two hundred and two..."

In my bones I could feel that she understood. I just knew it. Tiny wrinkles formed around her thin lips and her eyes narrowed behind the thick lenses. Her count slowed down and turned into a whisper. When she finished counting she sighed, closed my notebook and took off her glasses. She wiped them with the corner of her shirt and looked in my direction.

Without those glasses her eyes looked small and blind and lost. Not threatening at all. She put her glasses back on, got up from her chair, and walked to my desk. "Go take a shower, and then straight to bed," she said, putting the notebook in front of me.

She turned away and went toward the blackboard to fetch her white chalk and lock it in the drawer. I looked at my notebook and decided to show her one last time. I tore the useless page from my notebook. Rip. And another useless page. R-r-r-rip. Out of the strong came something sweet.

Her back was facing me. I thought her shoulders stiffened up, but I was not absolutely sure. I crumpled up the torn pages into a big paper ball and aimed at the plastic wastebasket that stood behind me. Then, like a seasoned basketball player, I threw the paper ball up in the air and it landed in the basket.

Oh, how thrilled I was to see it land so perfectly inside the empty basket. I closed the damaged notebook, slid it into my drawer, and left the classroom. And for one split second I felt eternally invincible.

When I crossed the dining room all the kids were already in their bedrooms, reading books or playing quietly by themselves. The *metapelet*, Zehava, poured a bucket full of soapy water on the floor and told me to walk near the wall. I tiptoed between the slippery water puddles, avoiding the rag that was chasing me around, as she was spreading the water evenly all over the dining room floor with a gray rag. Her eyes rested on me when I stopped to talk to my roommates, Nir and Daphna. I wanted to tell them how I outwitted the teacher and laugh at her with them, but one word from Zehava diverted me back to the shower route.

"Maya," I heard her voice cut the air. It had a clear intonation that exuded impatience, exasperation, and a hidden threat all at once.

Almost as a reflex, my head sunk between my shoulders. Nir slid under his thin blanket with his plastic soldiers, but not before he stuck his tongue out and made a nauseous sound. He always liked to make practical jokes that brought the wrath of everyone upon him. Maybe because he was the youngest kid in our class. I was the second youngest. But I was taller than he was. And smarter.

I ran to the shower with my hand over my mouth, swallowing a giggle Nir's funny face had forced out of me. I closed the door behind me and took off my clothes. Very slowly. I wanted to postpone the moment I had to go to bed, without raising the *metapelet*'s suspicion that I was playing instead of taking a shower. When I finished soaping every corner of my body under the lukewarm waterfall, I closed my eyes and began to sing my favorite song from the musical I was going to see. It was a quarrel song between two women in the marketplace; each woman was telling the other how ugly and stupid the other one was. I started to laugh. Then my hands hit the wall. I opened my eyes and saw that I sprayed water all over the floor during my grand rehearsal. I turned the water off, grabbed the floor squeegee, and standing in the middle of the shower room, pushed the water toward the drain. Suddenly the door flung open by the substitute *metapelet*. I jumped behind the stone partition and carefully looked out.

"What's going on here?" the substitute asked, looking at the wet floor. She walked in, poked her head behind the stone partition, and said, "So, did you leave us some water in the Sea of Galilee?"

I knew it was her special way of telling me that I betrayed our drought-stricken country, that my shower lasted too long, and that I was a nuisance. The grown-ups were always so worried about us wasting precious water. On our last field trip one of the kids drank from his canteen without asking for permission from our teacher.

To teach us a lesson she told us to spill on the ground all the water we had in our canteens so the next time we go for a long hike we remember to conserve water and control our thirst. They called it "water discipline." I nodded sheepishly, guilty that the entire country was suffering from a water shortage because of me, and covered my nakedness with my hands.

"Get dressed and run to bed," she ordered me, motioning with her head at the direction of the bedrooms. "I already closed the shades and turned the lights off. So be quiet. I don't want to hear a whisper," she said, waving her pointing finger at me. Then she turned around and left without closing the door.

I waited behind the stone partition until I was sure she was far enough, jumped out, and quickly shut the door. Then I wrapped myself in a big towel, climbed on the wooden bench, stretched my neck as far as I could, and looked out the window. Sometimes I could catch a glimpse of my brother playing soccer with the boys from seventh grade. It was a lot more interesting than going to bed. I was not tired at all. I was only sorry that I missed the reading hour, and that I had to go to bed and try to fall asleep. It was the only way to make the time pass faster. Otherwise, I was bound to die of boredom.

When I got out of the shower room the children's house was quiet and dark, even though it was the middle of the day. I climbed on my bed and tried to make myself comfortable on the flat pillow. Nir turned to look at me, and lifted his light blanket to show me his plastic soldiers standing in a circle underneath. I pushed my blanket down to my knees. It was too hot to sleep. Except for two flies that buzzed near the ceiling everything else was standing still in the room. I already felt sticky even though I just came out of the shower. Daphna started rocking in bed. She groaned and sighed under her blanket. When she finally pushed the blanket down, her eyes looked like the glass eyes of a doll. Looking nowhere in particular.

"Erez, I said be quiet," we heard the substitute barking somewhere at the southern end of the bedroom row. I watched the flies chase each other into the lamp that hung from the ceiling, and began to search the wall for shapes of mountains, trees, and clouds. Nir was talking to himself under his blanket.

"Nir, what do you think you're doing?" a loud voice startled me, and the flies flew out of the lamp. She caught him, I thought in desperation. Oh, please God, don't let her see the soldiers and confiscate them. Please.

"I'm not doing anything," Nir protested with an exaggerated whine in his voice, and peeped at her from underneath his blanket. He sounded truly offended. I was so glad he could lie so well. I praised him in my heart. The substitute stared at him and finally nodded to herself. It looked like she was going to believe him. I decided to believe in God for a while and maybe sacrifice something to him. A candy or a cookie. Maybe even make a vow of something when we get up from the afternoon nap.

"Then cover yourself up, turn your face to the wall and shut your eyes," she ordered him. "I want to see you fall asleep at once."

I shrunk quietly into my pillow. Nir turned to the wall and covered his head with his blanket. Then Daphna focused her glassy eyes on the substitute and asked, "Can I go to the bathroom?"

"No, you can't," the substitute barked at her before she even finished her question. She never allowed anyone use the bathroom or drink water during afternoon nap. She thought that we asked to go to the bathroom because we were bored, or because we wanted to sit behind the closed door and play, or read a book. Which was partly true, but not always. I was hoping Daphna didn't really have to go. Otherwise she would have to hold it until we got up at three thirty. Or cry.

Then it was my turn to be yelled at.

"You too, Maya. Cover yourself well, turn to the wall, and shut your eyes. I don't want to hear anyone talk in this room," she spat out her warnings, and darted out to scare the kids in the next bedroom.

Why do I have to cover myself with a blanket in the middle of the summer, I wanted to shout after her. But I didn't. Instead, I pulled the blanket up to my chin and turned my face to the wall. To make the time pass I counted the grains and scratches I saw on the whitewashed wall. I moved my finger from a grain to a stain and drew little squares, and triangles, and circles on the wall. I was open to do anything to divert my attention from the time that simply refused to move forward.

After the substitute completed her round of threats down the bedroom row the children's house was finally quiet. I tried to fall asleep but my mind wandered to other places. I put my finger in my mouth and thought about the musical we were going to see. There was going to be a special show in the nearest town for all the kibbutzim children of our county. We were going there in the yellow buses that took the children from the older grades to the regional high school. I was absolutely ecstatic about the musical. I already memorized most of the lyrics because Tikva let me listen to the record her father gave her when he came to visit her on the kibbutz.

I heard the members say that he "descended to Canada." He used to send her postcards with pictures of Indians dancing around totem poles and beautiful toys from a city that they called Vancouver. I didn't envy her for getting so many special presents because it was wrong to be envious of other people. Besides, I knew that she hardly ever saw her parents, and she always agreed to show me her postcards.

Her mother did not live on the kibbutz either. She worked in a nightclub in Tel Aviv and wore long black eye lashes and a mini leather skirt that matched the color of her bright red lipstick. People on the kibbutz thought she was a cheap woman; I thought she was very skinny. Her daughter, Tikva, was what we called "an outside girl." Most of the kids in the group did not like her because she did not understand the kibbutz rules, especially the rules about gifts. She also used to infect us with lice every time she came back from visiting her mother in the city. Then we would have to sleep with kerosene in our hair and later have the *metapelet* comb our hair with a special comb to ensure that all the lice were dead and the nits fell out. But I did not like to make fun of her, partly because it was not all her fault that she had a cheap mother. So sometimes, I went to her foster family's room after naptime, and we listened to the record her father gave her and looked at the pictures on the jacket.

Because I saw the pictures, I already knew what King Solomon and the shoemaker were going to wear. I even knew what the palace was going to look like, and the marketplace. I could not wait to see the dark theater swarming with people I have never seen before; and the huge stage; and the long velvet curtain opening slowly, slowly. There was even a good chance we would get to eat ice cream in a cone. It was so exciting to think about everything, I wanted to jump out of my bed and dance on the floor like the Indians in Tikva's postcards.

The quiet sound of chuckles and whispers broke my train of thought. I glued my ear to the wall and heard giggles on the other side. Something was definitely going on next door. I wondered what Iris, Noam, and Hadas were doing there. They knew they had to be very quiet and pretend to be asleep. Zehava threatened us more than once to be quiet and not give the substitute too much trouble or she would come up with something.

What was going on there?

I lay in bed and waited for the whispers to stop. But they didn't. Actually, they got worse. I heard a loud laughter. Noam was out of control. I recognized his voice. That was it. There was no way the substitute could not hear him. She was sitting on the stairs outside, talking to a substitute from another children's house who was going to join the army with her at the end of the summer. I heard them laugh, and then I heard another wave of giggles rolling down the bedroom row. I turned in bed and waited, holding my breath. Finally Dorit called from the first bedroom, "Children, be quiet."

"These kids are crazy if they think they can talk like this without getting caught," I whispered to Daphna, who lay still in her bed and stared at the curtains. Nir mumbled in his sleep. The noise did not wake him up. One of his soldiers fell on the floor. I jumped from my bed and picked it up. Noam's laughter burst out of the last bedroom. I rushed back to bed and lay still, my face turned to the wall.

"Children, what is going on here?" I heard the substitute's roar sweep the children's house. Tensed silence grasped the air. Nir woke up and looked around in confusion. Blinking at me he asked, "What did she say?"

"Nir, get out," she screamed, standing with her hands on her waist at the entrance of our bedroom. None of us had noticed her before she yelled at Nir. In her constant search for prey, she liked to tiptoe near the walls, and hide behind our doors to catch us by surprise.

"What did I do?" he complained.

"Don't argue," she barked, "I said get out. Go sit in the shower room."

Nir curled up in bed. Before we collected ourselves she dashed into the room, snatched his blanket, and grabbed his wrist. Then, with all her might, she pulled him out of bed and dragged him across the room. Nir started to cry. He was completely disoriented, still half-asleep. His bare feet gave away and he almost fell down. "Out," she shrieked, and I heard his bare feet stagger to the shower room.

"Anyone else wants to sit in the shower room?" she threatened us, and raced down the bedroom row to hunt for other criminals.

No one answered. Then a muffled giggle trickled out of Noam's room. Everyone stopped breathing. Even the two flies froze for a moment in midair, sensing that something out of the ordinary was taking place below. The substitute galloped by our room looking determined to crush the new spurt of dissent. Before I could count to three I heard a loud mixture of laughter and screams. "What is this supposed to be? Are you out of your minds? What do you think you're doing? Who did it?"

I heard more laughter, giggles, chuckles, but no words.

"Who did it?" her voice squealed in fury.

Still no answer.

I waited. Then she started again. "I'm getting out of here now, and while I'm out I want this mess to be cleaned up. Do you hear me? I Don't want to see a sign of this mess. Or I'm telling you, someone's going to pay very dearly for this. Do you hear me? I want this mess cleaned immediately."

Finally she bolted out of the children's house. I sighed in relief. A few seconds of abysmal silence descended the bedroom row. Then we all heard Nir's excited battle cry coming from the shower room. "Who did what?"

Before the echo of Nir's loud cry receded, I saw Dotan and Shlomi, another "outside boy," trot by my room to the end of the bedroom row, to look at the source of all the mysterious clamor. They burst out in wild laughter once they reached their destination. Nir followed them. Dressed in his white underwear, he ran around the three dining room tables, jumped above the chairs, and shouted, "Noam, what did you do?" over and over, and then gasped and croaked while trying to laugh backwards. When he got to Noam's room it sounded as if Shlomi caught him and twisted his arm. Nir screamed, "Drop my arm, you stupid monkey. Shlomi let go of me, you piece of shit." Shlomi chuckled wickedly.

I never liked Shlomi. He was much bigger than Nir, and he knew it was not fair to fight with someone so much smaller than him. I turned to Daphna. "You coming?" I asked her with a hope that bringing her as reinforcement would enhance my power to stop Shlomi.

Daphna shrugged and pulled her favorite book about Montezuma from under her bed. She was not interested at all in the commotion outside. Her Aztec heroes and their human sacrifices fascinated her a lot more than a bunch of childish boys next door. I waited for a few seconds to see if she was going to change her mind. She seemed deeply absorbed in her heavily stained and chafed book which she was reading, by the way, for the eighth time. Finally I had no choice but to accept that all the laughter in the world would not separate her from her bliss. I got myself out of bed and went next door to find out, once and for all, what was going on.

By the time I got there the kids were standing in a circle in the middle of the room, dressed in their white cotton underwear, looking at something on the floor, and talking excitedly to each other. Iris was sitting on her bed, her bare feet swinging in the air, her eyes watching the agitated group idly. As usual she looked bored and detached, as if whatever happened there had nothing to do with her. Hadas stood by the window by herself, her shoulders stooped and her left hand twisting a long strand of brown hair. Noam looked at me behind his steamy glasses, pointed at Hadas, and between bursts of wet laughter announced, "She did it."

"What did she do?" I asked Dorit who stood near me.

"She peed on the floor," Noam answered before Dorit had a chance to say anything, and all the boys burst out laughing and choking.

"Awhoooo, it stinks here," Nir yelled cheerfully from the other side of the circle and jumped backwards.

"Not true," Hadas argued in a tiny voice, "it doesn't stink."

"Yes, it does. It stinks. It stinks," Nir cheered again.

"It only stinks a little bit," Dotan corrected him and his face darkened.

"If you stand closer you'll be able to smell it," Erez said quietly with his typically honest approach to complicated situations.

"I don't want to stand closer. It's disgusting," Nir shouted and shook his blond head with excitement.

"Nobody asked you," Shlomi snorted and pushed him with his elbow.

"Stop it, let go of me, you idiot, ugly monkey," Nir screamed.

Noam started to laugh again. "His foot touched it," he chuckled, pointed at Nir's bare foot, and pushed his glasses up his nose.

"It didn't," Nir argued, trying to save his face. "Put your stupid glasses on."

While everyone joined the argument whether Noam could see anything without his glasses on, I climbed on his bed to look at the floor. I didn't climb on Iris' bed even though it was closer to the pee puddle because I knew she would get all flustered about it. She did not want other kids to step on her bedspread. She was afraid it would get dirty. We all knew that she did not like to share her things with us. Her parents spoiled her because she was so pretty. She had a long thick braid, big brown eyes, a small nose, and a real gold necklace with a Star of David that her mother gave her for her birthday. She was the only girl in the group who had a gold necklace.

"There's nothing to see," she said indifferently when I stretched my neck to see the pee on the floor. It was yellowish and it didn't look disgusting at all to me, but I was standing quite far from it. "Why did she do it?" I asked, guessing the answer.

"She couldn't hold it anymore," Iris shrugged. Still bored.

"Did she ask to go to the bathroom?" I asked again, knowing the answer.

She nodded and played with her gold necklace. "Twice, but the witch didn't let her. She tried to cry but she couldn't so she peed on the floor."

"In front of you and Noam?" I asked.

"We turned to the wall," she said.

"Aha," I said. Now I understood what happened. Ever since the new substitute started to forbid us to go to the bathroom during afternoon nap it was clear that something bad was bound to happen. We could not persuade her to change her mind. Even when we told the *metapelet*, Zehava, about it she took the substitute's side. She said that we should go to the bathroom before she turned the lights off. Then she said that if we tried to sleep we wouldn't have to go to the bathroom all the time. So it was our fault, she claimed. "People don't go to the bathroom when they sleep," she said and that was the end of it.

So the boys found a solution. They peed into empty jars and hid them under their beds. Later, before they went to their parents' rooms at four o'clock, they poured the pee out the window, making sure the wind was blowing in the right direction. Sometimes they used bottles. Then they threw the sealed bottles out of the window. Later, during recess we would go look for the bottles under the bushes and make bets who had the courage to open them. The only problem with that system was that we, the girls, could not pee into bottles. Once Tikva tried to do it and got all wet, and afterwards none of us ever tried again. We ended up having to cry.

"Children, who wants to clean this?" Dorit stopped the heated argument and tried to take control of the situation. Noam and Erez giggled but no one answered her.

"I don't mind cleaning it, but not by myself," Tikva surprised us and volunteered, her black eyes glowing with unknown determination.

"Me too," Daphna called from the door. Apparently, her curiosity won and she left her Aztec warriors to find out what happened.

"Let's have a meeting outside and decide what to do," I said to Dorit.

"Children, let's have a meeting outside," she repeated to me loudly.

We left the stuffy bedroom and sat around one of the dining room tables. Daphna put the flower vase on another table, and folded the tablecloth neatly, to make sure it would not get stained and wrinkled during the meeting. Then, unanimously, we elected Dorit to be the moderator.

"Anyone has an idea how to clean this mess?" Noam asked after Dorit gave him permission to talk, and started to laugh again.

We all looked at each other questioningly. Hadas raised her hand and whispered that she would clean it by herself since it was her pee.

No one agreed. What had happened to her was *our* problem and all of us should solve it together, we told her. Hadas nodded, looking smaller than ever. Then Iris waved her hand up in the air and said, "I know, I know what we have to do."

"Quiet, be quiet children," Dorit reminded us, drumming on the green Formica.

"We have to wash the floor with a lot of water," Iris said like we didn't know.

"But how? No one wants to step in the pee," Noam confronted her, annoyed.

"We can wear rubber boots and wash them outside afterwards," I suggested.

"But they're in storage and it'll take us hours to get them out," Dotan said.

"I have an idea," Hadas whispered again.

"Hadas has an idea," Dorit announced, and the loud argument between the boys about who was going to win the national soccer tournament came to a halt.

"We can stand on chairs," Hadas whispered after Erez, Tomer, Noam, and Dotan stopped arguing. I could see that she was painfully embarrassed about the entire affair. After all, it was her pee no one wanted to stand in.

"Great idea," Dorit declared, and hit the Formica with an open palm as she got up from her chair to get everyone's attention. "Let's take a vote."

"A vote?" Shlomi asked, alarmed. He was too busy pinching Nir's arm and slapping his head to hear Hadas' idea.

"Who's for the boots and who's for the chairs?" Dorit asked.

"Everyone is for the chairs," Dotan announced before anyone had a chance to make a decision. I waited for someone to object, but no one seemed to care, and the decision to drop my idea to wear rubber boots was accepted without a formal vote.

We split into two groups. One group arranged a line of chairs that stretched from the contaminated room at the end of the bedroom row across the dining room past the bathrooms, and all the way to the entrance of the children's house. The other group filled buckets with water and soap and brought them, the floor squeegees, and the cleaning rags to the dining room, where the chairs were placed in a straight line. By the time we took our places on the chairs we all felt invincible and euphoric. It was fun. We began to enjoy the adventure and our bursts of laughter grew louder and louder. The new turn of events seemed so wild nobody cared anymore that we had to touch bodily fluids.

Hadas received the honor of pouring the first bucket of water. To the applause of Noam, Dotan, and Dorit, the oldest kids in our group, who stood in her room on three chairs, she poured the water and jumped on her chair. Then each one poured a bucket of water and the rest of us, perched on chairs in the dining room, started to push the water with the floor squeegees and the brooms distributed by Daphna and Tikva. My chair rocked dangerously in the middle of a raging river. I tried to direct the water down the line but without much success. Everyone around me cheered each other to push the water faster before the river turned back into the last room. I fought the high tide with my squeegee, as fast as I could, trying to balance myself on the edge of my chair, making sure not to slip into the polluted river. When I looked up to check if the river had reached the end of the line, I saw that Daphna, who volunteered to coordinate us, was trudging through the river in black rubber boots. I wondered where she found them but I didn't stop to ask her. Controlling the flash flood that swept everything under my chair was more urgent. I could not stop, however, from feeling proud of myself. At least someone liked my idea to wear rubber boots in the middle of the summer.

When the torrential river was reduced to small puddles, Daphna and Tikva, now in rubber boots, wrapped their squeegees in dry rags and wiped the floor underneath the chairs. Afterwards, they pulled the curtains open to let the warm summer breeze blow into the children's house and dry everything. Victoriously, we held our brooms and squeegees, and standing in attention on our chairs, we sang the national anthem over and over at the top of our lungs until the floor dried. And Nir did not dare to push Shlomi from his chair until Daphna gave us the signal to get off the chairs.

"Boys, you put the chairs back around the tables, and the girls will take the buckets and squeegees outside to dry," Dorit announced when she came out of Noam's room with three empty buckets.

At four o'clock we went to our parents' rooms with a new sense of unity and accomplishment. My parents' room was quiet. The shades and bedroom door were closed. I heard my mother waking up from her long afternoon nap; coughing and sighing and moving things around. Finally, she opened the door, looked at me sitting on the couch in the small living room, and went to the bathroom. When she got out I was still sitting on the couch, making knots in my hair and untying them.

"Why do you sit in the dark? Open the shades," she said on her way back to the bedroom. "And stop playing with your hair. You're destroying it," she called from inside the bedroom.

I got up from the couch and opened the shades. Then I turned around and sat on the rocking chair. There was nothing else to do. I was hoping my brother would show up and we would go play outside, but he never came home before it was time to go to dinner. I heard the neighbors, whom I saw earlier sitting on a blanket on the front lawn drinking afternoon coffee, talking loudly to their children. Their stupid dog barked at anyone who passed in front of their room.

"I'm going to make myself a cup of coffee. Do you want something to drink?" my mother asked when she came out of the bedroom wearing a sundress.

I shook my head.

"Why don't you go to the kitchen and bring ice water. I'll make lemonade."

"I don't want lemonade."

"No, no, no. That's all you can say. And stop playing with your hair."

I sighed.

"Did you do your homework?" she asked while she was preparing herself a cup of instant coffee. All she had in that tiny kitchenette was an electric pot, a few glasses, a jar of sugar, some ancient cookies no one dared to eat, and a small aluminum pitcher full of milk that she remembered to bring from the kitchen after lunch.

I mumbled something and nodded.

"Now, where is your father?" she suddenly asked impatiently, looking at her watch, "it's almost five o'clock."

Probably organizing a lecture or a slide show for the kibbutz members, I thought.

She came into the living room with her cup of instant coffee, sat on the couch and started to read the newspaper. I rocked in the chair, bored. I could not think of anything to do. I already read all the interesting books I found in my parents' room, not just the children's books my mother arranged on a special shelf in the bedroom.

"Why don't you go look for your brother?" she startled me. "I can't understand why he never comes home anymore."

Because there is nothing to do here, I wanted to tell her. All our books, and toys, and clothes are in the children's house, and all you do is sit on the couch, listen to the radio and read the paper when we come here. But I didn't think she could understand it, so I jumped from the rocking chair and said, "Okay."

I ran outside and headed to see Tikva in her foster family's room. With a little luck I could find her there and listen to the record one last time before we went to see the musical. I wanted to make sure that I remembered the lyrics correctly, and looked at the beautiful pictures on the jacket until they sank inside my eyes and stayed there forever.

Tikva was learning how to ride her new red bicycle, which her mother bought in front of her foster parents' room. Her eyes lit up when she saw me. She stopped pedaling and asked me if I wanted to try riding it. "Can we listen to the record instead?" I asked breathlessly before I even bothered to say shalom.

She thought about my question for a few seconds and then, generously, said yes. She carefully leaned the bicycle on the wall by the stairs and I followed her inside. We listened to the record and looked at the pictures until Tikva's foster parents came in and announced that they were going to the dining hall to eat dinner. Only then did I remember that I was supposed to find my brother and ask him to come home. I left them standing on the walkway in front of their room and ran across the lawns, yelling my brother's name over and over, until I reached my parents' room.

The signal of the seven o'clock news program greeted me when I entered.

"Where were you all evening?" my mother asked, irritated.

"I went to visit Tikva."

"Don't you think you have to spend some time with your family?" she asked, looking at my father, who came home during my absence. Avner hid himself behind a newspaper. I knew he was not reading it, just making sure he was out of her line of fire. He also came home late, like all of us.

I shrugged. I knew they could not understand me. That was why I did not bother to tell them that I planned to run to the children's house immediately after dinner, and calculate how many hours I had to wait before I could see the musical.

"Did you hear what happened here yesterday afternoon?" I heard the *metapelet*, Zehava, whisper the next morning to the teacher.

It was just after breakfast. All the kids went to play outside and I stayed in the dining room, trying to finish my cheese and olive sandwich, and listened to the conversation between the *metapelet* and the teacher. By now I already knew that they were going to make instant coffee and drink it in their own glasses instead of the scratched plastic cups we used. I also knew that if they thought I wasn't listening, they would say things they would not dare to say in front of the children. They usually talked in low voices when they drank their instant coffee, believing I could not hear them. But I could. I only pretended that I wasn't listening.

"No, I didn't," the teacher said.

A huge wave of anxiety grappled my throat. Suddenly the cheese on my bread tasted like cement and I wanted to spit it out.

"You wouldn't believe me when I tell you," the *metapelet* said, waving one hand in the air. A fly landed on the rim of her glass and she shooed it away. It took off and landed inside the empty salad bowl that stood in front of me.

"After all the years I've worked with these kids, nothing can surprise me anymore," the teacher said, shook her head, and shrugged with apparent lack of interest.

"Wait till you hear this," the *metapelet* promised her and looked in my direction to check on me. I fixed my eyes on the Modigliani that hung under the clock and took another bite from my sandwich. Immediately I regretted it. But I was glad to see that my behavior convinced her that my thoughts were elsewhere.

"Margalit, the substitute who worked yesterday, came to my room last night and told me something I couldn't believe. I simply couldn't believe it." The *metapelet* enunciated each word carefully, and I knew that I was listening to very bad news.

"What did they do?" the teacher finally asked with growing curiosity, adding with typical self-righteousness, "You should have prepared her. You know them better than all of us. Did they break anything?"

"Worse," Zehava said, and waved her hand in the air. The fly didn't notice it.

"Worse?"

"She told me that when she came back from the laundry house she heard a lot of noise and went to check what it was. And do you know what she saw?"

"They put a frog in the silverware drawer and when she opened it...," the teacher tried to guess, and her voice trailed off before she finished her thought.

The *metapelet* only shook her head, right to left, left to right, trying to increase the tension and prolong the suspense as long as possible. Then, slowly, emphasizing each word, she broke the news. "She went to Noam's room and saw that someone had pissed on the floor. Can you believe it? Can you believe it?"

"Did they tell her who did it?"

"No. She said that they just laughed at her. They wouldn't tell her who did it," she said, and puffed on her cigarette until it hissed angrily between her lips.

"I see," the teacher said, and I felt the olives climb all the way from my stomach to my throat. The bitter juice almost choked me.

"What do you think we should do?" the *metapelet* asked.

"Who cleaned it?" the teacher asked with a frozen voice. She always wanted to get all the details before she made her final decision.

"They did. After they refused to tell her who did it, she told them to clean it up and left. Then she came to check if they cleaned the mess. And do you know what they did? They used brooms to mop the floor. Brooms. And now I have to go to Moshiko and ask him to give me new brooms. They ruined all the brooms. Who taught them to mop the floor with brooms? I don't understand it. I simply don't understand these kids. They behave as if they grew up in the jungle, as if they've never learned anything." She finished her speech with more shakes of the head, took another puff from her cigarette, and threw it inside her empty glass.

"Maya, did you fall asleep over there?" the teacher's voice startled me.

"What?" I said with genuine confusion, forgetting I was a jaded spy.

"Why don't you go play outside? Go out. Get some fresh air. Children your age need to run a little. You're behaving like an old lady sitting here all day. Go play with the rest of the kids," the teacher ordered me, and I knew I had to obey.

Now that both of them knew about what happened yesterday we might be in big trouble, I thought when I stumbled out of the dining room. They might be plotting something. I didn't know what to expect. I had to put it out of my mind. I didn't want to say anything to anyone yet. It could be nothing. After all, we had cleaned everything except for those three brooms. I decided to talk to Daphna. She might know what to do. She was older than me and I had a feeling that the *metapelet* liked her because she was a responsible girl. Boring, yet responsible.

Daphna was sitting at the top of the stairs, watching the boys chase one another around the rose bushes planted on top of the bomb shelter. I sat next to her.

"Daphna," I said and touched her shoulder slightly with my shoulder.

"Hmmm," she murmured.

"Do you think we ruined the brooms yesterday?"

"Which brooms?" she asked, scratching her bare knee.

"The brooms we used to mop the floor."

"Of course not," she waved me away and checked her mosquito bites more closely. One of them was bleeding.

"How do you know?" I insisted.

"Because we put them upside down to dry," she said impatiently. "And anyway, why do you care about these stupid brooms?" she asked and jumped from the third stair to the ground.

I watched her run up the hill to look for Tomer who had disappeared on the other side of the bomb shelter. I stayed on the stairs by myself feeling like a total nudnik. Then I decided not to worry about those brooms.

"Children, come in, I'm going to start the music lesson," the teacher called us, standing at the door in her blue balloon shorts and ringing her copper bell.

The boys ran down the hill that hid the bomb shelter, trying to push each other into the rose bushes, and screaming loudly when they passed near the prickly stems. "Dotan, Erez, Shlomi, Nir, Noam, Tomer," she called each name, trying to catch their attention with the copper bell. Ding, ding, ding, ding.

I rose from the stairs and walked to the classroom. Before I entered I saw Shlomi chase Nir up the hill into a rose bush. All the boys laughed wildly when Nir dodged him and ended up rolling downhill unharmed. I sat in my chair and watched them climb the stairs "like a herd of elephants." I have never seen elephants climb up a staircase, but that was what every *metapelet* who worked with us said when the boys ran up the stairs and shook the entire children's house.

Nir was the last one to enter. His clothes were covered with dirt and his hair was completely messed up. He stopped by the sink, turned on the tap, and sucked the water right from the nozzle. The teacher stood by her desk, her arms crossed under her breasts, and waited with the eleven of us until he sat down. Then she turned to the blackboard and wrote the lyrics of a song she was trying to teach us during the last three music lessons.

"Now everybody sing together," she finally said, and pointed at the words on the blackboard. Waving a small wooden stick in the air like a real conductor, and knitting her eyebrows together, she motioned to the five girls on my right to begin. I waited with the boys until they got to the third word and started singing my line, "Doom-du-lee-doom-du-lee-doom."

I let my voice sing with the boys, but my thoughts were wandering around the room, contemplating, trying to predict the future. Even though Daphna said the brooms were fine, I was almost sure that the teacher would come up with a new punishment for us. I did not want to be punished again, but I had to prepare myself. What could she do to us, I wondered. Make us copy an entire chapter from the Bible? Probably not. What happened yesterday had nothing to do with the Bible and it was not even during a lesson. It had to be something else. Maybe she would cancel the four o'clock snack. That was fine with me. I did not like those jelly sandwiches anyway. Maybe they would change the time of lights out in the children's house to eight o'clock instead of nine o'clock for a whole week. It would be quite embarrassing to go to sleep at the same time with the children from kindergarten, but I could live with it. Only for a week, though.

"Doom-du-lee-doom-du-lee-doom-doom-doom."

The last time we were seriously punished was just before Hanukah. The *metapelet* got mad at us for burning too many candles one Friday night, after a lightning storm left us in complete darkness. She threw all the candles in the garbage and said that we would not celebrate Hanukah. But it ended up as a big joke because we dug the candles out of the dumpster and hid them in our drawers. And then, to punish her, we mixed kerosene with water and poured it on the floor and she slipped on it, and nearly broke her back.

"Doom-du-lee-doom-du-lee-doom."

The only problem was that the teacher and the *metapelet* always came up with the weirdest punishments. And sometimes those punishments could be quite awful. I was hoping she would not force us to go to bed immediately after lunch and make us sleep until four thirty. I hated those afternoon naps. And what if she never allowed us to go to the bathroom again? Who knows? Maybe I could pray to God. Maybe they would not punish us at all.
"Doom-du-lee-doom-du-lee-doom-doom-doom."

Our teacher, I already knew, believed in God. She was the only member in the kibbutz who believed in him. No one else ever talked about him the way that she did. We didn't even have a synagogue. She told us that God punished people who lied and did not obey his commandments. She wanted us to believe that he punished people so we would be afraid of him and do everything she said. She thought we believed he was on her side because she was already a grown-up, and God was always on the side of the grown-ups. Of course I was not completely sure about it, but I didn't know any stories in which God did good miracles for children. In all the stories I read he only talked to important people. Prophets, kings, generals, judges. Besides, I have never seen him making miracles or punishments like he used to do in the Bible. On the kibbutz everything was happening on its own, without any reason.

"Doom-du-lee-doom-du-lee doom . . . doom . . . DOOM."

A loud knock on the door startled me. The singing stopped abruptly and we all turned to see who it was. The teacher said, "Come in," and the *metapelet* opened the door and motioned something to her. The teacher nodded, told us to remain seated in our chairs, and left the classroom.

I had a feeling that I had to whisper something and prepare them, but I didn't know what to say. So I looked at the orange fish that were swimming in the aquarium. After a few minutes the teacher returned to the classroom with the *metapelet*, and an extra chair from the dining room. They crossed the classroom side by side. The *metapelet* put the chair she brought with her in front of us and sat down. The teacher remained standing by her desk. She leaned on her desk and examined us behind her glasses. We waited. Nir fidgeted in his chair in front of me. Tomer sighed. The fish swam quietly in the aquarium under the bubbles, oblivious to the world.

"Children," the teacher finally opened, "this morning, after breakfast Zehava told me what happened here yesterday during afternoon nap." She stopped and looked at each one of us.

"Does anyone want to tell me what happened?" the teacher asked with a hidden threat in her voice.

Silence. Lots of fidgeting went on for a few seconds.

"I want to know who urinated on the floor in Noam's room."

Silence. No one moved. No one looked up. I knew it even though my head was bent down, my eyes following the black lines on the tile floor under my desk.

"Iris?" she called the first name.

"I didn't do it," Iris complained.

"Noam?"

"I didn't do it," Noam sulked, punching his desk with his fist.

"Hadas?"

Everyone stopped breathing. Suspense gripped us. A whole eternity went by.

"I didn't do it," she finally squeaked.

Sigh. Erez sneezed.

"Very well," the teacher said, and motioned something secret to Zehava.

"I'm asking again - who urinated on the floor?"

No answer.

"This is the last time I'm asking. Who did it?"

Still no answer.

Dorit raised her hand. "Can I say something?" she asked before she got permission to speak, and kept her hand up in the air.

"What do you want to say?" the teacher asked, exasperated.

"The kid who did it had no choice because the substitute doesn't let anyone go to the bathroom during afternoon nap," she explained.

The teacher looked annoyed. "No one asked for your opinion, Dorit," she said and nodded the secret code to Zehava. Now the *metapelet* got up to talk. She cleared her throat and exhaled all the air that was inside her.

"Children," she opened, and looked around the classroom, the white inside her eyes moved slowly from one desk to another, "we told you time and time again, when the substitute comes at two o'clock you're supposed to be already asleep. No bathroom or drinking water, or reading books, or playing games. When the substitute comes at two everyone is asleep. It's that simple. How many times do I have to tell you that? Every time a new substitute comes to this children's house something else happens. What is it supposed to mean? Huh? Do you think you can behave like savages without paying for it?" She asked and I knew that it was coming. The blow was finally coming. "Why do I have to hear about the noise and the mess you make here every time a new substitute comes to work here? Do you think that's what I want to do all my life? I am not going to let this go on. I am going to put a stop to this behavior. Do you understand? Do you understand what I'm talking about?" She asked again and pinched her lips together.

No one dared to think about the answer. No one.

"Do you think you can just urinate on the floor and not be punished?" she persisted. I knew that no one could answer that question either. I was looking at the floor so hard I felt it might open up any moment and swallow me. I was hoping it would. I couldn't bear the suspense. "I'm asking you for the last time - who did it?"

No one answered. I blinked up quickly and saw the two of them exchange glances and nod their secret code to each other.

"Well, since you don't want to tell us who did it," the teacher whistled through her lips, "and since, again, you made noise during afternoon nap, and...," she paused because the *metapelet* coughed a signal and got up from her chair.

"And since you think you can ruin the brooms as if your father were a millionaire, or as if we had an endless supply of brooms," the *metapelet* added and sat down.

"We decided that you are not going to see the musical tonight."

No.

I tried to breathe.

My stomach grumbled and turned upside down. I pulled a strand of hair from my head. By the roots. It hurt. I was trapped inside the classroom. I wanted to get out. I didn't want to be there. I didn't want to be. I had to call someone for help. Please. Someone. Let me out of here. I can't breathe. Someone. Help me. Get me out of here. Air. I need some air. Where is all the air? Floor, open up and swallow me. Now. A giant rock settled in my chest. I couldn't breathe. No. I was not going to cry. I couldn't do it anyway. I just had to concentrate on my breathing because the air was not going down to where it was supposed to go. My hand went into my mouth. I started to chew my knuckle. I just had to concentrate on my knuckle. I chewed it. And I breathed. Just chewed and breathed. The skin started to peel. I didn't feel anything. I felt my knuckle bleeding. I chewed another knuckle. And I breathed. Slowly. I could chew all of them until I stopped feeling the rock inside my chest. I didn't know what to do. I knew she didn't mean it. She only said it to scare us so we would tell her who peed on the floor. She didn't mean it. She knew how much I wanted to see that musical. She couldn't take it away from me. I just had to keep breathing and chewing my knuckles. She didn't mean it. She said it only because she was angry but in the afternoon she would not be angry anymore. And the brooms were fine. Daphna said we put them upside down. She could see that they were fine. She would even understand that we had to go to the bathroom even during afternoon nap. She must understand. I could chew another knuckle until she understood. My ears. What happened to my ears? I couldn't hear a thing. I knew they were talking. Their lips were moving. But I couldn't hear a thing. Then the *metapelet* left the classroom.

"I said you are not going to the musical, and that's final," I heard a voice. Final.

"What if we tell you who did it?" Iris tried to bargain.

"It won't make any difference now. And you know how ugly it is to snitch on a friend," the teacher berated her.

Of course she knew. She was just testing her. She would have gotten herself in big trouble if she snitched on Hadas. She wasn't going to say anything. I was not worried about it. I just had to figure out a way to talk to that teacher later and make her change her mind. Have a good plan and say the right thing. And then everything will be all right again.

"One sheep, two sheep, three sheep, four sheep, five sheep, six sheep," I was counting sheep and placing them in the alfalfa field down the hill, between the road that climbed up to the kibbutz and the ancient carob trees. What can I do? What can I do?

The silence in the children's house was eerie. No one wanted to cause another storm during afternoon nap. We all lay quietly and waited. For what? I was not sure. Daphna turned in her bed and stared at me. I looked back at her and she turned her head and stared at the ceiling. Nir rocked himself on his stomach, looking at the dining room table that stood outside, in front of our door. The table was covered with a green tablecloth and in the middle stood a vase full of fresh flowers. There were always fresh flowers in the children's house. I looked at the flowers and started counting them slowly. "One carnation, two carnations, three carnations, four carnations." I preferred counting carnations, but there were only four of them in the vase. I started counting them again.

I had to think. I had to keep my mind busy to block the loud silence that surrounded me. How am I going to persuade the *metapelet* to change her mind?

The bang of wooden shutters being pushed into a dark slot in the wall startled me. I had to wait for the substitute to slam the shutters in the second room before she came to my room. Only after she slammed our shutters into the wall and flipped the light switch I got out of bed. I did not jump out of it as I usually did. I was too preoccupied and worried. I knew that everyone was going to walk quietly to the bathroom and behave politely to each other. We always behaved ourselves in times of crisis.

I went to get dressed.

Dorit was braiding her hair in front of the mirror in the shower room. "Dorit, do you want to go with me to the *metapelet*'s room at four o'clock and ask her to change her mind?" I asked.

"I think everyone should go together to talk to her," Dorit said, wrapping a green rubber band around the tip of her braid.

"Did you ask anyone already?" I asked her, hoping the delegation was already preparing for the task with brave enthusiasm.

"Erez said he'll go only if Noam also comes," she reported.

"I'm going to ask Tikva to come," I said. I was sure she would like to join us because of the record, even though she did not say anything to me since it happened.

"No one listens to Tikva," Dorit shrugged my idea off, and emphasized what she really meant by adding, "you know what the *metapelet* thinks about her mother." She pulled hair that was stuck in her brush, and, while rolling it into a concise hairball, she asked, "Why don't you ask Daphna?"

"Ask me what?" Daphna asked when she entered the shower room.

"Do you want to come with us to talk to Zehava?" I asked her.

"Talk about what?" she asked and sat on the edge of the wooden bench. She was tall enough to see herself in the mirror even when she was sitting down.

"We want to ask her to let us go to the musical," I explained.

"She won't change her mind," Daphna said, firmly.

"How do you know?" I questioned her, annoyed.

She shrugged. "Because she's not going to change her mind."

"But you could still come with us," I insisted.

"Okay," she compromised, "I'll go with you, but I'm not going to talk. I'll just stand behind you." She tucked her shirt inside her pants and asked Dorit, "Is Tomer going to come too?" I was waiting for her to ask that question.

"He said he'd come with us only if I convinced at least four more kids to go."

"Go where? Can I go with you too?" Iris asked. She was standing near the bathroom, wiping dust from her black patent leather shoes with her bare hands.

By the time the big clock on the wall showed ten to four all the kids decided to participate in the delegation. The rumor that we were planning to go talk to the *metapelet* had traveled around the children's house and filled everyone with new hope. The boys joined us near the bomb shelter. For the first time ever they did not fight one another. They just waited with us for the substitute to poke her head out and yell at the top of her lungs: "Children, it's four o'clock. You can go home."

We sat at the entrance to the bomb shelter and tried to predict how she would react once she saw that none of us went anywhere at four. We laughed and giggled with growing excitement and anticipation. We were also a little embarrassed and self-conscious about the new unity that landed on us. Suddenly, boys and girls were on the same side, together striving to achieve the same goal. Like true grown-ups, we were acting jointly upon our determination to overturn injustice. When the substitute finally poked her head out with her daily announcement, we were certain that the musical was within our reach. We knew that once the *metapelet* saw all of us standing in front of her room she would not be able to say no. She would have to change her mind.

The substitute noticed that none of us had moved from the bomb shelter when she got out of the children's house. She stopped on the pavement, a few feet away from us, and lit a cigarette. Looking at us above her cigarette, she asked, "Aren't you going to your parents' rooms today?"

She definitely looked nervous. She took a long puff from her cigarette and said, "Iris, I'm sure your mother is waiting for you." A cloud of white smoke hid her face from us for a long moment.

Iris shrugged and said, "Not true." Then she turned to look at Dorit for reassurance. Dorit frowned and shook her head. Erez and Tomer started to giggle.

The substitute looked at us without trying to hide her contempt, threw the cigarette on the ground, dug a hole in the dirt with her sandal, buried it, and walked away. I could swear she mumbled something to herself. It sounded like, "I don't understand these disturbed kids."

Once she disappeared behind the bomb shelter, Dorit got up from the stairs and said, "let's go," as if the whole idea to go and talk to the *metapelet* was only hers. I did not mind it, though, because she was the oldest girl in the group. She raised one finger, and with the confident resolve of a well-trained army platoon, we got up from the stairs that led to the bomb shelter and began to march. We had to avoid crossing the lawns that stretched between the children's house and the *metapelet*'s room because of the gardener. He was completely fanatic about keeping the lawns green and healthy during all seasons, so whenever he caught us walking on the well-tended lawns, defying the "Do not step on the watered lawn" signs he spread all over the kibbutz, he got so angry that his face turned bright red and his thick mustache splattered dangerous sparks. There was also the rumor we heard that he shot a cat with a Czech rifle just because she ruined his jasmine bushes. That was what the kids from seventh grade told us when they found her corpse near their classroom with a bleeding wound on her forehead. They buried her between two tall cypresses by the western side of their children's house, and the white headstone they placed above the grave reminded us not to take any risks even when we were in a big rush.

When we reached the *metapelet*'s room some of the kids decided to hide in the bushes that covered the left wall of the building. They were tall leafy bushes with tiny white flowers that attracted gangs of bees and other stinging insects. I stayed with Dorit, Iris, Shlomi, and Noam on the pavement. I already decided that no matter how terrible I felt about letting the members of the kibbutz see me beg the *metapelet* to change her mind, I was not going to hide in the bushes. I did not want to be stung by a bee, or bitten by a snake right before the musical and ruin everything.

"So who wants to go talk to her?" Noam asked us, knowing that no one would volunteer. He knew that Shlomi could not persuade the *metapelet* to do anything because he was an outside boy from a broken home; Iris was not smart enough to represent us during crises; and I was too young and shy. Besides, I never went anywhere first. Especially when everyone was watching.

We looked at Dorit and waited for her to volunteer. She did not hesitate and agreed to go. She climbed the three concrete stairs and knocked on the door five times. I looked at her standing by the door, at the top of the stairs, and my heart filled with admiration for her.

"Just a minute," we heard a voice behind the door.

Dorit jumped off the stairs and joined us on the pavement. Noam and Dotan, who came out of the bushes, snorted nervously. After more than five minutes the door opened and the *metapelet* stood there in a house robe. She frowned at us, looking sleepy. Her curly hair was matted on one side and her eyes blinked fast getting used to the bright light. I realized that we woke her up from the sacred afternoon nap. It was a bad sign, but I quickly put it out of my mind. Before she had a chance to say anything, Dorit took one step forward, and said, "We came to ask you to change your mind about the punishment. We want to go to the musical." Then she stepped backward, and joined us on the pavement.

"Whose idea was this?" the *metapelet* asked, irritated. "Whose idea was it to come here and wake me up? Huh?"

The moment her "Huh" dissolved, the faces of the kids hiding in the bushes popped out. She heard the movement in the bushes and turned to look what it was. Her frown became even deeper when she saw the entire group gathered in front of her room.

"It was everyone's idea," Dorit told her and we all nodded behind her.

The *metapelet* looked at the group on the pavement, then she looked at the faces in the bushes, then she shook her head, and rolled her eyes up to the sky. We looked at her with growing anticipation. "You know very well why you were punished," she said, and tried to fix her hair. "You are not little children anymore. We decided that you are not going to the musical and that's it. We told you it was final," she said, and tightened the belt around her waist.

"We promise we'll never make noise during afternoon nap," Noam stepped forward with an offer we did not discuss among us. His glasses were covered with nervous steam and breadcrumbs.

"Of course you're not going to make noise during afternoon nap," she said.

"And we'll apologize to the substitute," Iris offered another bargain and received a few dirty looks from the bushes.

"True, you should apologize to her," the *metapelet* agreed and I felt a blink of joy pass inside my body.

"So if we promise not to make noise again and apologize to the substitute, are you going to let us see the musical?" Dorit tried to close the bargain and finish the negotiations. We had to start rushing her to say yes. The buses were going to arrive at the parking lot at any moment.

The *metapelet* looked at us and sniffed, "Of course not."

"Why not?" a long cry came out of the bushes.

"It is time you understand that we are serious when we tell you not to make noise during afternoon nap," she scorned us. "And besides, I did not make this decision alone, and I am not going to let you go without your teacher's consent."

I felt the familiar taste of despair touch me lightly at the nape of my neck. What else could we do to reverse that decision? What other sacrifice did she want? Think. I had to take every nuance in account. I had to trap her. And I had to be fast. But what could I do? My mind raced to find an answer and I heard myself finally say, "we could go and ask the teacher. Will you let us go if she says yes?"

I could not believe it. I entered the negotiations. I have never done it before. Not out loud anyway. Usually I heard entire conversations inside my head but I never spoke out. I was afraid to make a fool out of myself. And I hated being yelled at in public. But the situation was so severe I had to overcome my fear and speak up. I had to dare. I felt her eyes rest on my face for a moment with something close to hatred. She hated me for coming up with such a great idea. But I did not care. I felt so proud of myself. I was invincible again.

"You can do whatever pleases you, Miss Maya," she addressed me, as if I were the only kid who wanted to go to the musical. "Now, I'm going inside to get dressed, if you don't mind," she announced, and walked back into her room.

The moment her door closed Dotan said, "I'll go if Noam comes with me."

No one had to persuade Noam to go with Dotan. He knew that we were running out of time and that he needed to act fast. The teacher lived on the other side of the kibbutz, near the soccer field. It was going to take at least fifteen minutes to find her, to tell her about what happened, persuade her to change her mind, and then walk all the way back here with her. We knew that the *metapelet* might not believe them if they came back alone and said that she agreed to change her mind.

We all sighed in relief when the two of them disappeared behind the old azedarach tree. Daphna and Tikva came out of the bushes and joined us on the pavement. Everyone was sure that the teacher was going to change her mind once she found out how far we were ready to go to get her forgiveness. I listened to the optimistic predictions and my heart began to sink. I could not explain it, but inside me I felt suddenly that I was not going to see the musical after all. Stop it, I told myself. You're going to make it. Don't forget: out of the strong came something sweet.

Then we heard the buses puffing and groaning as they were crawling up the asphalt road behind the *metapelet*'s room, their engines sighed when they reached the top of the hill. Suddenly, like magic, children from younger groups showed up, running to the parking lot, screaming in delight. They were dressed in their Friday evening clothes; all the boys in their ironed white shirts, and the girls in fluttering dresses and black patent leather shoes. All of them were followed by hurried parents who tried to keep up with their excited pace.

My heart was going to explode. I wanted to join them, run to the parking lot, get into the yellow bus, and sit near the window. I had to force myself to stay on the pavement, or my legs would run to the bus on their own, without waiting for the *metapelet* to come out of her room and announce that she had changed her mind, that we could go to the musical.

"Children, what are you doing here?" I heard a man's voice behind me. "Hurry up or you will miss the bus."

Moyshaleh, Erez's father, was standing behind me in his blue work clothes. I had just seen him walking Erez' younger sister to the parking lot. "Erez, don't you want to go see the musical?" he asked in bewilderment.

Erez choked. His chin turned red, then his nose, then the rest of his face. He looked like he wanted to hide in the bushes. His hands went into his pockets, and out and in again. Then his left hand went to his ear and scratched it. Then he got the sniffles and gulped. I wanted him to stop sniffling and start breathing, before he got another asthma attack. It was painful to watch him squirm in front of his father. "We g-got p-punished not t-to s-see t-the musical," he stammered, looking at his feet.

"Ah," Moyshaleh said, scratching his head and just stood there, not knowing what to say. Finally he asked, "Do you want to walk with me back home?"

"Could you ask the *metapelet* to let us go?" Nir called from the bushes. He was swinging on a thick branch, up and down, up and down. "Could you convince her to let us go to the musical?" he asked again, the branch creaking dangerously under his weight.

Moyshaleh shook his head and smiled apologetically. I already knew he was not going to do it for us. None of our parents ever dared to argue with our *metapelet*. They thought she knew how to educate us better than they did, only because she had studied education in The Seminar near Haifa. Besides, it was against the rules to argue with her, they said. Erez looked at the grass. Trying to control his tears, he stuttered, "You have to talk to her quickly, or it's g-going to be t-too l-late." He started to cough and wiped his nose with his bare forearm.

"We didn't do anything wrong," Nir protested from his spot on the branch, and began to swing violently on it. I was afraid he would fall down and break a bone or something.

"You know I can't tell her what to do," Moyshaleh begged us to get him off the hook, scratching the stubble on his neck. In his youth, Moyshaleh had joined the partisans instead of going to the ghetto with his parents; he had blown up trains in Hungary, he had saved Jews from certain death, he had fought the Nazis; at the end of the war, on his way to Palestine, the boat he was on was captured by the British Navy and he was sent to rot in a prison camp in Cyprus - he survived every danger one could imagine, but he did not dare confront our *metapelet*.

I wanted to drop in front of him and beg him to talk to her, but my body did not know how. I was tired of controlling the tears that kept forcing their way into my eyes. I did not even know if I still wanted to go to the musical. I was too tired to argue with the *metapelet*. And I did not want to be near all the young children, who were happy and excited, fighting for a good seat by the window. I wanted to go away and hide somewhere. And sleep.

"Please, talk to her," Iris joined in. But he didn't listen. He walked away, shaking his head and waving one hand in the air.

These kids had no pride, I thought to myself and thanked them, too. I wanted to be able to stop him, and beg, and cry, and insist, but I couldn't. I just couldn't bring myself to fight for my lost musical anymore.

Once again we faced one another on the pavement, counting the last minutes. The drivers had started the engines and the flood of children running to the parking lot had diminished. We were the only kids on the kibbutz who were not going to the parking lot. No one but Erez' father asked us why we were not yet sitting in the bus. No one. I saw some of the parents come back from the parking lot and look at us questioningly, but none of them asked why we were still standing near our *metapelet*'s room; why we were not running to catch the bus.

"Maybe one of us should go to the parking lot and ask the driver to wait a few more minutes," my voice betrayed me again. I knew it was not fair that I always came up with ideas and never volunteered to do anything. I hoped someone else would have the guts to do what I wished I could do myself.

Before we started discussing my idea, Noam and Dotan showed up behind the old azedarach tree. "We could not find the teacher anywhere," Dotan said, fighting his tears. All the shoulders around me drooped when Noam added, "We even went to look for her in the library, but she wasn't there."

The only sounds that disturbed the silence surrounding us belonged to the yellow buses that rushed down the hill, and the voices of children singing and clapping hands. We stood in front of the *metapelet*'s room until the sound of the engines faded away. Until we could not hear the singing, only the typical sounds of the kibbutz: dogs barking in the distance, cows mooing on their way to be milked, birds fighting for a good spot on a branch before night fall, a tractor returning from the wheat fields. We looked at one another and we knew that there was nothing else we could do. Dorit sighed, Erez sneezed again, and Nir finally jumped to the ground. "Ai," he groaned on his way down.

Suddenly the door opened and the *metapelet* came outside holding an empty milk jar. She was going to get fresh milk from the kitchen for the afternoon snack, as if nothing happened. "Children, what are you doing here? Go home. All of you," she waved her arm, shooing us away like irritating flies.

Without exchanging glances, without protesting, we turned and left. We did not look back. We walked straight ahead. Ashen faces. Heads down. Shoulders stooped. Feet dragged on the grass. Fists tucked inside tight pockets.

I went to my parents' room. No one was there. My mother was in charge of the kitchen evening shift for the entire week, my father was not back from work yet. I sat on the rocking chair and stared out the window. For a long time the blue horizon moved up and down, up and down. My father came in when the color of the sky turned dark orange and purple. He sat on the couch, took off his sandals, yawned, leaned back, and closed his eyes. For a while he looked as if he was asleep. I kept rocking in the chair as if he were still not there, completely silent. Finally, he opened his eyes, sighed, reached for the newspaper and started to read the front page.

"Weren't you supposed to go to the musical today?" he asked me from behind the newspaper.

"We were punished and couldn't go," I said.

"Why? What did you do?" He asked without putting down the newspaper.

I shrugged without answering his question. I couldn't talk.

"Did you tell mother?"

"No, she's in the kitchen," I said, staring out the window.

After a few minutes my father got up and turned the lights on. The light hurt my eyes, forced them to close. I didn't open them until he took my hand, the one that rested on the arm of the rocking chair, and looked at it. I knew what he was looking at. On each knuckle of each finger there was a red scab, marking the spot where I had chewed the skin raw. Now that the torn flesh was drying I could not bend my fingers and they rested listlessly on the chair. I pulled my hand away from him and put it between my knees.

"Did you do this to yourself?" he asked.

I shook my head without looking at him.

"How did it happen?"

"I fell during a basketball game," I lied.

"Does it hurt?" he asked.

"No," I said. "It doesn't hurt. It doesn't hurt at all."

Chapter Six

I didn't believe it would happen to me so soon. According to what I had heard it was supposed to happen when I was much older. I didn't want to tell anyone about it. I was afraid that the girls in the children's house would think that I was a freak of nature if I'd told them that I had found bloodstains on my underwear. None of them had gotten their period yet. Not even Dorit who had already celebrated her bat-mitzvah. I had to find a way to live with my awful secret until all the other girls got their period. But I couldn't keep my secret from everyone. The cotton wool and pads were stored in the "small supplies room" and only grown-ups could order them from Amos. If I'd go and ask him for that stuff he would ask me why I needed them and what was I supposed to say?

I had no choice but to tell my secret to Carmela, my new *metapelet.* Luckily, she was different from all the other *metapelets* we had before. She liked to laugh. She never yelled. She listened to contemporary music on the radio, not only to the news. She made us feel comfortable around her even though she was a grown-up. And she could get me the sanitary pads I needed.

I found her sitting in the dining room. Breakfast was over and apart from the greedy flies that had never left the children's house no one was around. The sink was full of dishes and the tables were a mess but she looked completely relaxed. She was listening to the radio, smoking a cigarette, and enjoying a cup of Nescafe. I approached her and whispered that I got my period.

"Are you sure?"

I nodded.

She pointed the cigarette at the chair next to her and motioned to me to sit down. I plopped on the chair. She took a long drag from the cigarette and looked at me with half a smile. "*Mazal tov*, now you're a woman," she said and exhaled a cloud of smoke.

I did not want to become a woman. Not at the tender age of ten and a half, and not in the children's house where I would have to sneak into the bathroom with folded pads in my pockets and inexplicable stains on my shorts. I was too young to carry the burden of that messy inconvenience and I was mad at my body for inflicting womanhood on me. I whispered that I didn't want to be a woman.

Carmela smiled a grown-up smile and said something only a *metapelet* could say: "You'll get used to it. You've got no other choice."

I knew I had no choice but how could anyone get used to bleeding for days? In the summer I would have to go to a stupid summer camp, pretend that I was a mammoth hunter, sleep in a tent and pretend it was a cave. I wouldn't be able to take a shower or use a real toilet for three days. And what about going to the beach? I would have to stay in the children's house when everyone else goes swimming. And I still had to share the toilets with a bunch of boys who couldn't piss into a toilet bowl without missing. How could I ever get used to being a woman?

"Believe me, Maya. You'll be fine," she tried to console me when she saw the expression on my face. "And you should be happy that you understand what happened to your body. When I was your age no one explained anything to me. My mother didn't talk to me like I talk to you. She didn't prepare me for any of it."

She was right. I was pretty lucky. When I saw the bloodstains on my underwear I didn't think for one second that I was going to die or that I'd caught a terrible disease. I knew exactly what it was because Carmela had prepared me.

Two weeks earlier she had asked all of us girls to come to her room after dinner for "a serious talk." Because she didn't say what she wanted to talk about, I started to worry that she was going to punish us for something we did, even though we didn't do anything wrong as far as I could remember. Since she started working with us we were quiet during naptime, we didn't trash the house, and we hadn't sneaked out of the children's house even once after lights-out. I also wondered why she did not invite the boys. What had we done that they hadn't?

At dinnertime I saw Iris eating with her parents at the communal dining hall. I went to her table and asked if she wanted to walk with me to Carmela's room, which was located far from the dining hall and the well-lit walkways. I thought that she might feel the same about walking alone in the dark.

Iris gave me her famous shrug of indifference, looked at her mother, Bruria, from under her pretty eyelashes, and mumbled "all right," as if she were doing me a great favor.

Bruria put down her fork and rolled her eyes behind her glasses. "Why can't your mother go with you?"

"Let them walk together," Iris's father said, before I could explain that my mother had gone to the regional high school to study drama in the adult education program. Unlike Bruria, who was not interested in anything but her daughters, my mother wanted to learn to be an actress like Elizabeth Taylor whom she said was the most beautiful woman in the world.

"I didn't say they can't walk together," Bruria backfired, insulted.

I could swear that Bruria knew what Carmela was going to talk about, but I did not dare ask after the look that she gave me. I went with Iris to the dishwashing room to dump our dirty dishes in the tubs and together we left the dining hall.

The boys from our class were playing cowboys and Indians on the lawn in front of the dining hall. It was warm enough to play outside and too early to go to the children's house. When they saw us come out of the dining hall they surrounded us and pointed their plastic guns at us. "A girls' talk," Shlomi chuckled. "What do you girls talk about?"

I told Iris to ignore him but she stopped and said, "Admit that you're jealous because you were not invited."

"You're jealous, you're jealous," Nir imitated her. He pointed his plastic gun at us and commanded: "Endz-up."

"Leave these babies alone, Iris, let them play their stupid games," I said with all the maturity I could mobilize into my voice.

"Babies," Iris echoed and turned away from him.

The walkway up the hill was as dark as I had expected. The sky was moonless and cloudy and a row of cypresses blocked the faint light that the tall lamppost threw on the ground. We had to let our eyes get used to the darkness and walk slowly or end up walking into the oleander bushes that grew by the side of the walkway. A night bird swooshed by us, flapping heavy wings. I was glad Iris was walking by my side.

Carmela's house was a one-story, flat-roofed rectangular box situated behind pepper trees and hibiscus bushes. Recently built on the other side of the gravel road that encircled the residential area of the kibbutz, it was a unique building designed to accommodate only two married couples. All the other buildings on the kibbutz housed four married couples and looked like army barracks. Identical and uninspiring.

A bare light bulb dangling above the front door threw yellow light on the stairs and attracted clouds of flying insects. I started up the stairs, waving my hands in front of my face to protect it from a giant flying cockroach, when Anna burst out of the bushes and started barking at us. Anna was an old bitch, much too small to pose a serious threat to anyone who could kick. Iris ignored her and knocked on the door.

"Quiet, Anna," we heard Carmela's voice and the door opened.

The loud barking changed into a low growl then into a whine.

"Don't be afraid. She doesn't bite," Carmela reassured us.

I entered the small living room cautiously. Daphna, Hadas, Dorit and Tikva were sitting tight on a brown couch. Four tall glasses and a plate of over-baked cookies stood on the coffee table beside a thick book with a blue cover.

"Sit down, girls, feel at home." Carmela's voice resonated with courtesy, which according to my experience, was reserved until now only for grown-ups.

Once Carmela left the living room Iris became interested in the ceiling. She crossed her arms over her chest and fixed her eyes on the elaborate light fixture that hung above the coffee table. I sat on one of the two armchairs, crossed my legs and arms, and stared at the titles of the books lined on the shelves.

"Iris," Dorit whispered and motioned her head and eyes in the direction of an upright chair standing by a writing desk. Iris tried to pretend that she did not understand the hint but once she saw that all the girls were glaring at her she succumbed to the silent pressure and dragged the chair to the center of the room. She placed it next to the couch and sat down. We waited quietly and tried to act mature and serious. Carmela came in with two glasses of lemonade, put them on the coffee table, and sat on the other armchair facing the couch.

"We can talk freely tonight. Oved is working the second shift in the kitchen and will not be back for another hour," she said, leaning into the armchair.

Dorit cleared her throat. Daphna scratched her head. I reached for one of the glasses. There were three ice cubes in the glass. I fished one of the ice cubes and sucked on it. Ice cubes were a luxury that we had only recently started to enjoy, after the majority of the members decided that buying a small refrigerator for each family would not destroy the kibbutz social life. The ice cube was quickly melting in my mouth and Carmela was still silent. Her silence made me tingle with edginess. What did she want from us?

"Do you girls know why I asked you to come here tonight?" she finally spoke up.

We shook our heads and looked to one another.

Carmela leaned forward and opened the book that lay on top of the coffee table. She asked us to come closer and look at the drawings. Immediately I understood why she asked us to come to her room. She was going to tell us how babies come to the world. Nothing new to me. During the summer I asked my mother to eat a lot of potatoes and bread, and when she asked me why, I told her that I wanted her to get fat and make me a baby sister. My mother sighed, got a book with a picture of a transparent baby floating inside a balloon, and told me the whole story. Well, not all of it. Now I was hearing the bad news. Sometime in the near future I was going to become a woman and bleed for about one week every month for the rest of my life. Bleed in my underwear. For days.

I could not have been more devastated.

Until Carmela finished explaining how grown-ups make babies and told us that married couples slept naked in bed.

"Not every night," she tried to soften the blow when she saw the horror on our faces.

I was appalled. I could not imagine doing something as disgusting as lying naked in the same bed with a man. It was the worst thing I had ever heard, yet, Carmela was completely calm. She was telling us terrible, terrible news and she didn't seem upset at all.

That night I had a nightmare. I was running naked around the kibbutz looking for my clothes in the laundry house, unable to find even a handkerchief to hide my nakedness, while the members stood around and did nothing to help. The next morning I looked at Carmela and tried to imagine how she coped with her secret. She seemed so tragic even when she laughed. She was hiding something terrible under her clothes, yet she behaved as if she were untouched by catastrophe. For days I tried to comprehend the enormity of her affliction but my mind shrunk into a little corner and trembled. And before I could get used to the idea, my body had matured overnight and I became a woman right before breakfast.

Carmela patted my hand and said, "Your mother will be so happy when you tell her the news."

My mother? What did my mother have to do with it? There was nothing she could do for me. I was not planning to tell her anything. I stopped sharing my problems with her a long time ago and I was not interested in listening to another corny speech about the wonders of womanhood. She certainly was not someone I would tell about my life's misfortunes. Let her be a happy woman and leave me in my misery.

To my surprise I did get used to being a woman. I learned to take care of my body, and in spite of the occasional painful cramps and stained underwear, I was able to keep my secret intact even during hiking trips and countless picnics on the beach. I learned to hide my soiled underwear at the bottom of the laundry bag and fabricate explanations as to why sometimes I was taking a late shower or did not feel like swimming. Carmela also kept our secret pact. She brought packs of pink pads from the "small supply room" and put them in the first aid cabinet, conccaled behind bottles of iodine and sterile rolls of gauze. I never even had to remind her that I was running out of pads. Whenever I needed them, there they were, hiding behind the first aid stuff.

Then Carmela decided we needed to have another "girls' talk." This time it was going to take place in one of the bedrooms at the children's house during the ten o'clock recess. No need to go all the way to her room, she said. I wanted to avoid the "talk." If she had more bad news for us, I did not want to hear it. The boys, on the other hand, were very curious. They stood behind the bedroom door and tried to eavesdrop, snorting and chuckling and pushing one another until Dorit yelled, "Babies, go away, leave us alone."

I sat on the bed and waited with a heavy heart for Carmela to start the "talk."

"I have good news for you, girls," she said.

Someone sighed. I looked up to see who it was but all the girls were staring blankly at Carmela. Carmela clapped her hands and announced that it was time to separate between boys and girls. From now on, the girls would share two bedrooms and the boys would share the other two bedrooms. All we had to do was to decide who was going to move where.

That was great news. At last we could get rid of the boys. Since I had started wearing a bra I wanted Nir to move out of my room. Every day Daphna and I had to ask him to turn his face to the wall while we got dressed or leave the room. Nir was very considerate and never protested, but it started to be more and more difficult because we really didn't want to share the room with him. I was so glad Carmela finally thought about it. She really understood us. She was nothing like Zehava, our old mean *metapelet,* who would never have thought about separating us from the boys.

Three years earlier, when I was in second grade, I told Zehava that I didn't want to take my showers with the boys anymore and she made fun of me. It was all because of a game of doctor and patient I played with some of the kids. Dotan, who played a doctor, checked me under a blanket with a flashlight and diagnosed my illness as having grown hair on my private parts. I pushed him away from me and ran to the shower room to examine myself in the mirror. The only hair I could see was attached to my head, but my mind was made up. I told Zehava that I was not going to take a shower with the boys ever again.

Zehava thought that my behavior was the silly caprice of a girl who wanted attention. "Do you think you've got something that we haven't seen before?" she ridiculed me in front everyone. "You've got nothing to be ashamed of."

She was right, of course. I had no reason to be ashamed of my body. I was not too fat or too thin. I had no ugly birthmarks anywhere or strange deformities. I wasn't even sure what was changing inside me. I only had a gut feeling that something was changing and with it grew a new, unfamiliar need for privacy.

When Zehava saw me waiting for the boys to leave the shower room before taking my clothes off, she insisted that I take a shower with everybody. She had no patience for anyone who dared to interrupt her routine. Every afternoon, the moment the kids got out of the shower, she charged into the shower room with disinfecting soap and Brillo pads and scrubbed the walls and sinks and floors as if they were infected with a contagious disease. Her disregard for my feelings, however, did not shake my conviction that something was happening to my body. In my mind I could see my body growing into monstrous proportions, and although nothing much had changed, Dotan's words kept echoing in my ears.

"I see hair on your pee-pee."

I asked the girls to join me even though I wasn't sure they understood my plight. Together we kicked the boys out, blocked the window of the shower room with a towel, and took turns guarding the door from their assaults. Then, standing under the hot water, we discussed the hopeless immaturity of boys and compared the size of our breasts.

Zehava surrendered only because we didn't relent. She designated one shower room for boys and another one for girls, and allowed us to close the door. To show her our appreciation, we helped the boys move their towels and toothbrushes to their new shower room, then we went to our shower room and scrubbed the white walls and sink to a blinding shine. On Friday, during the Shabbat ceremony, we celebrated our victory with a song I wrote and performed with Dorit. The girls gave us a standing ovation. The boys snorted and belched in protest.

"I can move into Maya's room," Tikva's voice reminded me that I was supposed to think about the new sleeping arrangements rather than about my fight against Zehava.

"And I'll move in with Iris and Hadas," Dorit said.

I was glad Tikva volunteered to sleep in my room. I liked spending time with her even though she was an "outside girl" from Tel Aviv. I liked going to her foster family's room and listening to the records her father had sent her from Canada. Dorit, on the other hand, liked to play soccer with the boys. I didn't like to play soccer and I also didn't feel very comfortable in her parents' room. There were always too many people sitting on the lawn in front of her parents' room, eating sunflower seeds, drinking Turkish coffee, and joking about stuff I didn't understand.

I was certain that the "talk" was over when Carmela asked me to sit down and be patient. There were a few more things we needed to discuss. She said that she had decided also to designate one toilet for the girls and put a small trash can with a lid behind the door. "Don't throw cotton wool or sanitary pads into the toilet," she added. "In the last two months both toilets got clogged and I had to call Avram to come and unclog them. He said someone was throwing pads into the toilets. Don't do that, girls, use the trash can from now on."

I knew that she was talking to me. Who else could have done it? I wanted to kill her for giving away my secret. How could she do this to me after she promised to keep my secret? Now everyone would blame me for clogging up the toilets. I wanted to leave the room and slam the door but that would definitely appear as an admission of guilt. I was so embarrassed, I didn't know what to do. I looked out the window. On the mountainside, two yellow bulldozers were pushing large boulders and fallen trees to break an access road to the border. Until last year no one gave much thought to the border. It was an invisible line that ran somewhere on the top of the ridge separating us from Lebanon. But now, with the Six Day War behind us, the army decided "to demonstrate its presence" on the ridge even though no one ever crossed that border. The black goats had stopped crossing many years before and the Lebanese army had never posed a threat. Every kid on the kibbutz knew it. But last year the "situation" had changed and we had to be prepared. So now, every few days big explosions rattled the windows and raised huge clouds of dust, and afterwards the bulldozers came to remove the debris.

"It's about time," I heard Daphna's quiet voice. She was sitting on the bed near me, braiding her brown hair into many thin braids.

"Exactly," Dorit agreed from across the bedroom.

If one of the bulldozers grew wings, flew into the room through the window and started dancing in front of me I could not have been more surprised. Daphna and Dorit, the oldest girls in the group, practically admitted what I was so careful to conceal for months. Even when Carmela took the three of us to the communal clothing house to try on our first bras, they never said a word. And surely, I was not going to be the first one to confess.

"If there is anything else you need, girls, you should come and ask. Don't expect me to guess everything," Carmela said, not looking at me. She was talking to Daphna and Dorit who had the courage to talk.

"I have something to ask," Dorit said, straightening up her shirt and pulling on the strap of her bra as if it needed to be fixed. "I want to stay in the children's house when I get my period instead of going to work in the children's farm."

She was articulate and decisive and sounded so mature I nearly choked with jealousy. I wanted to tell them that I also knew the aches of womanhood. I was not a little girl with a flat chest and no hair anywhere like Iris and Hadas and Tikva.

"I'll talk to Moshon and see what we can do," Carmela promised.

I was not surprised to hear Dorit's request. I would have come up with the same request if only I had time to think. All the girls wanted to get away from the children's farm once in a while. Especially on hot days when Moshon, who was in charge of the children's farm, assigned us to shovel donkey shit from the floor of the stuffy stable. The flies were huge and green and fearless and the smell was deadly. We the girls would complain to Moshon about how much we hated doing it but he wouldn't budge. He said that he saw no difference between boys and girls and that all of us, without exception, had to do whatever needed to be done on the farm. "Children, work is our life," he recited with an evil smile whenever we complained that work was too hard and we were hot and tired.

Secretly, I also didn't want to ride our old donkey, Aphrodite. In the past, riding Aphrodite to the cowsheds to bring bales of hay or down the hill to get fresh alfalfa for our sheep and goats used to be the best job in the children's farm. It meant sitting in a wagon and doing very little for an hour. But after the war, the soldiers began to show up around the kibbutz and I no longer wished to ride old Aphrodite to the alfalfa field. I didn't want the young soldiers, who were traveling in open jeeps to the base at the border crossing, to see me sitting in a squeaky wagon dragged by a miserable looking donkey and think that I was an Arab kid. As far as I knew only Arabs rode donkeys. They used them for transportation and to carry stuff, and sometimes just for fun. We had to ride a donkey because we needed to learn that work was our life. But by now I felt that not only had I learned enough about the value of work, my new sense of femaleness began to crave gentility, finesse, and a glance of admiration from the passing jeeps. And how could I ever enjoy the ultimate pleasure of being admired by a man in uniform when I was seen riding a donkey?

"I want to ask something, too," Daphna stirred from what looked like a self-induced trance. "I don't want to participate in P.E. class when I get my period."

Carmela said she would talk to Zvi, the P.E. teacher, who was not a member of the kibbutz. Once a week he came from a neighboring town to teach us to play all kinds of sports and prepare us to pass the national fitness test which had different standards for boys and girls. I was sure that he didn't think that boys and girls were equal like Moshon, since he never insisted that we achieve the same records as the boys.

"Anything else?" Carmela asked.

I tried to think of something but nothing came to my mind. During the months I had lived with my secret, it never occurred to me to ask for special privileges. I worked and exercised and shoveled donkey shit and even went to summer camp without ever complaining about cramps and the lack of showers. Now nothing was entering my mind except for the thought that I did not want to ride Aphrodite to the alfalfa field. But asking not to ride Aphrodite to the fields would sound too stupid. What did my period have to do with riding a donkey? The girls would guess right away that I didn't want the soldiers to see me. They'd laugh at me. I had to think of something else. But I needed more time and time was running out. Dorit raised her hand and said that she didn't want to wear shorts for P.E. class during her period.

"I don't want to wear shorts, either," Iris joined in. "Every time we go to P.E. class the Arab construction workers stare at my legs."

She was absolutely right. The Arab construction workers were working on two new children's houses next to our children's house and every time we passed by them on our way to the basketball court they would stop talking and look at us. Their silent curiosity made us girls really nervous and we would huddle together and walk as fast as we could to get away from them.

"They're not used to seeing girls in shorts," Carmela explained.

"Someone should tell them it's not nice to stare," Tikva suggested.

"It's not fair that only Dorit and Daphna can have special privileges. Everyone should have the same privilege," Iris pouted her piece, though no one cared to hear it.

"Stop whining, Iris," Dorit scolded her, "you've got enough privileges."

"Not true," Iris persisted.

"Girls, this is not the right time to argue about who has more privileges. Let me talk to Zvi and Moshon and see what they say," Carmela interrupted before we were all dragged into their stupid argument. Then recess was over and we had to go back to class.

For days after our "talk" I tried to think of a special request, but my brain was paralyzed. I simply could not think of anything and I didn't want to ask for the same privileges as Dorit and Daphna. It would look too childish, like I was trying to imitate them. Besides, the girls wouldn't believe me if I suddenly said that I also got my period. I was the youngest girl in the group. They would think I made it up to get away from work and that I was lazy and a liar. I had no choice but to keep my secret; find the right moment to make my request.

But waiting for the right moment was not easy. The first time Dorit was excused from going to work in the children's farm, I was so jealous that I almost started to hate her. What about me, I wanted to ask Carmela. Iris was right. It was not fair. I should have been excused, too, without having to ask. We should all be excused from work without having to ask. Otherwise it would be like asking a favor and asking a favor from a grown-up was the last thing that I wanted to do. It would give that person too much power over me. And they could take it away from me if I did something wrong. I wondered if Carmela told Moshon why Dorit couldn't go to work. Did she tell him the truth? And did that mean that he knew? I couldn't imagine telling Moshon. I'd die of embarrassment. I'd rather shovel donkey shit all my life than tell him why I couldn't go to work.

When Dotan asked why Dorit did not have to go to work, Carmela said that she needed someone to help her in the children's house. Iris looked at me and rolled her eyes up like her mother, and Dotan, who did not notice it, asked if he could stay and help, too. Carmela said that there was not enough work for two. All the girls knew that she was lying, but of course we did not say anything. She had to lie. If she'd said anything, the boys would have started giggling and pointing fingers and behaving like babies. They were too immature to understand these things.

Then Daphna was excused from P.E. class. This time none of the boys asked why she stayed in the children's house. Dotan whispered something in Tomer's ear and they both started laughing. They have found out, I guessed. Someone had told them. I wondered who it was. Daphna didn't look like she cared that the boys had found out. I think she wanted them to find out. She wanted them to think that she was a mature girl. I went to P.E. class feeling like a total idiot. I was as grown up as Daphna and Dorit, yet no one knew. Even my mother didn't know. How long was I going to keep a stupid secret that no one cared to keep anyway?

The second time Dorit was excused from working in the children's farm I went to work full of resentment. Why did I have to work in the children's farm, anyway? We did not even enjoy the fruit of our work. No one I knew ate the vegetables the garden had produced or the eggs the chickens had lain. Whoever sheared the wool from our sheep was also a mystery. And whatever happened to all the goats' milk we sent to the communal kitchen every day in a tall aluminum jar? I had no idea.

Now we had to clear a square plot of land, build a fence, and get ready to receive a shipment of cute little ducklings, because Moshon decided that we should raise ducks and sell them to factories that made pate' from their liver. With the money we'd make from the ducks he planned to buy a horse.

I was glad that we were going to get a horse. It would be so much nicer to ride a horse to the alfalfa field than an old donkey. But make pate' out of the ducklings? That was disgusting. Only millionaires ate pate'. No one I knew ate that stuff. On the kibbutz people didn't even know what pate' looked like. I couldn't understand Moshon. He always had such weird ideas. Like when Tikva came to work in the children's farm for the first time Moshon gave her a toothbrush and told her to brush the teeth of all the goats. Tikva, who lived all her life in the city and knew nothing about taking care of animals, thought he was serious. She chased the goats and tried to shove the toothbrush into their mouths while the boys hid behind the chicken coop and almost died laughing.

Moshon told us to grab hoes and finish clearing up the area behind the stable from weeds and rocks. We still had a lot of work to do, he said, and we should stop wasting time standing around and doing nothing. Digging those stubborn weeds was hard work. The hoe I was using to dig out the weeds chafed the palm of my hand and small blisters appeared at the base of my fingers. I tried to pop them with my teeth. One of the blisters broke and salty liquid oozed out. I licked it.

"I have to go wash my hand," I told Moshon, who was loading a wheelbarrow with rocks.

"Don't forget to come back," he said. He always thought we were looking for excuses to get away from work. Which was true many times. Feeding the animals and watching the sheep graze in the alfalfa field were the only fun jobs in the children's farm. The rest was hard, thankless work.

I went to wash my hand at the tool shed and covered the blisters with a Band-Aid. It was so nice to take a little break from work. But I couldn't stay there for too long. It would raise Moshon's suspicion and he'd come looking for me. I returned to work. I was fighting a stubborn bush with my hoe when I saw a fat brown earthworm crawling out from under a little rock.

An earthworm. We called it *shilshul* - the same word for diarrhea. A deserving name. I'd rather startle a family of black scorpions than look at a disgusting earthworm. Scorpions were exciting. Earthworms were yucky.

Moshon shook his head in bemused disapproval when he saw me flinch in disgust. "Don't you know that earthworms are the farmer's best friends?"

"I do, but I don't like the way they look."

"Why not?" he asked. "Look how cute they are." He plucked the long earthworm from the moist ground and put the slimy thing on his palm.

I jumped backwards and covered my eyes. I couldn't stand looking at it writhing all over his hand.

"Give me your hand," he said.

I put my hand in my pocket. I knew what he was planning to do. Behind me the boys leaned on their hoes and watched us, giggling.

"It's about time you get used to these harmless creatures," Moshon decided. "You can't work in the children's farm if you're scared of earthworms."

"Then maybe I shouldn't work here," I said.

"Come on, give me your hand."

I gave him the hand with the Band-Aid.

"Not this hand. The other one," Moshon kept pressing.

I extended my hand and closed my eyes. He put the squishy, wet earthworm on my open palm. The boys were laughing in the background.

"See? You're still alive," Moshon patted my shoulder after a few seconds that felt like an eternity. He took the worm from my hand and threw it on the ground. "They don't bite even pretty girls like you."

I have never felt more humiliated. I was mocked in front of a laughing crowd. I decided to boycott the children's farm for good without asking anyone for a favor, special days or not.

The next day when we were on our way to work in the children's farm I dragged behind the group as slowly as I could. The boys were talking, as usual, about their favorite soccer teams, the girls were quiet. No one noticed when I stepped behind a carob tree and waited until everyone disappeared behind a bend in the road. I waited for a few minutes and went in the opposite direction. I decided to avoid the children's farm and find a nice spot to spend the next few hours. I wasn't worried about what the kids were going to think about my disappearance. They would understand why I didn't go to work.

I was still within a hearing distance from the children's farm when I looked down a limestone cliff and saw a small patch of green grass where the rock met the ground. Thorny bushes covered with tiny yellow flowers and tall dried oats surrounded the grass. The winding footpath that cut through the children's farm and led to the beach passed only a few meters away from the grass, but I could tell it was completely undiscovered. I made my way down the cliff, one step at a time, careful to avoid loose rocks and sharp corners and landed on a dusty footpath. No one but me was around. I parted the bushes growing by the side of the trail and slowly made my way back toward the cliff.

The grass was gorgeous. It was soft and silky and so inviting. I didn't even know that such beautiful grass could thrive without irrigation and the constant warnings from a zealous gardener. I took off my shoes and dropped on the grass, burying my fingers in it. My feet could easily touch the bushes surrounding the grass patch when I stretched my legs, but I didn't mind. That pristine patch of grass was my special secret hideout. I could hide there for as long as I wanted and never go back to the children's farm.

My plot to avoid the children's farm forever was torpedoed as soon as the children returned to the children's house and reported to Carmela that I didn't show up for work. Less than an hour later Moshon came to the children's house demanding a disciplinary inquiry. When I finally arrived, totally relaxed and unsuspecting, Carmela informed me that we were going to have a meeting with Moshon and find out what had happened.

We met in the classroom. Carmela acted as a mediator and a buffer between the scandalized Moshon and my new rebellious self. "Why didn't you go to work?" She opened.

I looked at her without saying anything.

"You know you have to go to work like everyone else," she said.

I looked at her, silent.

"Working in the children's farm is as important as any other activity," she explained. "You can be punished for missing work."

"Punish me, I don't care."

"What happened? Why don't you want to go to work?" she implored.

"Ask him," I shrugged without looking at Moshon.

She turned to him.

"I only tried to teach her about earthworms," Moshon said.

"He made fun of me in front of everyone," I accused him.

"I only tried to teach her about earthworms," he repeated.

"What can we do to make you go back to work?" Carmela asked me, practical as always.

I was too surprised to say anything. And flattered. No one had ever cared about what I thought. I was more used to being called a nuisance and a troublemaker. Suddenly someone wanted to hear about my grievances. I had to think about what I wanted, weigh all my options, consider all the pros and cons, make a rational decision and present my demands like a grown-up. Clear, assertive, and articulate. After all, I already was a woman.

"I want him to apologize," my mouth blurted out.

"And then you'd go back to work?" Carmela asked.

I nodded. I didn't know why I had said it. I have never thought about asking for an apology from a grown-up. Not when my kindergarten *metapelet* forced me to eat tomatoes until I threw up, not when old, mean Zehava insisted that I take showers with the boys, not even when my teacher crumpled up my beautiful painting because I took too long to finish it.

Moshon looked at Carmela. There was uncomfortable silence in the classroom. Carmela looked at him, squeezed her forehead upward until four tiny parallel lines formed on it, then she gave him a small nod. Moshon's eyes slowly moved and rested on me. I looked at my knees. Suddenly he was seized by an urge to scratch inside his ear. He stuck his little finger into his ear and shook it up and down so fast, it made me think of a hummingbird's wings. Finally he took the finger out of his ear and wiped it on his blue work shirt. I could see him do that even though my eyes were fixed on my knee. I hoped Carmela would give him another look. Moshon sighed and said he didn't mean to hurt my feelings, only to teach me that earthworms were friendly creatures. He said he was "Very sorry," and promised that it would never happen again.

No one had ever said, "I'm sorry" to me. I didn't know where to look. Suddenly my anger and resentment dissolved into embarrassment. I wanted to tell Moshon that I didn't mean what I had said, that I didn't really want him to apologize.

"Maya, did you hear? Moshon said he was sorry," I heard Carmela's voice. Soft and encouraging. Her voice made me feel like crying. I didn't want to cry in front of him. I nodded and still not looking at him agreed to return to work. But I had two conditions: no donkey rides to the alfalfa field and no shoveling shit into heavy wheelbarrows.

"Don't worry about Aphrodite, her days are numbered, Maya'le," Moshon said, not embarrassed at all. He extended a hand crisscrossed with dirt-filled crevices and old scars, took my hand, and squeezed it. His hand felt dry and rough like sandpaper. "Friends?" he asked, holding on to my hand. There was a little smile in his eyes, a begging smile.

"Okay," I said, not knowing what else to say.

After he left the classroom Carmela looked at me and smiled.

"Well done, Maya. You behaved like a real grown-up."

A grown-up, she said. A real grown-up.

Chapter Seven

I was balancing myself on top of a tall ladder picking olives. Summer was officially over but the air was still suffocating hot and humid. The sun was pounding on the olive grove, painting the sky in hazy white all the way to the mountains in the horizon. On my neck hung a big canvas sack almost full of olives, dangerously pulling me to the ground. Insects buzzed around my face threatening to bite and dust coated my hair, my clothes, even my tongue. The minutes dragged slowly, burning like hot wax. I had to find a way to make this work less torturous. Maybe invent an olive-picking machine for the next generation of young hard-working kibbutzniks. I wanted the week to be over. And the week after that as well. Why couldn't I be picking apples in the green valleys of Switzerland? Fresh, sweet, crunchy apples that cooled the hands that touched them and delighted the eyes that looked at them? Let me sink my teeth in apples instead of plucking hard, bitter olives. Let me feel raindrops on my forehead instead of sticky perspiration. I could not bear the oppressive heat of the Jordan Valley. I wanted to put down the heavy canvas sack and rest in the shade.

Most of the kids in the group, which had now grown from twelve to twenty five, had thought it was a great idea to spend three weeks at kibbutz Neveh Midbar. These kids came from different cities to live on the kibbutz with us because they either did very poorly at their schools or had too many problems at home. Some came from poor neighborhoods and large families who couldn't make ends meet, others who came from well-off families just wanted to live away from their parents. No one came because of a strong belief in our socialist ideals of equality and communal ownership. They knew little about kibbutz life, especially about our work ethics and discipline, but they still preferred going to work in the Jordan valley over spending time in the classroom, laboring over Hamlet and his family disputes or analyzing the causes of the French revolution. For me, the "work camp" in Neveh Midbar was another arduous assignment designed to turn me into a better kibbutznik. All that organized group activity got on my nerves. What I really wanted to do was to sit in a quiet, air-conditioned library, and write a letter to my boyfriend, Yonnie.

"One more hour to go," Doobie's voice traveled between the branches. Doobie was one of the pioneers who founded kibbutz Neveh Midbar after the war of sixty-seven. Every day he woke up before the birds, shaved his neck, put on his faded blue work clothes, and prepared bitter Turkish coffee in a large beat up aluminum pot before going to wake us up for work.

"Only one more hour guys," Gideon, the youth leader, repeated with his contrived camaraderie. All day he monitored our pace, sweating more than everyone, making sure we showed Doobie that we were diligent workers. After he emptied his canvas sack in the wooden crate, he took a walk around the grove, trying to energize us with lame jokes no one cared to hear. He was a bigger pain in the neck than my heavy canvas sack. We were all too hot and tired of listening to his annoying voice and participate in his stupid game of "let's show Doobie how excited we are to help your struggling young kibbutz."

The announcements that we had only one more hour to work didn't change our pace. Even the birds were too exhausted to twit a warning to their sisters waiting for us to leave. I looked at my watch in spite of my firm decision to ignore it and heard the radio blast the familiar signal of the eleven o'clock news. A dramatic voice began delivering the daily news: Two soldiers were killed last night during a chase after terrorists who had crossed the Syrian border. A pregnant mother and her four-year-old boy were killed in a car crash near Dimonah. The Prime Minister was trying to get more loans from the American government. The nurses promised to end their strike tomorrow. The weather was going to stay the same, unusually hot and humid. In short, everything was going to stay the same.

At five past twelve I climbed down the ladder and emptied my canvas sack for the last time. With the rest of the group, I lay on the ground under an olive tree and waited for Doobie to finish counting the full crates and drive us back to kibbutz Neveh Midbar. When Doobie finally arrived with the tractor, I took a seat on the hard bench and found myself almost enjoying the bone-rattling, five-kilometer ride. The boys tried to guess what the members of Neveh Midbar ate for lunch on Thursdays.

"Steak and chips," Erez said.

"Don't forget the ketchup," Dorit snorted, and everybody laughed.

My mind drifted away from the lame conversation. I had something more important to think about. I might get a letter from Yonnie. Even though it had been only three weeks since his last visit to the kibbutz, I felt as if I hadn't seen him in years. I had written to him almost every day long, detailed letters full of stories about my stay at kibbutz Neveh Midbar and about how much I had missed him.

At the entrance to the dining hall I heard that there was a letter for me in the pile. When Gideon handed it to me my heart almost burst out with happiness. I squeezed the wrinkled envelope to my dirty shirt, wishing that the letter would last on many, many pages, and contain wonderful confessions of love for me. I decided to skip lunch - meatballs in tomato sauce and greasy noodles - and hurried to the room I shared with Iris, Tikva, and Annette, one of the latest additions to our group. I wanted to be by myself when I was in the presence of my boyfriend's words; to savor every word without having to worry that someone may come in and bother me. I had been waiting for too long to let anyone spoil my pleasure.

I opened the envelope carefully and read the precious words. And yes. There was one person in this world who missed me as much as I missed him. And he was awarded with a twenty-four hours leave. Could you come to the kibbutz this weekend? his funny handwriting asked.

Of course, I could come, I wanted to shout. I would go to the end of the world if I had to. Even if all we had were a few precious hours. I'd do anything to be with you, Yonnie.

I folded the letter and put it in my backpack with all his other letters. The moment I finished zipping my backpack, Iris walked in and announced that her boyfriend wrote that he was coming to the kibbutz for the weekend, and that she was planning to go see him. I told her that Yonnie was coming, too and she said, "Let's go together, then."

I was glad Iris wanted to go. With her long silky brown hair, pretty face, and perfect figure we would have no problem catching a ride with one of the bored drivers who passed through this suffocating, miserable valley. We decided to tell Gideon that we wanted to go away for the weekend.

"Why should I allow you two to leave while all the others have to stay? Just because you two have boyfriends in the army you think you're more privileged?" Gideon asked with his typical condescending raise of the eyebrow.

"Everyone doesn't seem to want to go away for the weekend," I said.

"But what if they did? Would I have to let everyone go?"

"Why do we have to worry about it if it didn't happen?" I said, already feeling the familiar frustration rise inside my body.

"It's a matter of principle," he began to recite his slogans. "Since everyone else is staying here during the weekend, you two have to do the same. No exceptions. You are not better than anyone here and I don't see why you think you deserve any special privileges just because you have a boyfriend. I refuse to create a precedent and generate a mass emigration. We came here as a group, we stay here as a group and we leave as a group."

"But I want to see my boyfriend," Iris whined.

"You can see him next time he comes to the kibbutz. I don't know anyone who died of waiting to see her boyfriend," he smirked. "I am sure you can wait a few more weeks. You too, Maya."

"But I don't want to wait," Iris argued.

I could never express my feelings as openly as Iris, especially to Gideon of all people. But I agreed with her. I didn't want to wait three more weeks. And I refused to stay in Neveh Midbar and participate in the pretentious group dynamic Gideon was planning to moderate on Friday night. He thought that his psychological experiments would create some solidarity between us kibbutz born kids and the urbanites who did not respect or understood our values and traditions. I did not want to stay and watch him intimidate those kids again with his poisonous remarks. I just wanted to spend the weekend with my boyfriend.

"There are a lot of things I don't want to do and I still do them," he sneered at Iris, who looked more angry than usual.

I had to force myself not to ask him to be more specific. What exactly is it that you don't like to do? Where else would you get a chance to intimidate so many people? Listening to his stale arguments built up an uncontrollable rage inside me, but I had to be careful and not let the situation escalate. I had to conduct myself in a way that would help me win. I had to consider all the options I hadn't explored yet. Think. Conspire. Be original. Try to talk to Jeff.

Jeff was from Chicago. He wore John Lennon eyeglasses and spoke Hebrew with a heavy accent that made him sound refreshingly disarming. His problem was that he was still nurturing strong Socialist tendencies and exhibiting his Zionist vigor with an innocence that belonged only to young Americans. He was studying psychology at the Hebrew University in Jerusalem. Sadly though, he was learning how to work with kibbutz youth groups by following our vicious dictator, Gideon. We didn't know for sure if he was going to be our next youth leader, but for the time being he was Gideon's assistant. In spite of all that disadvantage, he could understand youthful rebellion and was much closer to our age than Gideon.

Gideon. My enemy. I sighed and shook my head.

"Don't pretend that you don't care, Maya," Iris said and nudged her elbow into my waist. "I know you want to go too, so tell him."

"It seems like we're wasting our time," I shrugged, crossing my arms over my chest. I was determined to solve this problem later with less strife. "Can't you see he's not going to change his mind?" I asked and walked away.

Iris shrugged her famous shrug and followed me to our room.

"What's the matter with you?" she pouted. "Why didn't you say anything to him? I know you want to go tomorrow. Why did you pretend you didn't care?"

"Because I'm going to talk to Jeff," I said, dropping on one of the beds. A cloud of dust rose from the gray army blanket covering it. "I am not going to spend my life arguing with that maniac. I refuse to keep feeding his ego," I declared, feeling articulate and mature.

"Then why didn't you tell me?" she complained.

"In front of him?"

At last, I saw some comprehension spread on her pretty face. She understood. Now all I had to do was execute my plan and collect the prize. After dinner I stalked Jeff from the dry bushes. When he came out of the room he shared with Gideon I pretended that I had just walked by, and smiling cheerfully I asked him about his girlfriend, Judy.

"She's fine, thank you," he said.

"Good." I tried to sound friendly, but not too friendly. I didn't want to raise any suspicion. I wanted to bring up my request as casually as possible. Jeff asked how I felt in Neveh Midbar, I lied that I really enjoyed working in the olive grove and that the swimming pool was out of the world.

"Feel like going for a swim?" he asked in simulated excitement. I said yes.

After we raced in the pool, we lay on the wet steamy concrete floor surrounding the pool and watched Shlomi trying to drown Nir in the deep end. These guys were so childish, I thought. Ever since our days in the children's house they've been playing the same lame games, trying to kill one another, push one another or hurt one another for no apparent reason.

"How's Yonnie doing? Did you hear from him?" Jeff asked, turning lazily on his back. "Did he finish officers' training already?"

I couldn't believe my luck. I started to believe that God loved me, and asked him to make sure no one would get out of the pool and interrupt our conversation.

"Not yet. But I got a letter from him today. He wrote that he had passed another important test," I said off-handedly.

"That's great," Jeff said in English. My favorite language.

I loved it when he spoke English. It made me feel so worldly, like one of them. I understood English quite well because I spent a lot of time with the American and the Australian volunteers who worked in our kibbutz. English was the language of the friendliest people in the world. People who spoke English traveled all over the world. Had been to rock concerts of famous bands. They knew the lyrics of the songs we heard on the radio. On the walls of their rooms they hung posters of Bob Dylan, Women's Lib, and Woodstock. They lit candles instead of lightbulbs at night. They played Frisbee and swam naked in the irrigation pool. They had more fun than we did. They were not as boring as the members of the kibbutz who could only talk about how many tons of bananas were picked last season and worry about the news they heard on the radio every hour.

"Right," I replied in Hebrew. When he nodded, I quickly added, "He's got a pass for twenty four hours and he's going to the kibbutz for the weekend."

There. I said it.

"So you want to go to the kibbutz for the weekend?" he asked.

I knew that he could understand me only because he was an American. They were more easy-going about big principles, morals, rules, and stuff like that.

Jeff looked at me and waited. I had to think about an answer. It was my big chance and I had to take it. I knew it was a risk to lie, but what did I have to lose?

"Sure, I want to go to the kibbutz," I said, with all the nonchalance I could mobilize into my voice. "But I need to get permission to leave," I added, watching the boys push and curse one another in the pool.

"What did Gideon say?"

Gideon? The man who thinks organized group activities were more constructive to the soul than pure adolescent love? The man who thinks the smell of perspiration mixed with dust was more pleasant than perfume? The man that every cell in my body resented with mountains of passion? I felt Jeff's eyes rest on me, innocent and trusting. "He said it was up to you to decide whether I could go or not."

I couldn't believe I did it so smoothly. I didn't even blink. I sounded completely convincing. I was a filthy, rotten, immoral person, and a wonderful, gifted, brilliant liar.

"Does anyone else want to go to the kibbutz for the weekend?" Jeff asked.

I simply couldn't believe my ears. These Americans were amazing. I had to hold myself back before I lost control and started kissing him. "I think Iris does," I said, and put my hand in the pool. I needed to keep myself a little cool.

"Well, as long as you guys make it back for work Sunday morning, I don't see any reason why you shouldn't go," he said, rolled into the water and disappeared in a whirlpool.

Right on, Jeff. Neither do I.

The last bus to the kibbutz had already left the station when Iris and I got off the truck in front of the old soccer stadium. But we were not concerned about it. We thanked the truck driver and headed to the main intersection, congratulating ourselves, feeling excited at the prospect that soon the tiresome journey would be over. However, our good mood, as well as our plan to catch a more comfortable ride up to the kibbutz, evaporated quickly when we saw how many soldiers were already competing for a ride at the same spot. It was obvious that even Iris's pretty eyes could not help us.

We decided to walk to a smaller intersection and try our luck there. It was the best way to catch a ride with the sneaky drivers who pretended they didn't see the tired soldiers and preferred to pick up pretty girls like us.

I volunteered to take the first shift. Many cars stopped at the busy intersection we left behind us, but the line of soldiers did not get any shorter. Other soldiers kept coming from nowhere, guns and backpacks slung over their shoulders. The sun began to descend behind the rooftops, and the leaves of the dusty eucalyptuses along the asphalt road rustled in the evening breeze. None of it made any effect on the temperature. The air was still hot and stuffy.

An old horse pulling a wooden wagon full of watermelons stopped on the other side of the road. A young boy dressed in rags jumped from the wagon. "Watermelon, red, sweet," he announced in a singsong voice every few minutes. The minutes between his announcements dragged on endlessly.

Finally it was time to change shifts.

Before Iris extended her hand, a brown Ford stopped. She looked at me questioningly. Shall I approach this car, her eyes asked. I shrugged, unsure of what to say. I wanted to get in the car, but at the same time we both knew that most drivers who rushed to pull over were too sleazy. We tried to avoid them as much as possible, unless we were totally desperate. Iris decided not to approach the car.

Two army reservists got out and thanked the driver with a casual salute. They hung their guns and backpacks on their shoulders, checked out Iris from behind their Ray Ban sunglasses, and walked away. Iris curled one side of her mouth in a contemptuous smile. Apparently the driver did not stop for us. Damn.

"Iris, Maya, come on in," someone inside the car called.

We looked at each other in relief. No horny drivers this time. It was Lazer Kowalski, who worked in Tel Aviv for the kibbutz movement or the Jewish Agency or something similar. He drove a pretty nice vehicle because of his important job in the city. It even had air conditioning. Iris climbed over the passenger seat to the back, and sat next to a silhouette of a soldier sleeping under a large backpack. I sat next to Lazer.

"Have you been waiting for a ride for a long time?" he asked.

"About half a century," I said, exaggerating as usual as I leaned back and sighed.

A hand touched my shoulder. I turned to see what Iris wanted and saw Yonnie, my beloved sleepy soldier, smiling in my face. I wanted to jump to the back seat, hug him, ask him a million questions, tell him how I bluffed Jeff and Gideon, and kiss him, but I couldn't move underneath my backpack.

"Do you guys want me to pull over so you could switch places?" Lazer asked.

Before Yonnie had a chance to say yes, I said no. I could wait ten more minutes. I didn't want Iris to be stuck with Lazer in the front seat without anything to talk about, while I had all the fun with Yonnie in the back. Besides, I didn't want to give Lazer any reason to gossip about me later. I could already hear him tell his wife how he gave us a ride and how I jumped all over my boyfriend and then say, "Where did she learn to behave like that in public? This girl has no manners at all, she forgot she is only sixteen, and she almost destroyed the back seat, and blah, blah, blah, blah, blah."

I could wait a few minutes. I already knew how to endure anticipation. I had years of experience.

When we stopped at the parking lot and got out of the car, I fell into Yonnie's arms, forgetting Lazer and his wife. I could hardly believe I was in Yonnie's arms at last. I wanted to spend every minute we had in his arms. But, once again, I had to wait. I had to visit my parents and go through the Friday night aggravation ritual.

When I entered my parents' room, my mother was just coming out of the shower with one towel wrapped around her body and another around her head like a turban. My father was sitting on the couch in the living room, reading a newspaper and listening to a symphony that was playing loudly on the classical radio station. I closed the front door and looked at him to assess the situation. Ever since my bat mitzvah I couldn't stand dinner with my parents on Friday night. My mother always became frantic about what she was going to wear, and insisted that I get dressed up for the occasion. "At least put your shoes on," she would whine, standing in front of the bedroom closet crowded with dresses that she never wore and complaining that she had nothing to wear.

My father, who heard me close the door, jumped from the couch, an expression of utter stupefaction on his face, and spread his arms. "I thought you were supposed to be in kibbutz Neveh Midbar until the end of next week," he exclaimed excitedly, giving me a hug and a wet kiss on the cheek.

"I came to see Yonnie."

"Did you ask for permission?" My mother's voice came from the bedroom.

"No. I sneaked through the metal bars, broke the locks on the gate, and killed the guards," I answered.

"You're such a smart girl," she said.

"Maya, don't start now," my father begged.

"It's not her business if I asked for permission or not," I answered, already in my fighting mode.

"She only wants to make sure you don't get yourself in trouble," my father said, hiding behind his newspaper.

"How do I look?" she asked, stepping out of the bedroom.

I couldn't see any difference between that dress and any other dress she had ever worn, so I didn't say anything. My father, though, fulfilled his obligation and said, "Prettier than Miss Israel herself."

I wanted to strangle him and his stupid jokes. Now she was going to believe him and stroll around the dining hall like a peacock in the zoo.

"Are we ready to go?" he asked, putting down his newspaper and looking at me with his hopelessly optimistic, peace loving grin. My God, this man is so oblivious, I thought. I couldn't believe that after all these years he still didn't remember that she had to put on her makeup.

"I'll meet you in the dining hall," I mumbled under my breath, rushing to the door, hoping to escape the final aggravation on the weekly menu.

"You're not going anywhere," I heard her voice, now coming from the bathroom. "Yonnie will not disappear if you don't see him during dinner."

Now I wanted to strangle her, too, but my father winked in a desperate attempt to keep me from blowing up. He already knew who he was dealing with. This verbal exchange was not new to any of us.

"I promised to meet him there, and I am not going to spend my entire life waiting for you to get ready," I persisted, ignoring my father's silent plea.

"She'll be ready in two minutes, Maya," my father said quietly. His good mood seemed to vanish.

I fell on the couch and sulked. I agreed to wait for my father's sake. That was the reason I did not take off right that minute. She only wanted me around to show off her family, to pretend that we were a normal family. Of course if she really cared about me it would have been different. But she didn't. She never did. I knew that. She only cared about herself and the kibbutz. Permission. That's what she was worried about. That I behaved myself. What for? So Gideon would tell everyone that her daughter was a responsible girl? Why would I want to be responsible? To make her look good? Or proud of me? What do I need her pride for?

"Where's Avner?" I asked my father, just to appease him. I knew very well where Avner was. With his girlfriend, Shula, in Jerusalem. They served on the same base and Avner spent most of his free weekends in her parents' place. Too bad Yonnie's parents decided to move to the kibbutz when he was in high school. Otherwise I would have had the best excuse not to show up at my parents' room at all.

"In Jerusalem, with Shula," my mother answered.

"I didn't ask you," I mumbled to myself.

"I'm ready," she announced, stepping out of the bathroom made-up and looking like a clown. I didn't like all that makeup she put on her face. Why was she trying to look so good anyway? It was always the same people. And what would she say if I used makeup? Gideon already gave us a long lecture that we were too young for it, that it made us look like sluts, that people who lived on the kibbutz didn't use nonsense like makeup and fancy clothes. Maybe I should have told her that she was a bad influence on my pure soul. Then I would have a good excuse to ignore her when she criticized my behavior or when she tried to tell me what to do.

"You look wonderful," my father said. Folding his newspaper, he rose from the couch with renewed hope.

"Do you really mean it?" she asked on their way out, using her coquettish voice to force another compliment out of him.

No, I thought as I followed them on the concrete pavement on the way to the Friday night parade in the dining hall. He didn't mean it. He only said it to make you feel good. Don't you know that women your age don't look good anymore? They don't need to look good. They have husbands, children, and varicose veins. Besides, how can they look good after working in the dining hall all their life? Or after getting up so early in the morning to work with children that they can't stand, or cook for people who never seem to like the food. And who was going to care that you looked so good anyway? Avri, who worked in the cow shed all his life and looked like a cow himself in spite of the low-fat, low-salt diet he was on? Or Yakov, who could only nag about the brave old days and vote against you in the general assembly? Or Tzvika, who always limped behind his wife like a puppy, carrying her eggs and flour so she could keep baking more apple strudels and gossip about everyone in their room? Or Natan, who cheated on his wife with Naomi until her husband caught them doing it in the bomb shelter? Pretend, pretend, pretend that everything was wonderful, that we like one another, and then stab one another in the back.

"Shabbat Shalom" my mother said to a woman's silhouette near the cactus triangle.

I tried to stay out of sight. I didn't feel like pretending that I was pleased to see that woman or her husband. I always tried to avoid her. But it was not that easy. Sometimes I had to pretend that I didn't see her until she greeted me. Then I felt really stupid. I knew that she knew that I only pretended not to see her. A lot of people on the kibbutz did the same to me. They walked by as if I were transparent, as if they didn't see me. But I didn't really mind. I preferred it that way. The problem was that some people were really fanatic about greeting one another, and criticized the young generation for our bad manners when we ignored them. I thought it felt awkward to run into people that you knew all the time and greet them every five minutes.

"Shalom, Maya," my notorious grammar school teacher said. I could guess the lecture she would have loved to have given me if I had been just a little younger.

I mumbled a quick "shalom" without glancing at her and kept walking before she had a chance to ask anything. I couldn't stand the hypocrisy. If my parents were not around I would have ignored her.

"Why do you always have to be so rude?" my mother complained, after the teacher and her husband were out of hearing range.

Because I hate this woman for what she did to us when we were under her control, and you should know it, I wanted to tell her. But as usual I didn't. Instead I said, "Because I like to be rude."

"I don't understand this girl," my mother complained to my father. "I never taught her to behave like that. Why is she so angry all the time? What did I do to her?"

I decided to ignore her. Pretend that I didn't hear anything because of the noise in the dining hall. It was just not worth it. Arguing with her was a total waste of time. She refused to understand the way I felt about that teacher.

"I'm going to look for Yonnie," I told my parents, who had stopped at the message board to read the latest announcements. A hand-written reminder from the librarian to return books overdue, a note from Tzippi, who lost an earring near the basketball court, an announcement about dogs' vaccinations on Monday, personal phone messages, a list of names under the headline Orthodontist, a final reminder to the soldiers that the laundry room would be locked at nine thirty, a flyer about the lecture on Kenya. Boring. I left my parents by the large corkboard and walked through the glass doors into the dining hall.

Yonnie was sitting with a bunch of other soldiers and their girlfriends by the wall near the window. Thick cigarette smoke hovered above their heads. Eran and Yalik burst out in loud laughter. Sasha, who we called "the prophet of wrath," got up from his table, and by the look on his face I knew he was going to tell them to shut up. None of us liked him. He behaved as if he were the kibbutz policeman, as if he owned the place. He got a kick out of walking around telling everyone how to behave. Whenever he saw us put our legs on a chair, or wipe the table with paper napkins he scorned us with biblical vehemence, "Do you also do this in your own home?" as if the dining hall was not a part of our home.

"Guys, really, why do you always have to make so much noise? Can't you see people are still eating here? Go to your rooms and make as much noise as you want and let me eat quietly here with my wife."

Rafi, Iris' boyfriend, snapped, "Okay, okay," with a motion of the head that meant, "We heard you, now get lost." Iris stared at Sasha with undiluted hate.

Everyone around the table knew about the historical animosity between Sasha and Rafi. It started before Rafi joined the army, when he was still an "outside boy" from a good family in eleventh grade. One night, Sasha caught him driving a tractor back from the beach and rushed to tell the kibbutz secretary. The members' committee almost kicked Rafi out of the kibbutz for stealing a tractor. Rafi could not forgive Sasha for snitching on him. Everyone "borrowed" tractors without permission once in a while to go to the beach at night with their girlfriends. It was not such a big deal. Even Yonnie and I did it a few times. But no one else was ever put on the spot like Rafi.

"Fucking shmuck," Rafi seethed under his new
"Stinking son of a cockroach," Eran added. Yalik kicke
chair. It dropped loudly on the floor. All the guys arouṇu
laughed loudly.

"Hooligans," Sasha murmured, shaking his head.

"Aren't you going to sit with us?" My mother reminded me of her existence when I headed towards Yonnie's table.

"No," I said without turning around. I was not going to waste one more minute with that mother. I had already paid my dues to her.

"What about dinner?" she insisted.

"I'm not hungry," I retorted. I had already checked the food on the counter: greasy potatoes and sliced beef with disgusting fat streaks. Yuk. It made me lose my appetite. Maybe later I'd go to Yonnie's parents' room and see if his mother had anything interesting in the refrigerator.

When I got to Yonnie's table he hugged me and kissed me right on the lips in front of everyone. I kept my eyes open. He scooted over and I sat next to him. Eran, who was leaning on his girlfriend, Efrat, took a long puff from his cigarette and buried it in a mound of yellow rice that was left on his plate. Disgusting. I wanted to kick him but I decided to keep my leg near Yonnie. Let Efrat teach him manners.

"Everyone is going to the dance in the bomb shelter later. Want to go, too?" Yonnie whispered in my ear. Each hair on the back of my neck stood on end.

"Only if you want to," I whispered, and he tickled my knee. He knew I would do anything he wanted as long as we could be together.

"First I've got to take my stuff to the laundry room," he said.

Missy, a volunteer from Australia, walked by our table and stopped when she saw me. She looked like she had just come out of the shower. Her blond hair was still wet, sticking to her back, wetting the pink tank top she was wearing. It clung to her tan back and everyone could see she wasn't wearing a bra. Yalik, who didn't have a girlfriend, gaped at her as if he had never seen a woman before. Luckily, he didn't drool. I wondered if I should tell him that she had a boyfriend in Sydney.

"Hi, Maya," Missy said, ignoring the devouring eyes. She was used to seeing men fall all over her. "Aren't you supposed to be somewhere picking oranges?" she asked in English. I knew Yalik would have killed to have her talk to him.

"I just came for the weekend to see Yonnie," I answered, also in English.

"Hi, Yonnie." She smiled her perfect Australian smile and asked, "How's everything in the army?"

Yonnie took her hand and kissed it like a true knight. "Could have been much better if you were there with me," he said in Hebrew, which I translated for her.

She pulled her hand back and laughed. Yalik's face turned green with envy. Not only did she talk to Yonnie, she also let him kiss her hand. Yonnie was such a heartthrob. His mischievous brown eyes made him irresistible. When she left, I kicked his leg and he groaned.

"Let's go," he finally said. I jumped from the chair. Now we could get away from everyone and start doing something by ourselves.

On the way to the laundry house Yonnie asked which room I wanted to spend the night in and I realized that he had forgotten that my two roommates were in Neveh Midbar. I was now living in one of the old long houses which used to house the founding members in the early days of the kibbutz. We had a lot more privacy there but still, we were not used to having a room to ourselves for an entire night. Usually we squeezed in my single bed and waited until my two roommates fell asleep before we dared to do anything. And even then, we couldn't do much because we were afraid they'd wake up and catch us in the middle of whatever we were doing. So we lay in bed, touched each other everywhere over our clothes, perspired profusely until Yonnie couldn't take it anymore and went outside to smoke a cigarette.

Sometimes I felt sorry for him. I knew that he had already done a lot more with his previous girlfriends than he had with me. But it was not completely my fault. Because our roommates were around us all the time we couldn't do much. We could not even take our clothes off.

When I told Yonnie that we could stay in my room without having to deal with roommates, his eyes lit up. He threw the bundle of dirty uniforms into the laundry cart and approached me with his daredevil grin. "Let's forget about the bomb shelter and go to your room now," he whispered, squeezing me to his body.

Maybe tonight was going to be our big night, a small thought occurred to me, tingling my skin from the top of my head down to my thighs. I tried to ignore it. It was still too scary for me. A gust of hot wind from inside the laundry burned my face. I almost choked. My heart fluttered. I wanted to fly to my room, drop on my bed, and let Yonnie take my clothes off. I shivered, but not from the sudden breeze. I wanted him to kiss me all over, and squeeze me with his weight until it hurt. I wanted to touch all the places that I never dared to touch before. I wanted to feel his hands everywhere. All night long. I wanted to roll in my bed with him, completely naked, until... until... I didn't know what to expect.

"Are you sure?" I squeaked.

"We can go down to the bomb shelter and check it out first if you want to," he said, pulling army issued towels from his bag.

I was glad he couldn't see my disappointment in the dark. I was hoping that he would insist on going to my room, but he didn't. Maybe he felt there was no need to rush. Now I had to pretend that I wanted to go dancing so he wouldn't think I was a sex-crazed slut.

"It could be fun," I lied.

We went to the bomb shelter. As we began descending the staircase, the shrill echoes of disco music deafened me. Then the smell of perspiration, dust, cigarette smoke, and fresh whitewash choked me. I was tugged by Yonnie, and pushed to the wall by a stream of sweating people, who stamped up the stairs like a bunch of deranged rhinoceroses to get a breath of fresh air. We passed a menacing iron door placed at the bottom of the stairs to block radioactivity from leaking into the main hall, just in case a nuclear bomb dropped on the kibbutz one day. We entered a stuffy room full of naked arms and legs, loose hair, and sweaty faces. The compact space that other people called "the dance floor" was lit by a naked red light bulb that cast monstrous shadows on the walls. The hall was tightly sealed and the thick air pushed into my face. I felt like I stepped into an oven. I looked around to see if there was any place to sit down, and bumped into Ziv, Yonnie's younger brother.

"Hey, Maya, want to dance?" he screamed into my ear.

Before I answered, he grabbed my arm and pulled me into the center of the concrete floor. Everyone was frantically prancing, jumping, twirling, twisting, and yelling jointly what sounded like the lyrics of a Beatles song. A new volunteer from New Zealand danced on my right, moving her lips as if she were singing, but no sound came out of her mouth. I tried to build up some excitement and loosen up. I knew I shouldn't feel so self-conscious, but I just couldn't forget what a terrible dancer I was.

"You don't know how to move," the girls in my group always criticized me. "Try to move your shoulders a bit. And listen to the music."

I had to calculate every step. My stiff shoulders embarrassed me terribly. I tried to ignore the growing self-consciousness that almost paralyzed me, and follow Ziv around the room. Slowly I started to get excited. Just like everyone else. The drums were beating inside my bones, and the music didn't sound so loud anymore. I had almost forgotten Yonnie and the promising night that lay ahead when two invisible hands grabbed my shoulders and turned me around. I looked up and saw Yonnie's devilish smile.

"Want to go out for some air?" he asked breathlessly as he bit my earlobe.

"Now?"

I didn't really want to leave. I was having so much fun jumping, sweating, and screaming "she's got it, ya' baby she's got it," with everyone. But my weekend belonged to Yonnie.

"Let's get out," he said and took hold of my hand. I followed him up the stairs against a stream of people who almost crushed me on their way down. We emerged from the steamy underworld into a cooler world. Yonnie climbed the hill that covered the bomb shelter in his bare feet, unintimidated by sharp objects, thorns, snakes, or the scorpions that may be waiting under the rocks, and looked for a place to sit down. He lighted a cigarette and pointed at an old frazzled armchair someone had dumped among the rosemary bushes.

It was only when we squeezed into the dusty armchair that I realized how exhausted I was. I sat on Yonnie's lap and rested my head on his chest. A mixture of rhythms vibrated the hollow ground below us. Yonnie took long puffs from his cigarette and carved a tiny cross on the filter with his fingernail. A night bird flapped dark wings in the air and landed on one of the pomegranate trees that grew near my room. I tried to kiss Yonnie on his lips but my twisted position allowed me to bend only as far as his forehead. In the distance I could hear the monotonous hum of the navy patrol boat rushing up the coast to Lebanon. Sometimes they were looking for small boats full of terrorists trying to land on the beach and kill civilians who lived near the border. A bright yellow flare descended from the sky and burned out before it reached the water. It left a smoky trail above the dark horizon.

"Do you mind if we go to your room now?" Yonnie asked, burying his cigarette butt under a rock with his big toe.

At last. I'd been waiting for this moment all evening. I tried to get up but my left leg was too heavy and tingly. "My leg fell asleep," I complained, hoping to get his sympathy.

Yonnie picked me up and carried me down the hill. I hung on to his neck with my eyes closed, and ignored the whistles that came from Yalik and Barak, another soldier on vacation, who were standing at the bomb shelter's entrance. They were still engaged in their Friday night recreation, i. e., trying to seduce the innocent, or not so innocent, female volunteers to spend the night with them. I knew their tactics by now. Missy told me they always said the same thing: either, "Let's go listen to my record collection" or "Come over for coffee." She said that she learned what those invitations meant the hard way. And I believed her.

When we entered my room the stale smell of trapped air hit my nostrils. I rushed to open the windows. The sound of conversations and laughter traveled all the way from the bomb shelter.

"Every time we go away Annette locks the windows as if somebody was going to break in and steal her stuff. She thinks she still lives in the city," I apologized.

Yonnie dropped on my bed.

"Wait, let me make the bed," I asked, and he rolled to the floor.

"I slept only three hours last night. I had to study for a test in meteorology," he mumbled, and I realized that my romantic night might not be what I had expected it to be after all. I looked at him lying on the floor, and decided not to ask him to wash his feet, even though he walked barefoot all over the place.

"I'm going to take a shower," I told him.

Yonnie opened his eyes and pulled me on top of him. "Don't take too long," he whispered and kissed me on my lips.

"I won't," I promised, knowing he would be asleep by the time I came back.

I got out of the shower and checked myself in the mirror. After deciding that a few curves around the hip area was not a curse but a sign of femininity, I put on a t-shirt and underwear and crossed the darkened porch into my room. Yonnie was already asleep, curled up on my bed, a pillow stuffed between his knees, breathing peacefully unperturbed by the light. I already knew that once he got in this position nothing could wake him up. Nothing.

"Are you awake?" I tried my luck after I crawled into bed.

"Mhmm," he murmured and sent his hand under my T-shirt to caress my breast. After a few minutes his hand dropped to my stomach, and slowly slid down below my waist until it found a comfortable spot between us.

I lay awake on my back and listened to Yonnie's quiet breath. I didn't want to wake him up. I just wanted to lie near him and feel his body next to mine. But then the thoughts started to sneak into my head. One by one. The thoughts that come to me in the middle of the night, when everyone around me is asleep. I had a tiny hope that one day I would feel much better about my life. That one day I would be a lot happier. Not so lonely. I was sick of pretending that everything was all right when it wasn't. And I was bored. Except for Yonnie, nothing could make me feel happy inside. And I already knew that Yonnie would not be mine forever because all good things had to come to an end. I already dreaded facing the next day. At two o'clock Yonnie would pack his uniform, walk downhill to catch a ride to his base, and leave. On Sunday morning I would have to return to Neveh Midbar and face Gideon and his principles again.

I woke up scratching an itchy hive on my shoulder. Scratch, scratch, scratch. I was not completely awake, but at least I knew I had escaped the terrorist. Sigh. He was not going to kill me after all. Scratch, scratch. My hand felt another mosquito bite on my knee. And another on my forearm. By the time my hand found another bite on my leg I was completely awake. But I couldn't stop myself. The sour feeling on my skin sucked every ounce of will power I had. Nothing else mattered. A mosquito buzzed above my head. That's it! I couldn't take it any longer. I had to put an end to the cruel attack on my body.

I slapped the wall, thinking that I had spotted a tiny shadow on it. From under the pillow, Yonnie mumbled, "Maya, what are you doing?"

"There's a mosquito in this room," I whined in misery.

"A mosquito?" Yonnie asked in feigned alarm.

"It's biting me everywhere," I complained, hoping to get his attention.

"Where?" he asked with the same voice.

I knew that my panic was mere exaggeration but I liked getting his attention in the middle of the night. I took his hand and put it on my hip. "Here, and here, and here." I led his hand on my skin, hoping to awaken his interest in more than just the bites. Yonnie kissed each bump and then kissed me on my lips. "Does it still itch?"

"Yes."

Yonnie sat up and turned the light on. He leaned on the wall and waited for the mosquito to make a mistake and land near him. He knew how to wait for his prey. In the beginning of the summer, he caught a snake and brought it to my room. He was very proud of his snake and wanted to give it to me as a gift. I nearly died when I saw it.

"Isn't it cute?" he asked. "Do you want to touch it?"

I only shook my head. I was too scared to talk. What if the snake heard my voice and didn't like it?

"Don't be afraid. It's not going to bite you," he promised.

I kept shaking my head until he understood and left with his cute snake. A few minutes later he came back and explained that snakes were polite creatures that never bothered anyone, unless someone bothered them first.

Slap.

Yonnie's hand shot in front of my face and hit the wall. Mosquitoes were not polite creatures and Yonnie had no mercy for them. "Got it," he announced proudly, showing me his open palm. A fat mosquito was sprawled inside a bloody blotch in his hand. It was my blood that smeared my hero's hand, I thought, and my heart was flowing with love and admiration.

Yonnie took his shirt off and wiped the blood from his hand. Then he turned and helped me out of my T-shirt. He turned the light off. It was too bright anyway. We lay down. Yonnie was on top of me. I liked to feel his weight on my body. His lips felt warm and soft. I wrapped my legs around him. Yonnie took my hand and put it on his underwear. I felt his hardness underneath but had no idea what to do. Yonnie slid down to kiss me between my thighs. I didn't dare to ask him what to do. I didn't know what he planned to do. We never really talked about that stuff. I didn't even know if I was going to like it. My body was cramping with anticipation. I wanted to take off my underwear but I was too embarrassed. My underwear felt wet. I hoped Yonnie would not notice. Everything was so embarrassing. And Yonnie was panting above me, his back was starting to get all wet with perspiration. I hoped he would do something to release my crampiness without hurting me. Sometimes he did something and I felt spasms all over my body until I couldn't take it even one more second. And then I didn't want him to touch me anymore. When he did it to me I tried to be as quiet as I could. I was too shy to let him know how much I liked it. I didn't want him to think that I was a cheap woman. And now that my roommates were not around he might have some new ideas. I had to figure out what to do. I adjusted myself to his pace. His hand went to my underwear but once again it stopped without removing them. I wished he would remove them for me. I didn't know if I should do it by myself. I wanted to feel him even more but I was afraid it would hurt. I didn't feel so brave anymore. I wanted him to moan or something so I would know what was going on. But he was just thrusting above me, faster now, and his body was rubbing against my underwear, chafing my insides, until it hurt.

When Yonnie stopped thrusting, both of us were swimming in perspiration. He kissed me and rolled over, leaving a puddle of sweat on my belly. It was hot. A bird twittered sleepily. "I'm going to smoke a cigarette outside, want to come?" he asked, checking his underwear.

I shook my head. I wanted to change my wet underwear first. I didn't want him to know that my underwear was all wet. I watched him put on his shorts and walk out to the porch. I jumped out of bed and took off my wet underwear. I threw them at the bottom of my closet and chose a clean pair. As I approached the door, dressed in my new underwear and a long white T-shirt I heard a man's voice greet Yonnie. "Good morning," the voice said.

"Good morning," Yonnie answered.

"Still partying, huh?" the voice asked.

Very funny. Now the whole kibbutz would find out that Yonnie was awake at four in the morning, smoking a cigarette in front of my room. Damn. I looked out to see who it was. Yakov, my parent's neighbor. He was one of the night guards that week. Otherwise he had no reason to walk near my room at that hour, wearing his blue work clothes, and carrying an Uzi and a flashlight.

"What else is there to do?" Yonnie answered.

I didn't get mad at the comment because I knew that whatever he said would incriminate me. "I could go for a swim now," Yakov said. Checking his shirt pocket, he took out a pack of cigarettes and realized it was empty. He crumbled it and put it back in his pocket. I watched them through the window and tried to decide what to do. Yakov looked at his watch, put his Uzi and flashlight on the stairs and sat next to Yonnie. "Can I bum a cigarette from you?" he asked.

Shit. Didn't he know he should be guarding us from terrorists instead of sitting in front of my room with my boyfriend at this hour?

"Good morning, Maya," he greeted as I opened the door, determined to ignore the grim consequences of my hasty decision to join Yonnie on the porch. "Don't you kids ever sleep at night?"

"No," I said, faking a yawn, "we prefer to talk politics."

"You know, Maya," Yakov said, nodding and blowing smoke through his hairy nostrils, "that's exactly what we used to do when we were your age. But when we were your age things were different. You guys are so spoiled."

I tried not to get mad at him and his glorious past. I had heard his stories so many times that I could puke. I hoped that he was not going to start talking again about how they used to dance around the bonfire until dawn, and how they argued whether Ben Gurion was right or wrong when he decided to disband the *Palmach* - the army that won the "liberation war" - and found the IDF (Israel Defense Forces) in its place, and how tedious life had become in the last twenty years. They all liked to accuse us of having no values whatsoever.

He chose another facet of his wonderful past. "We didn't have rooms like you have today. When I wanted to be alone with Shoshana, we had to go to the barn. There was no other place to go. We had to share our room with a third member, the "primus" we called him, even after we got married. We lived three in one room until Ofek was born."

Right. We heard that story a million times. My mother told me that one of the reasons she and my father decided to get married was because it was the only way to get on the waiting list for a family room, which was exactly the size of my bedroom today. Actually my bedroom was the first room they moved into after they were married. One small room and a bathroom on the porch. Big deal. I think I understood now why these people thought about their past with so much nostalgia. They had no privacy at all.

"I guess it's time to wake Yankaleh up for the morning milking," Yakov sighed. The eastern horizon already looked paler than the rest of the sky, and the stars began to disappear.

After he left, Yonnie and I burst out laughing. "Can you imagine, Yakov and Shoshana naked in the barn?" I chuckled.

"The worst place to do it," Yonnie said, waving a dry twig in the air, trying to catch the attention of the neighbors' German Shepherd. "The worst place to screw is on a bale of hay."

"How do you know?" I asked, jealous.

He looked at me with his you-don't-really-want-to-know look until I shrugged and gave up. "Okay, don't tell me."

Maybe I pretended to be hurt more than I really was because Yonnie slid onto the stair next to me, hugged me, kissed my neck, and begged for my forgiveness. "I was just kidding, sweetie, you know I was just kidding."

Although I couldn't be sure he was kidding, I decided to forgive him and we went back inside.

The sun was hanging in the middle of the sky when we woke up. Outside, kids were riding noisy tricycles, crunching leaves and dry branches under my window. "I caught you, I caught you," they screamed in turns. A mother scolded her little daughter, "Limor, easy, be careful. He's just a baby." The baby started crying.

It was Saturday morning.

"Why can't they go to the beach like everyone else?" I yawned, lifting the pillow that covered Yonnie's face. "It's after nine o'clock."

"They want to make sure you wake up first," Yonnie mumbled, trying to grab back his pillow.

"Well, I'm awake," I declared, getting out of bed.

Yonnie turned to watch while I dressed; cutoff jeans, striped tank-top, rubber flip-flops. When I came back from the bathroom, Yonnie was standing in his shorts by the opened window smoking a cigarette.

"Of course there are snakes here, very poisonous," I heard him tell the kids who played under my window.

A little girl screamed. "Liar, not true, I don't believe you, where?" a mix of excited children's voices came into the room.

Yonnie blew smoke into the air, and smiled mischievously. He knew I was going to give him a hard time about that snake. I was sure he wouldn't release it right under my window." I took the snake to the children's farm," Yonnie whispered, blowing a smoke ring into the air. I didn't believe him.

"Yonnie, come save me from the evil snake," cried Shira, an incredibly sweet five year old. I could tell she was in love with him. Little girls fell in love with him right and left. He had a way with women, no matter how old they were.

Yonnie winked at me, opened the window screen and jumped outside, barefoot. All the kids ran away screaming and giggling. Except for Shira. She stood by the pomegranate tree with her eyes wide open, a tiny hand over her mouth, and waited for the brave soldier to come to her rescue. Yonnie grabbed her waist, lifted her up in the air, and put her on his shoulders. The little girl squeaked with pleasure. "Where is the snake, where is it?" she sang, bending over Yonnie's head.

Yonnie walked around the three pomegranate trees in search for the evil snake, pretending to see something under every leaf. Finally he whispered to Shira, loud enough for me to hear, "The snake ran away because of all the noise."

"Snakes are afraid of noise?" she asked in disbelief, her hands hugging his neck.

Yonnie nodded. He told her that if she wanted to help him catch the snake she had to make sure that all the kids from kindergarten walked very quietly under my bedroom window. Otherwise, he would never be able to catch it. As he put her back on the ground he added, "And sometimes, when snakes are in a bad mood they even bite kids who make noise."

"There is nothing snakes hate more than noise," he said, "especially on Saturday."

Five hours later we were back in my room, getting ready for Yonnie's departure. Yonnie went to take a shower and shave for the first time since he came to the kibbutz. I started packing his clothes, and tried not to think about the long three weeks I had to endure until the next time he could come back to the kibbutz. Time will pass fast, I tried to encourage myself, it will be really easy. I zipped the backpack and sat on my bed. I felt so heavy inside.

"Don't look so gloomy," Yonnie said when he got out of the shower.

"I'm not gloomy," I lied and tried to smile.

"I'll write to you every day," he promised and kissed me on the lips. Tears came into my eyes. I didn't want to say good bye. I was not ready to see him leave. I watched him put on his clean pressed uniform.

"Will you write to me too?" he asked when he finished getting dressed.

I nodded, hanging on to him, unable to let him go. He lifted his backpack from my bed, put it on his shoulder, and kissed me one last time.

"It's time to go," he apologized and lit a cigarette.

"I'll walk you to the gate," I said.

On Sunday morning Iris and I woke up before sunrise to start our trip back to Neveh Midbar. In the parking lot we ran into Lazer again, who luckily had to be back in his Tel Aviv office before seven o'clock. He asked us to squeeze in the back seat and let Moshon, our old children' farm supervisor who was now studying agriculture in Rehovot, sit in front. Ten minutes later he let us get off at the central bus station.

I checked my watch. I wanted to get to Neveh Midbar as early as possible and go back to work just as I had promised Jeff, so he would not accuse me of cheating twice. We managed to catch the first Express bus headed toward the Jordan Valley. The ride was slow and uneventful. Iris was too sleepy to talk and I wanted to stare outside the window and dream about Yonnie. Shortly before seven o'clock we arrived at a small dirty bus station and got off our bus. In spite of the relatively early hour, the air was already heavy with the stink of urine, burned rubber tires, and steaming asphalt. The concrete pavement was covered with black wads of bubble gum and small mounds of cracked shells of sunflower seeds people spat out while waiting for their bus. A partly torn wrinkled poster advertising ice-cream in cones and popsicles lay face up on the ground until a warm gust of wind pushed it across the street. It floated a few centimeters above the pavement then wrapped itself around a signpost and stayed there. Factory workers already dressed in their working uniform were lining up at the bus station, some were reading the morning paper, others smoked cigarettes or listened to Arabic music coming from a small transistor radio; one of the men who was leaning on a metal pole yawned loudly. I noticed him eyeing us curiously and asked him where to find our bus stop. He pointed at a wooden bench covered with yellowing newspapers and got a choking cough attack. We collected the papers, shoved them into an already full trash bin that stood nearby and sat down. A few moments later the bus came.

Only three passengers were sitting in the bus. None of them looked up when we climbed in, paid the fare, and asked the driver to let us know when to get off. Iris followed me to the back and sat down. I stretched on the long bench at the end of the bus, but before I had time to get really comfortable the driver announced loudly, "Girls, next stop Neveh Midbar."

We got off the bus in the middle of nowhere. A small square road sign pointed the direction to Neveh Midbar. After walking about two kilometers from the deserted intersection we reached Neveh Midbar. It was about quarter to eight. We ran to our room, changed into our working clothes, and rushed to the dining hall to meet our fate.

The first eyes I noticed as I entered the dining hall belonged to Gideon. They stared at me expressionless as I greeted everyone. I could feel their flashes burn my face. I passed his table, fighting a terrible unease, preparing myself for whatever he was going to say, but he did not say anything.

Okay, if he wanted to play the ignoring game with me I didn't mind at all. I would not say anything either. Iris, who followed me along the row of ugly Formica tables, seemed unperturbed by Gideon's eyes and silence. I motioned my head in his direction to warn her. She only shrugged her typical indifference. An unoccupied table at the far corner of the dining hall promised a dignified refuge. I put my tray on the table, and before my bottom touched the seat Jeff showed up and asked if he could sit with us.

"My pleasure," I said in English, and pointed at the chair next to me.

"Maya," he sighed, and sat down.

I looked at him as blankly as I could.

"You've really disappointed me," he started immediately, sounding more solemn than angry, and scratched something brown that was stuck on the handle of his plastic coffee cup.

"You didn't tell me the truth. You cheated me," he whispered, and looked around to make sure no one heard his clumsy accusation.

I forced myself not say that he should rest assured that everyone already knew how I tricked him. This type of story traveled very fast; like a fire in a thorns' field, as they said on the kibbutz. I almost felt sorry for him. His authority was being mocked and undermined by a savvy genius.

"Jeff," I opened my line of defense and paused. Everything happened so fast, I did not have enough time to prepare a good speech. I grabbed the salt shaker and examined it closely. It was almost empty. I shook it above my open palm to see if the salt poured out easily. Sometimes the salt was so damp I had to unscrew the lid, pour the salt on my hand, and separate the rice from the salt before I could sprinkle it on my salad. I had to buy time. I was not ready to start apologizing so soon. Yet, I didn't want to antagonize him. He didn't know that he was my ally, not an enemy.

"We didn't do anything," Iris mumbled into her coffee cup without looking at him.

"Shut up, Iris. Nobody asked you," I hissed. I didn't want her to spoil my plan. She could ruin everything. She didn't know how to operate in such delicate situations.

"What's your problem?" she complained, shrugging her annoying shoulders.

I could tell that Jeff felt the same about her, but he couldn't talk to her like I did because he was our future youth leader. I knew that her opinion meant nothing to him. He wanted to hear what I had to say. After all I was the one who had conned him.

"Look Jeff," I said, putting down the salt shaker, "what I did was not fair but..."

"What you did was wrong," he interrupted.

That was a surprising turn. Jeff was too polite to barge in like that. He always said thank you and excuse me and please. Maybe he was too upset to follow his American social etiquette. I could understand his problem. I was determined to make him feel good about himself even though I had to fight my strong tendency to argue. He had to come out of the situation as a winner. "You're right, it was wrong of me, but..."

"You should have told me the truth," he barged in again.

"You're right, I should have, but..."

"I would have talked to Gideon and explained how important it was for you to go to the kibbutz and see Yonnie," he interrupted again.

That conversation was fun. All I had to do was repeat what he said, add a word or two, and he would do the rest. My tactic was going to work out just fine. I felt so smart.

"And you think you could have made Gideon change his mind about it?" I asked innocently, knowing that his pride would not allow him to doubt himself.

"Of course I could make him change his mind." He fell into my trap just like the wild pigs that fell into the traps at the banana plantation. That guy was so naive.

"Well, then I'm really sorry I didn't tell you the truth," I faked an apology, trying to sound honest. "I didn't know you could do it," I added to inflate his ego a little, make him feel better. I stretched it even farther for more effect. "I didn't think he would listen to you."

"I hope next time you'd trust me a bit more," he said looking much better already.

Oh, so that was what he wanted. Trust! Ha. They probably taught him that he needed to "gain their trust" in the youth-leader workshop he took in Chicago before he came to the kibbutz. These Americans were clueless.

"That's a possibility." I tried to smile and grabbed the salt shaker again. The situation was becoming a little too much. He wanted me to trust him so badly that I couldn't disappoint him. I didn't want to break his pure heart.

"Just trust me," he said, getting up from the chair with restored confidence.

"Okay," I said, looking straight into his eyes. "I promise to try."

"You too," Jeff told Iris without malice, leaving before she had a chance to spit something stupid in his direction and ruin everything.

When he got out of hearing range I drummed ceremoniously on the table and, holding my chin up, asked, "Well, what do you say about that performance?"

"What an idiot," she sniffed.

"You don't understand, do you?" I shook my head in exasperation.

"What is there to understand?" the fool asked, opening her almond eyes wide.

I got up and left her to contemplate her question. It wasn't my job to explain everything. Obviously, she didn't understand that we still had to face the real problem, i.e., Gideon and his principles. We still hadn't heard from him, and I was sure he had something quite ugly up his sleeve. I could tell by the way he glared at me when I passed him on my way to the tractor.

The next hours I spent hanging onto the ladder, speculating about my fate, and trying to predict the future. In spite of my strong premonition that something awful was about to happen, nothing happened. During our ten o'clock break I sat in front of him and he ignored me, looking right through me as if I had no physical substance. As if I were a ghost. He joked with everyone, passing the plastic jug with the stinging lemonade to Nir and Shlomi, who were sitting next to me. He avoided me. I watched him talk and got a feeling that he was trying very hard to be friendly to everyone but me. Damn him and his friendliness.

We finished work. We went to the swimming pool. We ate dinner. We met for the daily announcements and discussions. He still ignored me. At last Sunday was over. When I finally lay in bed and turned the light off I realized that I hadn't thought of Yonnie even once since I got off the bus.

Monday started at the break of dawn. I sat on the edge of a carriage pulled by the noisy tractor, my feet dangling just a few centimeters above the dirt road that rushed beneath in the opposite direction. The sun climbed slowly behind the purple mountains expelling the gray morning mist. Everyone behind me was bundled in long sleeve blue shirts too sleepy to talk or admire the view. His eyes scalded my back. I tried to ignore the discomfort and the tingling sensation in my spine.

When I jumped from the carriage I noticed that I was suddenly full of unfamiliar cheerfulness. I couldn't stop it. I had to pretend that going to pick olives at four in the morning, grinding dust between my teeth and breathing exhaust fumes while hanging on the edge of a wooden carriage was the best thing that had ever happened to me.

"Look at the sun, isn't it gorgeous," I exclaimed in excitement to Erez, Nir, Hadas, and Tikva who stared blankly, trying to swallow their yawns. I inhaled the dusty air and stretched my arms as high as I could. "Come on guys, wake up, enjoy the morning before it gets too hot."

None of them bothered to answer. They picked up their canvas sacks and disappeared behind the olive trees, dragging their sacks on the ground behind them.

What's the matter with you, I heard a little voice inside me complain. What are you trying to prove? Shut up and go to work. Stop pretending that you like to be up at this hour because you don't. Everyone can see that you're only trying to hide your terrible anxiety. They know you dread him.

No, they can't, I heard another voice. Just keep your fake enthusiasm and everything will be all right.

By the time we returned from breakfast I was trapped inside my act. I wanted to stop the meaningless chatter coming out of my mouth but didn't know how. I heard my contrived jokes and wondered why no one noticed how stupid they sounded. I couldn't stand myself. I had too much nervous energy and it exhausted me. After the ten o'clock break, I almost fell from the ladder when I tried to reach a high branch while showing off how brave I was to Shlomi. I screamed in exaggerated horror and generated a wave of laughter. I didn't know what to do with my overwhelming apprehension. I wanted to jump from the ladder and maybe break a leg, just to get away. Maybe they would carry me in a stretcher to the hospital and I would not have to see Him anymore. I didn't know how to get myself out of the situation. But at the same time I wanted to prove that I didn't care. Just convince yourself that you don't care about what He thinks and you'll be fine, I told myself as I tried to steady myself on the ladder. Just keep working and pretend that you're having a ball. Show everyone that you're a great sport. That it's fun to work with you. That you've got the right spirit and that you are invincible. That you have pinned down the values of hard work. Show everyone that neither he, nor the humidity, the heat, the insects that keep eating you alive, and the heavy canvas sack that hangs on your neck and threatens to pull you down, can defeat you because you are strong, determined, and fully committed to the kibbutz ethic of, "Labor is what our life is all about."

"Maya, tell me, did you swallow a radio last night by mistake?" my roommate, Tikva, asked on the way to our room after lunch.

"Did you ever hear the joke about the elephant and the mouse who were running in the desert and the mouse looked backward and said to the elephant....," I ignored her question and started another stupid joke.

"Everybody's heard it," she sighed, stopping my incessant stream of words. She called Iris who was walking in front of us. "I have something important to tell you," she whispered to Iris, looking at me over her shoulder.

I knew she was lying. She only wanted to get away from my stupid jokes. She is avoiding you, Maya, said the same small voice inside my head. You've been a nuisance all day. Look at yourself. You talk too much. Soon enough no one will want to be near you. Control yourself. Calm down. Relax. He is not going to do anything to you. Stop behaving like your Polish grandmother who's always preparing for another pogrom and worrying about nothing.

I was not going to argue with that voice anymore. I just hoped that the blow would come before the end of the week. I wanted to get it over with rather than feel it coming with every minute that ticked on my bat-mitzvah watch. If he had only acted I would have known what to do. But as long as he did nothing I was helpless. I couldn't take it anymore.

"Maya," I heard my name from far away, then my shoulder jolted.

"What, what happened?" I forced my eyes to open. I couldn't see anything. My heart pounded and my head throbbed. It took me a few seconds to realize that I had dozed off on the floor, leaning on the bed with my shoes and work clothes on. My neck felt stiff, and my left leg fell asleep like it always did when I tried to delay the future.

"We're going for a ride with some of the guys from Neveh Midbar," Iris announced breathlessly. "Want to come with us?"

I was stupefied. I was sure she noticed how crazy I acted all day and felt sorry for me. "No," I said, rubbing my sleeping leg.

"Come on," she insisted, "wash your face and you'll feel more awake. It's going to be fun."

I shook my head. I was not going to destroy the afternoon for her and the rest of whoever they may be and make a fool out of myself. I was going to stay in, read Siddhartha, listen to Simon and Garfunkel, and feel miserable.

"No, I really don't feel like going anywhere."

"We'll wait for you. Wash your face and don't forget to take your bikini. They said there's a natural pool somewhere in the hills," she said, throwing a towel on my bed. "The water is really cold there, and we might even see some rare birds."

"Iris, are you deaf or something? Don't you understand what I'm saying? I don't want to go anywhere. Why don't you just leave me alone, okay?" I snapped.

"What's your problem?" she asked.

"I just want to be by myself," I said, looking at the ceiling.

"Okay, okay." She finally pulled back. "We thought you might like to go too. Get out of this boring hole for a few hours."

I knew my behavior was inexcusable and mean, but I couldn't control it anymore. The heat and the suspense were killing me. It had nothing to do with Iris. "Yeah, it sounds like a great idea, but I'm just not in the mood," I apologized.

After she left I slumped on the bed and stared at the ceiling for a long time. A few minutes later I took my book and looked at the page. I read the lines but they didn't connect into sentences. I let the book drop on the floor and stared at the ceiling. I couldn't read and I couldn't concentrate. Even Siddhartha couldn't alleviate the feeling of impending doom.

What am I going to do? The question kept popping up inside my head. I wish I could be like Iris. So indifferent to everything. Why couldn't I be like her? Why couldn't I have some fun and forget my problems? Suddenly I knew what I had to do. I'd been doing it all along, only I was not aware of it. It was more like a reflex than a clear strategy. But now that I understood what I was doing I could refine my performance to absolute perfection. I was going to be cheerful, energetic, and ecstatic about everything. I was going to stay at the center of attention. I was going to act like the embodiment of fun and pleasure. I was going to outsmart him and his plans to retaliate. That way he would never be able to see how scared I really was behind my awful giddiness.

I spent all of Tuesday and Wednesday behind my cheerful mask, still expecting him to strike. But he didn't. For some reason, no one seemed to be bothered by my endless babbling, except for Daphna, who asked who I was trying to impress with my stupid jokes.

"No one. I just love it here," I lied, making sure that everyone could hear me.

On Thursday, I felt so confident about my new personality that even the anxious feelings that had wanted to throw me off the ladder and almost drowned me in fear only two days earlier began to disappear. Strangely though, I still missed a heartbeat every time he passed near my tree, or when I passed him in the dining hall, or when I heard his voice. I still felt his eyes pierce holes in my back, and the blood congealed in my veins when he picked up the pile of letters and distributed them. Luckily, Yonnie did not follow his promise to write every day and I was spared the humiliation of having to extend my hand and watch him stare at me with obvious disdain.

Finally Friday arrived; our last day in kibbutz Neveh Midbar.

The sense of doom that had tormented me since Sunday morning dissolved into the hot air and disappeared when I entered the dining hall. I resisted the urge to hug Iris and show her my true cheerfulness. At last my real self was able to emerge from beneath the layers of anxiety. I could breathe again. I looked at the desolate hills that surrounded Neveh Midbar and greeted them for the first time. At last I could stop acting happy because I was already happy and relieved. I could be myself again.

Back in our room, we mopped the floor and wiped the desk, the reading lamps, and the window sills from the incredible amount of dust blown indoors by the relentless desert wind; we took the brown blankets issued to us by the work committee of kibbutz Neveh Midbar to the porch and shook them vigorously; we made the beds, army style, each blanket showing eighteen folds and placed on top of the exposed mattress. When the room looked like it would pass the inspection, we picked up our backpacks and went out to wait for the truck.

I dropped my backpack on the yellow grass and lay on the ground next to Iris. Sitting on her backpack, she was obviously compelled to keep her clothes neat and free of foreign objects. I didn't mind the dry grass sticking to my clothes and hair as long as the ants and all the other crawling, biting things stayed away. I squinted at the sun and decided for the millionth time that the weeks we spent in Neveh Midbar were a complete waste of time.

Places like Neveh Midbar made me appreciate my own kibbutz. In my kibbutz I could open the window and see the waves crash on the white rocks; I could see our beautiful sand beaches and the sailboats in the far horizon; the cotton fields turning their pink flowers into white clouds of soft wool; the water reservoir sparkle in the sun; the red roofs of the beach resort that hosts police force officers and their families; the remains of the train tracks that used to run all the way up to Beirut, and the most glorious sunsets. I could take a walk to the mountain and lie in the shade of a carob tree that lived in ancient days. And if I felt like getting away from nature I could always walk down the hill and catch a ride to the nearest town and go to the movies with a friend, or feast on soft

American ice cream with a mountain of whipped cream on top and red sweet cherries. But in Neveh Midbar there was nothing to look at and nowhere to go. Only dry hills, olive groves, the mountains across the border and the sun.

"So it seems like we got away with it this time," Iris' voice broke my train of thought.

I sat up and stared at her dumbfounded. In a million years I would not have guessed that she was worried. I was totally, completely, and absolutely surprised. "Were you worried about what he was going to do to us?"

"Of course I was. Weren't you?"

"I reckoned Jeff would talk to Gideon after I apologized to him in the dining hall. You know how much he wants to prove himself to us," I said, inventing a twisted answer that I did not believe myself. But I couldn't tell her what a nervous wreck I was. No way.

"That idiot," she muttered, her eyes following him as he approached us, a goofy smile on his face, a pair of gray All Star sneakers on his feet, a tie-dyed T-shirt with the sleeves rolled up, a perfectly faded cut-off Levi's, and a bright orange nylon backpack on one shoulder. He tried so hard to be accepted by us. It was pitiful.

"Are you guys ready to go?" he asked in the acquired friendly tone people who work with youth use when they have nothing better to say.

"Mhmm," both of us nodded.

"Great," he said. Dropping his backpack on the grass near me, he sat down, hugged his knees, and swayed from side to side in the same phony friendliness, acting as if having authority didn't mean he couldn't behave like a mere human. Iris and I exchanged glances, and, as expected, he didn't notice.

"Ask him," Iris said, moving her eyes in his direction.

"Ask him what?"

"If he talked to Gideon," she whispered, covering her mouth with her hand. "And what Gideon said."

"Why don't you ask him?"

"What are you girls shushing about," Jeff asked, probably thinking we were talking about the color of his underwear or something.

"Maya wants to know if you talked to Gideon about us and what he said," Iris said. I felt the blood gallop into my face. I wanted to strangle that girl.

"You two worry about what you got to do and let me worry about what I got to do," he said with that soothing tone. I almost wanted to believe that he actually persuaded Gideon not to punish us.

"So you didn't talk to him," Iris decided.

"Iris, do me a favor," I said, interrupting her futile, tactless approach, "shut up."

"Don't tell me what to do, I can talk whenever I want to," she pouted. "It's a free country."

"Sometimes it's better not to say anything," Jeff said quietly, rising from the ground. I watched him pick up his backpack and walk away. He looked around and decided to join the guys sitting in a small circle near Gideon.

"See what you did," I confronted Iris, trying to control my anger and frustration. That stupid girl couldn't understand the ramifications of losing Jeff to the guys. Bad omen. A little muscle twitched inside me.

"Okay, listen," Gideon announced, standing up in the middle of the circle and clapping his hands as if we were still in kindergarten. "Why don't you all come closer so you can hear me better?"

Nir and Shlomi, who were sitting on the stairs, got up and dragged their backpacks to the circle. I didn't make any move toward the growing circle. Neither did Iris. She leaned on the trunk of a flimsy looking tree and pretended that she was comfortable.

"Girls, come join us," Jeff called.

Everyone turned their heads to look at us. They sat in a circle on the dying, yellow grass, leaning on their khaki backpacks, with Gideon standing in the middle like a flagpole, and waited for us to join them.

"I'm comfortable here," Iris said, crossing her arms over her chest.

"Come on," Jeff nudged while everyone watched.

I don't know how much time had passed, maybe an eternity. Finally I heard Dorit's voice. "Maya, Iris, come on, everyone is waiting for you."

I looked at Gideon. He didn't look back. He just stood there and waited, letting the others coerce us into the circle. My God, this is the most embarrassing moment of my life, I thought. I got up and joined the group. Iris followed me. I looked at Jeff for a sign but I couldn't read him. I could kill to find out what he was thinking.

"So how is everyone today?" Gideon started again. "Happy to go back home?"

An indistinct murmur passed in the circle. Wasn't it obvious?

"Good," he said, looking satisfied with himself. I couldn't stand him. He checked his watch. "The trucks will be here in about half an hour, so let's use the time to talk a little bit about what we've accomplished here."

I watched him pull a small notebook from his shirt pocket and leaf through it. He liked to use props that made him look important. A real actor he was. "The secretary of kibbutz Neveh Midbar was very pleased with your help. He said they've never seen such a serious and committed group of high school students here. I met him last night and he showed me some numbers, and I must tell you, it was quite impressive," he complimented the group. He looked at his notebook again for effect and put it back in his pocket.

"We picked more olives than any other group that worked here in the last four years," he summarized, as if anybody cared. "You guys should be very proud of yourselves. I'm sure every kibbutz in the Jordan Valley will hear about us."

After another pause for effect, he said, "Let me tell you guys, you've made a pretty good impression on the members of Neveh Midbar, in spite of the noise you made and the dirty dishes you left scattered around the swimming pool after the party on Friday night."

The boys looked at each other and chuckled secretly. Tomer pushed Nir's shoulder and whispered loudly. "So how was the Canadian volunteer who went to the rooms with you during the party? Huh? What did you say to her, you stinky fucker?"

Nir buried his head between his knees. "Shut the fuck up, you fucking asshole."

"I've got to tell you," Gideon continued, oblivious to the exchange between Nir and Tomer and the giggles that came from the other guys, "I was more than pleased to hear all this. I didn't expect you to impress a man like Doobie. But you did."

"And I got to give you all the credit for it. I think it was a great experience for all of us. I'm quite sure that in the long run you'll realize that during this month here you have grown up and became a lot more united as a group. You all did a wonderful job here," he said. And then, turning his head in my direction, he added, "Except for Maya and Iris, of course."

Ah-huh, now it was coming.

No one said anything.

"You two," Gideon said, "you two deserted this group in spite of what I said. You left your best friends to do your job only because you couldn't control your sexual urges. You just had to leave your friends here, ignore your duties, and rush to the kibbutz to sleep with your boyfriends. Poor girls. You couldn't wait to be with them. Like two little sluts."

When he spouted his last words I knew that I would never ever let him get away with what he said. Never!

The silence was simply unbelievable. I could hear a wasp buzz above me somewhere. An ant climbed up my leg. Before I brushed it off it stung me. I raised my head and looked right into his eyes. Nothing could stop me now. I was waiting for this all week. To launch my war against tyranny. My war against oppression.

"My sexual habits have nothing to do with you," I nearly screamed so everyone could hear me. I felt no shame. Only anger. Bitter anger. Overwhelming, blinding anger. "I have the right to see my boyfriend on my days off work and no one, not even you, can tell me what to do on my day off."

I was glad he was standing far from me. I could tell he would have slugged me if he were a little closer. Luckily, there were enough people between us and he couldn't strike me from the center of the circle.

"Don't you dare talk to me like that, do you hear me?" He threatened me through tight lips. The veins on his neck swelled and his eyes looked like they were going to pop out. "I'm warning you, do you understand?"

No one moved. His last words remained suspended in the air, echoing his warning.

"And I'm warning you," I spat back. I was so furious now, I could hardly think or breathe. "You can't talk to me like that either. And I don't care who you are, or how old you..." Before I could finish my assault Jeff jumped up and waved his arms in the air.

"Please, Maya, stop it, just stop it," he half-ordered half-begged as he rushed toward me. Only then did I notice that everyone was watching.

"Come with me Maya," he said, grabbing my arm.

I tried to pull it away but he had a firm hold. "Maya, stop it, control yourself," he whispered. He put his arm around my shoulder and gently forced me toward the long building we had just vacated.

"Okay, I'm not going to run away," I said once I got my breath. "You don't have to hold me like that." I didn't really know what was going on anymore. I was so blinded by rage I could hardly recognize myself.

"Let's sit here," Jeff said softly, leading me to the staircase.

We sat close to each other. Jeff was still holding my arm. It felt soothing. I felt safe again. I breathed quietly until my pulse returned to normal. I was still disoriented. I knew that my eyes were open but I couldn't see much. I was blinded by the glare of the sun. It penetrated my brain. Slowly, I started noticing blurry images on the balding yellow grass. I couldn't tell what these figures were doing. As time passed I realized that I was looking at people who were loading an army truck.

"My backpack is over there," I told Jeff, pointing at the sickly looking tree Iris was leaning on before everything started. My voice sounded strange, foreign.

"Don't worry about it," he said, squeezing my shoulder, still trying to help me calm down. "We won't forget it here."

I leaned on him. He didn't say anything. Suddenly I wanted to cry. I wanted to burst into tears and cry until there were no tears left in me. I wanted him to hug me and comfort me, and tell me that everything was going to be all right. I wanted to let all the scary feelings that choked me all week to come out of my body. I felt so small and bruised. I sniffled, looking straight ahead. Jeff's hand tightened on my shoulder. I didn't know if I wanted him to see how shaken I felt, but I wanted him to keep holding me. Rub my back. Murmur calming words in my ear. Tell me that everything was going to be okay. That he was on my side.

"Come on, let's go," Jeff said, letting go of my shoulder.

I followed. He picked up my backpack. I didn't dare go anywhere without him. I waited for him to make another move. I followed him to the truck. All the backpacks were already tied on the roof. Noam climbed down from the roof and told me to put my backpack inside the truck under one of the benches. I climbed into the truck, planning to move to the back, when I saw him blocking my way. I looked at him with the most undefeated glare I could summon.

"You'll pay very dearly for the way you've talked to me, I promise you," he hissed in my face.

"Don't try to scare me, Gideon. The one who will have to pay dearly for the way he speaks is you," I shot the words right back at him. I knew that Jeff was not around to stop me, and I was taking one more chance to give him a piece of my mind in front of everyone.

"Get out of my way," he ordered.

"I want to sit over there," I answered, pointing at a vacant seat behind him.

He shook his head. "You're going to sit at the front, just as I tell you."

"You can't tell me what to do. I can sit wherever I want," I said, trying to pass him. And suddenly I realized that Gideon had finally struck. He pushed me to the front and I began to fly, my back toward the opening of the truck. I was unable to stop my flight. A thought hit me as I tried to grab a bench, anything. If I fall on my back I will crush my neck. I've got to stop myself before I fly outside and hit the ground. I was suspended in the air, looking for the floor.

An arm caught me. Another arm helped me stand up. Then I felt two pairs of hands holding me. I looked down just to make sure I was still in one piece. The arms led me to the bench. I sat down and looked straight ahead.

"Maya, are you okay?" An unfamiliar voice echoed somewhere nearby.

I was not sure I could speak. My faculties were still trying to understand what had happened and where I was.

"She's fine," I heard him say.

The truck took off. I looked outside until kibbutz Neveh Midbar became a little black dot. When it finally disappeared behind the steam that rose from the parched asphalt, I decided to launch my final battle against Gideon. I was not sure about my strategy or what weapons I would use, but I knew without a shred of a doubt that I would do anything to win.

I sat between Noam and Erez, who were engaged in a loud argument about a certain soccer team and felt like a wounded outsider. The boys acted as if nothing happened. They competed who could burp louder and longer and laughed at the ugly noises they were making. Deep inside I was sure they knew as well as I did that it was only a matter of time before they would have to be at the center of unwanted attention. I already noticed how Gideon's reign of terror affected everyone around me. I watched them pretend that nothing had happened even though they witnessed everything. I saw them act as if fear was not an issue. And I resented it. I did not want to be guided by my hidden fear for one more second.

When we arrived at the kibbutz I went to my room, packed my clothes, books, and records and moved to Sharon's room. She had gone to Thailand and India and did not plan to return to the kibbutz until the end of the year and told me I could live there if I wanted. After I settled in, I announced to Jeff that I stopped recognizing Gideon as my youth leader.

"I don't think you can do that," Jeff said in bewilderment. He had never heard of such a possibility in a kibbutz. Defying a kibbutz authority was not a common phenomenon taught in the youth leaders' workshops in America.

"Why not?" I asked.

"Because..." he started.

I waited.

"Well, the educational committee will not allow it. At your age you have to belong to a group. Someone has to look after you," he explained the rules as if I didn't know them.

"The educational committee can't tell me what to do," I argued. They could not expel me from the kibbutz because my parents lived there. They could only label me a troublemaker and a nuisance.

Jeff flinched, realizing that he couldn't reason with me. "Maya, with this kind of attitude you are only going to isolate yourself from everyone. You're going to be ostracized," he said.

"I already ostracized myself."

"What will your parents say?" he asked in desperation.

"They don't have to know about it."

"You know that you can't keep it a secret for long."

"I'll deal with them when they find out," I said. My mother would certainly take the educational committee's stand and scold my rebellious attitude while emphasizing the "what will everyone say about you?" as the most dangerous outcome of my dissent. My father never said a thing.

Jeff gave up. I left him sitting in front of the dining hall, sadly staring at my back. His worries did not bother me. I felt good defying the rules and fighting the evil forces of oppression. I felt good being right and knowing it.

Chapter Eight

On Friday morning, two days before Hanukkah, I was jolted out of sleep by a loud burst of gunshots. It was not the first time I was awakened by the sound of gunshots. The latest rise in terrorist attacks in the Western Galilee put the soldiers who patrolled the mountain ridge above the kibbutz on edge. No one was willing to take a chance that the occasional rustle in the sagebrush indicated innocent wildlife activity. No one expected the tall electric fence to stop terrorists from crossing the border into Israel, either. So the report of machine-gun fire became a matter of routine for all of us. Only that this time the shots sounded awfully close. And they were fired in the early morning, which was very unusual. Most of the shootings took place before midnight when the soldiers were still alert and ready for action.

An edgy army reservist must have fired those shots, I decided, and pulled the pillow over my head. I had less than an hour to enjoy my warm bed and I was not going to waste it on staying awake and worrying about why the gunshots sounded so close. I dug deep under my blanket and dreamed about a startled porcupine waddling into a dark narrow cave away from the gunshots and the heavy rain.

When I woke up my mother was standing at the foot of my bed, unbuttoning her wet raincoat. A thick unattractive wool scarf she had knitted years ago covered her hair and shoulders. Fat raindrops clung to the brown wool. I looked at my alarm clock. In a few minutes I would have to get out of bed and get ready for school. The school bus, which was recently painted over in a strange green hue to mislead terrorists, was going to leave at quarter to seven and I could not afford to miss it. Our regional high school was a ten-minute ride from my kibbutz and there was no way I was going to walk there in the pouring rain.

"Maya, get up. You have to go to the bomb shelter near the basketball court," my mother said, picking up my jeans from the floor.

"Why? What happened?" I mumbled into my pillow.

"There's no reason to panic. There are soldiers everywhere," she said.

"Soldiers?" I asked, suddenly fully awake. I jumped out of bed and pulled open the curtains. Only because of what she said I was not surprised to see the soldiers standing outside my window. They were not the balding, slouchy, over-weight types who usually guarded the main gate and patrolled the fence that encircled the kibbutz, but the young good-looking kind that served in special combat units. One soldier was standing on the lawn, a pair of binoculars hanging around his neck and an M16 rifle slung over his shoulder; the other was lying by a shallow puddle, taking aim through the sights of a machine-gun mounted on a tripod. I opened the window, in spite of the heavy rain, and leaned out, hoping the soldiers would notice me, but my mother pulled me in and quickly closed it.

"Hurry up and get dressed. They're going to start the search at six thirty," she said.

"What search?"

"There was an infiltration last night. The Navy patrol spotted a rubber boat crossing the border from Lebanon at around two o'clock in the morning. They fired at them and sank the boat. They think there were three terrorists on the boat but they don't know what happened to them because it was too stormy, so they've been searching the sea and the beach all night. Then less than an hour ago someone shot Danny Brenner, so now the army's getting ready to comb the kibbutz," she concluded in a most matter-of-fact voice, speaking in the cool military jargon as if she were the chief-of-staff or something.

"Did they kill Danny?" I was afraid to find out.

"He lost a lot of blood, but they said he was conscious when they took him to the hospital," she said, picking up the rest of my clothes from the floor.

Did he see the terrorists? Where was he when he got shot? Did his wife go to the hospital with him? There were so many questions I wanted to ask, but she was not volunteering information and I didn't want to nag. I mean, why couldn't she tell me everything she knew right away?

"I'm going to see if they need help in the infants' house," she said, looking at her watch. "They said all the children must stay in the bomb shelters until further notice."

They? Who the hell are they? I almost asked. Sometimes I didn't know whether I should admire or despise my mother's total obedience to the invisible entity that she called "They." I had to assume that it was someone from the army. Who else could it be, otherwise?

I was putting my shoes on when she said, "I'll walk with you to the dining hall. We can have coffee together before you go to the bomb shelter. Just remember when you're outside that they asked everyone not to run and to keep away from the bushes."

"You mean somebody is working in the kitchen now with all these terrorists on the loose?" I asked.

"It's not the end of the world," she said, following me to the bathroom and watching me brush my teeth. "Someone has to prepare breakfast and lunch for the members and the soldiers. They've been up all night."

Her final piece of information sounded very promising. Not everyone was stuck in bomb shelters. Some people were still above ground. "You don't have to wait for me, I still have to make my bed," I said, looking at her reflection in the mirror.

She tried to argue that I didn't have to make my bed, but I insisted. I told her that I wanted to make a good impression on the search team when it came to look for the terrorists in my apartment. Except for me, every high-school kid on the kibbutz had to share a place with a roommate. My little apartment was all mine: the bedroom, the sitting area, the bathroom, and the tiny kitchenette. I loved it and was very proud of the way I had decorated it, with a real silk parachute hanging from the ceiling and posters of Bob Dylan and women burning their bras on the walls.

For some reason, my mother was not convinced. She went into the bedroom and picked up the Indian print bedspread from the floor. I was horrified. She was going to ruin my plan. "Let me do it," I said, grabbing the bedspread. "You should go to the infants' house now. Dinah's probably worried sick watching the babies by herself," I said, trying to look like I really cared.

"All right," she gave up and surrendered the bedspread. She made me promise to go directly to the bomb shelter and left without kissing me good-bye. As soon as she closed the door I opened the window and looked for the soldiers.

"Hey, you, close the window and go to the bomb shelter," the soldier with the binoculars called, waving his hand in the air to catch my attention. The other soldier did not even look up. He was aiming the machine-gun at a cluster of thick bushes and adjusting something on it.

I closed the window and left without making the bed. If the soldiers didn't want to talk to me, then I didn't care what they might think about my room. Let them plow through the mess and search for the terrorists under the blankets.

The kibbutz was eerily empty and quiet. No one dressed in blue work clothes was rushing to work, greeting me with a sleepy "good morning." As far as my eyes could see, I was the only person walking outside. A stocky soldier carrying a radio with a tall antenna on his back came out of nowhere and galloped by me, barking unintelligible words into a black telephone attached to the radio. I listened carefully but all I could understand was the word "over." I watched him run toward the children's houses, noticing the mud on his uniform and combat boots. Mud was everywhere. The beautifully tended lawn in front of the communal dining hall was crisscrossed by tire marks of heavy vehicles. Solid chunks of dark brown mud were scattered all over the rose beds and concrete walkways. I couldn't help thinking about what the gardener was going to do once he saw the trashed lawn. He'd make the kibbutz stink for days after spreading compost all over the place to help the grass recover from the trauma.

Once the soldier with the radio disappeared, I began to imagine a terrorist hiding behind every bush and on top of every tree. The muscles above my knees and around my eyes tightened and I felt a terrible urge to run. I had to force my legs to walk instead of run, look straight ahead, and breathe evenly. Pretend that I was out for an early morning stroll, enjoying the break in the rain.

From outside, the communal dining hall looked completely deserted. All the lights were on, but I could not see any movement behind the large windows. I raced up the stairs and quickly shut the glass doors behind me, as if they could protect me from real bullets. My heart was bouncing in my chest, forcing me to sit down. I looked around the dining hall, which could easily accommodate two hundred people at any given meal, and spotted Monica and Linda sitting at the other end by the coffee machine, filling salt and pepper shakers. These two came from America to work on the kibbutz and hang out for a few months with other volunteers from Holland, Australia, the United Kingdom, and Canada. Some of the volunteers from the United States were proud draft dodgers who called themselves "conscientious objectors;" the rest just wanted to travel and have fun in Israel.

"How come you're not at the bomb shelter?" I asked them, trying to catch my breath.

"We didn't feel like staying there," Monica shrugged, as if that was a valid excuse. She didn't live on the kibbutz long enough to know that no one here cared about what you felt or did not feel like doing. Here you had to play by the rules; that was that.

"The Ping-Pong table was already taken," Linda said. "And we got tired of playing backgammon."

The lucky volunteers had something to play with in their bomb shelter because during the week it was used as an improvised bar where they could go listen to loud music and drink cheap Israeli beer. In the youth society's bomb shelter there was nothing but bunk beds and the smell of whitewash and Lysol.

"Does Arazi know you're here?" I asked.

Arazi was in charge of security and the "weapons room" and his wife was in charge of the volunteers. It was impossible to believe that he would let Monica and Linda come to the dining hall to fill salt and pepper shakers while all the other volunteers hid in the safety of the bomb shelter.

"We'll stay here until he tells us to go back to the bomb shelter," Monica said.

So that's what it was: Monica could talk him out of it. All she had to do was smile and touch his forearm and he would let her do whatever she wanted. The men on the kibbutz were crazy about her. Even the married ones. They thought that she was the most gorgeous creature in the entire universe. Not only was she tall and blond, she also had a tan even in the middle of the winter. And no bikini lines, anywhere.

"I hope my parents don't listen to the BBC today," Linda sighed. Her parents lived in Boston and routinely begged her to come back home.

"Didn't you call them yet?" I asked.

"All the phone lines are occupied by the army. Even the one in the clinic. Arazi said we could use the public telephone near the parking lot, but I don't want to go there. Half of the IDF is there."

"Maybe they won't find out," I said, hoping to comfort her.

"Dream on," Monica said. "All they do is listen to the news."

The clock hanging above the coffee machine showed six twenty. Soon we would be at the center of national attention. There was no doubt in my mind that the terrorist attack would be at the top of the morning news. I was so glad that my kibbutz was located on the Lebanese border. Not only was I missing school - I was going to be a celebrity.

"Maya, what are you doing here? Don't you know you have to go to the bomb shelter?" Shoshana, who was in charge of the dining hall crew, scolded me on her way out of the dishwashing room. She was pushing a small stainless steel cart with two buckets of soapy water on the top shelf.

Before I had a chance to come up with a reasonable explanation, we heard the staccato of gunfire from the direction of the soccer field. We all froze. Then the shooting stopped. Shoshana exhaled loudly and said, "you girls should all be at the bomb shelter."

I almost admitted that she was right. Sitting in the safety of the nuclear-bomb-proof shelter, my peers were probably listening to Gideon, the youth leader, lecturing to them on why they were too young to watch the film "A Clockwork Orange." But if Shoshana could be in the dining hall while all the shooting was going on, so could I. I was about to ask her what I could do to help when she looked up at me and said, "I don't want you to walk outside when they're shooting like that."

Neither did I.

"Is there anything I can do here?" I asked.

"You can help me clean this mess," she pointed at a table next to her. The orange Formica top was littered with the remains of the early morning snack. Slices of a day-old rye bread in plastic baskets, empty cups of melted margarine, ant-ridden red jam in white ceramic bowls, sugar mounds, used paper napkins, dirty knives and teaspoons were scattered all over the place. "Or," she added as an afterthought, "you can be in charge of the Hanukkah decorations."

What a great idea. I could be in charge of something. "I'll clean the mess and then I'll do the decorations," I said quickly, before she would change her mind and send me to clean the toilets or scrub greasy pots.

Once the table was cleared, I followed her through the dishwashing room into the kitchen to get the art supplies. In the kitchen five women were standing around a rectangular stainless steel table, preparing sandwiches. The spirits around the table were high and so were the piles of the sliced salami and Swiss cheese. On a shelf behind the table, a small radio was playing contemporary music.

The women were surprised to see me. Tzipke, who walked in carrying a tray of sliced rye bread, wished me an automatic "good morning" and eyed me questioningly. The smell of the deliciously fresh bread stirred my stomach.

I returned the greeting and followed Shoshana to the storage room. Behind canvas sacks of sugar and flour, there were several cardboard boxes full of gouache paint containers and brushes. I took one box and followed Shoshana back to the kitchen. As we passed the women around the stainless steel table, Tzipke asked me why I was not in the bomb shelter with the rest of the youth society.

"She came to help me in the dining hall," Shoshana answered and patted me on the shoulder.

The women exchanged secretive disapproving glances. I was sure that they meant, "Maya never does what she's supposed to do." Since no one said anything, I dared and asked if there were any new "developments in the situation."

"Zorik said the chief-of-staff is on his way to the kibbutz," Dvora bragged proudly, separating a few slices of Swiss cheese from the pile in front of her.

"When did he say that?" Tamara asked in disbelief, digging her knife in a block of soft margarine.

"When he came to get sandwiches for the soldiers guarding the bomb shelter near the gym," Dvora said, annoyed at Tamara who doubted her.

"All the army will be here today," Ilana joined in, reaching over Tamara. She picked a handful of salami circles from the pile and slapped them on a slice of rye bread.

"I just hope they'll finish off the terrorists soon," Shifra interjected. She leaned over Ilana and added another sandwich to the pile on the tray, then started a tirade of complaints. "Yesterday Shlomo was digging behind my house and got all my windows covered with dust. I don't know what he's planning to put in that hole. Another swimming pool?" Without waiting for an answer, she continued: "Then, of course it had to rain and now my windows are completely dirty. With soap I'll have to wash them. With soap," she said in indignation. "Can you believe it? I don't know from where all this dust comes from."

"The Sahara," I mumbled under my breath.

All the women looked up at me. Shoshana, who was whispering at the other end of the table, motioned to me with her head to go to the dining hall. Tzipke tried to swallow a smile and Ilana shoved a salami sandwich into my hand.

"Eat something before you completely disappear," she said.

I left the kitchen with the box of art supplies and the sandwich. By the dishwashing machine, I stopped to dump the sandwich in the trashcan. I never liked salami. I wasn't going to eat it, no matter how hungry I felt. Behind my back I could hear Shifra go on. "Like a mad woman I work. And what do I get? Nothing, absolutely nothing."

Since there was nothing interesting to eat beside salami or Swiss cheese sandwiches, I decided to make myself a cup of hot chocolate. Standing by the hot milk dispenser, which we called "the cow," I could hear Shifra complaining again. "I was supposed to get my hair done today, but because of these terrorists the hairdresser had to cancel and I'll have to wait until who knows when. I can't stand the way my hair looks."

"Your hair looks fine. Doesn't it?" I could hear Ilana address the group.

"Maybe she'll be able to squeeze you in next week," suggested Aliza, who was quiet up till now. I really liked Aliza. She was the only woman on the kibbutz who knew how to prepare cosmetic wax from scratch and she was never too busy to wax my legs in the summer. Considering the fact that half of the women on the kibbutz needed her services, it was pretty amazing that she always found time for me, although I was not even a grown-up.

"Don't expect any miracles," Shifra whined.

"I don't understand why they don't hire another hairdresser. Nobody likes her," Dvora said.

I couldn't believe it. They completely forgot the terrorists. I really wanted to go inside and tell them to give the hairdresser a break, but a sudden series of machine-gun shots stopped me. I ducked behind a table. When the shootings halted Dvora said, "I wonder what that was all about."

"We'll find out when Zorik comes to get more sandwiches," Shoshana said and asked cheerfully if anybody wanted a fresh cup of coffee.

At seven a.m. the news signal split the air.

Like always it was easy to hear the news. Someone in the kitchen had turned the volume all the way up, so anyone within a radius of ten kilometers could hear it.

"What do they say?" Monica wanted to know.

I told her only what I thought she wanted to hear, skipping the stories about Sadat and Kissinger. The Navy had sunk a Zodiac full of terrorists one kilometer off shore after two a.m., the army was searching the area, and one kibbutznik was critically wounded.

"My mother will get a heart attack if she hears it," Linda sighed and spilled a bunch of black pepper on the table.

I decided to start working on my project. I pushed one table to the window, climbed on it and started painting the usual Hanukkah symbols on the glass. While I painted a *sevivon* (dreidel) an ancient looking oil vessel and candles, I looked out the window. The rain had stopped, but sluggish gray clouds still hung low, promising more rain. Thunder rolled in the distance, far above the Mediterranean Sea. Across from the dining hall, I could see a small team of soldiers search the apartments in the barrack-style buildings. One soldier stood on the patio, aiming a sub-machine gun at the front door, while the other kicked it open with his combat boot. It was like watching a movie. I knew what could have happened if the terrorists were hiding inside, but I was hoping that nothing awful would happen to the soldiers as long as I was watching them.

Zorik came in a few minutes before eight o'clock. His dark blue shirt and hair were sopping wet and his knee-high black rubber boots were covered with mud. Like all the men on the kibbutz he was helping the soldiers search for the terrorists. I saw him through the window lead the soldiers from one apartment to another, drawing with white chalk a large X on the doors of the cleared rooms. It reminded me of what God did to the doorways of the children of Israel before they escaped from Egypt with Moses. Only He did it with blood.

"Why aren't you in the bomb shelter?" Zorik asked me, pouring himself a mug of black coffee.

I already knew what to say. Instead of saying something selfish like "I didn't feel like getting stuck in the bomb shelter with everybody," I said, "I came to decorate the dining hall for Hanukkah." I knew it would get me off the hook. The grown-ups loved to hear that we kids wanted to contribute our time and energy to the kibbutz.

"That's wonderful," he complimented and yawned.

Since he didn't preach at me to join my peers in the bomb shelter, I decided to try my luck and ask for the confidential information about the chief-of-staff. "So what's going on? Any news about the chief-of-staff?"

Zorik stretched his legs under the table and shook his head. "All we know is that Danny was shot through the door when he got up to check why his dog was barking. We don't even know how many of them are around."

"How's Danny?" I asked, trying to sound like a grown-up. They always inquired about people's health even when they already knew the answer.

"Not so good. He got hit in three different places. One bullet went through his neck. But the doctors are optimistic."

I didn't know what to say. Was I supposed to ask where the other two bullets hit him? Or how his wife was doing?

Zorik got up from his chair and took his mug to the dishwashing room. I followed him, determined to get more information. "What were all the shots we've just heard?" I persisted.

"People are nervous. They shoot at anything. The terrorists can be anywhere for all we know," he said. On his way back into the dining hall to collect his umbrella he stopped and said, "Don't worry. They'll find them."

I watched him limp toward the kitchen. A few years ago he fell off a ladder while picking avocados and broke his leg. It never healed properly. That was why all he had to do was mark the doors with Xs and deliver sandwiches. When he disappeared behind the dishwashing machine I climbed back on the table and painted more candles and doughnuts and a brown vessel of oil with three yellow drops pouring out of the spout. Underneath, I wrote in Hebrew, "*Nes Gadol Haya Poh.*" Each word in a different color.

Linda and Monica, who finally finished wasting time on the salt and pepper shakers, decided to come help me. The first thing they asked was what the words I wrote on the glass meant. Instead of just translating each word, I told them the whole story of Hanukkah. I told them about the Jewish rebellion against the Greeks who defiled the holiest temple in Jerusalem with the statues of their Gods and Goddesses. How the Greeks forced the Jews to eat pigs. How one woman named Hanna watched a Greek general slaughter her seven children because they refused to eat pigs, and how the general poked her eyes out afterwards, or perhaps she blinded herself, I couldn't remember exactly how it ended. I also told them about Judas Macabee and how he defeated the Greeks and kicked them out of Jerusalem and when he came to light the menorah in the holy temple there was no oil anywhere. After a long search all over the temple, he found a tiny jug of oil that was nearly empty and lit the menorah and the oil lasted for eight days.

"And that's why we celebrate Hanukkah and write the words, a Big Miracle Happened Here," I concluded the brief lesson and showed them how to write only the first letter of each word: *Nun, Gimmel, Hey, Peh.*

First they practiced writing the letters on paper napkins, then they moved on to the windows. They were so proud of themselves. Every time someone passed outside they knocked on the glass and pointed excitedly at the letters they had painted. As usual, Monica received all the praise and attention, even though Linda did a much better job.

Meanwhile, a sporadic stream of soldiers and kibbutzniks passed through the dining hall. Some came to get something to eat; others came to relax for a few minutes over a cup of coffee. Zorik, who came in to get more sandwiches, looked at the decorated windows and muttered, "Yes, it will be a very big miracle if we find them and nobody else gets hurt."

"What did he say?" Linda asked.

"A big miracle, that's what we need, a miracle," Zorik sighed in a heavily accented English.

A second after he finished saying "a miracle," we heard a loud burst of gunfire and all the candles and the flames we had painted vibrated on the windows. I looked out between the letters *Nun* and *Gimmel* and saw a thin plume of smoke rise above the treetops, not far from the kindergarten area. I turned to ask Zorik what it was, but he was already gone.

I painted the windows in silence, absorbed in my own speculations. A few minutes later, two wet corporals and a sergeant entered the dining hall and marched to the soda fountain without wiping their muddy combat boots on the straw mat by the glass doors. I jumped off the table, rushed across the dining hall and asked if they wanted some coffee. They said they'd love it. As I filled the mugs, I felt the sergeant watching me and shivered. Was it pleasure or self-consciousness, at the time I didn't know, but I did know not to let them leave without giving me the latest scoop. I placed the steaming mugs in front of them and asked, as if I weren't really interested, "So what were all those gunshots we've just heard?"

"They found them," one corporal said.

"Really? Where? Who found them? How many are there? Did they kill them?" I asked. I was so excited to be the first one in the dining hall to hear the news that I didn't notice Monica and Linda join us at the table, sensing that something dramatic had happened.

"Your friends want to know what we're talking about," the sergeant motioned with his head toward Monica who was making all kinds of faces and questioning gestures to attract my attention.

"They found the terrorists," I said in English.

"They found the terrorists?" I heard a loud shrill behind my back. I turned and saw Shoshana coming out of the kitchen with a tray of fresh sandwiches.

"They found the terrorists," I said, this time in Hebrew, proud to be the messenger of good news.

Shoshana ran into the kitchen screaming the news, forgetting to leave the sandwich tray on the table. We heard more screams of surprise from the women and excited voices talking simultaneously. A moment later Shoshana came back with the same tray, put it on the table, and invited the soldiers to come inside the kitchen. I followed with Monica and Linda behind me. I listened as the young sergeant told the anxious women that during the search two kibbutzniks opened a bathroom door and the terrorists, who were hiding inside, shot one of them.

The women gasped. Dvora's hand grabbed her neck and the whites in her eyes almost popped out. "Who was it?" she asked in sheer terror.

The soldiers didn't know the name of the man who'd been shot, but assured the women that he was alive and walking. The bullet only grazed his forehead above the left eyebrow and the paramedics had already treated him.

After I translated what the soldiers said, Linda decided to go to the bomb shelter. "I can't stand it anymore," she whispered to me in English.

"Are you going, too?" I asked Monica, hoping she would stay with me.

"I don't know," she answered. "I think I'm getting a headache."

"Come on," I nudged her upper arm. "We can stand by the window and watch the action."

"No one is standing by any window," the sergeant stated authoritatively.

Until now I was sure he didn't understand English. I thought about arguing with him but he was not a kibbutznik. Besides, I still wanted to make a good impression on the soldiers, even though it appeared that they were a lot more interested in Monica, who looked gorgeous even in the kibbutz-issued blue work clothes.

"She thinks she is going to stand by the window and watch the show. What do you think this is, a circus?" Tzipke scolded me after the soldiers left. All the eyebrows around me rose in disgust.

"I think Maya can help us prepare lunch," Tamara decided.

With Monica and Linda joining their friends in the bomb shelter, I was afraid the women would send me to do all the shit work the Americans usually do. "What are we making for lunch?" I asked, careful not to give them any wrong idea like sending me to wash dishes or mop the floor.

"Don't pretend you don't know," Shifra, who was in charge of the children's kitchen, sniffed at me. "You've lived on the kibbutz long enough to know what we eat on Friday," she added, and the black hair that grew out of a nasty mole above her upper lip bristled when she spoke.

I did know the weekly menu. Even without working in the kitchen I would have known what was on the menu. Since the dawn of my childhood, and as far as my memory could go, every Friday we had hot dogs, spaghetti and canned corn for lunch. "Hot dogs?" I asked, incredulous. I couldn't believe they would prepare the same food on a day like this one. I mean, why couldn't we try something different for a change?

"Isn't she wonderful?" Shifra jeered.

I wanted to kick her. I was on the kitchen staff long before she joined us. I probably knew how to cook better than she could, too. "You want me to cook the hot dogs?" I said, trying to hide my anger.

"No," she said, her brown mole snickering at me. She wanted me to go to the walk-in refrigerator, get a huge bucket of machine-peeled potatoes dipped in freezing water, and with a sharp knife dig out the black eyes the machine had missed. Then, she said, she wanted me to make mashed potatoes for those who didn't want spaghetti.

I was so mad. For almost an hour I sat on an empty vegetable crate, alone in the dish room, dipping my fingers in freezing water and peeling slippery potatoes, while the women were keeping warm by the stoves and chatting about the day's events. Even

Monica, whom I had hoped would stay with me to the bitter end, went into hiding when she saw what I had to do. I hated myself for obeying Shifra instead of standing up for myself.

I can tell Shifra to get lost. What can she do to me? Tell my mother that I am a bad girl? Like I care. I don't have to do what she says. But then who would make mashed potatoes for those who don't like spaghetti?

I tried to ignore the annoying argument inside my head, but before I was able to resolve it, a series of loud explosions shook the building. The large windows above the stainless steel sinks rattled furiously and for a moment I was afraid the glass would shatter and rain all over the sinks and me. Everything around me vibrated and shook violently. The noise was deafening.

I ran out of the dish room. There was no fear in the kitchen's air. Only curious suspense. The women did not move. They stood silent in their posts by the large pots, clutching wooden spoons and ladles. Then Aliza said very quietly, "I wonder how long this is going to go on."

After several minutes that felt like an eternity, the shooting and the explosions stopped, but still we didn't move. It could have been just a break between explosions. I found myself thinking that the silence was scarier than the explosions because we had no idea what was going on.

I had to go somewhere, anywhere, out of the kitchen. I couldn't bear the silence. If I stayed around those serious expressions for one more minute, I would start giggling out of control. I went to the dining hall, sat down and stared at the breadcrumbs on the table. Shortly afterwards, people started to come in for lunch. The men came with M16s and Uzis slung over their shoulders, and slid them on the floor under their chairs. They looked tired and a bit relieved and the tension was completely gone from their faces. The women who did not have to stay in bomb shelters with the kids came to listen. Everyone was talking in low voices about the terrorists. No one complained about the lack of mashed potatoes, no one noticed the painted windows, and no one wondered why I was not in the bomb shelter with my classmates.

When I got up to collect the brushes and the paint containers I had left by the window, I overheard one of the men say that only one terrorist was found and killed.

"The commander of the northern region used the megaphone to call him to surrender," he said. "And other officers talked to him in Arabic and ordered him to come out with his hands above his head. But he didn't. So they blew up the place with hand grenades. There was no reason to take risks, especially because he was so close to the kindergarten."

"Luckily he wore a wetsuit," someone commented. "Imagine what it would have been like to get him out of there without it. We would have had to scrape him off the walls with putty knives."

Before sunset I went on a pilgrimage to the room in which the terrorist was killed. I was not the only one drawn to the center of the drama. In front of the house, on the trampled grass, there was a line of kibbutzniks, waiting to enter the room and witness the aftermath of the killing. I approached the line, embarrassed by my morbid curiosity but not enough to stop listening to the quiet conversations.

"It's a miracle the terrorist chose this room," Rivka, the gardener's wife, said. "Can you imagine what would have happened if Yogev had been there?"

Of course no one wanted to imagine what the terrorist would have done to Yogev, if he were sleeping in his bed instead of serving his country in an undisclosed army base in the Golan Heights. Like all the other soldiers, Yogev did not come to the kibbutz on Thursday nights; only on Friday. I wondered how Yogev would react once he found out that his new stereo system and record collection had been blown to pieces by hand grenades.

"How did he get in anyway?" Mona asked the people behind her, and started up the stairs without waiting to hear the answer.

"Maybe he found the key under the door mat," Rivka called after her.

"Maybe Yogev didn't lock it," her husband, the gardener, speculated.

"We sometimes forget to lock our door," Dinah said, getting to the front of the line.

"You forget to lock the door, not me," her husband corrected her.

"I started to lock my door only recently," Ayelet, who stood behind me crocheting a pink baby boot, said.

I stopped listening to them until Mona emerged from the room, shaking her head and rolling her eyes up. "When Yogev comes to the kibbutz someone should have a serious talk with him. This boy has to learn to hide his key in a better place," she said, walking away.

Finally it was my turn to enter the room, or what was left of it.

"Don't touch anything." Sasha, wearing a wrinkled pair of shorts revealing two white, skinny legs, warned before I stepped in. "And don't stay too long. There are more people waiting to get inside."

The destruction of the little apartment was uncompromising in its totality. A mound of debris erupted from a wide gash in the floor and met twisted metal bars that poked out of the ceiling. Concrete boulders were strewn around the mutilated walls, sharp and threatening. Layers of dust and metal grates lay on the exposed guts of the whitewashed wall that once separated the bedroom from the small living area. A jagged hole in another wall marked the kitchen window through which most of the hand grenades flew into the room. The lush ivy that hid that window from the morning sun was now lying lifeless on the rubble.

I stepped into the bathroom, where the terrorist was hiding during the last moments of his life, expecting to be overwhelmed by a gruesome sight. There were no bloodstains anywhere, or torn flesh, or even the stinking smell of gunpowder and burned hair. Evidently, as the soldiers said, the expensive diving suit had kept the terrorist intact, I thought, as I stumbled over a pile of empty twisted bullet shells. I picked up one shell from the floor, put it in my pocket and walked out of the room.

The soldiers were still searching the bushes, the roofs, and under the buildings for more terrorists, even though people inside the blown up room said that the commander of the northern region was almost certain that there were no more terrorists inside the kibbutz. At two thirty in the afternoon the army tracker found fresh marks on the gravel road that ran parallel to the border fence. They looked like the footprints of two men heading north into Lebanon. A new hole in the border fence marked their crossing spot.

At five p.m. the search was over and life was going back to normal. Friday night dinner was going to be served at the dining hall as usual, and the children were going to sleep in their own beds rather than in the stuffy bomb shelters. It was time to go to my little apartment to check the damage inflicted by the search team.

Muddy footprints led from the concrete walkway to the staircase. The stairs were smeared with mud and sprinkled with grass clippings and leaves. I climbed the stairs, avoiding the mud lumps, and opened the front door. From the entrance I could see that the bathroom door was wide open. My bath towel was lying on the floor between the toilet and the sink. I went in and picked it up. As I was turning to hang it on the hook, a flood of unexpected thoughts hit me. The terrorist died in an identical bathroom. He was probably hiding behind the shower curtain when the soldiers tried to talk him out of there. Someone in the blown-up room said he was about seventeen years old, maybe even younger. He was my age and he was already dead. I sat on the toilet, clutching the soiled towel.

Did you think that you could fool the entire Israeli army? I wanted to ask him. You? A teenager with no experience at all? Didn't they tell you in the training camp that you could die here, you stupid idiot? Didn't you know that you had no chance? That you were doomed the moment you entered the kibbutz? Do you know that in the dining hall people were laughing at you? They made hot dog jokes about you, while you were lying dead on a stretcher behind the fly-infested kitchen dumpsters, waiting for the ambulance to come get you and your fancy diving suit.

Of course, I could not mention these weird questions to anyone. Hardly even to myself. I knew that if the terrorist had survived the battle he would have been hunting for my blood because I was the Zionist oppressor; or at least one of their daughters. Yet, I could not stop thinking about his age and how he died behind the shower curtain. So I remained in my confusion and participated in the jokes. And at dinnertime, when everyone was celebrating our own miracle of Hanukkah, I was talking tough like all the other combat soldiers.

For days I could feel the dead terrorist following me in his expensive diving suit and swim cap. He was with me when I read, when I ate, when I listened to music, when I went to bed, when I was asleep. He pushed against my ribs, underneath my breasts, suffocating me with his shredded body. He did not let me rest. One morning I woke up before sunrise and knew that I was possessed, that my body had become a tomb.

"I want us to get out of here," he said.

"Where to?" I asked.

"Anywhere you wish to go," he said.

"I am not ready to go anywhere," I said. To myself I thought, there isn't any place I want to go with you, but I didn't want to hurt his feelings.

"Come on, you can't lie to me. I know you better than you think. I know you want to leave. " There was a sense of urgency in his voice.

"If you're so smart why don't you tell me where I want to go?"

"You want to go as far as possible, maybe to America," he said.

I couldn't understand how he knew my secret. I hardly dared to toy with that idea. I still had to finish school, serve two years in the military.

"You hate it here," he said.

"Shut up," I said. "What do you know about me? You're just a stupid dead terrorist with impossible dreams. If you were so smart you wouldn't be dead now."

"Maybe I'm a stupid dead terrorist, but I know that you decided to leave the kibbutz one day. "

"Don't tell me what I'm going to do or I'll kill you like the soldiers did," I threatened.

"I can't shut up," he said. "I have to talk to stay alive."

I didn't know how to kill a dead terrorist with impossible dreams so I skipped lunch and dinner, hoping that I could starve him. When I woke up the next day I didn't hear his voice. I started eating again. I thought I was rid of him.

A few months later I was window-shopping while waiting for a bus to take me back to the kibbutz. A tall, skinny mannequin wearing a blue bikini, sunglasses, and a wide-brimmed straw hat caught my eyes. I entered the fancy boutique to take a closer look at the display, knowing that I could not afford anything in that little store. A round rack laden with one-piece and two-piece bathing suits stood at the back. My hand reached for a bright red bikini. It was irresistibly adorable.

"Nice stuff," I suddenly heard a familiar voice.

My hand let go of the bikini. I was surprised and a bit embarrassed. A cute, little boutique for women's clothes was not an appropriate place for a young dead terrorist. I doubted that he had ever seen a woman in a bathing suit.

"You should get it," he declared.

"What does it matter to you?"

"You'll make heads turn," he chuckled.

"That's crazy," I snapped. "You should worry about your fight for self-determination, not fashionable bikinis."

"I can't," he said. "I can only fight your wars now."

"Well, I don't need this bikini."

"Who said anything about needing? Everyone likes to buy something new once in a while. It makes people feel good. You're going to look great in it."

I started to blush then I remembered that he couldn't see. "I already have a bikini. I don't need two."

"You really disappoint me," he said.

"Look," I started to feel defensive. "Where I come from people don't judge me by my looks. The way I behave and work is a lot more important. I know that you come from a different place and that you live by different rules, but you have to understand that on the kibbutz it's different."

"Ah," he said, "I didn't know you cared about all that stuff."

"Well, I don't, but sometimes I have no choice." He was confusing me with his questions.

"Of course you have a choice," he insisted.

"That's your opinion and I'm not interested in it." He was really starting to annoy me. "Why don't you just leave me alone? I don't want to hear you anymore."

I started to sleep longer hours to keep his voice in check. I didn't want to talk to him. I didn't want to hear him. But he kept showing up. I felt as if he was watching me from inside and hearing silent voices that I could not even hear myself. I could not stand it. I had to find a better way to rid myself of him. I decided to send a combat soldier to deal with him. I didn't want to pay attention to his constant blubbering. He was stubborn and not smart at all.

The combat soldier was very logical and patient at first. He explained to the dead terrorist how things were done on the kibbutz. He said that it was almost impossible to change things and that the rules were very clear and simple to anyone who lived there for more than a week. He said that some of the rules, the least important rules, could be sometimes changed by a majority vote during the Saturday night assembly. He told the terrorist about the long debate that had taken place only a few years earlier about whether or not to allow a small refrigerator in each apartment and how some members objected because it was against the principles. Then the same controversy repeated itself when some members thought it would be nice to also have a television set in every apartment. There were lots of heated arguments around the dinner tables in the dining hall about principles and ideals and the kibbutz social fabric, and the danger of succumbing to urban materialism. Even the decision whether or not to remove the *"kolboiniks,"* the little bowls into which the dining room eaters discarded eggshells and cucumber peels, had to be brought to the general assembly. I even reminded the combat soldier the funny stories my parents told about the long debates that had taken place in the early days of the kibbutz when some members wanted to have a radio in their rooms, and others suggested distributing an electric water kettle to every married couple. People were horrified at those suggestions, my parents laughed when they reminiscent about it. Those ideas reeked of the selfish contemptuous materialism of the petit bourgeois.

Our way of life, the combat soldier said for the hundredth time, was embedded in *"Takanon Ha'Kibbutz,"* the mysterious guidebook which no one saw or read, but everyone knew existed. Whenever we wanted to change something, we had to look at it to see if it agreed with the Kibbutz Movement's principles, values, missions. I imagined the *"Takanon"* as a big black book, its hard jacket faded and dusty and stained from years of neglect, its pages covered with long lists of rules that the movement founders had written years ago in old-fashioned Hebrew saturated with brave slogans about social justice and equality, love of the land and personal sacrifice.

One day, when I got tired of the constant quarrels and questioning, the combat soldier scolded the terrorist, "You always have something to complain about. Why can't you be happy with what you've got. Be glad that you're alive."

But the dead terrorist was not convinced. He insisted on being heard until the combat soldier got fed up and said, "Okay, you say you want privacy? You want to be on your own? I'll fight for it and I'll give you privacy."

And the combat soldier fought for my privacy so bravely that I ended up entirely alone. I had no one to talk to. The grown-ups annoyed me with their demands and constant criticism, my classmates bored me, my parents hardly noticed me. I even broke up with Yonnie. Or maybe we decided together it was time to end the relationship. It didn't matter to me anymore. I told Yonnie he could find a better girlfriend. That I needed to concentrate on my school work. We hardly ever saw each other anyway. He was busy with the army, doing secret things I did not dare to ask about.

"At least you proved to the terrorist that you could get what he wanted," I consoled the combat soldier when he realized what he had done. "You are strong and brave and I'm very proud of you."

Afterward, when the terrorist said that he wanted people to treat me nice, the combat soldier, who had become arrogant and cynical, told him, "Why do you care? I don't care about anybody, and nobody cares about me and that's the way I want it."

My combat soldier was so committed to the cause and strong as any other kibbutznik, I allowed him to guide me through the years. He taught me not to wish for what I could not have. He taught me to accept what I didn't like, how to hide my feelings, how not to care. He taught me to pretend. He erected high walls around me, dug deep bunkers and surrounded them with barbed wire and cannons. With his help I became an emotional survivalist. And a better liar.

And the dead terrorist kept reappearing in my life. Wanting and demanding, wanting and insisting, and begging, and failing, and trying again and again. Never giving up completely. Every few months I would hear his whisper wanting something and I would call the combat soldier and he would crush him with his fierce logic because I could not take the risk of listening. And the combat soldier, who by now had become an expert, marched on and buried the dead terrorist under my heart.

I stopped wanting. I forgot what I wanted. Wanting reeked of selfishness and greed and materialistic shallowness. I knew what other people wanted but I had no idea what I wanted for myself.

And I didn't care. At last I proved to myself and to the rest of the kibbutz that my heart belonged to a combat soldier who could face all dangers and defeat my greatest enemies.

Sadly though, I didn't realize that every time I asked the combat soldier to kill the terrorist I let him kill another part of me. The dead terrorist tried to fight back. But his voice became weaker and weaker. It trembled in the middle of the night. It sighed and whispered. Sometimes it even cried in a strange muffled voice. I pushed him away from me without any effort. I heard less and less of him until he disappeared.

Finally I could sigh in relief. I had won my battle. I killed the terrorist for good and adopted everyone else's wishes. No one would be able to say that I was a failure. I became the walking epitome of selflessness: I didn't want anything and I didn't own anything.

Without conviction I followed the rules, feeling dead inside, pretending that I was alive. No one knew the depth of my despair. People were protected by an enlightened ideology that preached sacrifice and emotional austerity. I had no excuse or ideology to protect me from these great ideals, only a silent voice that urged me to escape as far as I could go.

Chapter Nine

When I first mentioned to my mother that I was thinking about leaving the kibbutz she treated it as a childish caprice. I was almost twenty-one years old, and apart from the two years of mandatory service I had spent in a dusty, sun scorched army base, I had lived all my life on the kibbutz.

"Why should I stay?" I grumbled when she insisted that I should give the kibbutz a fair chance. "I stopped liking this place a long time ago and I am not going to start liking it now."

"How do you know you won't like it?" she argued. "You've never lived here as a kibbutz member. You were always just one of the kids. Give yourself a few years and you'll see. It'll be completely different. I promise..."

"How come you didn't ask Avner to stay?" I interrupted. My brother left the kibbutz less than a year after he completed his military service and she did not say a word about it.

"Avner is a man," she waved her arm in total disregard. "He made friends in the army. I knew they would help him. But with you it's completely different. You have no experience living in a big city. You don't know anyone. How are you going to survive? What are you going to do? Work as a babysitter? Is that what you want to do? To waste your life like that?"

"Yes," I sulked. "That's exactly what I want to do." Her arguments were very close to the truth, but I was afraid to admit it even to myself.

"You know your father and I can't help you," she began another line of argument. "We can't buy you a house or a car. We don't know anyone who could give you a good job. Besides, what do you think you're going to find in the city that you can't find here? Do you think life is easier in the city? At least here you can work as a teacher, a *metapelet*, a nurse. Here you can make a difference. People know you, they care about you. They say good morning when they see you on the way to work, they say good evening, they say shalom. But in the city no one is going to talk to you. Not even your neighbors.

"And who do you think is going to take care of you if you get sick? No one. No one is going to care whether you're dead or alive. It's a jungle out there. So many people everywhere, and cars, and garbage, and noise, and thieves. What do you need all this for? So you could say that you live in the city? No one is going to give you a medal or write about you in the newspaper if you do it. Anyone can live in the city. But not everyone can live here, in this paradise we built here for our children, not for all these parasites who only yesterday moved here from the city and now demand everything from the kibbutz as if they deserved anything. We worked here all our lives for you, not for them. So why don't you work here for one year before you make a decision? Show everybody that you care, contribute one year of your life to the kibbutz. It won't kill you. Besides, don't you think you owe it to the kibbutz after everything the kibbutz has given you?"

It was a waste of time to argue with her. She could go on like that for days, glorifying the kibbutz as if it were the best place on earth. I knew all these arguments by heart. Heard these lies a thousand times. In the kibbutz we cared about values and morals, not about making money and showing off. Our lives were richer here. We didn't have to worry about what the boss thought about us because there were no bosses. We didn't judge people by what they do or by the size of their house because we were all equal. We were free to pursue our interests and be who we really wanted to be. We truly cared about one another, blah, blah, blah. All lies.

"A year is too long," I tried to negotiate. I needed time to prepare myself for life in the big city, but a year seemed like an eternity.

My answer did not satisfy her. "I saw Jeff at lunch today, he said he wanted to talk to you," she said, suddenly becoming totally interested in her painted fingernails.

Of course Jeff would want to talk to me. As the new coordinator of the young generation committee his job was to talk to me, keep me in the kibbutz, make sure I didn't leave too fast. "About what?" I asked.

"Your future."

"I don't want to talk to him about my future."

"Nothing will happen to you if you talk to him for five minutes," she insisted, tight-lipped.

The next evening I found myself waiting for Jeff in front of the cultural center. I cursed myself for giving in. There were better things to do on a hot and sticky summer night than fighting bloodthirsty mosquitoes and listening to a lecture about the merits of the kibbutz from someone who lived most of his life in an affluent suburb of Chicago. I wanted to go back to my room, take a cold shower, lie on my bed, listen to the *Moody Blues,* and feel sorry for myself.

The concluding signal of the long, depressing news program burst out of the crowded television room and put me on alert. Soon Jeff would come out looking for me. I lit a cigarette, crossed my bare legs, and wondered what would be the fastest way to get rid of him and his tiresome ideals.

"I have a feeling you forgot it's Thursday night," Jeff announced the moment he spotted me sitting on the concrete bench.

"And what's so special about Thursday night?" I frowned, already irritated at his cheerful disposition.

"It's ice-cream night," he smiled and rubbed his hands in satisfaction. "Want vanilla, chocolate, or both?"

I could not stand him when he behaved liked that: pretending to be excited about nothing. In America, I was sure, he ate ice cream twice a day. Once I heard him brag that they had more than thirty ice-cream flavors over there. Like I cared.

"Vanilla," I said.

Following the crowd that spilled out of the stuffy television room, Jeff rushed to elbow his way through the double glass doors. Three tattooed giants from New Zealand, who worked with the banana plantation crew, were pushing to get inside and sent him to the end of the line. I knew that with his impeccable American manners he would never dare to push back, especially not the muscular giants.

I concentrated on my cigarette until he returned, sat next to me, and handed me a chipped ceramic cup full of melting vanilla ice cream. I put the cup between my knees and waited for him to start preaching.

"I heard you want to leave the kibbutz," he opened, looking wistfully at his ice cream and playing with the spoon.

"Mhmm."

Jeff raised one eyebrow and started to recite in his American accent all the familiar slogans. "Maya," he said, "what do you know about life? You've just finished your military service. You're too confused now. Why don't you take some time to think? Have some fun, enjoy your life. Don't make any decisions, yet. You still have all your life ahead of you."

"First of all, I am not confused," I opened slowly, ominously. "Second of all, I have nothing to do here, and third of all, I can't live here. The routine will kill me."

"What do you mean you have nothing to do here? There are tons of things to do here," he complained.

Show me one, I wanted to say, but I didn't want to start arguing with him.

Jeff licked his spoon and started speaking very slowly, his demeanor oozing dramatic confidence and secrecy. "What would you say if I told you that you could start studying agriculture next year at the Weitzman Institute of Science? I think the secretary and the education committee will approve it without putting you on the higher education waiting list. The secretary himself told me that the kibbutz is going to need an entomologist pretty soon."

"Me? Study bugs? I hate bugs. I don't want to study agriculture," I suddenly panicked. My plan to intimidate Jeff with cool indifference evaporated at the thought that I would have to chase insects and look at them up close.

"What else would you like to study, then?" he asked.

"Anthropology."

"Anthropology? Come on, Maya, you'll have to study something you can use here, you know that," he said what I had expected him to say.

"Of course, I know, but that doesn't mean I can't want," I said.

"I'll talk to the secretary and to the education committee and we'll see what we can do." He patted me on my knee to reassure me that everything was going to be fine.

I shrugged. I already knew that there was no way the education committee would let me study anthropology. I mean, what would an anthropologist do in the kibbutz?

It was almost ten o'clock when our conversation was over. Jeff asked if I wanted to go inside the cultural center for a game of backgammon but I was in no mood for games.

"Cheer up, Maya, everything will be okay," he promised. I could hear in his voice that he was not convinced.

I went to my room. I was not tired but I had to go to sleep. In a little over five hours I would have to get up and go to work in the greenhouses. I didn't like working there. Sasha was in charge of the greenhouses and he treated anyone who was under thirty like a slave. He constantly reminded us to work when we stood around and talked, insisted that we do things only his way, even if it took twice as long to do, and the moment I showed some initiative or started enjoying what I did, he would send me to do something else. It was a no win situation for me. Boring, boring, boring work.

I couldn't fall asleep. The windows were open but the hot air was still and heavy. Outside, the crickets were competing for attention and the dogs were carrying on, showing no consideration for humans who had to get up before sunrise. I pushed the sheet away and pulled the curtain open. What was I going to do? How much longer would I have to do this? Get up, go to work, eat, go to my room, sleep alone, get up and start all over again. How long would I have to live in this room, in the *Ravakia*, the singles' section, surrounded by other unmarried kibbutzniks fresh out of the army, with no boyfriend on the horizon and no way of escaping the numbing daily routine? Higher education was my only way out, but studying agriculture was not something I fancied.

Anthropology seemed so much more exotic and full of possibilities.

If only I had the courage to leave right now. Take the little stuff I had and go to Tel Aviv, rent a room, find a job, start a new life. But how? With what money? What job?

I surveyed the small square that was my private kingdom. Several potted plants I got from the nursery stood on concrete blocks under the window. The iron-framed full-size bed stood under the other window. A synthetic imitation Persian rug that used to belong to my parents covered most of the floor between the bed and the opposite wall. In the corner, I had hung two shelves and placed a round table and two chairs that were assigned to me by the furniture committee. A small radio, an ancient record player, a stack of records, an electric kettle, and a few Pyrex cups and plates were crammed on the shelves. The room was small and in need of more personality but I liked it. It was mine. I did not have to share it with anyone. I even had my own bathroom and shower. And I could live there for as long as I wanted to.

That was a scary thought. I could stay there for the rest of my life. Waiting for something to happen. Alone. In the kibbutz. For the rest of my life I'd be working under the command of men like Sasha, washing greasy pots and vegetables in the kitchen, mopping floors in children's houses, grafting avocado plants, weeding strawberries, picking lemons, trying to avoid old *metapelets* and teachers, eating in the noisy dining hall. At night I could pace the deserted walkways, go to the cultural center, look for someone to talk to, something to do.

I woke up with a start. Someone was knocking on the door.

"Maya, good morning."

It was the night guard. Luckily I didn't trust my alarm clock and put my name on the wake-up list, otherwise I would have slept till eight.

"Good morning," I mumbled to let him know I was awake. It was three thirty. I was tempted to keep on snoozing but I was afraid I wouldn't wake up on time. I jumped out of bed, splashed cold water on my face, got dressed, and was ready to go in five minutes.

As soon as I got out, a shiver passed over my body and the hair on my arms stood up. In a few hours it would get so hot I would have to take off my long sleeve shirt and put on a hat, but now the air was cool and sweet and so quiet, I wanted to breathe it all in. The color of the sky was quickly turning light gray and several bulbuls were already greeting the morning from the treetops. Dawn was my favorite hour. Once I was up and walking, I loved witnessing how the deep colors of the night burst into flames that brought the new day.

Since the greenhouses were situated less than one kilometer east of the residential area of the kibbutz, behind the cowshed and the barns, I decided to walk there instead of taking a bouncy ride with the tractor. I wanted to savor the magical moments of sunrise by myself, in silence.

No one was at the greenhouse area when I arrived. I entered the office and made myself a cup of tea with lots of sugar and lemon. As soon as I sat down, the rest of the crew arrived. After a short conference, Sasha sent me to prepare roses and baby's-breath for shipment with the help of two industrious Dutch volunteers. That was good news. It meant working in an air-conditioned room and away from the suffocating heat of the greenhouses. It also meant minimum contact with Sasha who spent most of his time supervising the work there.

I hardly spoke a word all morning. My mind was preoccupied thinking about my conversation with Jeff. I tried to convince myself that studying agriculture could be interesting. It would also get me out of the kibbutz for a few years. Give me time to learn about life in the city. And why not study agriculture? I could learn to drive a tractor, roam the fields by myself, be my own boss. Why not give it a try?

Because I don't want to do it, I thought. And I don't want to be a teacher or a *metapelet* or a nurse. And I don't want people to tell me what to do all the time.

Then what do you want? I heard the question bounce in my brain.

I want to travel, meet new people, learn new things, get away from this boring place where nothing ever happened. But how? Where will I get the money to do all this? I needed to talk to someone. But there was no one to talk to. No one I knew was interested in my torment. They just expected me to stay in the kibbutz and love it.

Shortly after eight o'clock Sasha came in and said that a tractor was waiting for us outside. We took off our gloves, returned the flowers to the walk-in fridge, and joined the rest of the crew. This time I took a ride with the tractor. I did not want to waste half of my morning break on walking. I wanted to have enough time to eat and relax before going back to work. I saw Jeff enter the dining hall when I went to the coffee machine to fill my coffee cup. I fought my urge to approach him and ask if he had already talked to the secretary. Jeff saw me looking at him, sent an automatic yet uncommitted smile, and continued toward the food counter. No, he had not talked to the secretary, I decided, otherwise he would have come to talk to me. I felt the kibbutz's gates close on me. I had to do something before it was too late. But what could I do beside waiting?

At lunchtime I surprised myself. As usual, the dining hall was crowded and noisy, the heat unbearable, the flies rude and greedy, and the food an insult to the eyes. Around the table behind me, four American volunteers in blue work clothes were smoking cigarettes, laughing loudly, and ignoring the stern gazes Sasha was sending them from a neighboring table. I looked at Sasha trying to intimidate the volunteers and decided to show him that his scowling didn't scare anyone. Or maybe I wanted to show the volunteers that not everyone on the kibbutz was stiff and humorless like Sasha. I got up, went to the next table, and in my best English asked the volunteers, "May I have a cigarette?"

One of the Americans handed me a pack of Israeli cigarettes, identical to the green pack tucked away in my loose pants pocket, and offered a lit match. With the cigarette between my lips, I bent over the lit match and inhaled slowly. Then, handing him back the pack of cigarettes, I looked into his blue eyes, nodded a silent "thank you," and returned to my table. Sasha looked at me and shook his head in disapproval. I dropped on the chair, turned my back to him, and puffed into the air less than perfect smoke rings.

I did not give my dining hall show-of-force much thought until the next morning when I found myself sitting on a hard bench of a blue wagon pulled by a noisy tractor, heading down the hill to work at the banana plantation. I was glad to get away from Sasha and his greenhouses. But I was not prepared to see the American volunteer, who had given me the cigarette in the dining hall, sitting right next to me. And recognizing me on top of it. I nodded to show him that I recognized him, too, leaned back, and closed my eyes. The ride to the banana plantation was rough and bumpy and more than once we were thrown against each other when the wheels of the tractor rolled into the deep ruts that scarred the unpaved road. The American was very polite and apologized, but I became too self-conscious to come up with anything witty, so I only said, "no problem."

"*Lo* problem," the American tried to show off his knowledge of Hebrew.

"*Ein be'aya*," someone behind translated for him.

"*Ein be'aya*," the American repeated.

"No problem," I said. I didn't like it when foreigners tried to be friendly by talking to me in Hebrew. I couldn't care less if he didn't speak a word of Hebrew.

When we reached our destination, the tough guys did not bother to use the steps. They squeezed through the metal railing that surrounded the wagon and jumped down. I stood in line for the steps. The American was standing on the ground watching me. I pretended not to notice. He offered a hand to help me down.

I took it. He smiled. I didn't. When my feet touched the ground I put my hands in my pockets and walked away from him. Barak, the member in charge of the banana crew, called everyone – about fifteen of us - to stand around one of the banana trees and watch him demonstrate how to use a machete when clearing the stalk from the layers of dry leaves. The American followed me and stood so close to me his shirtsleeve touched my arm every time he moved. I tried to concentrate on Barak's words, even though I knew exactly what he was going to say. As usual he took the time to scare the new volunteers with the famous yarn about someone from another kibbutz - no one knew from which kibbutz or how true the story was - who accidentally fell on his machete and stabbed himself to death. "Watch what you're doing with this thing," he grinned wickedly, as he handed us the rusty machetes and the belts.

The rows started at the dirt road and stretched far into the distance where they converged into a messy jungle brightened up by blue plastic bags that were used to cover the banana bunches. I chose a row and attacked the first tree with my machete. Inga from Denmark worked slowly by my side. She took Barak's story too seriously and was carefully pulling each dying leaf from the stalk, cutting it gently, and watching it fall down. The tattooed giants from New Zealand worked side by side a few rows down. I could easily hear their laughter, their machetes cutting the dry leaves and their work boots crunching them on the ground. They worked so fast, that in a few minutes their voices disappeared in the thicket. The American was nowhere to be seen.

It was hard and boring work, but suddenly I felt like acting as if cutting dry banana leaves was my dream job. I told silly jokes to Inga whose delicate frame and silky blond hair looked completely out of place. I flirted with the New-Zealanders every time they passed me, and never stopped admiring their tattoos. In turn, they laughed at what I said and complimented me on my slashing technique. The American was nowhere.

At seven o'clock Barak called Inga and I and asked us to go prepare breakfast for the crew in the large shed that was used for storage and occasionally, as an improvised dining room for the workers. The regulars liked to eat at the shed and save the time it took to drive back to the kibbutz. Eating at the plantation was also more satisfying for them because they could eat as many fried eggs as they liked, instead of eating the usual hard-boiled eggs that were served at the dining hall for breakfast every morning.

Inside the shed there was an industrial gas stove, a deep stone sink, and a few long wooden planks that were used as tables and long wooden benches to sit on. Inga started setting the tables and I settled in "the kitchen." I boiled water for coffee, washed vegetables and arranged them in large plastic bowls, opened containers of margarine and soft cream cheese and olives, and stacked piles of sliced rye bread in plastic breadbaskets. Then I started making the special treats. I fried onions and thin slices of salami, broke eggs on top and scrambled everything to perfection. I fried onions in melted margarine and added slices of Swiss cheese and eggs, I made salami omelets and added to them green and red peppers and onions, and Swiss cheese omelets with tomatoes and onions. The smell of fried eggs and coffee was divine.

At exactly eight o'clock the door flew open and the starved crew came in. Skipping polite conventions, the men attacked the food, piling their plates up high as if they had not eaten for days. I stayed by the stove to take special orders, but everyone seemed happy with the selection, so I joined them at the table.

The American sat at the other end of the table, facing me. I could see him talking to Inga, listening intently to whatever she was saying. Suddenly I felt jealous. No longer was I of any interest to him. Now she was getting all his attention. Of course she would. She was a pretty Scandinavian and all men were crazy about them. Thin, blond, blue-eyed princesses from Hans Christian Anderson's fairy tales, as gracious as swans. Why should he be interested in someone like me? A muscular kibbutznik with dark hair, a small forehead, brown eyes, scratched legs, bitten fingernails and so little finesse. My heart sank. I found myself not wanting to eat.

I got up and went to the sink with my coffee cup and cigarette. He could be friendly to anyone he wanted to. I don't care and I don't need to sit and watch him do it, I thought to myself. There was a ton of dishes in the sink waiting to be washed.

I was up to my elbows in soapy water when people started to bring their dirty plates to the sink and return to work. "Good job," Barak complimented me. "Thanks" another one said behind my back and strolled outside. "Best omelet I've ever had," the American whispered in my ear, leaning over me and squeezing my shoulder. His long curly hair tickled my face. It smelled of fresh shampoo.

It made me dizzy with anticipation.

When Inga and I were done with the cleanup we walked back to the plantation. It was hot outside. Flies were everywhere. I didn't feel like working anymore. I didn't want to think about what the American said to me. He confused me with his attention. I liked it when he talked to me, but when he was not around I started to think too much about him. It was no use. That was how they behaved in America. They were friendly. He just wanted to talk to someone from the kibbutz, improve his Hebrew or something and, by chance, I started a conversation with him the day before. It was nothing. I shouldn't have given it so much thought.

I tried to concentrate on my work, watch the machete go up and down the stalk. Who cares what he thinks about me, anyway? Tomorrow he would go back to America and forget he'd ever talked to me. I should stop thinking about him. Just work. That was my final decision. Just ignore him.

During break I saw him again. He offered me a cigarette but I declined, took a long gulp of warm lemonade from the plastic jug, and went to lie in the shade. I wanted him out of my system quickly, even though, my body refused to cooperate. My heart fluttered every time I caught him looking at me, my face blushed under my deep suntan, and tingling perspiration collected under my armpits and inside my bra. I was worried that he would notice the effect his blue eyes had on me.

At lunchtime he followed me across the communal dining hall, balancing a tray of vegetables and rice on one arm, the machete dangling from his leather belt. I spotted a vacant table by a window and sat down.

"May I?" he asked.

I shrugged and moved my tray from the middle of the table.

"You never told me your name," he said, sitting down.

"Maya."

"What a pretty name. Do you want to know my name?"

Sure I wanted to know his name, but what difference would it make? "Yes, I'm dying to know," I said. What else could I have said?

He laughed. "Ari."

"Hi Ari," I said stupidly, suddenly forgetting my entire English vocabulary.

"You're supposed to say nice to meet you," he said and shoved a forkful of rice into his mouth.

"Nice to meet you," I said.

He laughed again. "You're funny."

I wasn't trying to be funny. I wanted to be sophisticated and worldly like the women he probably knew in America.

"So where are you from?" he asked.

"From here," I said a bit surprised at the question. "Where else could I be from?"

"You mean you were born here?"

"Unfortunately," I answered, this time trying to be funny. But he did not take it as a joke.

"You don't like living here?" he looked curious, surprised, as if I had said something incredible.

"Not really," I said.

"Wow," he looked at me appreciatively. "That's really interesting."

He didn't ask me why I didn't like the kibbutz but I sensed he wanted to know. I started telling him stuff I didn't think I could tell anyone on the kibbutz. I told him about how bored I was of the predictable life I had on the kibbutz. That the only thing I could strive for was to get married and have at least three children. I told him how much I hated not being able to make my own decisions about anything, not even about what I ate. I told him about how frustrating it was to have to ask favors from people every time I needed something and then have to be grateful to them for the smallest thing they did for me. I purposely used the word "frustrated." I hoped he'd notice. It was a good word.

"Where would you go if you left?" he wanted to know.

"Tel Aviv probably. My brother lives there. He left a few years ago," I spoke fast, not entirely convinced.

"And what would you do there?" he asked.

"Now you sound like my mother," I said, annoyed more at the nagging question than at him. How could I know what I would do there? Let me get there first, then I'll try to figure out what to do. It's not like I was living in the land of endless opportunities where only the sky was the limit.

"It's just so interesting what you're saying," he sounded apologetic. "I thought everyone loved it here."

"It's like everywhere else, I suppose. Some people like it, some don't," I tried to sound magnanimous and philosophical, as if the kibbutz were really like every other place. I mean, how on earth could I explain to him that leaving the kibbutz was equal to denouncing a way of life that everyone I knew tried to instill in me since the day I was born? That leaving would be a reflection on my weak character and my inability to understand the true "greatness" of the kibbutz? How could I explain to him, a person who had never lived on the kibbutz, that all the ideas I was raised to believe were just ideas, big words most people practiced without honesty and conviction? How could I explain to him that people in the kibbutz confused equality with sameness? That from the day I remembered myself I was supposed to be like everyone else? Love the same things, want the same things, enjoy the same things, believe in the same things? How could I explain to him that in the kibbutz any sign of individuality was considered as a character flaw, as a sign of selfishness? That only blind obedience was appreciated and expected of me? How could I explain to him that everything I was raised to believe turned out to be a lie? That there was no real freedom in the kibbutz, only strict rules and regulations and narrow mindedness. How could I talk about the hypocrisy and about my disillusion and not sound bitter, mean, ungrateful?

I looked around. The dining hall was almost empty now. I was so engrossed in my internal monologue I did not notice it got so late. Apart from us, only the usual latecomers were still eating lunch, occupying two tables at the other corner of the dining hall. The servers already cleared the food counters and wiped most of the tables around us. I collected my dirty dishes and took my tray to the dishwashing room. Ari followed behind. On the way out he asked if I was going to work in the banana plantation again the next day.

"I'll have to look at the schedule tonight to find out," I said.

"I hope I see you tomorrow," he said.

We split. He headed toward the volunteers' section, I headed toward the *Ravakia*. On the way to my room my brain was driving me crazy again with questions. Why did he hope that I would work there again? Did he really mean it? He couldn't have. He was just trying to be nice. I could tell that he was more interested in Inga. She was so sexy, wearing a bikini bra and shorts to work in the banana plantation. And sunglasses. Whoever came to work wearing sunglasses? And why did I have to talk so much at lunch just because he sat at my table? I probably bored the hell out of him. How I hated myself when I behaved like that. Talking, talking, talking about myself.

I took a cold shower and dropped naked on the unmade bed without drying myself. It was so hot, I didn't mind getting the sheets damp. They'd be dry in no time. For a few minutes I stared at the ceiling, my mind completely blank. I got up, turned the radio on, listened to music for a while, turned it off. I felt empty and restless. What was he doing now? Was he sitting on the lawn in front of his room talking to her? Playing with the other Americans that weird game they called football? Maybe I could go to the swimming pool and check if he was there, pretend to be surprised if I saw him.

I got up, put on my bikini, a long t-shirt and flip-flops, grabbed a towel and a book and left. Two kibbutz women were doing laps in the deep side of the pool. The lifeguard was sitting under a beach umbrella listening to loud music that blasted out of a small radio. Inga and another volunteer from Sweden were lying on towels on the grass, baking themselves in the merciless afternoon sun. Dotan, one of my old classmates, was hammering something by the fence that surrounded the swimming pool area. He saw me, nodded and kept working, occasionally eyeing the blondes on the grass. I hardly ever saw or spoke to anyone from my class. Although some of us were living in the *Ravakia*, we did not hang out together. I guess, after living in such close proximity for so many years in the children's house we lost interest in one another.

I opened my book and tried to read. Every few minutes I looked up. Nothing. I went for a swim. Got out of the pool. Some high-school kids showed up and jumped into the pool. A few minutes passed and more kids came, jumped into the water, and started playing with a ball, screaming each other's name and laughing loudly. I collected my stuff and left. Disappointed.

There were more important things to worry about, I reminded myself on the way back to my room. I still had to talk to Jeff, find out what the secretary said. Make some decisions about my future. Stop obsessing about that guy. Go to my parents' room to tell my mother about the prospect of me studying agriculture.

The next day, again, I went to work at the banana plantation. Ari did not show up. At first I was sure he did not wake up on time and missed the ride. Then I became convinced that he got fed up with the hard work and decided to go back to America. After all, he did not have to do it. He did it because he wanted to do it. For him it was an adventure, an experience, something to write home about. Not real life.

At lunch I discovered why he did not show up for work. He was working in the dishwashing room. "Until Friday," he said when I came to unload my tray into the machine. "Someone got sick," he explained although I did not ask.

"Enjoy yourself," I said and turned to leave.

"Wait, wait," he called me above the noise. "What do you do later?"

"Nothing. What is there to do?" I said the first thing that came to my mind. Why should he care about what I'm doing, anyway?

"Want to go to the beach?" he asked.

"Sure," my mouth said before my brain registered all the implications. I always looked for someone who'd want to go to the beach with me.

"Good," he said. "I'll wait for you by the main gate at four."

All my doubts and self-criticism evaporated when I saw him lying on the concrete bench in the shade of the she-almond tree by the gate, waiting. An army jeep was parked next to him, but the guard was nowhere. I approached him quietly and stood right behind him. "I'm here."

He jumped into a sitting position, smiling. "Great. I was afraid you'd change your mind." For a split second I could swear he was checking me out, even though I was wearing an extra-large men's tank top over my bikini. He was wearing shorts and a white t-shirt, a blue baseball cap and the type of sandals we called Biblical sandals.

On the way down the hill he told me that his family lived near San Francisco, that he took a year to travel in Asia after graduating from college and was planning to go back to America in a few months. He said he wanted to go back to school to study photography. After traveling for so many months he decided he wanted to be a professional photographer, keep traveling all over the world, and take pictures of extreme weather patterns and nature and indigenous people, whatever that meant. I was tempted to tell him that I wanted to study anthropology for similar reasons, but I was afraid he would not believe me. Plus, I was almost sure that the education committee and the secretary would not approve and I would have to go study how to kill bugs.

It was still hot at the beach even though the sun was starting to descend toward the horizon. We crossed the gravel road that covered the old train tracks that separated the sandy beach from the corn fields. I took my flip-flops off and ran to dip my feet in the water. The sand was soft and burning hot and the water felt oily warm, not even a little ripple disturbing the calm. We walked further down the beach and stopped by a cluster of jagged rocks. I liked to lie in that spot. It made me feel protected from curious onlookers. Ari took off his t-shirt and ran into the water, making big splashes. I sat on my towel and watched him swim until he turned around and called me to join him.

The water was warm and full of slippery brown seaweed. I tried to avoid the seaweed, shoving it to the sides as I walked the shallow area toward Ari. He was floating on his back, kicking the water. I dived under the surface until I ran out of breath, came out for air, and swam back to the beach. Ari came shortly after me. I watched him walk toward me. He had no hair on his chest at all. Anywhere. I thought he looked like a Greek god. He shook the sand from his towel and lay next to me.

"Do you come here often?" he broke the silence the second I began feeling self-conscious about lying so close to him and saying nothing.

I started liking him. He wanted to know things about me. He was interested in what I had to say. He thought I was funny. He did not just say, ah, and yeah, and sure, and right when I asked him something. He could talk. He told me things about himself and his family. He made me comfortable.

I told him I used to go to the beach a lot more often before. He asked if I stopped going because of the occasional bombings and the skirmishes on the border.

"The *Katyushas* are not the problem," I laughed. "They fly above us and explode ten kilometers away from here. It's the perverts from the city who come here to gawk at young girls in bikinis that scare me. They hide behind the bushes over there and look at us like they've never seen a woman in their life." I pointed at some low bushes that grew by the road we crossed earlier.

"So I'm your protector now," he declared and flexed his biceps.

"Yes," I laughed. I was feeling more relaxed near him. He turned on his belly, rested his cheek on his arm and closed his eyes. I dug my toes in the sand, covered my eyes with his baseball cap, and before I knew it, I fell asleep. I woke up when the sun was quickly approaching the sea. The sky was on fire. Ari was lying next to me, asleep. I didn't want him to miss the best part of sunset when the sky presents the wildest spectacle of colors and shapes. I touched his shoulder and rocked him gently. He mumbled something. I touched him again. His skin was warm and silky. He opened his eyes and looked at me, sleepy and a bit disoriented.

"We can't stay here after dark. The soldiers will come and tell us to get lost," I said.

"Hmm," he agreed. He rose on his elbows, looked at the sun, pulled his body toward me, and put his head on my lap.

I needed to mobilize all my willpower not to let him feel the petrifying stupor that engulfed every muscle, tendon, and nerve in my body. I concentrated so hard on the sun, it looked green. I could feel his breath on my skin. My hand went to his head and caressed his hair. He made an indiscernible sound. The sun sank into the sea. He did not move. Then the armored personnel carrier passed behind us. I could hear the sound of the engine turning, then it stopped. It was time to go.

We walked back to the kibbutz in silence. I wanted to get there fast, before the mosquitoes found me. I also needed to take a shower. But most of all I needed to think about what happened between us. I didn't know Americans well enough to interpret what he did. They were different from us. More touchy-feely, open, comfortable with their bodies. I did not know what putting his head on my lap could mean. Friendship? More than friendship? A pillow?

"Will you come to the pub later?" he asked when we reached the gate. It was getting dark and I was anxious to get to my room.

"Maybe," I shrugged. The volunteers hung out in a bomb shelter behind the dining hall, where they drank free beer, listened to music, and played chess and Ping-Pong. I hardly ever frequented that place. It was dark and stuffy and there was nothing comfortable to sit on.

"I'll see you later, then," he smiled, putting his hand on my shoulder and letting it slide over my arm.

I didn't go to the pub that night. The next day I worked at the banana plantation and had breakfast with the crew at the shed. At lunch I went to my parent's room. He was working in the dishwashing room and I needed to avoid the dining hall.

My mother came in and asked about my conversation with Jeff. I told her he suggested I study agriculture because the kibbutz needs an entomologist.

"Do you want to study agriculture?" she asked in disbelief.

"Of course not," I said.

She wanted to know what I wanted to study instead. I told her. She said what I expected to hear: that the kibbutz did not need an anthropologist and what would I do with a degree in anthropology. How about biology? I could always teach biology at the regional high-school. The conversation was going to develop into a fight. I didn't want to talk to her about becoming a teacher. She was annoying me with her predictable questions and suggestions.

"You always think you know everything," she concluded, exasperated.

"Yes, I do," I shot back at her and stormed out.

I avoided the dining hall for the rest of the week. I wanted to see him badly, but I did not have the courage to face him. What would he say? What would I say? I missed him. I thought about him all the time. It was unsettling. I kept telling myself that he probably did not think about me at all. He was having fun with the volunteers, playing games, drinking beer, laughing all the time. What did he need me for? All I talked about was how much I wanted to leave the kibbutz, how much I didn't like the place. Why should anyone want to listen to this stuff? Suddenly life became even more awful. My loneliness tripled. While before I was just lonely and bored, now I was lonely with a purpose.

On Friday, long after lunch was over, I decided to go to the communal kitchen and make a chocolate cake. Everyone had a fresh cake on Friday. Even my mother who was a lousy baker baked a cake every Thursday night. The only difference between us was that she had an oven and a kitchen. I didn't.

"Hey, stranger," I heard his voice behind me as soon as I walked into the kitchen with all the ingredients in a plastic tub.

He was not supposed to be there so late. He was supposed to finish work at two thirty, three o'clock at the most. Instead, he was mopping the floor around the dishwashing machine.

"Hi, what are you doing here so late?" I tried to sound friendly but indifferent. Not too surprised.

"Where did you disappear? You were supposed to come to the pub the other day," he ignored the question, moving dish racks around and mopping underneath.

"I didn't feel like it," I shrugged as if it were nothing.

"Too bad," he said and approached me, dragging the mop on the floor. "What are you making?"

"A chocolate cake."

"Mhmm, I love chocolate cake. Can I help?"

"Okay," I said. What else could I have said? He was so friendly, acting as if nothing happened. Here I was tormenting myself for days and he did not notice anything.

He put the mop and rags away. I asked him to oil the baking pan. He watched every move I made and vocalized a lot more admiration than I deserved. When I put the cake in the oven he asked if I was going to eat it all by myself. I made a funny face. He wanted to know who was going to eat it.

"You," I said, completely off-guard.

"Great," he rubbed his hands together. "How about me going to take a shower while this is baking, then I come to your room and we have a tea party. I'll bring the cigarettes."

I had to be crazy to turn him down.

I forced myself not to open the oven every two minutes to check if the cake was done. At last, the knife came out dry. I put the cake on a tray, covered it with chocolate frosting I had prepared while the cake was baking, filled a small jug of milk, and carried everything to my room. My little kingdom was a mess. I needed to make the bed, sweep the floor, fold my clothes, wash dirty cups, scrub the toilet. I watered the plants, put a white tablecloth on the table, picked three red roses from the rose bush outside, arranged them in a bottle I found tucked in the cupboard, and went to take a shower.

When I got out of the shower, I treated myself to the luxurious body lotion Avner's wife gave me for my birthday, which I did not bother to open until that moment. I also took an unusual long time to decide what to wear. After much vacillation I decided to wear a white cotton dress that was kind of tight around the waist and a little lacy on the bottom. He never saw me wearing a dress before. I wanted him to see that I could also look feminine and charming, if I wanted to.

The cake was cooling under the roses. My room smelled clean and fresh. The windows were open, and the curtains were fluttering in the little breeze that passed between them. I sat on the bed and waited. And waited. And waited.

I realized that my body was tensing up every time I heard someone walk outside. I told myself to stop behaving like an infatuated teenager. He said he'd come. Give him time. I put "Wish You Were Here" on the record player. Side one finished playing and he still did not come. I started to get mad at myself. Stupid me. Getting all dressed up for nothing. I should have known. He probably met his friends and completely forgot about me. I looked at the roses on the table and felt totally pathetic. Stupid, stupid me. I changed the side of the record and plopped on the bed. I should read something. Get my mind off this whole thing. It was not like I expected him to come in the first place. I made that cake only because I needed to do something. I lit a cigarette, lay on my back, stared at the ceiling. I started to hate myself. Evening started to fall. Soon it would be night and I'd be sitting here like an idiot in my white Shabbat dress, waiting for Prince Charming to come and rescue me from boredom. Hanna'le is waiting for Eliyahu to help her instead of the other way around. I wanted to laugh, then I wanted to cry. I got up, went to look at myself in the mirror. My eyes looked sad and defeated. Why was it so hard for me to find some happiness in this place?

I didn't want to turn the light on. I found a box of Shabbat candles in the drawer and stuck two in my candleholders. I lit the candles and put them next to the roses. The Pink Floyd finished playing. I put Leonard Cohen on. His soft, deep voice and melancholic songs suited my mood. I lay on my bed and stared at the dancing flames until my eyes burned. The turmoil was slowly leaving my body. I began to relax, silence the constant chatter inside my head. Breathe in, breathe out, listen to the music. I fell asleep.

Someone was knocking softly on the door. I didn't want to wake up. The soft knocks persisted. I looked at my alarm clock. It was almost nine. My head was foggy, full of sleep. Too early to go to work. What day was it anyway? The candles were burning low, filling the room with huge shadows. I went to open the door.

"I'm so sorry, I fell asleep, I hope you're not mad at me, are you?" he begged, a painful smile on his face.

I opened the door wide and moved to let him enter. He walked in, squinting, unsure of his step. I turned the light on.

"No, no, please don't turn the light on," he covered his eyes with his hands.

I turned the light off. He dropped on my bed, rubbing his face and his eyes. I stood next to him, watching him, saying nothing. "I'm so sorry," he said again, shaking his head. He took my hand and held it between his hands. I would have been happy standing there forever, but the candles were dying fast. I went to get another pair of candles, lit them, replaced the old ones.

He sat up, looked at me. "I meant to come right away. I told you I would. I took a shower, smoked a little joint, and the next thing I fell asleep. I just wanted to rest for a minute, you know," he smiled his painful smile again.

I was too full of emotions to say anything. I stared at him stupidly. Didn't know what I felt anymore. "I can make some coffee if you want," I said.

"Thank you," he sighed in relief.

I needed to do something while he was squirming on my bed. I took the kettle to the sink in the bathroom and filled it with water. Back in the room, I pulled a chair and sat in front of him. "You shouldn't tell people you don't know really well that you smoked a joint. You'll get kicked out of the kibbutz, they'll deport you from the country, you'll get in trouble with the police."

He took my hand again and looked into my eyes, steady. "I'm telling it to you, not to everybody."

I looked away. I couldn't let him look into my eyes like that. "Okay."

He got up, looked out the window, took a deep breath. "Nice room you got here. You don't have to share it with anyone."

"I know. I like it this way."

He nodded. Then he started to talk about his traveling and how he hadn't slept in a nice room by himself since he left home almost a year ago.

"I don't feel sorry for you," I said.

He laughed.

Hearing him laugh made me feel better. He was getting back to himself. Talking about his travels, enjoying himself, not so apologetic and miserable. I made two cups of Nescafe and set them on the table. He followed me with his eyes, and that was when he saw the cake. He wanted to taste it. I cut a large piece and invited him to the table.

"I'm starving," he smiled.

I offered him another piece. No, he was full, he said. He got up and went to check my record collection. Chose Segovia, put it on the record player. Turned to me and asked if I felt like smoking. I told him there was a pack of cigarettes next to the record player.

"That's not what I meant," he said.

"Ah," was all I said.

He took a little tin can from his pants pocket and rolled a thin cigarette. He lit it, inhaled deeply, and offered it to me, coughing. I took it. Put it between my lips and inhaled. The tip was a little wet from his saliva.

"Who would have guessed that a little kibbutznik like you would know how to smoke a joint," he smiled.

"Actually, we don't smoke grass. We smoke Hashish," I said as if I were a big expert. When I was in the army I smoked that stuff several times but the risk made me too paranoid to enjoy it.

"Right," he said, coughing.

We smoked in silence listening to Segovia. My head started to spin. My mouth was dry. My thoughts were going nowhere. I caught myself staring at Ari's fingers handling the joint. There was a little cut on his thumb and a silver ring on the little finger. I asked him where he got the ring.

He looked at the ring for a long time and said in Hebrew, "*taba'at*." Took it off and said "India." The ring was made of two snakes wrapped around each other. He took my hand and dropped the ring on my palm. "You can have it," he said.

I put it on my little finger but it was too big. I slid it on my pointing finger and said, "thank you."

"*Toda*," he said.

"Your Hebrew is getting better every day," I spoke slowly, making sure my mouth was really saying what my mind wanted it to say.

"*Ken*, will you be my teacher?" he asked and sat on the floor in front of me.

"What do you want to learn?"

"How do you say, come sit next to me?"

"*Bo'i shvi le'yadi.*"

"Over here," he said in English and patted on the carpet. I sat next to him.

"How do you say I love you?"

"It depends on who says it, a man to a woman or a woman to a man," I said, trying to sound like a teacher, although my heart almost jumped out of my chest.

"How does a woman say it to a man?" he asked, concentrating on the tip of the joint and making sure it didn't burn his fingers.

"*Ani oh'evet otcha,*" I said, looking at the floor, picking at the carpet.

He tried to make the Hebrew *ch* sound and started to cough. Then he asked, "how does a man say it to a woman?"

"*Ani o'hev otach,*" I said slowly.

"*Ani o'hev otach,*" he repeated, taking my hand and putting it on his chest.

I didn't move. He kept looking at me. Then slowly, slowly, he moved closer and kissed me on my lips. I closed my eyes. His lips stayed on mine. I opened my eyes and looked into his eyes. He closed his eyes. He put his arms around me and I melted into him. Again, and again, and again. Thank you God for letting this happen, don't let this ever stop, I love him more than I can think, please God, let me feel him next to me forever, I'll do anything for you, just don't let it end.

We were up all night, reveling in each other, devouring each other, whispering words I'd never believed were possible to utter. It was not a wild dream I was living, but an enchanting movie in which I was the star. "I love you," he whispered in my ear every time he melted into me. We were making love in English, the language of famous movie stars, the only language I could say "I love you," without feeling like a total idiot. And it made me feel sublime, heavenly romantic, beyond anything I could imagine.

All day Saturday we stayed in my room. When we got hungry we ate chocolate cake. Going out to the world was out of the question. There was too much to find out about each other. We did not want to waste our precious moments on going outside, mingling with people ignorant of our love, and behaving as if nothing out of the ordinary had happened. On Saturday night we sneaked out of my room and went to check our schedule for the next day. Ari's name was written under Bananas. My name was written under Kitchen. Ari went to get his work clothes and came back to my room to spend the rest of the night with me.

Early in the morning, dressed in work clothes and ready to go to work, I realized that once we stepped out of my room, together, it would be a declaration to the world. Anyone who saw us by my room at such an early hour would arrive at the only possible conclusion, and a rumor would start floating around the kibbutz: Maya had a night visitor, she is sleeping with a volunteer. My neighbors would be curious. My mother would pretend she didn't know. I tried to explain the situation to Ari. He smiled. "I can't hide here all day," he said.

"I just wanted you to know that," I said.

"*Ein be'aya*," he said and followed me out the door. He closed the door and put his arm around me. Then he bent and kissed me on the lips. Outside, in front of my room. "Let them think whatever they want," he whispered in my ear and kissed me again.

"Okay," I said even though I wanted to bury myself. Not twenty meters away from where we were standing, I could see Tzipke walking by, on her way to the kitchen, pretending that she did not see him kissing me.

"Come on, it will be okay," he said with the typical optimism characteristic of people who've never lived on this kibbutz.

After our first weekend together, Ari started spending more and more time with me. At first he would come every evening after dinner. After a week he started coming before dinner and going to the dining hall with me. Then he started coming to my room directly from work. People started getting used to seeing us together and we stopped hiding in my room when we wanted to be together. We looked and behaved like a couple. Suddenly the kibbutz felt like paradise. Nothing mattered as long as Ari was near me. He brought most of his stuff to my room and hardly ever spent any time with the volunteers.

I did not dare to think about the meaning of our relationship. The present was so precious, thinking about the future was too dangerous. I knew that Ari would not stay on the kibbutz forever. Not even for me. His future was in America, studying photography, traveling around the world, living life the way he chose. My future was going to be decided any day by the secretary and the education committee. Study agriculture or anthropology and remain on the kibbutz, or pack my stuff and go to Tel Aviv. Make the big leap forward and see what happens. The only question was how much longer I would have to wait.

It took Jeff a month to bring me the news. The secretary brought my request to the education committee and the decision was not in my favor. However, if I really wanted to study anthropology I could put my name on the waiting list. "Things change," Jeff said, "next year there will be more money and you'll probably have a better chance."

I tried to hide my distress from Ari but he could see that something was wrong. He wanted to know what happened. Did he do something? Did he say something? I promised him it had nothing to do with him.

"Then what is it?" he insisted.

I told him about the committee's decision.

"Do you want to study agriculture?" he asked.

I shook my head.

"Then what's the problem? Don't," he said as if it were that simple.

"But I can't stay here forever doing the same thing every day," I finally started the conversation I was afraid to have; the conversation that would decide the future of our relationship.

"Who said you have to?" he was a bit confused by my frustration.

"No one says it. But now I have to leave."

"And?" He couldn't get it. For him things were so much simpler. "You always said you wanted to leave," he tried to make sense.

"I know, but how?"

"You pack your stuff, and leave."

"And what about us?" the question popped out of my mouth. I didn't plan to ask him that. I never meant to put him on the spot, that was why I never wanted to talk about the future, but it had to come, and it did. There was no way back anymore.

"You don't want to leave because of me?" he asked. I've never seen him so serious. I started to cry. "Not while you're here."

"Maya, am I making you stay on the kibbutz?"

"I was waiting for the education committee and the secretary to decide if I could go to study anthropology, but now that I can't there is no reason for me to stay here." I didn't want to say those words but I couldn't lie to him. And I didn't want to sound as if I were putting pressure on him. I was confused and afraid of losing him.

Ari said he wanted to go for a walk. He needed to think about stuff alone. I begged him not to leave. I was panicking and he could sense it.

"I need some time to think," he said slowly. "I'm not going anywhere, I just need to be by myself," he repeated. I always knew that somewhere inside he was a lot more pragmatic than he looked, more mature, more American. He did not panic so easily.

I paced in my room all evening, imagining the worst case scenarios, biting my nails and trying not to cry. He was leaving me, there was no question about it. He was leaving the kibbutz. It was fun as long as I did not say anything, but now he was going to leave. He was going to leave anyway, go back to America. He said that a long time ago. I was too desperate to think straight.

At midnight he returned. His breath smelled of cigarettes. His shirt smelled worse. He looked tired. The smile in his eyes was gone. He sat on my bed and asked me to sit next to him. I wanted to throw myself at his feet and beg him to forget the entire conversation, pretend that nothing has happened. "There's something I want to ask you," he opened. That was a bad opening. He had bad news and I did not want to hear it. I was exhausted. I just wanted him to hug me and tell me that he loved me and that somehow we would find a way to stay together.

"Did you ever think about going to America?"

My mind went blank. What was he trying to say? What does he want me to say? I couldn't remember anything. Did I ever think about going to America? I probably did when I was in high school. Or was it Australia, England, Holland?

"I can't remember."

"Would you like to?" He could see that my mind went blank. "Take your time."

I stared at him. America? I would go to the end of the world with you if that was what you were trying to say. "You mean, me? Go to America?"

He nodded.

"How? I don't know what I'm going to do in Tel Aviv and you ask me about going to America?" It was after midnight and he was asking me about America.

"Yeah," he said, completely serious. "Would you go to America with me?"

"With you?"

"Yeah."

"Do I have to say yes or no?"

"Yeah."

"I think I would," I said, slowly.

"That's a good start," he smiled.

I felt encouraged. "What have I got to lose? It's not like they really need me in the kitchen or anywhere else. I can leave, I always wanted to. And once I leave, it's all the same, isn't it? Tel Aviv, America, what's the difference? A big city is a big city." I was starting to feel much better, much, much better, almost giddy with excitement.

"Can we go to sleep now?" Ari asked, crawling under the sheets, pulling me with him. "We'll talk about the rest tomorrow."

I couldn't wait to break the news to my parents. At last, I had a plan. A vague plan, not very well thought of, but it was still a plan. I was going to stay with Ari. I would go to America. Our relationship was not over.

My parents wanted to know if Ari was Jewish.

"Yes."

"Are you going to get married?"

"Don't know."

"What do you mean you don't know?" my mother panicked.

"We didn't talk about it."

"Who's going to support you?" my father asked.

"I'll get a job."

"Doing what?"

"I don't know. I'll find something."

"How long are you going to stay there?" they wanted to know.

"I don't know."

"A month? Two months? Three months?"

There was no way I was going to tell them.

"I don't know. I'll go and see."

"Boaz, talk to her," my mother nudged his shoulder, irritated, as if I were not sitting in front of her.

"Maya," my father tried to reason with me. I knew it was hard for him. He wanted me to stay in the kibbutz forever. "Where are you going to get the money for a ticket? Where are you going to live? What do you know about this person, anyway?"

"I got money in my yearly stipend and I was hoping you'd lend me the rest. I'll pay you back as soon as I get a job," I quickly recited my plans, ignoring the other questions.

My mother looked at my father questioningly. "What about your studies? You were planning to go to the university," she demanded.

"I'll go when I come back."

"When are you planning to come back?" my father tried to trap me, negotiate with me.

"She told you she doesn't know," my mother barged in, directing her anger and frustration at him instead of at me.

My father nodded heavily, looking a bit defeated. "I'll give you the money, but I want you to promise me that you'll come back."

He did not dare ask me if I was planning to leave the kibbutz for good. I knew he couldn't talk about it. After Avner left the kibbutz the burden of their expectation that I stay almost choked me, but I was not going to give in. I did not want to spend the rest of my life in the kibbutz, and if they couldn't accept it, I could break the news gradually, make it easier on them. I told him I'd be back in a year.

"A year?" my mother shrieked and went to the bedroom, slamming the door behind her.

My father looked at the bedroom door. "Talk to the secretary," he sighed. "Tell him that you're planning to take a year off. Everyone has the right to take a year off. Go to America, see the world, enjoy your life, and come back. Remember that your life is here, in the kibbutz."

Chapter Ten

I didn't know what to expect. Of course I was nervous, but not scared. I knew that America was a huge country populated by skyscrapers, six-lane freeways, vast cornfields, and everything the highest, the biggest, the tallest, the deepest, the fastest, and the longest. But I also knew, from personal experience, that Americans were a friendly bunch who loved to play Frisbee in the afternoon, swim naked, play guitar, listen to the right music, and get stoned. I had nothing to be afraid of. If I ever got lost I could always ask someone for directions because I knew how to speak English, and that gave me all the confidence I needed.

The plane landed in San Francisco. I was jet-lagged, overwhelmed by the size of the terminal, and intimidated by the aloof immigration officer who stamped my passport after examining me suspiciously, as if I were an international terrorist or a dangerous drug smuggler. Ari met me at the airport and took me to his parents' home. There, less than two hours in America, I realized that knowing how to speak English was not enough. America was a completely different world.

It dawned on me when I entered the guest bathroom. It was beautiful. The ceramic tile, the floor mat, the shower curtain, the framed picture on the wall, the neatly folded towels, the sink, the garbage can, the shell-shaped soap dish. Even the decorative soap balls in the soap dish were of the same color and flower design. I did not dare touch the towels or the soap. I flushed the toilet, wiped my hands on my jeans, and tiptoed outside, hoping I didn't leave a trail of water drops or fingerprints on the marble surface that surrounded the sink. I felt clumsy, provincial, and out of place. I prayed that no one would notice my inadequacy.

I tried to hide my ignorance but there was no way around it. I had to learn everything from scratch. Even basic stuff like how to open cereal boxes, potato chips bags, salt containers, bottles of pills, milk cartons. "Don't tear it with your teeth, look for where it says, Open," Ari suggested once when he saw me struggling to open a bag of chocolate chip cookies.

I had to learn how to order food in restaurants and how to do it fast. Did I want it small, medium, or large? Did I like it rare, medium rare, or well done? Before I even knew what salad dressing was (in the kibbutz dining room we used only vegetable oil and lemon juice) I had to know if I wanted my salad with dressing, without dressing, or with dressing on the side. Waiters wanted to know if I liked my eggs scrambled soft, medium, or hard, up or over easy, over medium, over hard? Soft-boiled, hard-boiled, poached, fried, grilled, low-fat, nonfat, sugarless, decaffeinated? On white, rye, wheat, sourdough? On a sesame bagel, onion, garlic, poppy seed? The possibilities were endless.

Sometimes, even before we left the house, Ari wanted to know if I felt like seafood, or maybe I preferred Chinese, Italian, Indian, Mexican, Thai food? Suddenly I had to know exactly what I wanted, and how I liked it. And there was so much to choose from. I had no idea what I wanted.

The most embarrassing part, though, was learning to be polite. In the kibbutz people did not bother to be polite to one another. They hardly ever said "thank you," "please," or even "you look great." Most likely I would run into someone in the dining hall and she'd ask me if I had gained weight or would make a comment that my hair looked terrible and why can't I get a decent haircut once and for all. But in America I had to say "thank you," "nice to meet you," "please," and "excuse me" all the time. I had to learn to say "pardon?" instead of "what?" which translated into the simple Hebrew word "*ma*?" and made Ari cringe every time he heard me say it. I could not understand the subtle difference between "I'm sorry," and "excuse me," and ended up sounding a lot sorrier than I felt most of the time. Because in the kibbutz people never had to introduce themselves, I did not know how to behave during the introduction ritual. When people extended a hand and asked, "How do you do?" I always wanted to ask "Do you mean *what* do I do?" but I never did. Instead I taught myself to shake their hands and smile.

Shortly after I arrived, we rented a one-bedroom apartment in the city, Ari started school, and I had to decide what to do. Ari suggested I teach Hebrew in one of the Hebrew schools in town, but I wanted to be around grown-ups. I had had enough working with children on the kibbutz. It was time for me to try something new. But what?

The fact that my kibbutz experience was not very useful in San Francisco, I already knew. But working in a restaurant would probably be just like working in the dining hall with the volunteers, I thought, and I wouldn't have to wash dishes or get up before sunrise. I told Ari I wanted to try to find a job in a restaurant. He was not excited about my idea to become a waitress but he did not do anything to stop me.

I collected my courage, put on my new jeans, which would have cost me a fortune in Israel but not in America, a touch of lipstick, and went out to conquer the world. My first job interview took place in a nice downtown restaurant, not too big, not too small, comfortable seating area, very business-oriented, fast-paced lunches, drinks, good tips. Previous experience required.

I waited for my turn in a booth by the entrance. The interviewer was a tall blond who looked like a model from a sleek fashion magazine I saw at Ari's parents' house. She was wearing a black blazer over a white silk shirt, gold earrings, a thin gold chain and a bracelet, her makeup was perfect and so were her long red nails. Her short blond hair did not move when she walked toward me, unsmiling.

"Nice to meet you. Please, sit down," she invited me to sit opposite her in the third booth. I shook her hand as if I'd been shaking hands all my life, noticing the neat pile of printed resumes that was facing her on the square table. I did not bring a resume. I didn't have one.

"Thank you," I replied, desperately trying to smile. She looked so pretty, confident and professional, I felt my courage quickly dissolve into complete nothingness. My knees felt weak. I waited for her to open.

"Well, tell me about yourself," she said.

I went blank. What was I supposed to say? I was not prepared to talk about myself at all. Was I supposed to tell her about the kibbutz? The army? Why I came to America? What my father thought about it? "What exactly do you want to know about me?" I asked, meekly.

The light in her eyes went off. "Tell me about your restaurant experience," she said very politely, leaned back, crossed her arms over her chest, and looked at me as if I were an exotic animal from a distant zoo.

I knew she was not interested but I started blabbering on and on. I told her I worked in a restaurant in Israel near Beer-Sheva, in the south, not far from the Dead-Sea. Which was true because I did try to work in a restaurant once, when I was in the army, but the sleazy owner made a pass at me and I quit right away.

She nodded, still patient. I felt compelled to talk, even though I wasn't sure she understood what I was saying since she didn't ask me how long I had been in the country, a question everyone asked me the second I opened my mouth. Finally she stirred as if out of a trance, smiled absentmindedly, thanked me, still incredibly polite, and promised to call in a few days. Nice lady. If I was interviewing someone like me, I would have kicked myself out of there and tell me not to waste my time, but she was an American and Americans knew how to behave.

I didn't tell Ari about the interview. And luckily, he didn't ask. He had to prepare a big project and a presentation for school. My little struggles to fit into his culture were not on the top of his list.

I went to another interview. This time I was ready to talk about myself and my extensive, yet fabricated, restaurant experience. And I had a fabricated resume to prove it, too. But I was not ready to sit in front of three serious judges in a ballroom crowded with fifty nervous applicants. When I heard my name, I stood up and started walking toward the long table where the interviewers sat. I felt as if a firing squad was waiting for me behind that table. I was absolutely terrified. I thought I was going to faint. Fifty pairs of eyes were staring enviously at my back hoping I flunked the interview, and six judgmental eyes were examining my posture, measuring my smile, my enthusiasm, my confident walk.

I don't know what I said during that interview, and it doesn't really matter. Better yet, I hope nobody remembers what I've said.

I kept Ari uninformed and wondered if I had made a big mistake coming to America.

My third interviewer was the headwaiter of a 50s-style diner. He wore black pants, a white shirt, a bow tie, black shoes, and a diamond ring on his right pinky. He was incredibly friendly and talkative. Before the end of the interview, I found out that he came from the Philippines, that he could sing Hava Nagila, that he practiced selective Judaism, lived a few months in Israel, thought that Israeli men were the sexiest men in the world, especially those in uniform, and knew Imelda Marcos. I was hired on the spot. No experience necessary.

In a few weeks I was taught all the secrets of the trade. I memorized the entire menu, learned to add, subtract, and calculate the sales tax without using a calculator, and recite the ice-breaker "Hi, how you doin' today, folks?" with a genuine smile. I learned to spot a good tipper, anticipate patrons' needs, and charm the kitchen staff.

Because of my accent, almost all my customers thought that I was French. Sometimes people started ordering food in French before I had a chance to tell them I didn't understand what they were saying. But once I told them I was not French they always wanted to know where I was from. I told them I was from Israel. They wanted to know from where in Israel. I could never understand why people wanted to know exactly where in Israel. The chance they would recognize the name of my kibbutz was below zero, so why ask? To make them happy I usually said Tel Aviv, knowing that most people knew the name of that city. Only rarely did I go out on a limb and said Jerusalem. Jerusalem was risky because of all the religious and political connotations, so I tried to avoid being from there, unless a customer assumed I was from there before I managed to give my usual answer.

I did not tell strangers I grew up in a kibbutz. Speaking about the kibbutz entailed too many explanations. Most people knew very little about Israel or life on the kibbutz. Those who thought they did got most of their information from Leon Uris's "Exodus." For them, the kibbutznik was a courageous pioneer; a sensitive, muscular Rambo who danced around the bonfire until dawn, then marched to dry malaria-stricken swamps and fight hostile Arabs. The more informed individuals thought that Israel was a vast desert inhabited by tanks and camels, and that the kibbutz was a special army base situated on the border. They would have been surprised to find out that my parents still lived there, that they did not eat kosher food or own a bank account.

In spite of the discomfort I experienced during those countless interrogations, I loved working at the diner. It felt like hanging out with the volunteers from the kibbutz all day long, but without any of the criticism and pettiness of the kibbutzniks. Brightened by lots of chrome, neon lights, and cute little jukeboxes, the diner specialized in classic rock 'n' roll and huge sandwiches even hungry people could not finish. It was as noisy as the kibbutz dining hall, with the music playing in the background all the time, but it didn't bother me at all. I liked everything about that place. And I was making money, too, which was a totally new experience for me. The waiters became my best teachers and my best friends. From them I learned to sit in bars after work, treat myself to colorful cocktails in tall glasses during Happy Hour, go to the movies on the spur of the moment, stand around and talk about nothing at parties. I also learned that to be a true American meant to know how to have fun. Every Monday, when I showed up for work at ten o'clock, everyone would stop to greet me cheerfully and ask me the same question, "So, how was your weekend? Did you have fun?"

I didn't understand them. What was the big deal about the weekend? And why were they so obsessed with having fun? The concept of Fun was so foreign to me. I knew about personal responsibility, social justice, sacrifice, self-restraint, politics, the Middle East, but fun had nothing to do with any of it. When I asked them why they always had to have fun they teased me that if I could only lighten up a bit I would become an American in no time.

"Except for the accent," I always reminded them. That, I knew, would never go away.

After several months I got used to having fun, and I even enjoyed it most of the time. I even learned to ask, "So how was your weekend?" enthusiastically, energetically, as if I really meant it. It felt as strange as saying "Merry Christmas" and eating marshmallows, but I was determined to fit in, and neither Santa Claus and his reindeer nor the icky stickiness of the white artificial substance I happened to taste at Thanksgiving dinner could deter me from doing everything I could to become a true American.

The kibbutz was quickly fading out of my mind, and except for the occasional letter I wrote to my parents and to Avner describing the great fun I was having in America, I tried not to think about it at all. Ari noticed my progress and congratulated me. He liked seeing me "integrate so well," learning the ins and outs of American life. He encouraged me to consider going to college.

When my visa was about to expire we decided to get married. We had a small wedding ceremony at Ari's parents' home. I wore white satin shoes with heels significantly higher than anything I had ever worn before, a white dress (not the bridal kind) with a beaded lacy shawl over my shoulders, which Ari's mother insisted I wear as long as the Rabbi was present. Ari wore a suit, minus the tie, and a white yarmulke that disappeared as soon as the Rabbi completed the ceremony and left. He looked sexy, smart, and worldly. I felt like Cinderella, but looked like a kibbutznik who was persuaded by her future mother-in-law to dress up for a party. We kissed, took pictures, drank champagne, cut a three-tier-cake, and danced. I sent my parents a mini photo album with copies of the wedding pictures, and wrote them that I had decided to prolong my stay in America. They did not protest. They congratulated me, wished me the best, and added that they had informed the secretary of the kibbutz that I was not coming back as planned. I was relieved.

Now that I was a married woman I could really start planning my future. But I still wasn't sure about what I wanted to do. My English was improving, but not fast enough, and besides, I was having so much fun with my new friends and making so much money at the restaurant, I didn't feel pressured to make drastic changes. I need more time, I insisted, whenever Ari asked me if my aspiration was to be a waitress for the rest of my life.

I've never heard the word "aspiration" before. I had to look it up in the dictionary. Then I realized that I did not have any aspirations. I'd never thought clearly about my future. The kibbutz was all I knew, and life outside the kibbutz was an unknown mystery, I couldn't realistically think about it, only fantasize and dream. As a matter of fact, when I told Jeff I wanted to study anthropology, my heart was not completely set on it. I was only intrigued by the idea of traveling to distant places and meeting new people. I could have easily said "architecture" or "linguistics" that night.

Like every major change that took place in my life, the decision to embark on a new career was the result of a coincidence, not the outcome of much thought and planning. I was working at the restaurant, serving lunch to a curious middle-aged businessman who wanted to know everything about me immediately after I greeted him with my usual "hi, how are you today?" After I cleared up that question, and the next questions about where exactly in Israel I grew up, how long I'd been in the States, and if I liked living in San Francisco more than in Israel, he wanted to know if I was an actress.

"No."
"Musician?"
"No."
"Singer?"
"No."
"Artist?"
"No."
"Then what are you doing waiting tables?"

That was my wake up call. After that conversation I decided it was time to change directions. Ari suggested I write a list of all the things I liked to do. I took a piece of paper and wrote:

I like working in a restaurant, I like watching cooking shows on TV, I like cooking, and I enjoy shopping in small ethnic markets. But most of all, I am totally interested in food.

After eating the same food for nearly twenty years and knowing in advance what I was going to eat every day, the abundance and variety I saw in the stores and restaurants dazzled me. In the kibbutz, food was something I ate only when I was hungry and on a strict schedule. Here food was recreation. Food was Fun.

I decided to go to a culinary school. Ari teased me that if I ever decided to go back to the kibbutz I would have no problem getting a job. I told him that for the kind of food they served in the dining hall they did not need a certified chef. They needed hungry people.

Culinary school was a much bigger challenge than learning to work in a restaurant. It was like going to military basic training all over again. Suddenly I had to get up at dawn to get to school on time or lose some precious points. I had to wear a uniform, keep my station clean, stand at attention every day during inspection to show the "commander" that my weapon, i.e., my knife, was shiny and very sharp, that my nails were short and clean, my face without makeup. But I liked it. And for the first time in my life I also discovered what it was like to be around people who were really interested in what I had to say. It was intoxicating.

We always talked about food. When it was my turn to talk, I told them I had never seen broccoli before I came to America, that steaks I ate on the kibbutz looked and tasted like burned shoe soles. I told them that sour cream was one of the biggest delicacy of my childhood (the other was homemade French Fries). That on the kibbutz we had sour cream only on Tuesday for dinner and on Saturday for breakfast, and that what I liked the most about America was having the freedom to enjoy sour cream every day for breakfast, lunch, and dinner, if I only wanted to. Not that I ever did.

During the last semester I got an internship working in the spacious underground kitchen of a large hotel in downtown San Francisco. It was not as adventurous and creative as I had expected it to be, but I was not disappointed. I learned to present food on plates that traveled slowly on an assembly line, I scrubbed large pots and pans, improved my chopping technique, I fried, baked, sautéed, stirred, and washed huge quantities of foodstuffs. I pushed carts, mopped floors, and observed everyone around me with unending curiosity and respect. Ari was impressed and I was blissful. "Don't let my success go to your head," I teased him.

At the end of the semester one of the cooks transferred to another location and I joined the team. I knew that working in the hotel kitchen would not fulfill all my undiscovered aspirations, but

I didn't mind. My aspirations could wait. At last I had a full-time job with benefits and paid vacation. I was living the dream and I was having lots of fun like a true American. I also acquired a new identity. No longer was I merely a naive kibbutznik from the north of Israel. I was a chef, and I had a certificate to prove it.

My mother's card caught me by surprise.

It arrived on Friday afternoon in a large envelope covered with too many stamps and black ink stains. The address was written in hesitant English and the street's name was misspelled.

"I am not planning to sit here and mourn the loss of my youth," she wrote in her perfect handwriting, after bashing some right wing politicians and their bloated salaries. "Instead, I decided to organize a big birthday party and invite all our friends and relatives. To tell you the truth, I would rather let someone else organize the party and surprise me (like your father or your brother, for example), but I already know that I couldn't rely on them. So I decided to surprise them and organize a birthday party for myself! And I would disclose my age. I am not ashamed to tell everyone that I am sixty years old. I know I look good for my age. Everybody says so."

At the bottom of the page she scribbled, "I want your honest opinion about the card which I designed myself," and signed, "Ima."

I could hardly believe my eyes. My mother decided to reveal her true age? Impossible. She had all kinds of strange ideas about the way women were supposed to behave; like saving their virginity for their husbands, or faking their age like her life-long role model, whom she called in one breath, "Elizabetaylor."

Perhaps she was changing, I thought. Finally she understood that virginity and youth had no effect on a woman's happiness or the success of her marriage. But the realization that my mother was changing her ground rules did not make me feel better. On the contrary. I got mad at her. For ten years I'd been telling her I didn't want to go back to the kibbutz, so why was she inviting me to a party she knew I didn't want to attend?

"What shall I do?" I asked Ari. "What shall I say if she calls and asks when I am planning to come, and then tells me that *everyone* is absolutely dying to see me?"

"You don't have to pay attention to what everyone is saying," Ari said, exuding practicality and logic.

"But I don't want to go," I complained, feeling how my mature self quickly turns into the little whiny girl who had never left the kibbutz.

"Then tell her that you can't afford to travel right now, or that you can't take time off work, or that you were thinking about coming next year. There are lots of things you can say," he suggested patiently, supportive as always.

"And you think she'd believe me?"

"She might."

I always felt that I would never return to the kibbutz. But now, suddenly, after ten years in California, I had to consider going back. I could not bring myself to do it. I did not want to do it, in spite of the deep connection I still felt to the kibbutz.

Deep inside me I could still hear the sound of the wind whistling above the poplars and inside the pine trees; see the splashes of red and yellow wild flowers on the uncultivated hills and wadis; smell fresh hay on summer afternoons, taste the sweetness of the water flowing from the hidden spring into the reservoir.

I missed the dramatic sunsets and the mystical sunrises, the breathtaking immensity of the Milky Way on clear nights, the heavy clouds that climbed up the horizon and filled the skies with promise of rain, the sight of the moon sinking into the Mediterranean.

But I did not miss the feelings that my mother's card evoked in me. They were saturated with memories of childhood resentments, silenced angers, unfinished arguments, frozen helplessness. I tried to resist them, ignore them, placate them, but they forced themselves on me with the brutal fierceness only buried memories possess.

A week later, on my way home from work, I decided to go buy my mother a gift, then rush to the post office to mail it, maybe even Fed-Ex it, then try to forget about the invitation and the party. I was not going to allow my guilt drive me back to the kibbutz. To save the peace of mind I gained during my years in California, I had to stay away from her and everybody else. I turned my car around and drove to the first place that came to my mind. As soon as I entered the enclosed, sun-lit shopping mall I became sleepy. I forgot that shopping malls made me feel out of place, awkward, disoriented, even when they offered splendid architecture and live music from a grand piano standing amid potted ferns and marble benches.

At the entrance of a sprawling department store I visited only once before with Ari's mother, a pretty woman dressed in a pink suit greeted me with an inviting smile and the question, "Hi, how are you today?"

I wanted to snap back at her, "Why do you ask? Do you really care?" when I remembered it was just a polite gesture that did not mean anything. It was a simple acknowledgement of my presence, not an expression of genuine interest. I nodded and raised both sides of my lips. A contrived smile could give her an idea about how I felt, I thought, and bumped into a glass counter covered with a smart display of seductive perfume bottles and glossy brochures advertising promises to turn any pragmatic duckling like myself into a graceful swan.

From the far side of the counter a tall woman sent me a divine smile designed to perfection by the seasonal color of lipstick, moved toward me, and handed me a brochure that explained in scientific terms and charts how the products on the page could enhance my youthful look and rejuvenate my complexion. She suggested I buy a scientifically proved wrinkle concealer, claiming that, "You don't have too many of those, but it's also good for prevention," and explained the danger of UV rays. She also showed me a variety of eyeliners promising that the right one would give my eyes a dramatic overtone. "Such exotic eyes," she repeated, as if she were trying to convince herself.

Unfortunately, I did not believe a word she said. I thanked her politely and stomped away from the counter.

I hated myself and everything I stood for. I was embarrassed by my Spartan disregard for the lure of cosmetics and my adherence to socialist austerity. I wanted to be carefree and capricious, to buy fun stuff I didn't need. But I couldn't. Years of living under the impression that the collection of expensive things symbolized abject greed and a sick compulsion to outdo the neighbors had erased any shopping impulse I might have entertained otherwise. Only when I started eleventh grade did I discover that buying precious metals, real estate, designer clothes, expensive cars, and art, also symbolized success, power, and prestige.

I learned about it from an essay we read in class.

"Conspicuous consumption of valuable goods is a mean of reputability to the man of leisure. When he finds himself unable to display his opulence to the lady of the house it adds another duty to her daily tasks which is the vicarious consumption of goods," my English teacher read aloud from her book of essays, pronouncing each word slowly and clearly in her distinct New York accent.

I did not recognize more than half of the words. Even the word "goods" did not mean the opposite of "evils," even though it sounded like it. I had to look up each word in my dictionary and write the Hebrew version with a pencil above the English words. Only after the page was covered with my tiny handwriting, was I able to read the paragraph and answer all the questions.

I was glad I spent so much time working on my homework. Not only did I get a good grade, I also learned to verbalize my profound understanding of life on the kibbutz in English. Comparing our life with that of the "man of leisure," I wrote in my notebook the following: "People who live in the kibbutz don't have money because they get everything they need from the kibbutz. There are no shops and restaurants and movie theaters in the kibbutz like in the city. If someone gets something special from his grandparents who live in the city, like a record player or bicycles with ten gears, everyone can share it. We live in a society where we have equality and it is not necessary to be selfish."

I was very proud of knowing the words 'society' and 'equality' and tried to plant them in all my answers even when they did not belong there. They sounded so sophisticated and grown-up and full of merit.

As a result of my education I have never suffered from the capitalist shopping spree syndrome, even after I came to America and saw the sleek catalogues, the overflowing department stores, the giant billboards. Living for so many years under the close supervision of hardcore social justice fans, I adopted a belief that if I did not possess a certain object it meant that I did not need it. Which was absolutely true in most cases. I have never lacked anything I truly needed, like food and clothes and books and health care and even music lessons. I could never claim that I was deprived of materialistic needs. No one I knew needed silk pajamas, flannel sheets, and a feather bed to enjoy a good night's sleep. Lying on straw mattresses under heavy blankets stuffed with cotton wool achieved the same results. Fancy clothes and jewelry were also unaffordable, but regardless of their price, they were useless for people who spent most of their time in the open fields, taking care of domesticated animals, getting bitten by mosquitoes, and painful sunburns on their noses. Every drop of our sweat was devoted to the building of the state and protecting its borders. Austerity was an accepted way of life for all the citizens (or most of them), even those who lived in nearby towns. Only that, when the townspeople started to abandon their minimalist lifestyle for the sake of a little comfort, we in the kibbutz became its conscientious guardians.

Again and again I heard that happiness was not a commodity a person could buy with money, and I accepted it without my typical suspicion toward grown-up axioms. I never bought anything just to make myself feel better. I developed a conscious denial of self-adornment, despite the heavy burden it had put on my personality. In the back of my mind I knew that such efforts were bound to awaken a harsh response from highly critical observers.

Constant reminders were easily available.

"Did you see the new pearl earrings Aliza wore on Friday night in the dining hall? I bet she bought them with the money she got from the Germans," I heard Shifra whisper to Tzipke one early Sunday morning when I was in eighth grade. I was crouching on the ground, filling yogurt cups with fresh dirt mixed with peat moss, later to host young avocado plants the two women were grafting on the long table next to me.

"I don't understand why the kibbutz allows her to keep the money," Tzipke wondered, digging dirt from under her fingernails with her grafting knife.

"Shh, don't talk so loud," Shifra moved her shoulder in my direction.

"Even the walls have ears," I recited to myself the proverb I had heard so many times before. Was I one of those walls?

"Let her buy all the earrings in the world if that's what she wants to do with their dirty money," Tzipke shrugged self-righteously. "If it makes her happy, who am I to say anything against it," she added with an accusing tone, insinuating again to my juvenile ears that jewels could not cure painful memories.

"All the German money in the world will not bring her family back from Auschwitz," Shifra agreed with rare compassion in her voice, shaking her head and slashing a crisp stem with her sharp knife.

"Can you imagine," Tzipke assented, "hiding in sewer tunnels for months with nothing to eat." She wrinkled her big nose, pulled a long slimy earth warm from among the filled yogurt cups, and threw it on the ground away from me.

We worked in silence for a while. My thoughts drifted away to a beautiful beach where no annoying kibbutz women ever lived to question the merit of precious stones and metals. Then Tzipke contemplated again, "Maybe the kibbutz was right to let her keep that money. After all she lost all her family."

I didn't know what conclusions to draw out of that conversation. It sounded like they agreed that the German money could cure some of Aliza's losses and sufferings in the sewer tunnels. But then Shifra wiped her muddy hands on her blue pants and said, "I still don't think she should wear pearl earrings in front of everyone. First, she knows that nobody here cares about these things, and second, it's not fair that people who can't afford pearl earrings and want them should see her wearing them in the dining hall. Some people, like you know who," she lowered her voice dramatically and moved her head in my direction, "can be jealous about things like that and then talk about her behind her back. She doesn't need it."

"Of course not," Tzipke agreed.

I was completely confused and lost in the maze of their logic, but I learned that wearing pearl earrings on Friday nights was unacceptable. It could inflict jealousy on people like my mother (or was it me?) and that was the worst thing that could happen to anyone.

Without ever speaking about it, I knew that in the kibbutz one had to overcome the need to look different, to be more noticeable than others, especially if it entailed giving in to mundane temptations. And since the use of fashionable clothes and jewelry was a way of claiming some individuality, it generated a multitude of ideological quarrels between us pubescent girls and Gideon, our zealous educator.

"You should be happy you don't live in the city," he told me and my sixteen-year-old friend, Tikva when we argued that every city girl had at least one dress like the dress we shared. For him our insistence on wearing a dress with puffy sleeves was a sign of personal corruption; a serious deviation from the modest dress code he had developed during years of pumping values into challenging adolescents.

"If I lived in the city I wouldn't have to argue with anyone about which clothes I could or couldn't wear," I argued.

"If you lived in the city your parents could watch every move you make," he scorned, "and you wouldn't have the freedom you have on the kibbutz."

He was partly right but not convincing because I never had as much freedom as I wanted. With him snooping around all the time, and the gossipmongers sticking their noses everywhere, it was very hard to do anything without being spotted and punished promptly

"What's wrong with that dress anyway?" I questioned his vehement ideology.

"The dining hall is not a stage to show off clothes and jewelry," he recited his tired slogan, as if I hadn't heard two thousand times already. I wanted to tell him that my mother never went to the dining hall without spending at least half an hour in front of the mirror, making sure she looked perfect, but I didn't want to hear him badmouthing her too.

"You shouldn't be preoccupied with your clothes and your appearance at this age, anyway. There are more important things you should think about," he had to add for effect. He just couldn't resist it.

"Like what?" I dared him.

Of course I knew what he was going to say. I just wanted to annoy him. After all, I had lived on the kibbutz long enough to internalize all the correct values and behavior codes. I knew that my energy should have been spent at group activities and not in the private search to understand the changes that were taking place inside my body and my mind. I knew that I should have been grateful to the entity called "The Kibbutz" which took care of all my needs. I knew I had to concentrate on my participation in the general effort to complete this or that urgent agricultural assignment instead of trying to be me. Everything I ever got belonged to the kibbutz. Except for my life. The life I got I owed to my mother. And what could I have given in return?

I had no idea.

I left the shopping mall surrounded by bitter memories and questions, but without a gift for my mother. I had no experience buying gifts for her. I didn't know where to begin and how to do it. I wished I could find someone who would tell me what to do. Someone I could trust.

At night I called the terrorist.

I was not afraid to see him. I knew he would not want to hurt me like the terrorists who haunted me in my nightmares ever since he died. He had been suffocating inside me long enough to understand that our pain was linked; that if I would die, he would have to go with me. I was certain he would come to talk with gratitude. I kept my eyes open and waited in the dark, hoping to get a glimpse of him before he noticed me. I wanted to be ready for him. And I wanted to explain my cruelty even though I wasn't sure what I had to say. I scrutinized every shadow on the wall for a familiar sign. I counted the seconds, the minutes, and the hours. I concentrated on my heartbeat, on Ari's quiet breathing.

"Where are you?" I whispered.

He did not answer.

"Are you afraid I'd kill you?"

Still no answer.

"Please, talk to me, tell me what I am supposed to do," I begged. I didn't know what else to say. I had to find him in the dark. I felt an urge to promise him that I would never ever call the combat soldier to come and kill him once again. I thought about giving up but I didn't know how to surrender. So I kept waiting for him to reveal himself.

Finally I lost my patience. "You were right all along. You always knew exactly what I wanted, during all the years I was too scared to ask for it. I should have listened to you. I'm sorry I was so brutal, but I was young and frightened. Please tell me what to do."

I talked myself to sleep.

I woke up when my mother entered. I was not surprised to see her. The last time she came without knocking on the door the terrorist was alive, hiding in the bathroom, trying to be a hero. I thought he sent her with news for me, or maybe she came to tell me to stay away from him. I watched her glide across the room, her feet hardly touched the hardwood floor. She was wearing a floor-length black velvet dress adorned with intricate gold embroidery and round mirrors on the chest. Her shiny black hair was arranged in a beehive and the thin gold threads that were woven into it played with the moonlight that got trapped in the folds of the lace curtain.

The dress she was wearing looked like the dress she wore at my Bat-Mitzvah party. I remembered how embarrassed I was when she showed it to me and to my father a week before the party. She was so proud of her good taste. It was the fanciest piece of clothing I had ever seen. I knew she would never find another opportunity to wear that dress. People on the kibbutz would laugh at her if she wore it on a Friday night. Even the Passover dinner did not require such a glamorous costume. I told her I thought it was an ugly dress, even though, I didn't know if it was ugly or not.

"I know why you bought this stupid dress," I scolded her mercilessly. "You want Aliza to be jealous of you. I saw the way you looked at her on Friday night when she came to the dining hall with her new pearl earrings."

"Nonsense," she dismissed me as always, waving her hand in the air and turning away from me.

To avoid embarrassment, I went sailing with my brother and got a tan instead of showing up for my Bat-Mitzvah party. I was certain that my mother would become the laughing stock of the kibbutz once she stepped out of her room wearing that dress. When I finally came to collect the gifts, wearing my bikini underneath a knee-length, wrinkled T-shirt, my salty hair dried in clumps, my bare heels and toes smeared with residue of melted tar, and my straw bag pulled along the grass, my mother was too exasperated to talk. She shook her head and sighed and sighed and sighed, until my father asked her to stop and please attend to the remaining guests.

On my twentieth birthday she reminded me of my sin. "I'll never forgive you for not showing up at your Bat-Mitzvah. I didn't know what to tell the guests. We all sat at the cultural center waiting for you to come and give your speech and I had to pretend that everything was normal."

I snickered. "At least I showed up to get the gifts."

"Wearing a bikini?"

"It was better than that horrendous dress you bought."

Only then, when I was twenty years old, did she admit to me how much she disliked that dress. "I don't know what possessed me to buy that horrible *schmate'* and then have the audacity to wear it in public. I think I am ready to give it away. Do you think a new immigrant from Russia would like to have it?" she asked, smiling.

"Only if she is very, very poor," I said, trying to keep a serious expression on my face.

She took off her sandals, climbed on a chair, and started searching the top shelves of her bedroom closet. Old sweaters and polyester pants rained on the bed, showering me with partially evaporated moth balls and ancient dust, along with wool scarves she had started knitting years ago and never finished, some doilies she crocheted during long winter nights and decided not to use, and even one small bible.

"Here it is," she turned to me, waving the archeological find in the air. She climbed down from the chair, sat next to me on the pile of old clothes, and shaking her head in what looked like disbelief, caressed the dress not with affection but with the skilled hand of a woman obsessed with dusting. "I was so unsure about what to wear at your Bat-Mitzvah party. I looked at what other women bought and ended up buying this horrible thing," she suddenly confessed.

She turned the dress inside out, checked the black satin lining and the stitching along the hem and the sleeves. It was in perfect condition. There were no old stains or tears along the folds anywhere. It was obvious that she had not worn that dress even once since my Bat-Mitzvah party. "Isn't it the ugliest dress you've ever seen?" she said still caressing the dress. "It's hard for me to believe how ignorant I was in those days and how insecure. I didn't know anything about fashion. I was so naive, but I thought I knew everything, just like you did when you were a teenager. Always arguing, complaining, fighting against the world."

I didn't know whether she was talking about me or about herself fighting against the world, and I didn't dare to ask. She was in such a good mood, and she admitted I was right even though she did not remember it.

Now, again, she was wearing that awful dress. And there was not a party to go to. "Ima, what are you doing here wearing this dress again? I thought you got rid of it years ago," I asked the shadow sitting on the windowsill, still half asleep.

She looked at me with a mysterious smile. "What do you think about it now?"

"You didn't come here to show me an old dress you haven't worn in years, did you?"

"It's not an old dress, Maminka," she said softly. "It only looks like the old one we both hated."

I was so glad she remembered it correctly.

"Do you like the way I look in it?" she asked.

It was too dark to tell. "Come closer, let me look at you."

She stood up but did not approach my bed.

"I think you look very nice in this dress," I decided to compliment her, even though her shadow blended with the wall behind her and I was unable to see how the dress fitted her. Yet, in a way, she did look different, better than before. The way she carried herself was new to me, erect and confident, yet agile and graceful. For a change, she did not look as if she were trying to impress a judgmental crowd, but like a woman who enjoyed herself. "Why are you wearing it?"

"I was looking for an opportunity to wear it again. Maybe you could appreciate it now because you live in America and not in the kibbutz. You know how it is in the kibbutz. If I wear it to the dining hall on Friday night people would look at me funny. Even weddings do not require dressing up. Only when I go with your father to a special banquet in the city I can wear it, but how many of those do we go to?" she paused, then continued before I tried to answer her. "Look how well it fits me. The old one hung on me like a sack of potatoes, but this one is perfect, it makes me look taller and thinner," she giggled.

"Yes, mother," I had to agree. "You always liked to dress up; even when they talked behind your back you did not stop. I guess it was your way of fighting back, your way of rebelling against narrow mindedness and petty jealousy. You did not surrender to the convention that women were supposed to look unattractive, unfeminine, plain. With lipstick and nail polish and hair dye and high-heels you set yourself apart, they were your best ammunition."

She laughed out loud. "I am so happy you understand me so well and don't criticize me like all of them. Now I can tell you why I came."

I was awed by her new confidence. She had never spoken this way. Clear and assertive and full of spirit. She came to my bed and sat down, very close to me, and took my hand between her hands. I swallowed a gasp. My mother never touched me tenderly, never showed her feelings.

"I came to give you this reminder," she said, putting a card on my lap.

I picked it up and read aloud: "Our old sages of blessed memory said: Not into liberty we are born but into slavery. Only the power to liberate ourselves is given to us, and to use this power is our mission in life."

The words on the card made some sense since my mother's birthday was going to take place on the second night of Passover; a holiday that symbolized freedom from oppression. But they also confused me. I was not sure why she wanted me to have that card. I thought she came to my bedroom to show me that she was a different woman, clear and confident and full of new insights, but now I realized that she did not change. She was still talking in circles, in symbols, still trying to decide who she was and what she wanted.

As long as I had known her, she was not the kind of woman who would walk into my life to proclaim her revolutionary decisions. She would more likely stumble into my room and warn me that, "Gideon said you should not stay up so late," or "Zehava said you didn't mop the floor," or "Why do you complain to me about it? You know there's nothing I can do to change it. The kibbutz decided," and so forth. Throughout my childhood, my mother did not act independently on the communal stage. She volunteered to practice motherhood according to rules that were designed by the general assembly. Her only error was that she had sacrificed her motherhood for an ideology, assuming that my love for her was still included in the new arrangement.

She didn't know that even before I had learned to read and write, I learned to control my childish longing for her. It was the only way I could survive her inexplicable indifference. At the time, I didn't know that living in the children's house and saying good bye to her every night before she went to the other children's house where my brother lived was an exercise in social justice and equality. For me it was a daily ritual of learning how to cope with darkness on my own and without showing anyone that I was afraid. Later, every punishment that I received from my idealistic educators only reinforced my deep conviction that she did not care about me. So I avoided telling her about myself. I believed that if she truly loved me she would have seen my misery. And then, I thought, she would have rescued me, she would not have allowed them to hurt me.

Before I was completely awake I knew what I was going to do. Since it was Saturday morning and I didn't have to go to work, I had all the time I needed to accomplish my plan. I searched the Yellow Pages, made several inquiries on the telephone, told Ari I was going out for a few hours, got to my car and drove to my chosen destination.

The moment the man behind the counter of the very secured jewelry store opened his mouth, I knew he was an Israeli. "Yes, what can I do for you?" he barked suspiciously in a heavy Hebrew accent, looking at me as if I had come to rob him. No smiles, no friendly, "Hi, how are you today?" no compliments about my youthful look and exotic eyes. Only a laconic, straightforward question implying a subtle, yet very clear message: unless you're serious about doing business here, don't waste my time.

Perhaps I did not look like someone who visited jewelry stores very often, I thought to myself. Any salesman, even an unfriendly one who clearly felt imprisoned in a black suit and a tie, could see immediately that I was not wearing any jewelry, not even the inexpensive kind.

"I'm looking for pearl earrings," I said, hoping the confidence in my voice would reassure him that I was very serious about doing business.

"Israeli?" he shot at me, as if I had said something incredible. Within a split second his demeanor completely changed. He looked at me with keen interest, taking in the details he missed during my entry, a judgmental spark of curiosity replacing the suspicion in his eyes.

"Uhm," I had to admit reluctantly. If I could guess his nationality so easily by his accent, so could he, I assumed.

"You live in the city?" he asked in Hebrew, as he unlocked a drawer beneath the counter and brought out a display of earrings glinting on dark blue velvet.

"Ken," I answered in Hebrew.

"How long?" he asked, handing me a giant pearl encased in gold.

"Long."

"Married?"

"Yes."

"Children?"

"Not yet."

He shook his head then nodded. I wasn't sure if it was a sign of disapproval or an affirmation of an earlier observation.

"What do you do?" He took the earring, returned it to the tray and handed me a smaller version. I wanted to sigh in exasperation. The familiarity with which Israelis questioned other Israelis when they were away from the homeland reminded me so much of the kibbutz, I was tempted to tell him it was none of his business, but then I decided not to antagonize him. This was the grand rehearsal for what was lying ahead of me and I might as well go on with it.

"I cook."

"In a restaurant?" he assumed. Naturally.

I nodded and looked at the price tag. Immediately he said that he was ready to make me an offer if I buy a necklace, too. I agreed to take a look at the necklaces. He unlocked another drawer and pulled out a tray covered with long strings of pearls. He unhooked one of the strings and let me hold it. It felt cool to the touch, and so smooth and perfect, I fell in love with it right away. And so would my mother, I was certain.

"Where did you live in Israel?" he broke the spell.

"In a kibbutz up in the north," I answered, absentmindedly, and put down the pearls. I didn't want him to see how much I liked it.

The little experience I had shopping in Tel Aviv had taught me to assume a little indifference for the sake of getting a good deal.

"Which kibbutz?" he did not let go.

I told him the name of the kibbutz and watched him slide another string of pearls into my hand.

His eyes lit up. "I know someone from your kibbutz," he said victoriously, shedding some of the detached interrogator mannerism. "Yoav, I am quite sure his name was Yoav. A good guy he was. I knew him in the army. I remember him. Nice guy," he repeated, and launched into a nostalgic tale about how Yoav and him once got stranded in the middle of the desert with an empty tank of gasoline and Yoav volunteered to walk twenty kilometers to get gas while he waited in the shade of the jeep.

Now it was my turn to show surprise. As much as I resented the direction of the conversation, I found myself succumbing to the cliché of "what a small world," since Yoav had grown up in the same children's house with my brother.

For the next few minutes we neglected the pearls and the business propositions that hung above us, and my formerly unfriendly interrogator digressed into a lively monologue about his adventures in the army with "those amazing kibbutzniks who always volunteered to do everything." With a newfound thread connecting us, as flimsy as it was, he now talked to me like a lost relative found in a strange land, and even revealed his name. "Mike Avrahami," he extended his hand with a satisfied smile, "but you can call me Micha."

I shook his hand and introduced myself. Now I also had to tell him why I was buying the pearls.

"Good choice," he nodded in appreciation, and gave me the best deal he could give. Actually, he was losing some money selling the pearl earrings and the necklace for such a low price, he insinuated, but since I knew Yoav, it was worth it. "Tell him I said hi when you see him again," he said. I didn't tell him that the chance I would run into Yoav in the future was as low as his was.

He placed the earrings and the necklace in a padded box and handed it to me along with his business card. "Come again when she turns sixty one. I'll give you a good deal," he smiled with a conspiratorial wink.

"Thanks. Next time it will be diamonds," I promised, whether to myself or to him, I was not completely sure.

On my way out of the store, with the long padded jewelry box lying safely in my pocket, a mischievous thought occurred to me: eat you hearts out, Shifra and Tzipke, for all the dirty looks you gave my mother, I give you one right back.

Chapter Eleven

The successful landing awarded the pilot and flight crew with synchronized applause and ear-splitting whistles from the Israeli passengers who could not wait to step out of the plane and start pushing one another toward the exit door, trampling over handbags, and leaving a trail of destruction between the aisles. It was five-thirty in the morning in Ben Gurion airport. The sun was already splashing the horizon with hazy orange, pink, and yellow and the air was lazily waking up to another Middle Eastern day. I looked out the window and saw an Air China plane parked nearby. For a moment I thought that we must not have landed in Israel, but the bus that approached my plane and announced a welcome salutation in Hebrew, made me realize that I was wrong. It was a slightly different Israel from the one I'd left, a country reconciled with China, but it was Israel, indeed.

My brother was waiting for me outside the terminal with the rest of the anxious crowd who closely scrutinized every face that emerged from the custom checkpoint. I felt as self-conscious of my limbs as those long-legged nervous Amazons who compete for the crown in beauty pageants, only that I was far from feeling beautiful, and the grand prize I was hoping to snatch at the end of my journey could not be handed to me by any judging committee.

I noticed him before he saw me and my heart overflowed with joy. He was separated from the crowd, leaning on a concrete post and talking to a man I did not recognize. I galloped toward him, fighting the heavy luggage cart that insisted on pulling me in the opposite direction, and fell into his chest.

"Ah, I didn't see you," he coughed an apology, wrapping an arm around my shoulders.

"Have you been waiting long? This flight was endless. I hope you didn't come too early. How are you? You look great, I'm so happy to see you, how's everyone doing? You didn't tell them I was coming, did you?" I flooded him with every exclamation that came to my mind before he had a chance to utter a syllable.

He shook his head and smiled helplessly, unable to answer my questions. When I finally stopped to take a breath, he said, "This is Shabtai," and motioned his head toward the man he was talking to while I struggled with the stubborn cart. It was only then that I noticed that Shabtai was loading my suitcase into the trunk of a Japanese car. I had never seen a Japanese car in Israel before.

"Hi, Shabtai, I'm Avner's sister," I called as we walked toward the car. He turned around, slammed the trunk door and nodded. I didn't think for a moment that the introduction was incomplete, though for a split second I realized that if I were one of my American friends, I might have been shocked at the rudeness of my brother and his friend. During my early days in California, I realized that Israeli informality was often interpreted by the locals as plain rudeness. It took me quite a while to learn to perform the introduction ceremony as well as other ceremonies, without feeling odd. But now I was at home, ready to follow a completely different set of rules and I was feeling something close to comfort.

We drove to Tel Aviv.

The run-down apartment buildings we passed on our way to the City competed with huge billboards for my attention, announcing old and recent political debates that had gripped the nation, proclaiming, "The People are with the Golan Heights" and "The Prime Minister is a Traitor" on homemade improvised banners. I looked at Avner questioningly and he gave me an in-depth overview of the current situation, stopping after every few sentences to argue one point or another with Shabtai, who seemed to be the interpreter of the "people's sentiments," as Avner called it. I realized that family business might have to be postponed until much later, unless I was going to barge into their heated conversation.

"When are you planning go to the kibbutz?" I interrupted.

"I promise you that none of these people," Avner told Shabtai with cool assertiveness, pointing his finger out the window and ignoring my question, "has ever been to the Golan Heights. They probably don't even know where it is."

He sniffed and turned his attention to me. "Tomorrow, around one, one-thirty, maximum two o'clock."

"Did you decide what we're going to do? Are we going to call them today?"

"No, it'll ruin the surprise," he said.

"I am not showing up without calling at all," I said very firmly and with growing alarm, even though it was my idea to come to the kibbutz without notifying anyone but my brother. I wanted to save my parents the nerve-racking anticipation, the long drive to the airport in the middle of the night, and the house-cleaning frenzy that would agitate my mother out of her routine and my father out of his mind. But in spite of my careful calculations, I still wanted to somehow prepare her for my sudden decision to accept her invitation and come to the kibbutz.

"We'll stop somewhere on the way to the kibbutz and call," he compromised and I agreed. I knew that it would give her enough time to absorb the information, but not long enough to rearrange the living room, dust every corner in the house and send my reluctant father to the top of the hill on his ancient bicycle to buy vanilla ice cream, a variety of chocolate bars and factory made Passover cookies in case there was not enough food around.

"Absolutely out of the question," my brother's wife, Shula, declared when she heard our plan. She told Yaniv and Orly, who came running to see "what their aunt brought them from America" to finish getting dressed and then whispered, "Do you want your father to get a heart attack?"

Ignoring their protests and my dread at being called "An Aunt From America," she said, "Your parents are not young people anymore," and berated my brother in a tone that almost reminded me of my notorious *metapelet* from second grade. This time, however, I knew she meant no harm. Shula was what we used to call "an urbanite." Because she had always lived in the city she had more experience than we did when it came to acting like a family. She also had more experience when it came to dressing up for a party. Unlike me and Avner who liked to wear tennis shoes and jeans, she could wear a mini-skirt and walk on high-heels like no one we knew. She also knew how to apply makeup and wear jewelry, something I repeatedly failed to learn.

"Because of you two she already missed the pleasure of meeting you at the airport. The least you can do is give her some time to get ready," she continued. "If I showed up like that at my mother's house she would never forgive me."

I could not understand why her mother would be upset for saving her the trouble of anticipation, but I also didn't know how real families behaved on these occasions. We were always so nonchalant about celebrating our birthdays, weddings, graduations and anniversaries that I truly thought that waiting at the airport was an inconvenience, not an exciting family event. To defend my poor decision, I told Shula how Avner forgot to call me when she gave birth to Yaniv, and I found out about it two weeks later when I got a letter from my mother, and that in the first photograph I saw of Yaniv, he was already walking.

Shula sighed in exaggerated despair. "You and your brother," she said, shaking her head, and remained silent for a while. It allowed me to speculate about what she meant by her incomplete accusation. We were ignorant and inconsiderate; we were fools. Then, for the millionth time, she said, "I don't understand how they raised you in the kibbutz. What did they do to you?"

"You don't want to know," Avner shook his head and rolled his eyes, then agreed to let her call our mother.

After traveling north for almost two hours, the countryside began to shape into the familiar landscape I had known so well. The mountain range that guarded the border with the loyalty of an old soldier looked the same, except for the new red and white radio antennas that sprouted on one of its barren humps; the soft sand beaches were lacerated by rusting barbed-concertina wire, still intent on stopping future martyrs with their crooked teeth; the foamy waves were cradling seaweed-covered rocks and carrying the same unsuspecting fishes toward the fishing hooks of the local fishermen. I breathed the salty air and thanked all the gods who decided where I should be born. In spite of all the years of voluntary absence, I still felt that I was heading toward the most beautiful place in the world, toward the promised paradise.

Shortly after we left behind us the legendary Club Med resort, which did not cease to operate even during the worst shelling from across the border, our car passed a white truck with the letters UN painted in black on both sides. My brother, who was sitting in the front next to Shula, turned around and asked his eight-year-old daughter, Orly, if she knew what the letters meant. Before she could answer, Yaniv screamed excitedly, "United Nations." Shula, our driver and self-designated educator, tried to explain to Yaniv that what he did was unfair, that he should have let Orly speak first, and a cheerful argument broke out.

While everyone was debating whether Orly knew the answer or not, I gazed out the window. The banana trees on our left were applauding the sky with sheets of deep green leaves and large blue plastic bags that covered their small bunches. On our right, rows of avocado trees extended their heavy branches close to the asphalt road, welcoming me with their generous shade. I had to fight my urge to get out of the car and hug the trees, dip my fingers in the grass beneath them, smell the fresh dirt. The first white porches of the kibbutz apartment houses were already showing on the hill ahead of us.

I felt as if I had never left. Tall trees still graced the curves and corners of the two story buildings, their back porches still overlooking the beach. The argument around me stopped and the children broke into a familiar song: *"hevenu shalom aleichem"* screaming the word Shalom at the top of their lungs, until my brother ordered them to quiet down. Shula stopped at the gate. Slowly, it slid on its wheels, rattling and wiggling its iron parts, letting only the car's front tires cross the tracks. With obvious boredom, an armed, uniformed reservist scrutinized us through the small window of the guardhouse. He did not even bother to get up from his chair or put down his newspaper. Behind him a radiophonic voice of doom reported the latest death toll on the roads.

"We are from the kibbutz," my brother told the soldier before he asked him anything. Without bothering to remove his sunglasses, the soldier nodded and pressed an invisible button that brought the gate back to life. It rattled slowly to the end of the track and let our car enter the kibbutz boundaries.

I felt strange hearing my brother say that we were from the kibbutz. He was right, of course, but from the soldier's point of view we were not from the kibbutz because we didn't live there. We were only visitors, and my brother was a liar.

"I guess we could have been anybody," I accused my brother halfheartedly, already visualizing hostile agents coming in disguise with their sophisticated Russian weapons tucked under their car seats, ready to attack the members of the kibbutz who were enjoying their siesta, trusting that the reservist at the gate would stop the impostors.

"I used to give them Aba's name, but they never bothered to check the list," my brother shrugged. "So I stopped doing it. I just tell them I'm from here."

"What does it matter if you are from here or if your parents live here? It's all the same," Shula scolded both of us impatiently. "I don't see the difference."

Of course she could not see the difference. She had to be born on a kibbutz to understand us. "They put a guard at the gate to make sure the wrong people would not get in the kibbutz," I tried to explain, looking out the window.

At the top of the hill, on the right side of the road, where the old gate used to be, I saw a she-almond tree. It was the same tree I had known in my childhood. She looked exactly the way I remembered her; her lower branches concealing a narrow drainage canal, her upper branches leaning over a concrete bench placed in her shade for the use of those who had to climb the hill on foot. Tradition bestowed on her the honor of being the harbinger of spring probably because of the beautiful blanket of white flowers that covered her during the month of *Shvat*. In my childhood, we were faithful to that tradition; every year, armed with hoes and shovels and spirited devotion resembling pagan worship a lot more than secular appreciation, we hiked to the gate to celebrate her bloom; a hike that felt like a pilgrimage to a shrine rather than to an almond tree that failed to produce edible almonds. We recited to her our inculcated adoration, painted her image over and over on large sheets of crisp, white paper, cleared the dry branches that fell on the ground, planted pines and cypresses on the rocky hillside near her. Now the pines and cypresses growing on the hillside were mature trees, three times taller than I was. I could hardly believe I was one of the kids who planted them there.

"There is no way to do that," my brother's voice shook me out of my reverie. "Those reservists cannot guess who is telling the truth and who is lying. Any idiot can come up with a name like Cohen and get in. I'm sure every kibbutz has at least one Cohen family."

My brother had logic made of steel which none of us could bend. I nodded my surrender. Shula sighed, obviously annoyed at his stubbornness, and veered to a narrow asphalt road that ran along a tall fence, overlooking the sea, the banana plantations, the white cliffs, the old train tracks leading to Beirut, and the tunnel carved in the rocks. The landscape was magnificent as ever; the colors were so vivid, they made my heart ache.

"Did you know that for the longest time mom used to write her letters to me while she was guarding the gate on Saturdays?" I told my brother on my way out of the car, after Shula had parked it under a huge pecan tree I had never noticed before. "She used to call it the Hezbollah Gate, and vowed in every letter that if any terrorist dared to show up during her shift, she would chase him away with a broomstick."

My story elicited loud laughter from the kids and a warning glance from my brother, "Orly, Yaniv, be quiet. It's not four o'clock yet and everyone is still napping."

"Can we go play in the swimming pool?" they begged him in loud whispers, pulling at his shirt from both sides, and trying to drag him toward the swimming pool behind us.

"You know you can't do anything before four o'clock. Savta will be very angry with you if you wake up the neighbors. She'll have to apologize to each one of them," Shula told the kids, winking at me, and added under her breath, "and you know how much she likes them."

Her wink made me realize how well she knew my mother, and how well she understood one of the toughest rules of the kibbutz; no noise during nap time. I was also surprised to hear her call my mother Savta. Shula had such a talent to make us sound and behave like a real family.

An hour before we left Tel Aviv, she called my mother and told her to prepare for a big surprise. At first, my mother thought that Yaniv must have won an award in his martial arts class. But Shula said that she was not even close, so my mother tried again, thinking that Orly must have finished knitting the scarf that she had shown her how to knit when she was sick with chickenpox. But Shula insisted that it had nothing to do with the children. Finally my brother grabbed the phone from her hand and said, "We're bringing a guest with us."

My mother, sounding alarmed, said that she reserved only six seats in the dining hall for the ceremony and the Passover dinner to take place on the night we arrive. With obvious disappointment, she added that someone would probably have to stay home with "your guest" while everyone went to the dining hall.

My brother tried to comfort her. "There would be no problem to arrange for one more seat." Then he stopped and asked, "Do you want to know who the guest is?"

"Oh, you want me to guess who it is?" She sounded hesitant over the phone.

"Yes, and I give you one minute to do it," he said, covering the phone with his palm. "That will give her time to prepare. Now she's getting excited and when I tell her, she'll be ready to hear it."

"Why do you have to torture her?" Shula whispered in annoyance.

"Trust me, I know what I'm doing," he said. I didn't think he knew what he was doing at all, and neither did Shula, who kept shaking her head and rolling her eyes; but neither of us said anything.

"So who do you think it is?" he asked my mother before the minute had passed. I could hear my mother's voice on the other side saying that she had no idea.

"A young woman who lives in San Francisco," he said, waving the telephone in our direction so that we could hear my mother's reaction.

"Maya?" my mother answered hesitantly, after a long pause. "Maya lives in San Francisco."

And then she understood what he was trying to tell her and started to laugh. "You mean Maya is in your house? My Maminka? Really? When did she come? How is she? Boaz, did you hear, Maya is here," we heard her call my father, then return to the telephone, "Maminka? Are you there? Where is she? Let me talk to her."

My brother, looking proud of himself and the brilliant execution of his plan, agreed to surrender the telephone, but not before he told her all the details of my arrival.

When I finally got hold of the telephone, I told her that the decision to come to her birthday party was very sudden and that she shouldn't worry about the extra seat in the dining hall, since I was not planning to attend the Passover ceremony and dinner anyway. She paused for a moment before she answered. Immediately, my memory flashed back to the endless quarrels we used to have when I refused to pretend that we were a happy family and go with her to dinner at the dining hall on Friday nights. I began to prepare myself for the eternal argument.

"You can do whatever you want," she said in the most natural voice, as if all those quarrels were not a part of her past as well.

That was a good start, I thought, pulling my heavy suitcase from the trunk and wheeling it toward what we used to call "the parents' room." It stood in the same place as it always had, only now it looked more like a Mediterranean villa than a bombproof walled apartment built decades ago, according to the old standards of the kibbutz. The old apartment that I knew consisted of one bedroom, a tiny bathroom, a crowded living room, a kitchenette and a few small square holes in the walls for windows.

The kids, who appeared to take the marvelous sight for granted, as if the members of the kibbutz had always lived in spacious villas, ran in front, competing to see who would be first to reach the door and yell, "We're here," in spite of their parents' strict orders to the contrary.

I followed, noticing the rapid change in my heartbeat. My father's garden was celebrating the spring with the bloom of every flower I could name, and more exotic flowers one can see only in the tropics. Lush ivy shaded the front patio, its boughs heavy with bunches of sensuous pink flowers. I climbed the stairs and crossed the threshold, ready to embrace my biggest challenge. When I heard the kids gallop upstairs to shake their Savta out of her afternoon nap, I realized that without any warning, another me, a much younger Maya, stepped into the house.

I put my suitcase at a far corner of the living room, where it would not disturb the perfect harmony between dusted furniture and vacuumed rug and puffed up sitting pillows and decorative houseplants. I knew how much thought and energy my mother had put into preparing her house for our intrusion.

The big test has begun, let us see what *she* will do now, I thought, watching in alarm how carelessly my brother dropped on the white couch, threw the color-coordinated pillows on the floor, and stretched his legs on the coffee table; his foot resting dangerously close to a delicate Chinese bowl my mother had so thoughtfully placed at the center of the table. I will listen carefully and memorize every move she makes, and then I will pretend that I was happy to see her too, I decided, picking up the rejected pillows from the floor and arranging them in a row on the sister couch. Shula was too busy in the kitchen, preparing lemonade for the kids, to notice my brother's violation of the order. I was hoping she would stop to scold him; but she had to turn her attention to the kids who were running down the stairs, competing who would be the first to announce that, "Savta is getting dressed."

While I was wondering why my mother was taking so long, my father came down the stairs. He was barefoot, wearing jeans, a cotton undershirt, and a wide smile full of pleasure and excitement. He squashed me against his belly, with the repeated exclamation, "What a surprise, what a wonderful surprise." When he regained his composure, I told him about the flight, the weather in San Francisco, and asked about his health. As usual, he said that his doctor promised him he had at least another sixty years to go.

Finally she appeared.

Like the queen's yacht passing in the middle of the ocean, she sailed down from the second floor, graciously flapping the wings of her stylish housedress, and sent a royal smile to us, her humble citizens, waiting at the bottom of the stairs. "Maya," she said to all of us, walking to fetch her matching sandals from the closet by the front door. I stayed by the wooden railing and made a mental note that she looked a little heavier in reality than in the photographs she sent me.

When her feet were secured inside her high-heeled canvas sandals, she approached me with open arms and patted me lightly on both cheeks. "I can't believe it," she giggled, "you're here. Did you know it's my birthday party tomorrow?"

"No. She came because she loves the food they serve in the dining hall on Passover," Avner said facetiously.

"I can't believe it. Suddenly you're here," she said happily, ignoring my brother.

We exchanged kissing sounds on each other's cheeks and checked each other from top to bottom. "We didn't think you'd get here so soon. Your father thought you won't be here before four thirty because of the holiday traffic." She turned to my father and said, "I told you they'd get here before four."

"Four, five, who cares," my brother barged in impatiently, rising from the couch and kicking one of the cushions on his way to the kitchen. Oh, no, I thought in despair, the family drama is already going in full gear and I haven't been here even half an hour.

My father, sensing the sudden tension in the living room, clapped his hands, asked cheerfully, "Who wants coffee?" and went to the kitchen before anyone answered. Yaniv and Orly followed, asking for ice cream, oblivious to my brother's firm command to stay in the living room. Through the haze of my jetlag, I watched the five of them bump into one another around the kitchen table, then I turned to my mother, who was fluffing the pillows, straightening the rug, and wiping transparent dust from the coffee table with her bare hands, and complimented her on her dress.

"I bought it two weeks ago in the kibbutzim clothing store in Tel Aviv," she said. "If you want, we can go together and I'll use my ten-percent discount card. They finally learned something about fashion. I was actually surprised when I saw the new show room."

Yes, sure, I smirked to myself. Me, going to the kibbutzim clothing store on my own volition. What a joke. I'd have to be really lucky to come all the way from America and have the golden opportunity to shop at that efficiency-ridden place with a ten-percent discount card. I have despised that store since the day I was herded in with the rest of the girls to choose my first bikini, only because the prices in the clothes storage of the struggling proletariat were more reasonable than the corrupt bourgeois prices in the fancy boutiques of the big cities. I tried on every bikini that had been tossed in disarray in a plastic square cart, and in spite of the fact that I hated every single one, I ended up buying a horrid green bikini, not only because my limited budget did not allow anything else, but also because the *metapelet* insisted that it was perfectly fine and finalized my situation with the old rhetorical questions, "Why do you always think you're so special? Why should I allow you to buy it somewhere else when all the other girls can find something they like here?"

"And I want to dye my hair again," my mother continued, unaware of the effect her offer had on my equanimity. "I don't like this color. There's too much red in it. It makes me look older. Maybe you can help me dye it," she suggested, shaking her head elegantly and passing her fingers through her hair.

By the time the water boiled and my father finished pouring coffee into four blue cups, I was about to pass out. When he handed me the coffee cup on a matching blue saucer –"Unlike the way they serve it in your America," my mother puffed in contempt, "where they shove the cup in your face without giving you a saucer"–I told him that I needed to lie down for a little while to fight an overwhelming jetlag attack. My father took the coffee from my hand and, as I headed toward the guestroom, he said, "No, don't go there. Go upstairs and take a nap in our bed."

I climbed the stairs and entered their bedroom. I was pleased to see that my mother didn't take the time to make the bed before she made her dramatic entry. The pillows were flattened in their cases, the blanket hastily shoved to one side. The light in the small reading lamp standing on the nightstand was left on, and a hectic collection of facial creams, perfumed bottles, and books surrounded it; on the other nightstand, a collection of books, a newspaper, and an unattractive pair of man's reading glasses attested to my parents' matrimonial comfort. A ceiling fan cooled the air above me.

I was too tired to undress. I kicked off my sandals and turned the light in the reading lamp off. Next, I crawled into the cave my mother's body carved underneath the blanket, put my head on her pillow, at the spot her head was resting right before she woke up, and fell asleep, realizing that I had just snatched the grandest prize I could ever have wished for in my childhood: After all these years, I was sleeping in my parents' bed!

The house was quiet when I woke up. Outside the frogs in the neighbors' fishpond tried to out-croak one another, the crickets chirped their assiduous love songs to their blushing sweethearts, and bored dogs sent coded messages into the air. I listened to the orchestrated effort to chase away the silence and contributed a yawn. It was gratifying to know that everyone on the kibbutz was now gathered in the stuffy, overcrowded dining hall, fidgeting around long tables in their best clothes, and trying to enjoy the ancient celebration that marked our ancestors' passage from slavery to liberty, while I was privileged to stay in bed. I reminisced about the uncomfortable folding chairs, the greenish-orange Formica tables, the fierce neon lights, my eternal boredom at watching my mother's animated reading of the same esoteric lines year after year, "In your blood you shall live..." and I savored my freedom to miss the ceremony.

But I did not completely miss the dinner.

I heard my father whistle one of his favorite symphonies before I saw him marching with his grandchildren in the dark toward the house, carrying a square plastic container that I guessed was full of food from the Passover dinner. He entered the living room and invited me to the kitchen table. Sleepily, I got up from the couch and sat down, facing the sink, my back to the kids who were getting comfortable in front of the television set.

My father opened the plastic container and arranged broiled chicken legs, roasted potatoes, and what looked like overcooked sweet carrots on a plate he got from the cupboard above the sink. He popped the plate in the microwave, found a placemat in a drawer and put it on top of one of my mother's magnificent tablecloths. I watched him work around the kitchen, not wasting a moment to search for a dish or think about recipes, confident and organized, like a seasoned chef on a television cooking show, and had to admire his efficiency. Whistling Mozart's 40th symphony, he even provided his own background music. He opened the refrigerator, got a jar of cucumbers that he had pickled himself, stopped whistling to ask me if I wanted ice in my coke, chopped one cucumber into thin even slices, poured the coke into a tall yellow glass, added ice, took the heated plate out of the microwave, put it on the placemat in front of me, and said, victoriously, "*be'te'avon.*"

I knew exactly how the food on my plate would taste even before I took the first bite. Years of living abroad and eating like a foreigner could not erase that memory; and it was not a memory I cherished.

"Aren't you hungry?" he asked when he saw that I put down the fork after the second bite.

There was something so comforting about his concern that I had to tell the truth. "The potatoes are too salty and the vegetables are overcooked."

"Ah-ha," he nodded in sympathy, as if he had known all along but wanted to let me find out on my own. Then, with the same energy he had poured into putting the dinner together, offered to make me a sandwich. "Everyone loves my sandwiches," he vowed, "ask your brother."

I accepted the offer not because I needed an endorsement from my brother or anyone else, but because he seemed eager to take care of me and I liked it.

I watched him move around his modern kitchen and thought how odd it was that only twenty years earlier the majority of the founding members of the kibbutz had vetoed home refrigerators. They were convinced that such a luxury would destroy their communal life. "The members will prefer eating dinner at home with their family instead of going to the dining hall," they warned about the impending doom, and the decision to buy refrigerators was postponed. And again we had to walk to the dining hall after four o'clock to fill our green plastic bottle with ice water for lemonade and the battered aluminum jar with milk for coffee.

"Your mother is still in the dining hall. She had to stay and sing the last songs with the chorus," my father explained, as he piled sliced pickles and chunks of broiled chicken on top of two slices of tomato that he placed on a sheet of matzo bread.

"Dad, don't you have some real bread?" I wrinkled my nose at the sight of the matzo.

"What's wrong with this? Don't you like matzo?" he asked, faking to be surprised.

"Noooo. Don't you know what it does to you?"

My father raised a mischievous eyebrow.

"It makes you fart dust," Orly screamed from the living room and Yaniv followed by making an unattractive sound.

"Children," my father said with an amused threat, waving a finger in their direction. I had to laugh at their boldness. Still waving his finger, he turned to me and, trying hard to look serious, said, "Maya," as if I were also one of the kids.

"Don't pretend, dad, you know they're right," I laughed along.

"Okay," my father surrendered, and fished a loaf of Challah bread from the belly of the refrigerator. "I don't know who taught you to eat bread on Passover," he said in feigned disappointment, moving everything he'd put on the matzo over to a thick piece of Challah bread he sliced for me.

"God will punish you," Yaniv predicted loudly from the living room, where he was playing a video game on my parents' second television set.

"Is that what they teach kids today?" I asked.

My father put the sandwich he had made in front of me and said, "If not God, somebody else will make sure to punish you for eating bread on Passover. Last year some hoodlums burned down a Ramat-Gan grocery store that sold pita bread during the week on Passover."

"At least in the kibbutz you don't have to live by their rules," I comforted him. I knew that the growing political power of the religious parties troubled him. I also knew that regardless of his phenomenal ability to quote whole chapters of the Bible from memory, he was never a religious person.

"By whose rules?" my mother barged into our conversation, her voice sounding alarm. We did not hear her enter. Her eyes were focused on a beautiful red rose she had picked in the garden prior to her entrance, her hands carefully plucking leaves from the long stem.

"The religious parties," I said.

"The fanatics," she said, straightening the tablecloth. She took one red rose that looked a little wilted out of the vase, replaced it with the fresh one she had brought in, threw the wilted rose and the plucked leaves in the garbage, and sat down. "It's too bad the Labor Party did not get more seats in the Knesset in the last elections. We should have won fifty seats and then the Prime Minister would have been able to consolidate his power and get rid of the fundamentalists. They hold everyone by the throat. We should do anything we can to stop the right wingers."

I chewed slowly on the sandwich, savoring the sweetness of the bread, while she reflected on the latest scandal that had shaken one of the stronger religious parties and condemned its corrupt Rabbi-leader. I listened with amazement. My mother had the special gift of talking about politics when no one wanted to listen. It was her favorite topic in time of discomfort, or when she had nothing else to say. Once, on a transatlantic call, she started complaining about the policies of one of the Presidents of the United States, as if I were responsible for his inept decisions.

"They should throw him in jail," she concluded her speech, her voice resonating her familiar contempt for corrupt politicians, and glanced at my father to see if he agreed with her.

My father felt the same about those politicians, but was not in the mood to discuss them. He nodded tiredly and asked my mother to give it a rest.

"It's Passover today," he said. "What do you care about these politicians now? Orly is here, Yaniv is here, Avner and Shula are here, Maya is here all the way from San Francisco. All the family is here and you are worried about a moron no one had even heard about three years ago."

"Avner and Shula are not here," my mother squeezed the under her breath, and rubbed the edge of the beautiful table cloth she had crocheted during the Gulf-War between her thumb and forefinger. She was provoking him for no reason just because they were not right here at home with us. Yet.

My father finished washing all the dishes in the sink, wiped his hands with a dishtowel, and whispered to himself, "Don't start, don't start this now." Seething, he walked to the living room where Yaniv was still playing his video game, and asked if he could switch the channel and watch *Mabat La'hadashot*, the nightly news program.

The sudden tense silence made me feel the same way it did an eternity ago. I wanted to run to my bedroom in the children's house and hide.

"Your father gets angry a little too fast," my mother said calmly, smoothing the tablecloth that had wrinkled when she rubbed it.

I wanted to tell her that he had a pretty good reason to get angry, but I did not want to start taking sides so early, so I asked her about the ceremony in the dining hall.

"It was not as long as in previous years. I think they finally learned that no one wanted to sit in the dining hall for so long. Everyone is tired of it. So we sang, and read from the *Haggadah*, the children read the same lines they read every year, the girls performed their dances, and that was it. It was very nice," she said, elegantly moving a strand of black hair away from her forehead. She had a pretty hand, I noticed for the first time; her fingernails were painted in light pink nail polish, and no raised blue veins or brown age spots marked her skin. "You should have come with us," she continued. "Everyone was asking about you. They wanted to see you. Why are you so afraid to go to the dining hall? Nobody is going to bite you." She sounded annoyed at my reclusive behavior.

"Who is everyone?" I asked.

"Everyone," she said.

"Ima, I can't stand it when you say everyone, and they and we, why can't you tell me the name of the people who want to see me?"

"What is the matter with all of you today?" she complained. "Why do you have to criticize everything I say?"

"She just wants you to tell her who asked about her, that's all," my father called from the living room.

"Forget it, okay, Ima? Just forget it. It doesn't matter who asked about me. I don't care anymore, okay?" I said, getting up from the table. It looked like we were embarking on a big family quarrel and I felt no need to escalate it, let alone be the one who precipitated it.

I left the house to search for Avner and Shula, knowing that my father would accuse my mother of aggravating me and driving me out of the house. I hoped the darkness could help me calm down and collect myself. I wanted to talk to my brother about our parents. I regretted not calling around and asking for him before I left, but the telephone in my parents' house was such a novelty for me that I forgot about its existence in the heat of the moment.

I strolled aimlessly around the kibbutz, hoping to bump into my brother and his wife; but no one was outside. It was too cold to lounge on the patios with a cigarette and a cup of coffee and carry on a friendly conversation. Spring was evident in the small gardens that adorned the front of each dwelling, but winter did not yet surrender its biting wind to the caress of the mild evening sea breeze. Behind drawn curtains I could see shadows of people I knew since childhood walk in and out of rooms, getting ready to go to bed. Many television sets were on, spilling their flickering blue light into the dark night. It was hard to tell that only an hour and a half earlier the dining room was teeming with children and people celebrating Passover.

Without thinking about my route, I found myself standing in front of the row house I inhabited when I was in high-school, during the days I loved Yoni. It looked different now. Where was the old bomb shelter that was flooded by the rains every winter, and ended up being used as a dumping hole for old straw mattresses and puppy-chewed slippers? And where were the three bauhinia trees that grew around it.

I have never found out how they got there. By the time I noticed them, they were already grown trees and I was tall enough to reach their lower branches and pick a leaf. What I did know was that they were not native to the lawn they shaded. None of the trees that grew within the kibbutz boundaries was adopted from the wilderness that surrounded it. All of them, even the pines and cypresses that looked as if they had been braving the salty winds and the long, rainless summers for generations, came from nearby nurseries, their roots tucked inside tattered plastic buckets and their tops clipped by heartless hands.

During most of the year the bauhinia trees did not look strikingly different from the rest of the trees in their vicinity; but come spring time and suddenly those unassuming trees looked as if they had been carried to our kibbutz by the wind from an enchanted forest. Their giant flowers, painted in exquisite shades of pink and violet, burst out of hidden buds in a shameless celebration of shapes and texture no other tree could claim. Like young brides, they displayed limbs heavy with flowers, shed lovely petals on the grass beneath them, and whispered perfumed promises about everlasting happiness to passersby. The stout pines that populated the grove below the water tower, the proud cypresses that guarded the laundry house, the tall poplars that brushed against the southern wall of the old dining hall; even the acacia, carob, and oak trees that struggled for their survival outside the fence, all brought images of barren hills, dusty roads, and long hot summers; none of them produced flowers worth looking at or remembering. But the sight of the bauhinias in full bloom was beyond pleasing; it was magical. It evoked tales of passionate romances, images from the Garden of Eden, a yearning for a tropical paradise. Even the name, Bauhinia, invoked a mystic lure.

Now the bauhinias were gone. In their place stood a new apartment building, housing two families and their impressive fleet of bicycles, tricycles, and red scooters. A square patio crowded with potted ferns, colorful children's toys, and white plastic garden furniture identical to those my parents had on their front lawn, signaled that the inhabitants were friendly, hospitable, and blessed with many children. The mouth of the old bomb shelter that led brave adventurers like my brother and his friends to the abyss used to open at the spot I was standing on, but now there was only grass under my feet.

I turned away from the new building and continued my solitary walk. Near one of the children's houses, I ran into Daphna, my grammar school roommate. Daphna never left the kibbutz; she married a young man she met during her military service, convinced him to come to the kibbutz and had three children. In spite of the poor lighting around us, I could tell that the red lipstick she used was too bright and the thick black eyeliner surrounding her dark eyes made her look tired rather than exotic. The long brown braid which I so envied during the years we had lived together in the children's house was gone; her short wavy hair was now dyed so black it looked unnatural. The flowery cotton dress she wore had a touch of the current fashion, but it was made for a woman smaller than her. It exposed her square shoulders, strengthened by years of lifting, moving, and carrying heavy objects, and revealed two muscular legs which ended with wide ankles steadily secured inside high platform sandals.

"Maya?" she asked, recognizing me.

"Hi, Daphna," I said.

"When did you come here?"

"Today."

"How is it going?"

"Just fine, and how about you?" I didn't know what else to say.

"Tired. It took so much time to clean up the mess in the dining hall. Nobody wants to stay and help clean anymore. They just want to run back home and watch television. People today don't care about anyone but themselves, it's terrible," she sighed.

After a pause she said, "You still live in San Francisco?"

"Mhmm," I said. I felt so strange talking to her. For so many years we lived so close to each other, yet, we didn't know each other at all. Never talked about anything meaningful. Not even once. We faced each other without saying anything for a while. Then I asked if Nir was still living in the kibbutz.

"Nir? No. He married an Australian volunteer three years ago and they went to Australia after she converted."

"And Iris, is she still married to Rafi?"

"Yes. I just saw them in the dining hall. She comes to the kibbutz with her children every Passover."

"How about Dorit?"

"I think she lives in England, but I'm not sure," she said, looking at her watch.

I wanted to ask her about the rest of the group but it did not feel right. After a few seconds of awkward silence during which neither one of us knew what else to say, Daphna said that she had to run and put her kids to bed before they drove their father crazy and destroyed all the furniture.

"Aren't you glad you don't have to go put each one of them to bed in a different children's house like our mothers did?" I tried to sense how she felt about the kibbutz.

"Very glad," she nodded without elaborating. Then she said, "You're staying a few more days here, right? I'll see you again probably," and left.

I leaned on the wall of a concrete tunnel that led to a bomb shelter and watched until her large figure disappeared behind a darkened children's house, the same one that the two of us had lived in for six long and trying years. I stood in the shadows and felt a faraway sadness touch me. Like wings of butterflies it was so elusive and frail; almost transparent. I realized that we would never talk about our past, our experience in the children's house, our feelings toward the *metapelets*. We were as close and as far apart from each other as only two people who were forced to live together for too long could ever be. We were strangers by choice; we could not open up to each other.

    I looked around to make sure no one was coming and climbed the stairs of the children's house. The second stair was loose and rocked a concrete thump under my foot the same way it did years ago when the *metapelet* returned from the laundry house during our afternoon nap, always giving us the signal to stop the whispers and pretend we were asleep. Feeling like a trespasser, I tiptoed to the front door and tried to open it; but it was locked. I had to overcome the unease that gripped me when I looked for the key in the closet where we used to store the brooms, the floor squeegees, and the water buckets. How could I explain my behavior if I were caught by one of the parents? What if this parent came to live in the kibbutz after I left and did not even know me? What if they thought that I was trying to get my hands on the instant coffee and the cookies that the *metapelet*s kept on the kitchen shelves just like we used to do when we were recklessly young? What could I say? That I needed to take one final look at my fearful childhood? That I wanted to make peace with the walls that watched us struggle against unjust rules and did not crumble in protest?

    The key wasn't there.

    I went to the classroom door. It was unlocked. I walked inside and closed the door. I turned the fluorescent lights on. The wooden desks were now arranged in a circle instead of in two rows facing the blackboard, looking smaller than I remembered, and there was no trace of my teacher's perfect handwriting on the blackboard. The tap above the sink leaked lazy drops of water, leaving brown streaks on the stained enamel. The air was still and stuffy. I sat down in the same place where young Maya used to sit and calculate her careful moves, and waited to be overwhelmed by vivid memories, by locked emotions, by long forgotten voices, but all I could hear were some vacillating gun shots in the distance and a siren.

    I left the classroom and entered the living quarters. The deserted bedroom row stared at me from the dark, bewildered by my blatant intrusion, unable to recognize me or to understand what exactly I was looking for since I was not behaving like a thief. I peered into the first bedroom, hoping to confront old ghosts, but none were interested enough to greet me like a grown-up. I went to the next room, the one that used to be my bedroom, hoping to see something familiar, but the room was dark and quiet.

"Over here," I heard a soft voice behind me.

I flinched and held my breath. Should I be afraid? I didn't hear any footsteps on the loose stair. I was sure I was the only person in the children's house. Slowly, I turned around and searched for the voice. A young man's silhouette was sitting at the dining room table, facing the bedroom row and smoking a cigarette. The Modigliani painting of a long-necked woman in a blue dress, which I used to stare at during our long afternoon naps, was gone and in her place hung a pot of Wandering Jew. Underneath the plant a white refrigerator hummed, the forbidden luxury of my childhood.

"Do I know you from somewhere?" I asked, as I approached the silhouette, fighting a terrible urge to run out.

The last time I saw a mysterious silhouette in front of that window was on the night before I started sixth grade. I woke up when someone touched me. An unfamiliar shadow was sitting on my bed. Still half asleep, I asked the shadow, "Who are you?" The shadow ran away. I got out of bed and tiptoed outside. At first I couldn't see anything. I sat on the floor in the dark, until I saw a silhouette cross the porch back into the children's house. I followed it into the first bedroom and turned the lights on when it leaned over Iris' bed. For a moment he froze in place. Then he turned around and ran outside. His head and upper body were covered with a white sheet, but I recognized the hairy legs.

Iris didn't feel anything. I buttoned her shirt and went back to bed wondering what to do about the hormone-crazed teenage prowler. But as usual, I ended up not telling anyone.

"You certainly do," the silhouette said quietly. His voice had a touch of an accent, familiar yet elusive, soft and reassuring. I thought I had heard that voice before, but I could not remember where, neither attach a face to it. The dark shape was wearing a white T-shirt that asked in Hebrew, Arabic, and English to give peace a chance under a picture of a dove in flight, holding an olive branch in its beak. Looking at the outline of the silhouette, I could see that it was a young man, not very tall, quite thin, narrow-shouldered, with short curly hair; but the details still did not help me recognize him. Then I noticed the missing ashtray. Only a flower vase with wild chrysanthemums, strands of wild oats and asparagus fern stood in the middle of the table. I turned away from the shadow to look for an ashtray. My old *metapelet*s kept their ashtrays in the left drawer, along with the scissors, the aspirin bottles, the scotch tape, and the waterproof markers; I could not see why the new *metapelets* would use that drawer for anything else.

"Thank you, I don't need an ashtray," he said, puffing on his cigarette.

"How did you know I was looking for an ashtray?" I turned sharply to face him.

"I always know what you're looking for."

I froze in my place, finally recognizing the voice. Only then did I notice the strange phenomenon: his cigarette was not collecting ashes at the tip, even though a faint red glow hissed in the dark near his hand, and oval smoke rings floated out of his lips. He was so different from how I had expected him to look after all these years. There was no sign of a decaying diving suit, no scars on his face, no blood, no putrid smell; his wavy hair bounced freely on his shoulders; his arms and legs were intact, and there was no sense of despair and hopelessness about him. He looked quite relaxed and comfortable.

"Is it really you?" I asked, not knowing whether I should be happy or distraught at the sudden appearance of my dead terrorist. "Why didn't you come when I called you?"

"I was busy," he said nonchalantly, puffing on his eternal cigarette.

That was the last thing I expected to hear. I thought he was afraid of me. I thought he missed me. I thought he wanted my approval more than anything. "Busy? Doing what?"

"Many people need my attention these days," he said.

"But I needed your help more than anybody else."

He smiled. "Not really. You never did what I told you to do Maya, you preferred to kill me. And besides, I told you I was busy."

"Doing what?" I asked again, resenting the fact that I had to share him with others. I wanted him to be all mine even though I knew how much I had hurt him.

"Take a look around you," he said.

"You can't expect me to see anything in this darkness," I protested, annoyed with him, and annoyed at myself for not out guessing him.

"It's very noticeable."

I couldn't see anything. Even the three dining room tables stood at the same old spots. "My old ghosts?" I asked facetiously. I had to protect myself, somehow.

"The children, Maya. The children are not here and it's way past ten o'clock."

"Of course they are not here. They are in their parents' rooms, ruining the furniture," I smirked.

"And how do you think it happened?" he asked.

I remembered how I always had to explain to him what life on the kibbutz was all about, so I told him what I knew.

"Several years ago the general assembly voted to change the system and the kids moved to their parents' rooms. I guess they had enough money to add more bedrooms to each apartment."

"No, Maya," he said with half a smile, a forgiving smile. "The kids did not go to live in their parents' rooms. The kids went back home because many parents wanted their children to live with them, and they fought to change the system."

"How do you know that? That's not what I heard."

"I know because I made them do it," he said, leaning back. "You see, Maya, you think you were the only one who heard me, you think you were alone, but you were not. At least not all the time. When I died I was angry and desperate. I wanted revenge. I didn't want to go into eternity without leaving my mark on this world, on your people. I needed to do something. But I didn't know what to do, or how to do it. I was too young; I had no experience, no guidance, and no company; I was alone, I was hurting, and I wanted someone to talk to. So I adopted you. I liked you; you were my age and you understood me better than the rest of them. You understood I had an impossible dream and that I was reckless enough to die for it.

"When I saw you pick up the empty shell from the floor and hide it in your pocket in spite of what they had told you, I decided to help you fulfill your dreams. But you fought me so hard, you killed me so viciously every time you heard my voice, I had to give you up. I thought I'd give you time to learn from your mistakes. I was hoping that one day you'd understand what I was doing and call me back.

"That's why I decided to stay around. I told you I was not ready to leave this world before I got my revenge. I decided to destroy the people who killed me with impossible dreams. I wanted to teach them a lesson.

"I came back to the kibbutz and settled in your people's hearts. And just like I reminded you of each dream you had, every hope, and wish, and fear, I tormented the members of this kibbutz. I woke them up in the middle of the night and reminded them of all the secret wishes that they ever had. I shook the dust off their best memories and their forgotten aspirations when they slept, and when they woke up they couldn't think about anything but what they really wanted. I encouraged them to fight for what they saw as an ideal scenario. When I felt really powerful I even planted new ideas in their minds and tried to scare them with thoughts about more terrorist attacks on their children's houses. I whispered in their ears, 'If you don't protect your children from me I will take them away from you.' I planted fear and hope inside their hearts. For you. I did it for you, Maya. I wanted you to trust me. I wanted you to see what I can do and come back to me. I wanted you to listen to me. And I succeeded. Nothing is the same in the kibbutz. At last the children live at home, and you dared to come back here."

My eyes were warm with tears. I never thought that the grown-ups also suffered. So many years I spent thinking that I was the only one who wanted something else.

"So what's going to happen to you now?" I sniffled.

"You don't need my help, and neither do the members here," he said. "They learned their lesson. I'm not angry anymore. I got my revenge and I know they understand me better now. And you, just remember that I'll always watch you and applaud your courage to fulfill your dreams."

I asked him to stay, to keep talking to me, but he said it was time for him to go. I wanted to laugh with him, hug him, thank him, wish him peace of mind, but except for a transparent cloud of smoke that was left above the dining room table, the children's house was completely still.

When I came home Yaniv and Orly were sleeping in the living room on a pile of blankets that cushioned the rug, their arms and legs spread out in all directions and an expression of innocent bliss on their faces. My brother and Shula, who mumbled something when I entered, were close to falling asleep among their children's limbs and demonstrated rare contentment and ease. My father was sleeping upstairs reciting his paternal snores, and my mother, who could not guess whom I had just met, was watching a late night program on television, looking wide awake on her spotless white armchair.

"Where were you?" she whispered, still caught in the drama she was watching.

"Walking around."

"Do you want something to drink?"

"Don't get up. Let me do it," I said, before she made a move toward the kitchen.

"Would you also like some tea?" I asked, without any intention to be polite. I knew she would not insist on making us tea. She was never too fond of her kitchen, as small as it was, and as little as she had to use it.

"I can't compete with all the other women anymore," she wrote in one of her letters, "I gave up baking." Then she told me about the last time she agreed to bake a cake for one of the numerous bar-mitzvah parties. Instead of baking the cake herself, she went to the kibbutz's general store and bought a bakery-made cake.

Rebellion!!! She declared.

How fortunate my father must have felt, I thought, when I read her declaration of independence. From that moment on she could concentrate on improving her instant coffee making skills and let my father take over the kitchen and learn how to use the coffee machine.

"I'll have a glass of sherry," she said.

Voilà, I thought. My mother, the hard-core pioneer, prefers a glass of sherry before she goes to bed. No more muddy, bitter coffee and scorched potatoes by the bonfire for this dainty lady. "And where do you keep your sherry, madam?" I asked.

She pointed to a small cabinet behind the television set. I opened it and found a small collection of hard liquor and kosher wine bottles, a hectic variety of shot glasses no one ever knew what to do with, a used California travel book, a key holder without any keys attached, two chipped flower vases and a broken pair of man's sunglasses.

"What a mess, mother," I said, after poking my head inside and finding the sherry bottle buried at the back. It looked like no one had touched it since my high school graduation.

"It's all your father's," she chuckled, pleased to dump the blame on him.

"Sure, Ima, it's always someone else's fault," I couldn't resist saying.

"I can't run after him all the time anymore, you know how he is, everything drops from his hands the moment he gets home," she said with so much familiarity I finally started to feel like her daughter.

"I'm sure you can do something about it, just like you do with the rest of this palace," I said, trying to locate the sugar, the tea bags, and a mug.

"I can't find anything here," I finally gave up. "Where do you hide the sugar?"

"Somewhere on the bottom shelf near the refrigerator."

"And the tea bags?"

"I think it's on the bottom shelf above the microwave."

"And the mugs?"

"Try the top cabinet by the left side of the sink. No, the right side"

"Actually, do you have honey?"

"Last time I saw it, it was in the cabinet under the left drawer."

By the time I finished collecting everything to make a cup of tea, I was well acquainted with the kitchen.

"I can't believe I have to spend so much time to make a cup of tea here," I complained. "Why do you have the plates on one side of the kitchen, the cups on the opposite side, the silverware hidden somewhere else, the pots and pans all stacked up on top of each other in a big mess, and the spices all over the place? How can you find anything here? How can you cook like this?"

"First of all," she said, not offended at all, "I don't do anything in this kitchen. It's your father who cooks here." She paused for effect, sipped her sherry and put her tiny glass on the coffee table. "And second, if you don't like the way the kitchen is organized, I wouldn't mind if you rearranged everything in it."

"Ima, you know it's hopeless," I said. "Last time I was here I rearranged your kitchen."

"What's wrong with that? I like the way you do it. You're so organized."

I decided not to argue. I knew she liked it when I organized her shelves but it was such a Sisyphean task, I refused to be seduced by her compliment. This time I was going to learn to live with her annoyingly illogical kitchen and her suffocating, neat living room. It was much easier to surrender and accept that contradiction than constantly fight to change it.

We sat together and sipped quietly from our glasses while another British nursing student got herself mysteriously poisoned to death on the muted television.

Suddenly, she broke our silence, looking at my brother's little family piled on the living room floor. "Look at them," she said. "Look how beautiful they are."

Her eyes were full of maternal satisfaction I had never noticed before. She licked the brim of her tiny glass and partly to herself, partly to me, she reflected, "Ever since you left, there is always a touch of sadness in my heart. I miss all of you and I wish I could be near you. I want to see my grandchildren grow up near me. I have two wonderful children, and so rarely I enjoy your company and conversation, it's sad. What a waste. Since you were a little girl I have been waiting impatiently for your visits. Sometimes I forget that I don't have to get up from my afternoon nap anymore and wait for you and your brother to come home from the children's house. I get dressed and sit in this chair, drinking my coffee until your father comes downstairs and says that I have no reason to get out of bed so quickly because the news program starts only at five o'clock.

"It took me more than thirty years, maybe forty years, to realize how worthless, stupid, and wrong our educational system was; a system we worshipped as if it were given to us by God. Now I know that we were a group of fanatics, uptight, brainwashed idealists, and I'm so glad I'm not as narrow minded as some of my neighbors, who still believe in this nonsense. At least I can understand my children and why you had left.

"I don't understand how I could think that living on the kibbutz was the best way of living. I had no idea it was possible to live in a different way. In a nice home, with all my family around me, not scattered all over the world. Sometimes, I guess, one has to be shaken so hard to start seeing the truth. With my own eyes I saw how from a traumatic crisis something more real, different, new, could come out. Today I will not settle for anything less than the real thing, anything less than the truth.

"But still, it's not easy to watch the neighbors spend every evening with their children and grandchildren around them, even if their children are not half as bright as you and your brother are, you know. Rutka is completely crazy about her grandchildren. I see how she chases the little one all day long, shoving cookies and candies into his mouth as if he needs it. I don't know why she does it. Maybe she's trying to buy his love. I would never do this to my grandchildren. I'd be ashamed of myself. "

She sighed and continued without waiting for my response. "I look at her and say to myself, 'Why can't I have my grandchildren near me every day. What did she do that I didn't?' I know I was a good mother. I was known as 'the worrying mother' who never believed that the responsibility for her children's wellbeing depended on the *metapelet*, the teacher or the nurse. I always interfered, and I never allowed them to treat the two of you as they saw fit. For many years I have been trying to overcome my worrying. I worry about you living so far away by yourself, and all I can hope for is a telephone call or a letter once in a while. And your brother, you know him, he is so busy and forgetful. If it weren't for Shula I would probably see him twice a year, once on Passover and once on Rosh Hashanah. He knows that we don't own a car and to travel by train or a bus all the way to Tel Aviv at our age is not that easy anymore."

I wanted to tell her that I never thought she was a good mother, that I never felt she was worried about me or cared at all, but I did not want to be cruel. I did not want to shatter her belief. So I just said, "Don't you have a special arrangement in the kibbutz that each member can get a car once a month or so?"

"Yes, but you know the way we are, we don't like to ask for favors," she recited one of her oldest and most familiar lines. "Especially your father."

"I'm not afraid to ask for a car once in a while if I want to go see a good movie, or if I want to go to a concert or a play. I don't care what *they* think about me anymore. *They* already said everything they could possibly say about me, but he is the one who had to drive and he has to go get the keys, so I try not to ask for it too much not to upset him," she said, motioning her head toward the bedroom upstairs. "Well, most of the time I will not insist because I also know that it's not that easy for him to drive to Tel Aviv and back anymore. He has been so tired lately and his lower back bothers him a lot. He thinks I don't know he's in pain, but nothing escapes me. Never did."

"But it's your right to use a car, you can't be stuck here all the time," I argued, afraid to hear her talk about my father's deteriorating health and age.

"You still have to ask for it," she said very calmly, as if it were a basic law of nature, which, in a way, it was. That was what I found so difficult to cope with during my last years on the kibbutz. I couldn't bear thinking that control over the least important as well as the most important decisions of my life was attached to the tip of other members' voting fingers, or typed on one of the countless forms of the movement's regulations.

Always having to ask permission made me feel that I owed favors to those who complied with my requests, even if according to the rules they were supposed to provide me whatever I needed. As the years passed by, my debt grew into such monstrous proportions that my only way to get out of the whirlpool of accumulating more favors and debts was to leave the kibbutz, start paying for what I get, and learn to accept favors without feeling trapped.

"It's much easier if the member who makes the car schedule is a friend of yours," she said suddenly, as if she could read my mind. She sucked the sherry from the rim of her glass with a pensive gaze. "Luckily, Ezra, who does the cars' scheduling became a good friend of mine last year, when we rehearsed for the play we produced for the kibbutz anniversary party. It was such a wonderful play. I wish you had seen it too. Everyone said I was great as the good fairy. It was his idea that I should start taking acting classes. I wrote to you about it, didn't I?"

I nodded. My mother always had a soft spot for drama, and Ezra, who saved her life when she nearly fell from the stage in a moment of blind exhilaration, became an avid supporter of her secret dream to become the kibbutznik version of Elizabetaylor, her venerated model of the invincible feminine spirit. His explicit admiration for her won her loyalty and her genuine respect because, as she wrote to me after her first acting lesson, "If he could notice my talent, he must be smarter than the rest of them."

"The problem now is that I don't want to take advantage of him and ask for favors. I don't want to behave like the rest of them, so here, we are at the same place we started," she smiled with a shrug; undefeated but realistic.

"No matter what you do you can never win here," I said.

"No," she shook her head, "that's not true at all. Today, if I really want something I fight for it and I don't give up until I get what I want. Ask Hadassah and Dahlia and Shukie. They'll tell you. You can ask *everyone* and they'll tell you that when I want something, I go all the way to get it and nothing can stop me. I 'whistle one long whistle' at all those who say anything against me. I don't care anymore about what they say. I learned my lesson. For years I was so afraid of what *they* say about me, but now... I tell them exactly what I think, and what I feel and I'm not afraid. They already said everything they could say about me behind my back. I only hope that the gossipmongers are satisfied at last. I'm just waiting until they learn to appreciate what I do and if they don't learn, I don't care either. I'm no more that little frightened kibbutznik who worries about what people say all the time. I'm free of that. Even a long time ago I did not care that much. When you were five years old and I heard how your *metapelet* forced you to eat tomatoes, I raised such hell they decided that she should not ever work with children. It took a long time for them to see that I was right, but in the end I won. And I did the same with your brother. When I heard about the brutality of his *metapelet* and what she did to him, I fought so hard to get her out of that children's house that people thought there was something wrong with me. I can't remember now how I found out that she dislocated his arm, not once but twice, but I do remember how much I screamed at her. I lost my voice for three days, afterwards. But I didn't care. I got what I wanted. So you see, even then I raised my voice against them. I did all I could do, then and now. But today, today I would not even think twice or hesitate to raise my voice. I don't feel that I have to report anything to anyone. And *they* know it very well. I'm a lot more confident than I used to be. If I have new ideas or demands, I fight. Like when I fought to add another floor to this house, in spite of the opposition of some "important" members, who think they understand finances better than everyone. Peh. Members like Misha and Debaleh who still believe in all the old fashioned pioneer nonsense. Today I don't give up until I win. I'm not afraid to express my opinions to anyone, and believe me, to suggest change into the dreary conservatism of this place is as easy as climbing the Everest.

"Yes. I am glad to see how I improved with the years. I am open to change and I still have a lot more to say about the way *they* treat us, the older generation, the founders of the kibbutz, and the place of women. I am not like all these other silly women who still believe in the old ways, who cannot see that this system is wrong and corrupt. That it's not working anymore."

I was not sure whether the faint chuckle I heard somewhere above the ceiling came from my imagination or from the dead terrorist. I watched her as she turned the television off with the remote control, while telling me that the murderer of the nurse was not the boyfriend, which was what they were trying to make us believe, but the skinny head nurse who treated the nursing students like a Nazi in a concentration camp. She was so confident, I didn't dare doubt her.

We said good night and parted without kissing. She turned off the last light in the house, and I went to the guest bedroom that used to be my parents' bedroom before their house turned into a two-floor Greek villa. That room was added to the building during the years the kibbutz was under the constant threat of rockets flying over the mountain. For years, the thick concrete walls and the tiny square that posed as a window were used as my parents' designated fortress; with its lack of proper ventilation, the oppressive heat, and the temporary protection it provided, not for nothing was it named, "the secure room."

On my way to bed I found a thin paperback on the tall bookshelf. It was a compilation of interviews of women born and raised in various kibbutzim during the 1930s and 1940s. In the introduction, the interviewer, a kibbutznik herself, wrote, "For years I have been walking around with the feeling that the first generation who was born on the kibbutz paid a terrible price... We grew up in Sparta."

It was the first time I had read that someone else had felt like me. In the kibbutz we have never talked about feelings, the way we grew up, the way we were treated by our educators. Our childhood was not a topic of conversation, unless we reminisced about the beauty of the countryside. Until that moment, I thought I was the only person in the world who carried the burden of resentment, loneliness, shame. It didn't occur to me to share my stories, not even with my mother.

Hours later, when I finished reading the last interview I turned the light off, hoping I'd be able to fall asleep. But I couldn't. I was lying wide-awake, thinking that without my knowledge, my mother had fought to dismiss my *metapelet*, and she had never said a word about it.

Chapter Twelve

"No, don't wake her up, let her sleep as long as she wants," my father's voice woke me up from a dreamless sleep.

"But the guests might get here any moment," my mother argued in a whisper.

"We got two more hours before they'll start coming, by then I promise you she'll wake up," he said, trying to soothe her.

"I have a feeling that once she wakes up and sees people she doesn't know, she'll take off to the beach and we won't see her until the last guest leaves."

"Where did you get that idea?" my father asked, sounding a little annoyed at her exaggerated anxiety.

"Don't you remember how she disappeared with her brother on the day of her bat-mitzvah and we didn't know what to tell the guests? Especially your friend Elisha who brought her the record player and you had to thank him instead of her because we didn't know where she was?"

"Alma, that was almost twenty years ago," my father sighed.

"I promise you that she hasn't changed," she said.

I almost got out of bed to protest, but I wanted to continue eavesdropping. It was such a once-in-a-life-time opportunity to hear my parents talk about me that I didn't want to miss it, even at the price of letting my mother get away with her wrong assumptions.

"She looks more relaxed than she used to," my father tried to save my honor. I heard him open a drawer. For a few seconds it sounded like he was sorting silverware.

"And her hair is so long and beautiful. I don't understand why I let her *metapelet* cut her hair when she was a little girl. It looks so healthy and shiny. I wonder what kind of shampoo and conditioner she uses." She paused for a second and added, "Maybe it's the air in San Francisco."

For a few minutes they were busy unwrapping items that had been packed inside cellophane paper, opening and closing cabinet doors in the kitchen. I started to lose patience. Was that all they were going to say about me?

My mother finally broke the silence. "You know, Boaz, when I heard Maya's voice on the telephone yesterday I simply couldn't believe that she was here. In my wildest dreams I didn't expect her to come to my birthday party."

I heard the refrigerator door open and the sound of soda poured into a glass. My father said, "I thought you sent her the invitation we printed in Haifa."

"I did, but I only wanted her to tell me if she liked it or not. I just wanted her to see it that's all. I didn't dare ask her to come to the party in my letter. For one moment I didn't dream that she would come. You know how she is. She never misses an opportunity to tell me how much she doesn't like to come here, and that if I want to see her I should come to San Francisco. I didn't want to impose myself on her, and I didn't want to put any pressure on her to come if she doesn't want to. I don't want her to blame me for aggravating her "intentionally" as she always does. I want her to be comfortable, and I want her to do what she wants. That's the most important thing. So I decided to save her the aggravation and said nothing about coming to the party. I'd rather see her here when she want to see me, not when I ask her to come."

I could not believe what my ears were hearing. She did not expect me to come to her birthday party. She just wanted me to compliment her on the invitation she designed. God, what a fool I was, assuming that she would ask me to do something she knew I wouldn't want to do. After all these years I was still blinded by my childish resentment of her. What else am I going to find out?

"Un-be-lieveable," my father broke my trail of thought with his favorite exclamation, emphasizing each syllable, and ending with a crescendo.

"What's so unbelievable?" my mother asked. I could tell his declaration irritated her. For him, everything that happened unexpectedly was either unbelievable or a miracle.

"That she came of her own free will."

"Maybe what I did was subconscious," my mother said, suddenly changing her mind. "Maybe deep inside I felt that if I didn't ask her to come I'd have a better chance to see her because she would have no one to say no to."

"Maybe," my father said, sounding unconvinced.

After a few silent moments, she gave herself the compliment that he wouldn't award her. "I still have good mother instincts, even after all these years," she said. "Maybe I know her better than I think."

"Maybe you should stop talking like that," my father sealed the conversation, decisive.

The kettle started to whistle. It gave me an excuse to "wake up" and stop my mother's analysis of my character and her maternal gifts. I waited in bed until the whistle stopped and made my entry.

"My sweet little daughter, shall I make you a cup of coffee?" my father asked eagerly, as I opened the sliding door and entered the kitchen dressed in one of my mother's pajama shirts.

"Boaz, let her wash her face first, can't you see she's not awake yet?" my mother reproached, pouring a mixture of peanuts and sunflower seeds into several glass bowls.

"Do you need help?" I asked.

"No, we're fine," my father said quickly. My mother was looking frantically for something in one drawer. "Boaz, I don't understand it, where did I put the paper plates?" she called out in alarm and frustration

"What time are the guests going to be here?" I asked with an innocent expression, watching my father open another drawer and pull a stack of paper plates from under a pile of kitchen towels. He knew her kitchen like the palm of his hand.

"At eleven we meet our relatives and old-time friends from outside the kibbutz, and at five o'clock we'll have a party for the *chaverim*, and your father will tape everything on the video camera," my mother said proudly in one breath, as she took the paper plates from my father's hand.

Instead of thanking him, she asked, "Did you remember to load the battery?"

He did not answer. His silence told me that this was not the first or last reminder, and his expression predicted an upcoming quarrel.

I left the kitchen quickly, knowing that my presence would add more fuel to the argument, and went upstairs to take a shower in my parents' new spacious bathroom. It was much nicer than the tiny bathroom they had downstairs, a relic of a lifestyle they endured before a certain committee in the kibbutz decided to upgrade the standard of living and poured millions of shekels into the concrete mixers that added another level to the modest one bedroom dwellings.

When I got out of the shower, still undecided about whether my mother's decision not to invite me, consciously or unconsciously, was an act of love and mercy, or plain forgetfulness and carelessness, Orly came upstairs to tell me that my father was preparing breakfast especially for me, and wanted to know how I liked my eggs. Then she proudly said that she already had breakfast in the dining hall and that Yaniv reminded my brother to bring me more bread from the kitchen. While I dressed, she chattered cheerfully, forgetting to tell my father that I didn't want any eggs, and told me how much she liked to come to the kibbutz during the holidays and eat in the dining hall.

"I wish I could eat there every day, because after we eat we can go outside and play hide-and-seek with the kids. And there are so many places to hide in. I wish we lived on the kibbutz," she sighed, skipping down the stairs on one leg while steadying herself on the wooden railing, which caused my mother to gasp and hold on to her throat.

I caught my brother's eye and raised an eyebrow without commenting on her wish. "Did you also play hide-and-seek when you were kids?" she asked, falling breathlessly into his arms from the second stair.

"No, we played hunting for the treasure and flags," he said.

"I think it's more fun to live here than in Tel Aviv," Orly announced. Pulling on my brother's arm, in a whining voice, she asked, "Why can't we come to live here with Saba and Savta and play flags like you did?"

"Orly, stop nagging," my brother said impatiently, pulling his arm away from her.

"Why not come to live here?" my mother interjected. "I can take them to the swimming pool in the summer, Saba can take them to pick olives in the afternoons, and you'll be able to go out in the evenings without worrying about a baby sitter. At least here they won't have to sit at home all day and watch television."

"Don't put any ideas into your head, Ima," Avner said coldly.

"But Avner, don't you know that the kibbutz is a paradise for children?" I couldn't resist, and added my own little facetious remark to the conversation.

"You know, Orly," my father said in a pacifying voice, ignoring my sarcasm, "very soon we are going to stop eating breakfast in the dining hall on Saturdays, so when you come to visit us you'll have to eat here."

"Not true," she pouted.

"The general assembly decided to cancel breakfasts on Saturday and keep the dining hall closed, because finally everyone realized it is a waste of time to open the kitchen and keep the staff working all day. Nowadays, hardly anyone eats breakfast in the dining hall on Saturday. The young generation sleeps in, the children stay home to watch the morning programs on channel two, and even we, the elders, prefer to take our time in the mornings and eat at home," my father explained patiently, adding green olives to the vegetables he finished chopping on the kitchen counter.

"Seems like the sour cream has lost its appeal," my brother smirked.

"Avner, stop being so smart," my mother scolded on her way outside with the paper plates. I realized that in spite of all her criticism of the system she still couldn't bear hearing us say anything bad about the kibbutz.

Later, when I attacked her for being a hypocrite, she defended herself in a whisper, "At least not in front of the children."

My father, determined to keep a cheerful disposition, placed a bowl of finely chopped vegetables on the table before me, handed me a bottle of olive oil and said, "Orly, do you want to hear a story?"

"Yes, yes, we want to hear a story," Yaniv, who just walked in with his mother, joined Orly and jumped on my father's lap chanting the same line over and over. I had a feeling that I knew what was coming and so did Avner, who suddenly had to go look for something in the guest bedroom.

"When Avner was your age, Orly, we used to have sour cream every Tuesday night for dinner. I would make a big salad and mix the sour cream in it and Avner would eat everything and lick his spoon afterwards. But Avner didn't remember that we had sour cream only on Tuesday nights and sometimes he would ask me to make him salad with sour cream when we didn't have it. So you know what I did? I took yogurt and mixed it with cottage cheese and put that on his salad and he always ate everything and wiped the plate clean with a piece of bread. Then one Tuesday evening, we came to the dining hall to eat dinner, and again Avner asked for salad with sour cream. I went to the counter as I always did and saw that all the sour cream was gone. So I returned to the table and said to Avner that there was no more sour cream. Do you know what he said to me? He said, Aba, do what you always do, take some yogurt and mix it with cottage cheese and put it on my salad."

We burst out laughing. Avner poked his head from the guestroom and snorted. "What's so funny? We heard that story two million times."

I ignored him. My father's stories about our childhood amazed me. His anecdotes were the best proof that we were not completely separated from one another. And I always laughed, no matter how many times I heard the same story. But I wasn't sure Yaniv understood the point because he was laughing too loud to sound convincing. Orly, whose shy smile showed me that she understood her father's cleverness, said, "Yuk, daddy likes sour cream on his salad."

"I'm going for a walk, does anybody want to join me?" Avner announced, returning to the kitchen with a pair of binoculars.

"Where to?" Shula asked.

"The stables, the cow sheds, the banana plantation, the water reservoir, the beach. Wherever my feet want to take me."

"I'll stay here and help your mother prepare for the party. Just do me a favor and make sure your feet don't take you too far," Shula said.

I was glad she wanted to help my mother. It absolved me from volunteering. I didn't want to be around when my parents' old friends showed up. Ever since I was twelve I had been hearing them say how much I looked like my mother when she was my age. "Like two drops of water," they exclaimed with awe every time they saw me. It forced me to relive her looks decade after decade, as if my face belonged to her as well, not only my life.

"Do you want to go with us?" my brother asked.

I couldn't decide.

"Don't worry, half of the members are not on the kibbutz on Passover," he reassured me, knowing how much I wanted to avoid crossing the kibbutz in full daylight and running into prying questions about my marital status, my career, and my unpatriotic choice to live abroad.

"Where do you think you're going?" my mother asked with apparent annoyance when we went out.

"To see the cows," Yaniv and Orly yelled, running down the stairs to chase the neighbors' aging cocker spaniel, which appeared more confused than delighted by their juvenile friendliness and enthusiasm. Now she won't be able to show her friends what a wonderful family we are, I thought, as I heard a deafening shriek. "Maya? Is this Maya? My goodness, it's Maya."

I turned around. It was my parent's neighbor, Rutka, the woman whose children stayed on the kibbutz. She approached with a small plastic bucket full of soapy water and put it on the floor. She wiped her hands on her housedress, extended one arm and took hold of my right arm. Immediately I remembered that on the kibbutz people didn't greet each other with a kiss on the cheek like in America. They didn't shake hands either. Ceremonial touching was not a part of the kibbutz etiquette. "How are you?" she asked without looking into my eyes and letting go of my arm.

"Excellent."

"Look at your hair, it's so long," she said, speaking to an imaginary person behind me. I smiled without knowing what to say. I knew I was going to hear the same observation many times during the next few days.

"You came for your mother's birthday?" she asked, although it really wasn't a question. I nodded.

"How long are you going to stay with us?" she asked again.

"Two weeks."

"What a wonderful daughter you've got, Alma. To come all the way from America to be with you on your birthday," she called across the porch. She fished a hand towel out of the soapy water, squeezed out the water, and began wiping the dust that settled on the leaves of the potted plants that decorated her front porch.

My mother, who was adding greenery to the flower vases that stood in the middle of each round table my father placed earlier on the lawn, looked up, raised her arms, palms up, and returned to the flower vases without saying anything.

"Did you come alone?" Rutka surprised me with another question. In the same breath, she asked if I knew that her daughter married Flavio, the Argentinean lifeguard who had come to live on the kibbutz three years ago.

Before I had a chance to answer, my mother blurted with subtle contempt, "She came with Avner."

She was getting protective. She didn't like when people tried to get personal information about her family. And she detested anything that smelled of petty gossip.

"Amnon, come see who's here," Rutka called her husband, disappearing into her apartment. My mother looked at me above the rose bush and frowned.

"It's okay," I reassured her with a whisper. But she still shook her head and knitted her eyebrows in discontent.

"Come on, Maya, we're all waiting for you," called Orly, who had given up on the uncooperative dog, pushing Yaniv away. Yaniv dropped on the grass laughing wildly and kicking the air like a cockroach who had fallen on his back.

"When are you coming back?" my mother demanded.

"An hour, a couple of hours," said Avner, giving his usual noncommittal answer.

"Boaz, please tell him to come back at a reasonable time," she asked my father who emerged from the house looking at me through the lens of his video camera.

"As long as I know you're in this country I'm happy," my father said, hugging me and offering his new familial philosophy that ignored my mother's request. "You don't have to be with me all the time to make me feel good. Go wherever you want, just don't forget to come back."

We left Shula in my parents' deserted living room and headed east, toward the cowsheds, where my brother had worked before he left the kibbutz. Orly and Yaniv ran ahead, competing for their father's attention, challenging each other to look for scary reptiles under bushes, and chasing big black crows that landed on the wide lawns to look for a snack. One of these crows was probably the great grandson of Tarzan, a mean-looking crow who lived on Yoshi's roof when Avner and I were little children. I used to believe that Yoshi could speak the language of wild animals, and the proof for that special talent was his friendship with the evil crow who liked to sit on his shoulder and feed on blind, naked chicks that fell from their nests on windy winter nights.

"Remember Yoshi's crow?" Avner broke my train of thought as if he could read them.

"I hated that bird."

"I was scared of him. I thought he would fly through the window one night and peck my eyes out while I was asleep and then I'd wake up blind."

"But how could he peck your eyes when they were closed?"

"I was a kid. I didn't think about it. I was afraid and that was it. Now I know that kids have fears of things that to us seem illogical, but I didn't know that until I had my own kids. I thought I was the only coward in the group when I was a kid. But now with Yaniv and Orly I learn that they will have fears no matter what I do for them. Yaniv, for example, is afraid of dinosaurs."

"How do you know?"

"He told me," Avner said, as if all the kids in the world told their parents about their hidden fears.

"What is Orly afraid of?"

"Jackals."

"Where did she see a jackal?"

"She has never seen one. She only hears them howling on the mountain every time we come here."

"She did? I haven't heard a jackal howling near the kibbutz since First Grade."

"Tonight you'll hear them probably. They're all over the place."

"What made them come back?" I asked in excitement. The possibility of hearing the jackals howling on the hills after so many years aroused so much nostalgia inside me, I was surprised to find out that I, too, succumbed to the same malady that afflicted the kibbutz founders; the same nostalgia I resented so much in my youth.

"The theory is that the pesticides sprayed on the fields killed them after they ate the poisoned rodents, and those who survived were scared away by the constant shooting on the border. But now, they say, they don't use those pesticides anymore, and the buffer zone in Lebanon moved most of the action away so they're slowly coming back."

"Daddy, look what I found, isn't she cute?" Yaniv came running and showed us a ladybug sitting between his palms.

"Can I take her home and put her in my room?" he asked.

"How would you feel if someone you don't know caught you and decided to take you to his home because you were cute?" Avner asked. Yaniv, without saying anything, opened his hands and blew air on the ladybug until she spread her dotted wings and flew away.

"I can't believe it Avner, you're such a father," I teased.

"The best thing that ever happened to me," he said, lifting Yaniv up in the air and placing him on his shoulders. "It's a great experience."

"Is it?" I asked, unable to hide my doubts. "Did I ever tell you that even now that I'm married, I am afraid to have children? I'm afraid they'd hate me." I didn't tell him what I really was afraid of: that they'd run away from me like I ran away from her.

"It's a tricky business, this parenthood thing," he said, nodding seriously to himself. "To be honest with you, I didn't imagine what I was getting myself into even when Shula got pregnant. Only after Orly was born did I realize that my concept of what a family meant was totally different from Shula's. I had to look at her interacting with her family to learn what it meant. You know how it is. What do we know about sense of belonging or loyalty to the family, or let's say, mutual support, and unconditional love? Nothing. I knew one big round zero. I could hardly tell the difference between what I got from mom and what I got from the kibbutz. Every time she spoke to me I heard the entire kibbutz talking behind her."

I knew exactly what he meant.

"You know, Maya, I think we have to accept the fact that we were a bunch of Guinea pigs. We grew up in a laboratory for human relationship in which the family was interpreted as a bourgeois institution that had to be eliminated. Our greatest educators didn't realize that a stupid *metapelet* could not fulfill the basic need for maternal love, and that a community composed of mostly mediocre people could not replace the parents.

"It took me years to see that our relationship with our parents was a joke compared to what realistic family dynamics are like. In the city, everything is so much more intensive. The pressures are stronger, the demands are more acute and immediate, and the conflicts are a lot more painful. And you learn to cope with everything without resorting to oppression. You learn to listen to what your children say. In my house there is no *metapelet* who can take care of my children when I'm tired or irritable or busy doing my own thing. I can't ignore their needs, I can't brush them away, and I can't take them back to the children's house at eight o'clock, dump them in their bed and leave. Raising children is a high maintenance operation. It entails a lot more time and attention than what the kibbutz movement and those who taught education in "The Seminar" prescribed for our parents and for us," he concluded, his eyes glowing with deep conviction.

My brother knew how much I admired his speeches about our family and the kibbutz lifestyle. I liked to listen to him even during the years I still believed he was going to be one of the kids who ended up living on the kibbutz, those whose spirit, I believed, was crushed by the system and the cruel *metapelets*. Unlike me, Avner had great relationships with most of the members; he enjoyed getting up at three o'clock in the morning to milk the cows; he belonged to the right social clique; he was a youth leader himself, and unlike Gideon, the kids admired him; he participated in many committees, especially those that involved the preparation of fun-oriented activities; and he could convert almost any Capitalist to become a devoted Socialist with his clear-cut logic and well-constructed arguments.

It was a miracle that I learned to like him so much. As a small girl I hardly knew him at all. He lived in another children's house and spent most of his days playing with boys much older than I was. Our friendship started to bloom when I entered high school and he was preparing to join the military. He taught me how to sneak into the cultural center, open the lock on the refrigerator in which the ice cream was secured, and enjoy a forbidden moment of sweetness. Later, he taught me how to ride a horse. Sometimes we would ride side by side to the beach to watch the sunset, gallop to the rusty lifeguard's tower, tie the horses to a pole and swim around the rocks until the sun sank into the sea. Other times we would climb to the top of the hill, tie the horses to a pine tree, sit on a warm rock and talk about our future plans and the endless conflict with our neighbors.

For years I didn't know if sisters were supposed to love their brothers the way I did, and I had no one to ask, so I kept loving him in my quiet special way. Once I told him that he understood me better than anyone I'd ever known. His response was, "because we have the same mother."

I asked him if he thought she loved us.

Yaniv was kicking excitedly and begging to go to the cowsheds. He put him on the ground, patted him on the back and said, "Go bother your sister. She knows the names of all the cows."

"Orly, Daddy said I have to bother you, now," Yaniv yelled and stomped in her direction. Orly, who was watching a white heron peck in the cow feeders, turned abruptly and tried to silence him. But it was too late. The startled bird flew away.

"Now look what you did," she said, disappointed.

"Can we go jump on the cotton?" Yaniv changed his mind, and pointed at a white mound of fuzzy cottonseeds inside a partially enclosed barn.

"Sure. I'll race you," Avner challenged him with contrived enthusiasm. He started to run, but the moment Orly joined the race he abandoned it and turned to me.

"It's really strange, but every time we come here these kids change. They become normal. I love bringing them here and watch them play together," he said, watching his kids roll down the white mound and scream with pleasure. "When I first brought Yaniv here he was afraid of the cows and the horses but now he lets them eat from his hand. I think it's great. Much better than playing video games and watching television all day."

"Did you ever think about coming back to live on the kibbutz?" I asked.

"No," he said, looking pensively at his kids. "I couldn't live here."

"But you feel connected, don't you?" It was strange how in spite of our decision not to live on the kibbutz we still felt a deep connection to the trees we had known since childhood, to the smells of wet grass and salty air, to the fields that kept changing colors, to the thorny bushes, to the mountain silhouette at night, to each rock on the beach, to the sunsets, to the hills, to the sound of the sprinklers.

"Only to the place, not to the people," he said.

"I would have died if I had to stay here for the rest of my life."

"I believe you. You've never really fit in."

"Don't you think she should have stood by my side when I was going through all the shit with Gideon and the education committee?" I asked.

"I don't think you can judge her now for what she did or didn't do almost twenty years ago. Things were different then. She couldn't stand up and fight the entire kibbutz. Don't you remember how scared she was of what people would say about you or me or her? Why don't you just give her a break? She didn't want to stay here all her life, either."

"Avner, I know all that but I still can't stop wishing that she would have gone to him and said something."

"Well, he's dead now, Maya. There's no one she can talk to."

"But I'm alive," I insisted.

"Don't you think it's time to put the past behind and live in the present? Live with what you've got now, not with what was taken away from you. Stop expecting her to do what you want her to do. She can't do it. She never did it and you can't teach her to do it now. You can be sure she's doing the best she can already. I'm sure she meant every word she said to you last night. And it's not the first time she had said it either. So why don't you just accept that we didn't have a normal childhood and go on from there? At least you have the freedom to experience the kind of motherhood she didn't have."

"Forgiveness? Is that what you're saying? You think I should just forget everything?"

"You can call it whatever you want. I call it pragmatism. It's that simple. For a long time I was angry, too, but it didn't solve anything. It only made things worse. There was no room inside me to enjoy anything because I was too busy thinking about my childhood, talking about it, analyzing it as if it were the most important thing in the world. Luckily, these two kids showed up and taught me to enjoy what I've got now and stop worrying about what kind of life I missed because I was born on a kibbutz," he said, motioning his head in the direction of his kids.

"Daddy, look at me," Yaniv yelled from the top of the white mound, diving into the cotton, head first.

"You see? That's what I mean. We've got another chance. She didn't."

We sat on two folding chairs that we found leaning on a bale of hay and watched the kids climb and roll down the cotton mound, screaming joyfully, chasing each other, competing to get to the top, until they came asking for another adventure. Avner stopped searching the mountain with the binoculars and suggested we climb up the hill and look for an old tank that was abandoned by the army near the fence after one of the invasions of Lebanon.

As he expected, the kids were beyond themselves with curiosity. We were almost dragged by the two of them up the hill. When they spotted the rusty tank half buried in the bushes, I told Avner I had to leave them for a few minutes.

"Don't take too long. We still have to pretend to the guests we're a little happy family," he said with a wink.

I left them standing by the bushes, calculating how to get to the aging tank through the natural barrier it had grown around itself without getting too many scratches. I cut across an avocado grove and started climbing the road. A row of tall cypresses stood erect on both sides of the asphalt road that led me to my destination. They bowed their tops, reluctantly, when a gust of warm wind swept the mountainside, raising a cloud of choking dust. I passed through an iron gate, feeling the trees scrutinize my back with a thousand suspicious eyes, wondering who I was, why I came to disturb the peace with my noisy rubber flip-flops. At first I wanted to turn around and run away, but when I saw the first gravestones hiding in the shade between the jagged rocks, I forgot the cypresses and my discomfort and went to look for my grandma's grave.

My brave grandmother had left her home, her language, and her large family and had gone to conquer an unknown land in the early twenties, propelled by ideals and dreams she never spoke about. I could never think of her as the quintessential pioneer. To me she looked like a tired old woman with sagging breasts and lots of wrinkles; an old woman who spoke a mixture of Yiddish and heavily accented, old-fashioned Hebrew; an old woman who wore a tattered house robe and apron all day long and perspired, perspired rivers. I used to think that she was at least a hundred years old, even though my mother often claimed that *Savta* looked younger than her age. I didn't know her very well, or the man who was my grandfather. They lived in Tel Aviv in a small one-bedroom apartment whose walls were decorated with black and white photographs of relatives I'd never seen and one enlarged colored photograph of my mother at sixteen.

Before they came to live in the kibbutz, near my mother who could help them in their later years, we used to visit them during my summer vacation, which was the worst time of the year for such a visit. The oppressive heat and the humidity suffocated my poor grandmother, who suffered from various ailments that afflicted the aging Eastern European pioneers, and left her breathless and exhausted.

"Where do you hide the clean towels," my mother would scream at the top of her lungs at the moment I made myself comfortable on the couch with one of the books I found on the cabinet every time we came to visit. "Maya has to take a shower."

My grandmother, acting deaf only in my mother's presence, would pretend that she did not hear the question and retreat to her steamy kitchen to prepare us lunch. Her meal included rye bread with caraway seeds which I plucked out one by one, Deviled eggs, Vienna schnitzel with boiled potatoes, her special homemade pickles, an authentic chicken noodle soup, and chilled apple and prunes compote with lots of raisins, served in that order on her best china and accompanied by audible encouragement to eat some more. It took me years to realize that by complying with her requests, and by watching her maneuver around the kitchen, I learned not only about my culinary heritage, but also got the comforting proof that even years of pioneering in an inhospitable land could not wean a fantastic cook from her recipes.

After we finished eating I liked to lie on the couch in the darkened living room and listen to the homey clinking sounds that my grandma's china made when she washed the dishes. For me, those clinking sounds were the closest thing to comfort, family, security, and even love. I would close my eyes and pretend that I was safe at home, away from a *metapelet* who routinely forced me to eat food I did not like. Then the clinking sounds would stop, and overwhelmed by old anxiety and fear, I would run to the bathroom and throw up every bite I ate.

As I strolled around the cemetery that had witnessed only three emotionally restrained funerals before I left the kibbutz, but had since grown several rows of well-kept graves with unfamiliar names, I noticed that the left side of the cemetery was dedicated to the kibbutz members while the right side was allocated as a burial ground for members' parents who came to spend their final years on the kibbutz, like my own grandparents. I went to the right side of the invisible divider and there, just as I expected, I found my grandma's resting-place. Next to her rested my grandfather, who passed away shortly after her. They were the only couple resting for eternity next to each other. No empty spaces were reserved for spouses on either side of the divider. The kibbutz cemetery was organized like a military cemetery. Each grave stood by itself; no family plots were allotted on the rocky mountainside. Parents were buried on one side of the divider, children on the other side. Just like during life, so in death, parents were separated from their children, only that now, the children belonged to my parents' generation.

I sat in front of my grandmother's grave, looked around to make sure no one could hear me, and started to talk.

"Now, tell me the truth, Savta. Don't hide underneath your grave and pretend that you forgot or that you cannot hear me. Why did she always yell at you when we came to see you in the holidays? Why did you pretend you couldn't hear her? And why does she insist that you were a good mother and forgets how she used to storm out of your house claiming that you were crazy? What kind of a mother were you? Did you love her? Did you ever tell her that? Did you hug her and kiss her the way you hugged and kissed me? Did she ever blame you that you didn't love her like I blamed her all my life? Did you really give her as much love and attention as she insists you did? And if you did, then how come she couldn't understand that I needed her love and attention, as much as she did when she was a little girl? How could she believe those who said that her children could be happier if they lived away from her in the children's house?

"And how about you, *Savta*? What kind of mother did you have? Did she love you? What did she say when you told her you were leaving home to go to Palestine? That you were going to be a pioneer? Did you run away from her like your daughter ran away from you? Like I ran away from her? Why didn't you ever talk about your mother? Was she crazy too? Or deaf? What did she look like? What was her name?

"I hope that one day, *Savta*, I will be able to live in peace with your daughter, accept her without criticizing her, without hurting her, as much as she hurt me when she was blind to my sadness, my fears, my loneliness. I hope one day the daughters of our family will stop running away from their mothers and later come back to blame them. I hope we will learn to love each other. Do you think that if I ever have a daughter I will be able to give her what she needed, freely and with joy, without driving her away from me?

"I know you cannot answer me now. Don't try. I am not ready to listen to what you have to say, yet, anyway. I already know that she will never give me what I want, the way I want it, because she can't imagine what I missed and how much I still want it. I will try as hard as I can not to demand anything from her, I will try to believe her when she says she loves me. I will do my best. I promise.

"There was a moment yesterday, I wanted to tell her what they did to me but I am not going to. Not after what she had told me. I don't want her to remember my pain; she has enough of her own. But if you can, *Savta*, please, tell her that I didn't mean to hurt her. Tell her that I didn't know any other way to make her understand me. Tell her I'm sorry I didn't know how to be a loving daughter, because there was an ocean of ideology separating us. Tell her that I am not so angry anymore."

Now I was done. I did not mean to say everything I said. I did not even know what I was feeling yet, it was so new; my mother talking about the past, my brother's experiences and new understanding. I was still attached to my old feelings, my old way of thinking, but deep inside, I sensed a shift and it made me giddy with anticipation.

I picked up a stone from the ground and put it on my grandma's grave. Then I said goodbye and trotted down the dirt road, feeling lighter as if a terrible heavy burden was lifted off my body. A few minutes later I heard my brother give Yaniv and Orly a stern ultimatum to climb down the tank.

"Come down, now, the two of you. I promised your mother to bring you home in one piece. Don't break any bone on your way down, be careful. Orly, do me a favor, give Yaniv a hand before he loses an eye over there."

We left the tank and headed back to our parents' home in pairs; Yaniv riding on Avner's shoulders, and Orly, holding my right hand and counting the white sails dotting the calm blue sea. A lazy atmosphere surrounded the kibbutz. Apart from a flock of swallows chasing insects up in the sky, no one was around. Only the faint sounds of a familiar symphony indicated that a celebration was in progress behind the tall trees and the quiet houses. In the distance a large banner hanging between two tall trees announced in bright red letters and colorful balloons: Happy Birthday, Alma.

We passed under the banner and saw that the party was already going full blast. The lawn in front of my parents' house was teeming with people talking loudly to each other, children running around tables, babies crawling on the grass, a variety of barking dogs, and balloons floating in the air. In the crowd I could see my father looking through his video camera at two women who were waving their hands awkwardly and acting happy. Shula was carrying a cake to one of the tables. Orly and Yaniv, spotting their mother in the crowd, broke away and ran toward her, bumping into chairs and people's legs. I stayed near Avner, trying to decide whether I should try to hide somewhere or go inside and get the gift I brought for my mother, when a man I did not recognize stood up, waved his smoking pipe in the air and called, "We also wrote something for Alma. Listen, everybody."

The loud conversations quickly died down.

The older man unfolded a piece of yellow paper, coughed ceremoniously and started reading.

"Alma, a beautiful woman in the middle of the road. You carry the years like a feather on your shoulders, and we, the youngsters, are a little jealous of you. Can you teach us how to do it?" he paused to let the guests laugh before he continued reading. "Alma, the brave, the fighter lady who cannot give up her dreams. So many times you won your battles, and even when you lost them you kept your spirit. Since our days together in the youth movement, you were ready to fulfill your call with pride and perseverance. You went to live on the kibbutz to accomplish the ideals that you believed in: equality, communal life, love, and camaraderie.

"And what does the future hold for you? We're sure you've got yourself new challenges to conquer, which you will, with your knowledge, diligence, and courage, with your experience and depth."

When he finished listing her accomplishments, her virtues, and her blessings, the guests applauded warmly.

I did not join the applause even though I knew how much she loved to get compliments, and how rarely they came her way. I crossed the lawn, looking for her, trying to avoid familiar faces and lame conversations, but to no avail. A loud voice behind me jerked me back into my past, reminding me that in the eyes of the members I was still a daughter of the kibbutz, a little girl, no matter where I chose to live and how long I stayed away.

"Maya, how dare you come to the kibbutz without letting your mother know about it? She should slap you for doing such a thing, you could have given her a heart attack," a loud woman's voice scolded with excitement, as if I were still in kindergarten. I turned around, fighting a conditioned reflex to explain myself, and bumped into Bruria, Iris's mother. She was standing by a roofless cage on wheels that was built in the metal shop in the early days to carry clothes from and to the laundry house, and was now converted into a stroller. A blond baby stood among plastic toys thrown in disarray on a pink blanket, holding on to the metal railing and rocking itself according to an inner rhythm.

"Look at you, your hair is so long," she exclaimed, as if she was the only person who could notice it.

"I just let it grow," I apologized.

"Do you know whose baby she is?" she tested me.

I shook my head, feeling like a little girl who had been caught unprepared for her most important test.

"It's Dana. Iris' daughter. My granddaughter. Isn't she adorable?" She bent down, kissed the baby on top of the head, and squeezed both her cheeks. I could not resist remembering that I had never seen her kiss her daughter in the children's house.

"She's very cute," I agreed.

"Of course she's cute. Just like you," she patted me on the cheek. "Now go to your mother. She's been looking for you."

Again, I had to comply. I elbowed my way around the crowded tables, declining invitations to sit down and talk about my life in America, and headed toward my mother. She was standing at the top of the stairs, wearing a flowery dress and a wide-brimmed white straw hat, receiving a gift from Ora, my elementary school teacher. Ora looked so small and harmless now, it was hard to believe that she was once my greatest enemy, the carrier of bad news, the woman I feared so much in my childhood.

My mother, sensing my presence, raised her eyes, looked at me for a few seconds, then looked down and opened the gift box Ora handed her. With an elegant turn of the wrist, she pulled out a blue silk scarf, thanked Ora, and appreciated the shiny silk.

"That's a beautiful scarf," I said, climbing the stairs and nodding an acknowledgment to Ora.

"You like it?" my mother asked, wrapping the scarf around my neck. Ora stood by her side, looking more agreeable than ever.

My mother took two steps back, examined me, brushed an invisible speck of dust from my shoulder and hummed an approval. Behind her my father was feeding a new tape into the video camera.

"You'd look great in it," I said.

"She would," Ora agreed on her way down the stairs.

"Even at my advanced age," my mother joked.

"Don't worry, Ima, you don't look a day over fifty-nine," I recited one of my father's well-known lines.

"Fifty-eight," my father corrected from behind the camera.

"Right," I laughed and bowed to the camera.

My mother passed her hand over the slippery wrinkles of her new scarf, and nodded enigmatically more to herself than to the camera. I noticed the pride in her dark eyes, the contentment in her smile, the tenderness with which she touched me; and at that very moment, no longer did I mind pretending, for her sake as well as for my own, that we were an ordinary family in celebration.

Glossary

Aba   father in Hebrew

Be'te'avon   bon appétit in Hebrew

Bible   always refers to the Jewish Bible, the Old Testament, or the Tanakh

Boker tov   good morning in Hebrew

Challa   braided Jewish bread eaten on Friday, Saturday and holidays

Chaverim   members of a kibbutz, also means friends in Hebrew.

Haggadah   the Hebrew text that sets the order of the Passover Seder (ceremony and meal) and is read by the participants.

Hash'kava   bedtime in the children's house

IDF   Israel Defense Forces

Ima   mother in Hebrew

Katyusha   a Russian made rocket launcher. This word is used interchangeably for the multiple-rocket launcher and for the rocket that is launched from it. These rockets are used by militant groups located in Lebanon and occasionally fired into northern Israel.

Kibbutznik/kibbutznikim   a member/members of a kibbutz

Kolboinik   a plastic or stainless steel bowl placed on the table and used for discarded eggshells, fruit and vegetable peels, chicken bones and leftovers. HaKol-Bo means everything is in it in Hebrew.

Metapelet   the woman in charge of the children's house, the daily routine of the children, and their discipline.

Mazal tov   literally "good luck" but used in Hebrew as "congratulations."

Nes Gadol Haya Poh   a big miracle happened here in Hebrew.

Palmach   the acronym for Plugot Mahatz (in Hebrew "strike forces") the elite fighting force of the underground army of the Jewish community during the British Mandate for Palestine. The Palmach was established in 1941 and disbanded soon after the establishment of the state of Israel.

Ravakia   the area where young unmarried kibbutzniks live.

Savta   Grandmother in Hebrew. Sometimes pronounced as Safta.

Sevivon   also called dreidel in Yiddish, is a four-sided spinning top played with during Hanukah.

Schmate'   an old and tattered article of clothing in Yiddish.

Takanon ha'kibbutzim   the collection of all the regulations related to life on the kibbutz, including mission statement, definitions, goals and rules.

Uzi   an open-bolt submachine gun designed by Major Uziel Gal in the late 1940s, manufactured in Israel and used by the Israel Defense Forces.

Wadi/Wadis   a word that entered Hebrew from Arabic referring to a ravine, a gulch or a dry riverbed. Sometimes water runs through it during heavy rains.

Printed in Great Britain
by Amazon